ON THE TERROR WARD—

"The Autopsy" by Michael Shea—Sometimes when the dead rise again, it's not a medical miracle, it's the ultimate invasion of privacy!

"The Case of Lady Sannox" by A. Conan Doyle—For noted surgeon Douglas Stone, his passion and his skill may prove his own undoing. . . .

"The Needle Men" by George R. R. Martin—On the track of a bizarre, poison-laced story, a reporter discovers that seeking medical advice is not always good for your health. . . .

"Herbert West—Reanimator" by H. P. Lovecraft—When you spend too much time experimenting with the dead, your work may come back to haunt you. . . .

INTENSIVE SCARE
It's just what the doctor ordered!

INTENSIVE SCARE

EDITED BY
KARL EDWARD WAGNER

DAW BOOKS, INC.

DONALD A. WOLLHEIM, PUBLISHER

1633 Broadway, New York, NY 10019

First Printing, January 1990

1 2 3 4 5 6 7 8 9

PRINTED IN THE U.S.A.

ACKNOWLEDGMENTS

The Dead Line by Dennis Etchison. Copyright © 1979 by Stuart David Schiff for *Whispers* No. 13–14; Copyright © 1982 by Dennis Etchison. Reprinted by permission of the author.

The House of Horror by Seabury Quinn. Copyright © 1926 by the Popular Fiction Publishing Company for *Weird Tales,* July 1926. Reprinted by permission of Kirby McCauley Ltd., agents for the author's estate.

Casey Agonistes by Richard McKenna. Copyright © 1958 by Mercury Press, Inc. for *The Magazine of Fantasy & Science Fiction,* September 1958. Reprinted by permission of Mrs. Eva McKenna.

The Body-Snatcher by Robert Louis Stevenson. First published in *Pall Mall Christmas Extra,* 1884.

The Autopsy by Michael Shea. Copyright © 1980 by Michael Shea for *The Magazine of Fantasy & Science Fiction,* December 1980. Reprinted by permission of the author.

Back to the Beast by Manly Wade Wellman. Copyright © 1927 by the Popular Fiction Publishing Company for *Weird Tales,* November 1927. Reprinted by permission of Mrs. Frances Wellman and of Karl Edward Wagner, literary executor for Manly Wade Wellman.

The Incalling by M. John Harrison. Copyright © 1978 by M. John Harrison for *The Savoy Book.* Reprinted by permission of the author.

The Case of Lady Sannox by A. Conan Doyle. Reprinted from *Round the Red Lamp,* Copyright © 1894.

The Needle Men by George R.R. Martin. Copyright © 1981 by Mercury Press, Inc. for *The Magazine of Fantasy & Science Fiction,* October 1981. Reprinted by permission of the author.

The Shifting Growth by Edgar Jepson and John Gawsworth. First published in *Crimes, Creeps and Thrills*, 1936.

Camps by Jack Dann. Copyright © 1979 by Jack Dann for *The Magazine of Fantasy & Science Fiction*, May 1979. Reprinted by permission of the author.

Herbert West—Reanimator by H.P. Lovecraft. First published in *Home Brew*, 1922. Reprinted by permission of the author's estate and the agents for the Estate, Scott Meredith Literary Agency, Inc., 845 Third Avenue, New York, New York 10022.

The Little Black Bag by C.M. Kornbluth. Copyright © 1950 by Street and Smith Publications for *Astounding Science Fiction*, July 1950. Reprinted by permission of Curtis Brown Ltd., agents for the author's estate.

The editor would also like to express his gratitude to Jack Dann, David Drake, John Rieber, and Charles Waugh for their help and suggestions in making these selections—and special thanks to Jim Killus, who suggested to me the title for this anthology, and to Dr. Sharon Farber, who told it to Jim in the first place.

To James Groce, M.D.

Classmate and roommate from medical school days, best of friends for many years after, and exemplary proof that there really are good doctors.

CONTENTS

10 *Contents*

INTRODUCTION
Trust Me. I'm a Doctor.

Trust me. I'm a doctor. I'm always right, and I never lie.

Can you feel anything when I do this?

Just tell me where it hurts.

Relax. You may feel a little pinprick.

Just relax . . .

There are probably more intensely terrifying experiences to endure than to enter a hospital and place your life and well-being in the rubber-gloved hands of some masked and impersonal medical team. Just maybe.

For most of us, this will do very well, indeed. It's a common dread. And it's a very *real* fear. Odds are that you will never be assaulted by a peckish werewolf or some chainsaw-wielding zombie, but you very well may be stricken by acute appendicitis while you lie snug in bed, or suffer a subdural hematoma if you fall off your ten-speed while cycling to your health spa, or discover a lump in your breast one sunny morning, or. . . .

Health is such a chancy thing. And so precious.

That's why there are doctors.

That's why you go to them.

But you are *afraid* of them. Afraid of their offices and hospitals. Afraid of their questions and examinations. Afraid of their poking and probing. Afraid of their pills and needles. Afraid of their scalpels and sutures. Afraid of lying helpless and naked beneath the sterile murmur of fluorescent lights.

Helpless.

Can you understand their jargon, their professional aloofness? The half-heard words, distracted frowns, and flutter of charts and lab reports? The impersonal cluster of peering faces over your bed?

Best not to try. Just lie there and trust. And pray. What's your choice?

There are only two things worse than being the patient.

One is to be the doctor, who worries what might be wrong with you.

But it's far worse to be the doctor who is also the patient—and who *knows* what's wrong.

You see, we don't believe in our own rituals. We know the fear that we try to mask with our magic. We know that our spells and charms are often for our consciences alone. A miss is as good as a placebo. Anyway, we tried.

Sometimes we cure. Sometimes you may recover despite all that we have done. Sometimes . . .

If this is cynicism, it is cynicism born of experience. I earned my M.D. from the University of North Carolina School of Medicine in 1974. Not long after that I left my psychiatric residency at a state hospital in order to write full time.

Burned out. I'd had enough. Watching some close friends die, thanks to the misdirected machinations of the present medical system, fed fuel to the burnout. But—to be truthful—my first interest had always been to be a writer. You can never be a good writer or a good doctor if your loyalty lies elsewhere. It means cheating your readers or your patients, and if you have any valid commitment to yourself and your work—and to those who look to you for that commitment—then you have to make a choice.

So, I've been a full-time writer these last fifteen years. And I've never regretted it. It's what I *really* wanted to do. Whatever, the ties remain. Too deep a commitment to ignore, and I still jump when someone yells: "Is there a doctor here?" (Yes, that really does happen.)

So, then, you can never forget medical school, nor the horrors made commonplace that every practicing physician must deal with. I remember carrying a chart into the examining room as the attending physician (a man who spiritually guided my soul and doggedly hauled my ass through medical school) was telling a young woman that her double radical mastectomy had not contained her cancer. They were both in tears. Meeting his eyes in that instant, I discreetly backed out. Five minutes later he was making rounds with us. Callous? *No.* He was bleeding inside and always would remember the pain. But there were other patients who needed him; there were medical students he must teach. His was a courage I can never forget nor equal.

What I'm saying here is that in some ways it is more terrifying to be the physician than it is to be the patient. Your patient is relying on you; you are calling upon every bit of your knowledge and art to respond to that need. No second-place finish in CPR. Mistakes kill, and even your best efforts may not be good enough.

It all makes for a really scary scenario. The patient needs help. The doctor wants to help. Most of the time it works out that way.

But then . . .

Suppose the doctor *isn't* just what you imagined?

Suppose the patient *isn't* really what you thought?

You're lying there on the bed, vulnerable and half-naked in a humiliating hospital gown.

You're called in to a case, and suddenly you sense that something isn't right.

You see, scalpels don't care who they cut.

And no one ever gets well in a hospital.

You're never closer to death. Never more helpless. This is *real* terror.

So, here you are: thirteen heart-stopping tales of medical horror. They span a century, proving that not much changes except for the hospital bills. Here are good doctors and bad doctors, kindly doctors and mad doctors, doctors who risk their lives to heal and doctors who sell their souls to destroy.

Please *don't* give this book to a friend who is about to undergo surgery.

Please *don't* read this book as you fidget in your doctor's waiting room.

Please *do* give this book to anyone who is contemplating a career in medicine.

It's too late for me.

Now, then—who's next?

Trust me.

I'm a doctor.

KARL EDWARD WAGNER, M.D.
Chapel Hill, North Carolina

THE DEAD LINE

by Dennis Etchison

1.

This morning I put ground glass in my wife's eyes. She didn't mind. She didn't make a sound. She never does.

I took an empty bottle from the table. I wrapped it in a towel and swung it, smashing it gently against the side of her bed. When the glass shattered it made a faint, very faint sound like wind chimes in a thick fog. No one noticed, of course, least of all Karen. Then I placed it under my shoe and stepped down hard, rocking my weight back and forth until I felt fine sand underfoot. I knelt and picked up a few sharp grains on the end of my finger, rose and dropped them onto her corneas. First one, then the other. She doesn't blink, you know. It was easy.

Then I had to leave. I saw the technicians coming. But already it was too late; the damage had been done. I don't know if they found the mess under the bed. I suppose someone will. The janitors or the orderlies, perhaps. But it won't matter to them, I'm sure.

I slipped outside the glass observation wall as the technicians descended the lines, adjusting respirators, reading printouts and making notations on their pocket recorders. I remember that I thought then of clean, college-trained farmers combing rows of crops, checking the condition of the coming harvest, turning down a cover here, patting a loose mound there, touching the beds with a horticulturist's fussiness, ready to prune wherever necessary for the demands of the marketplace. They may not have seen me at all. And what if they had? What was I but a concerned husband come to pay his respects to a loved one? I might have been lectured about the risk of bringing unwanted germs into the area, though they must know how unlikely that is with the high-intensity UV lights and sonic purifiers and other sanitary precautions. I did make a point of passing near the Children's Communicable Diseases Ward on my way there, however; one always hopes.

Then, standing alone behind the windows, isolated and empty as an expectant father waiting for his flesh and blood to be delivered at last into his own hands, I had the sudden, unshakable feeling that I was being watched.

By whom?

The technicians were still intent on their readouts.

Another visitor? It was unlikely; hardly anyone else bothers to observe. A guilty few still do stop by during the lonely hours, seeking silent expiation from a friend, relative or lover, or merely to satisfy some morbid curiosity; the most recently-acquired neomorts usually receive dutiful visitations at the beginning, but invariably the newly-grieved are so overwhelmed by the impersonalness of the procedure that they soon learn to stay away to preserve their own sanity.

I kept careful track of the progress of the white coats on the other side of the windows, ready to move on at the first sign of undue concern over my wife's bed.

And it was then that I saw her face shining behind my own in the pane. She was alert and standing for the first time since the stroke, nearly eighteen months ago. I gripped the handrail until my nails were white, staring in disbelief at Karen's transparent reflection.

I turned. And shrank back against the wall. The cold sweat must have been on my face, because she reached out shakily and pressed my hand.

"Can I get you anything?"

Her hair was beautiful again, not the stringy, matted mass I had come to know. Her makeup was freshly applied, her lips dark at the edges and parted just so, opening on a warm, pink interior, her teeth no longer discolored but once more a luminous bone-white. And her eyes. They were perfect.

I lunged for her.

She sidestepped gracefully and supported my arm. I looked closely at her face as I allowed her to hold me a moment longer. There was nothing wrong with that, was there?

"Are you all right?" she said.

She was so much like Karen I had to stop the backs of my fingers from stroking the soft, wispy down at her temple, as they had done so many, many times. She had always liked that. And so, I remembered, had I; it was so long ago I had almost forgotten.

"Sorry," I managed. I adjusted my clothing, smoothing my hair down from the laminar airflow around the beds. "I'm not feeling well."

"I understand."

Did she?

"My name is Emily Richterhausen," she said.

I straightened and introduced myself. If she had seen me inside the restricted area she said nothing. But she couldn't have been here that long. I would have noticed her.

"A relative?" she asked.

"My wife."

"Has . . . has she been here long?"

"Yes. I'm sorry. If you'll excuse me—"

"Are you sure you're all right?" She moved in front of me. "I could get you a cup of coffee, you know, from the machines. We could both have one. Or some water."

It was obvious that she wanted to talk. She needed it. Perhaps I did, too. I realized that I needed to explain myself, to pass off my presence before she could guess my plan.

"Do you come here often, Emily?" It was a foolish question. I knew I hadn't seen her before.

"It's my husband," she said.

"I see."

"Oh, he's not one of . . . them. Not yet. He's in

Intensive Care." The lovely face began to change. "A coma. It's been weeks. They say he may regain consciousness. One of the doctors said that. How long can it go on, do you know?"

I walked with her to a bench in the waiting area.

"An accident?" I said.

"A heart attack. He was driving to work. The car crossed the divider. It was awful." She fumbled for a handkerchief. I gave her mine. "They say it was a miracle he survived at all. You should have seen the car. No, you shouldn't have. No one should have. A miracle."

"Well," I told her, trying to sound comforting, "as I understand it, there is no 'usual' in comatose cases. It can go on indefinitely, as long as brain death hasn't occurred. Until then there's always hope. I saw a news item the other day about a young man who woke up after four years. He asked if he had missed his homework assignment. You've probably heard—"

"Brain death," she repeated, mouthing the words uneasily. I saw her shudder.

"That's the latest Supreme Court ruling. Even then," I went on quickly, "there's still hope. You remember that girl in New Jersey? She's still alive. She may pull out of it at any time," I lied. "And there are others like her. A great many, in fact. Why—"

"There *is* hope, isn't there?"

"I'm sure of it," I said, as kindly as possible.

"But then," she said, "supposing. . . . What is it that actually happens, afterwards? How does it work? Oh, I know about the Maintenance and Cultivation Act. The doctor explained everything at the beginning, just in case." She glanced back toward the Neomort Ward and took a deep, uncertain breath. She didn't really want to know, not now. "It looks so nice and clean, doesn't it? They can still be of great service to society. The kidneys, the eyes, even the heart. It's a wonderful thing. Isn't it?"

"It's remarkable," I agreed. "Your husband, had he signed the papers?"

"No. He kept putting it off. William never liked to

dwell on such matters. He didn't believe in courting disaster. Now I only wish I had forced him to talk about it, while there was still time.''

''I'm sure it won't come to that,'' I said immediately. I couldn't bear the sight of her crying. ''You'll see. The odds are very much on your side.''

We sat side by side in silence as an orderly wheeled a stainless-steel cleaning cart off the elevator and headed past us to the observation area. I could not help but notice the special scent of her skin. Spring flowers. It was so unlike the hospital, the antisepticized cloud that hangs over everything until it has settled into the very pores of the skin. I studied her discreetly: the tiny, exquisite whorls of her ear, the blood pulsing rapidly and naturally beneath her healthy skin. Somewhere an electronic air ionizer was whirring, and a muffled bell began to chime in a distant hallway.

''Forgive me,'' she said. ''I shouldn't have gone on like that. But tell me about your wife.'' She faced me. ''Isn't it strange?'' We were inches apart. ''It's so reassuring to talk to someone else who understands. I don't think the doctors really know how it is for us, for those who wait.''

''They can't,'' I said.

''I'm a good listener, really I am. William always said that.''

''My—my wife signed the Universal Donor Release two years ago,'' I began reluctantly, ''the last time she renewed her driver's license.'' Good until her next birthday, I thought. As simple as that. Too simple. Karen, how could you have known? How could I? I should have. I should have found out. I should have stopped your hand. ''She's here now. She's been here since last year. Her electroencephalogram was certified almost immediately.''

''It must be a comfort to you,'' she said, ''to know that she didn't suffer.''

''Yes.''

''You know, this is the first time I've been on this particular floor. What is it they call it?'' She was rattling on, perhaps to distract herself.

"The Bioemporium."

"Yes, that's it. I guess I wanted to see what it would be like, just in case. For my William." She tried bravely to smile. "Do you visit her often?"

"As often as possible."

"I'm sure that must mean a great deal."

To whom? I thought, but let it pass.

"Don't worry," I said. "Your husband will recover. He'll be fine. You'll see."

Our legs were touching. It had been so long since I had felt contact with sentient flesh. I thought of asking her for that cup of coffee now, or something more, in the cafeteria. Or a drink.

"I try to believe that," she said. "It's the only thing that keeps me going. None of this seems real, does it?"

She forced the delicate corners of her mouth up into a full smile.

"I really should be going now. I could get something for him, couldn't I? You know, in the gift shop downstairs? I'm told they have a very lovely store right here in the building. And then I'll be able to give it to him during visiting hours. When he wakes up."

"That's a good idea," I said.

She said decisively, "I don't think I'll be coming to this floor again."

"Good luck," I told her. "But first, if you'd like, Emily, I thought—"

"What was . . . what is your wife's name? If you don't mind my asking?"

"Karen," I said. Karen. What was I thinking? Can you forgive me? You can do that, can't you, sweetheart?

"That's such a pretty name," she said.

"Thank you."

She stood. I did not try to delay her. There are some things that must be set to rest first, before one can go on. You helped remind me of that, didn't you, Karen? I nearly forgot. But you wouldn't let me.

"I suppose we won't be running into each other again," she said. Her eyes were almost cheerful.

"No."

"Would you . . . could you do me one small favor?"

I looked at her.

"What do you think I should get him? He has so many nice things. But you're a man. What would you like to have, if you were in the hospital? God forbid," she added, smiling warmly.

I sat there. I couldn't speak. I should have told her the truth then. But I couldn't. It would have seemed cruel, and that is not part of my nature.

What do you get, I wondered, for a man who has nothing?

2.

I awaken.

The phone is silent.

I go to the medicine cabinet, swallow another fistful of L-tryptophane tablets and settle back down restlessly, hoping for a long and mercifully dreamless nap.

Soon, all too soon and not soon enough, I fall into a deep and troubled sleep.

I awaken to find myself trapped in an airtight box.

I pound on the lid, kicking until my toes are broken and my elbows are torn and bleeding. I reach into my pocket for my lighter, an antique Zippo, thumb the flint. In the sudden flare I am able to read an engraved plate set into the satin. TWENTY-FIVE YEAR GUARANTEE, it says in fancy script. I scream. My throat tears. The lighter catches the white folds and tongues of flame lick my face, spreading rapidly down my squirming body. I inhale fire.

The lid swings open.

Two attendants in white are bending over me, squirting out the flames with a water hose. One of them chuckles.

Wonder how that happened? he says.

Spontaneous combustion? says his partner.

That would make our job a hell of a lot easier, says the other. He coils the hose and I see through burned-away eyelids that it is attached to a sink at the head of a stainless-steel table. The table has grooves running along the sides and a drainage hole at one end.

I scream again, but no sound comes out.

They turn away.

I struggle up out of the coffin. There is no pain. How can that be? I claw at my clothing, baring my seared flesh.

See? I cry. I'm alive!

They do not hear.

I rip at my chest with smoldering hands, the peeled skin rolling up under my fingernails. See the blood in my veins? I shout. I'm not one of them!

Do we have to do this one over? asks the attendant. It's only a cremation. Who'll know?

I see the eviscerated remains of others glistening in the sink, in the jars and plastic bags. I grab a scalpel. I slash at my arm. I cut through the smoking cloth of my shirt, laying open fresh incisions like white lips, slicing deeper into muscle and bone.

See? Do I not bleed?

They won't listen.

I stagger from the embalming chamber, gouging my sides as I bump other caskets which topple, spilling their pale contents onto the mortuary floor.

My body is steaming as I stumble out into the cold, gray dawn.

Where can I go? What is left for me? There must be a place. There must be—

A bell chimes, and I awaken.

Frantically I locate the telephone.

A woman. Her voice is relieved but shaking as she calls my name.

"Thank God you're home," she says. "I know it's late. But I didn't know who else to call. I'm terribly sorry to bother you. Do you remember me?"

No luck this time. When? I wonder. How much longer?

"You can hear me," I say to her.

"What?" She makes an effort to mask her hysteria,

but I hear her cover the mouthpiece and sob. "We must have a bad connection. I'll hang up."

"No. Please." I sit forward, rubbing invisible cobwebs from my face. "Of course I remember you. Helló, Mrs. Richterhausen." What time is it? I wonder. "I'm glad you called. How did you know the number?"

"I asked Directory Information. I couldn't forget your name. You were so kind. I have to talk to someone first, before I go back to the hospital."

It's time for her, then. She must face it now; it cannot be put off, not anymore.

"How is your husband?"

"It's my husband," she says, not listening. Her voice breaks up momentarily under electrical interference. The signal reforms, but we are still separated by a grid, as if in an electronic confessional. "At twelve-thirty tonight his, what is it, now?" She bites her lips but cannot control her voice. "His EEG. It . . . stopped. That's what they say. A straight line. There's nothing there. They say it's nonreversible. How can that be?" she asks desperately.

I wait.

"They want you to sign, don't they, Emily?"

"Yes." Her voice is tortured as she says, "It's a good thing, isn't it? You said so yourself, this afternoon. You know about these things. Your wife . . ."

"We're not talking about my wife now, are we?"

"But they say it's right. The doctor said that."

"What is, Emily?"

"The life-support," she says pathetically. "The Maintenance." She still does not know what she is saying. "My husband can be of great value to medical science. Not all the usable organs can be taken at once. They may not be matched up with recipients for some time. That's why the Maintenance is so important. It's safer, more efficient than storage. Isn't that so?"

"Don't think of it as 'life-support,' Emily. Don't fool yourself. There is no longer any life to be supported."

"But he's not dead!"

"No."

"Then his body must be kept alive. . . ."

"Not alive, either," I say. "Your husband is now—and will continue to be—neither alive nor dead. Do you understand that?"

It is too much. She breaks down. "H-how can I decide? I can't tell them to pull the plug. How could I do that to him?"

"Isn't there a decision involved in *not* pulling the plug?"

"But it's for the good of mankind, that's what they say. For people not yet born. Isn't that true? Help me," she says imploringly. "You're a good man. I need to be sure that he won't suffer. Do you think he would want it this way? It was what your wife wanted, wasn't it? At least this way you're able to visit, to go on seeing her. That's important to you, isn't it?"

"He won't feel a thing, if that's what you're asking. He doesn't now, and he never will. Not ever again."

"Then it's all right?"

I wait.

"She's at peace, isn't she, despite everything? It all seems so ghastly, somehow. I don't know what to do. Help me, please. . . ."

"Emily," I say with great difficulty. But it must be done. "Do you understand what will happen to your husband if you authorize the Maintenance?"

She does not answer.

"Only this. Listen: this is how it begins. First he will be connected to an IBM cell separator, to keep track of leucocytes, platelets, red cells, antigens that can't be stored. He will be used around the clock to manufacture an endless red tide for transfusions—"

"But transfusions save lives!"

"Not just transfusions, Emily. His veins will be a battleground for viruses, for pneumonia, hepatitis, leukemia, live cancers. And then his body will be drained off, like a stuck pig's, and a new supply of experimental toxins pumped in, so that he can go on producing antitoxins for them. Listen to me. He will begin to decay inside, Emily. He will be riddled with disease, tumors, parasites. He will stink with fever. His heart will deform, his brain fester with tubercules, his body cavities run with infection. His hair will fall, his skin yellow, his teeth splinter and rot. In the name of science, Emily, in the name of their beloved research.''

I pause.

''That is, if he's one of the lucky ones.''

''But the transplants . . .''

''Yes, that's right! You are so right, Emily. If not the blood, then the transplants. They will take him organ by organ, cell by cell. And it will take years. As long as the machines can keep the lungs and heart moving. And finally, after they've taken his eyes, his kidneys, and the rest, it will be time for his nerve tissue, his lymph nodes, his testes. They will drill out his bone marrow, and when there is no more of that left it will be time to remove his stomach and intestines, as soon as they learn how to transplant those parts, too. And they will. Believe me, they will.''

''No, please. . . .''

''And when he's been thoroughly, efficiently gutted—or when his body has eaten itself from the inside out—when there is nothing left but a respirated sac bathed from within by its own excrement, do you know what they will do then? *Do you?* Then they will begin to strip the skin from his limbs, from his skull, a few millimeters at a time, for grafting and re-grafting, until—''

''Stop!''

''Take him, Emily! Take your William out of there now, tonight, before the technicians can get their bloody hands on him! Sign nothing! Take him home. Take him away and bury him forever. Do that much for him. And for yourself. Let him rest. Give him that one last, most precious gift. Grant him his final peace. You can do that much, can't you? *Can't you?*''

From far away, across miles of the city, I hear the phone drop and then clack dully into place. But only after I have heard another sound, one that I pray I will never hear again.

Goodspeed, Emily, I think, weeping. *Godspeed.*
I resume my vigil.
I try to awaken, and cannot.

3.

There is a machine outside my door. It eats people, chews them up and spits out only what it can't use. It wants to get me, I know it does, but I'm not going to let it.

The call I have been waiting for will never come.

I'm sure of it now. The doctor, or his nurse or secretary or dialing machine, will never announce that they are done at last, that the procedure is no longer cost-effective, that her remains will be released for burial or cremation. Not yesterday, not today, not ever.

I have cut her arteries with stolen scalpels. I have dug with an ice pick deep into her brain, hoping to sever her motor centers. I have probed for her ganglia and nerve cords. I have pierced her eardrums. I have inserted needles, trying to puncture her heart and lungs. I have hidden caustics in the folds of her throat. I have ruined her eyes. But it's no use. It will never be enough.

They will never be done with her.

When I go to the hospital today she will not be there. She will already have been given to the interns for their spinal taps and arteriograms, for surgical practice on a cadaver that is neither alive nor dead. She will belong to the meat cutters, to the first-year med students with their dull knives and stained cross sections. . . .

But I know what I will do.

I will search the floors and labs and secret doors of the wing, and when I find her I will steal her silently away; I will give her safe passage. I can do that much, can't I? I will take her to a place where even they can't reach, beyond the boundaries that separate the living from the dead. I will carry her over the threshold and into that realm, wherever it may be.

And there I will stay with her, to be there with her, to take refuge with her among the dead. I will tear at my body and my corruption until we are one in soft asylum. And there I will remain, living with death for whatever may be left of eternity.

Wish me Godspeed.

THE HOUSE OF HORROR

by Seabury Quinn

"*Morbleu*, Friend Trowbridge, have a care," Jules de Grandin warned as my lurching motor car almost ran into the brimming ditch beside the rain-soaked road.

I wrenched the steering wheel viciously and swore softly under my breath as I leaned forward, striving vainly to pierce the curtains of rain which shut us in.

"No use, old fellow," I confessed, turning to my companion, "we're lost; that's all there is to it."

"Ha," he laughed shortly, "do you just begin to discover that fact, my friend? *Parbleu*, I have known it this last half-hour."

Throttling my engine down, I crept along the concrete roadway, peering through my streaming windshield and storm curtains for some familiar landmark, but nothing but blackness, wet and impenetrable, met my eyes.

Two hours before, answering an insistent 'phone call, de Grandin and I had left the security of my warm office to administer a dose of toxin antitoxin to an Italian laborer's child who lay, choking with diphtheria, in a hut at the workmen's settlement where the new branch of the railroad was being put through. The cold, driving rain and the Stygian darkness of the night had misled me when I made the detour around the railway cut, and for the past hour and a half I had been feeling my way over unfamiliar roads as futilely as a lost child wandering in the woods.

"*Grâce à Dieu*," de Grandin exclaimed, seizing my arm with both his small, strong hands, "a light! See, there it shines in the night. Come, let us go to it. Even the meanest hovel is preferable to this so villainous rain.''

I peeped through a joint in the curtains and saw a faint, intermittent light flickering through the driving rain some two hundred yards away.

"All right," I acquiesced, climbing from the car, "we've lost so much time already we probably couldn't do anything for the Vivianti child, and maybe these people can put us on the right road, anyway."

Plunging through puddles like miniature lakes, soaked by the wind-driven rain, barking our shins again and again on invisible obstacles, we made for the light, finally drawing up to a large, square house of red brick fronted by an imposing white-pillared porch. Light streamed out through the fanlight over the white door and from the two tall windows flanking the portal.

"*Parbleu,* a house of circumstance, this,'' de Grandin commented, mounting the porch and banging lustily at the polished brass knocker.

I wrinkled my forehead in thought while he rattled the knocker a second time. "Strange, I can't remember this place," I muttered. "I thought I knew every building within thirty miles, but this is a new one——"

"Ah bah!" de Grandin interrupted. "Always you must be casting a wet blanket on the parade, Friend Trowbridge. First you insist on losing us in the midst of a *sacré* rainstorm, then when I, Jules de Grandin, find us a shelter from the weather, you must needs waste time in wonderment why it is you know not the place. *Morbleu,* you will refuse shelter because you have never been presented to the master of the house, if I do not watch you, I fear.''

"But I ought to know the place, de Grandin," I protested. "It's certainly imposing enough to——"

My defense was cut short by the sharp click of a lock, and the wide, white door swung inward before us.

We strode over the threshold, removing our dripping hats as we did so, and turned to address the person who had opened the door.

"Why——" I began, and stared about me in open-mouthed surprise.

"Name of a little blue man!" said Jules de Grandin, and added his incredulous stare to mine.

As far as we could see, we were alone in the mansion's imposing hall. Straight before us, perhaps for forty feet, ran a corridor of parquetry flooring, covered here and there by rich-hued Oriental rugs. White-paneled walls, adorned with oil paintings of imposing-looking individuals, rose for eighteen feet or so to a beautifully frescoed ceiling, and a graceful, curving staircase swept upward from the farther end of the room. Candles in cut glass sconces lighted the high-ceiled apartment, the hospitable glow from a log fire burning under the high white marble mantel lent an air of homely coziness to the place, but of anything living, human or animal, there was no faintest trace or sign.

Click! Behind us, the heavy outer door swung to silently on well-oiled hinges and the automatic lock latched firmly.

"Death of my life!" de Grandin murmured, reaching for the door's silver-plated knob and giving it a vigorous twist. "*Par la moustache du diable,* Friend Trowbridge, it is locked! Truly, perhaps it had been better if we had remained outside in the rain!"

"Not at all, I assure you, my dear sir," a rich, mellow voice answered him from the curve of the stairs. "Your arrival was nothing less than providential, gentlemen."

Coming toward us, walking heavily with the aid of a stout cane, was an unusually handsome man attired in pajamas and dressing gown, a sort of nightcap of flowered silk on his white head, slippers of softest Morocco on his feet.

"You are a physician, sir!" he asked, glancing inquiringly at the medicine case in my hand.

"Yes," I answered. "I am Dr. Samuel Trowbridge, from Harrisonville, and this is Dr. Jules de Grandin, of Paris, who is my guest."

"Ah," replied our host, "I am very, very glad to

welcome you to Marston Hall, gentlemen. It so happens that one—er—my daughter, is quite ill, and I have been unable to obtain medical aid for her on account of my infirmities and the lack of a telephone. If I may trespass on your charity to attend my poor child, I shall be delighted to have you as my guests for the night. If you will lay aside your coats''—he paused expectantly. "Ah, thank you''—as we hung our dripping garments over a chair—"you will come this way, please?''

We followed him up the broad stairs and down an upper corridor to a tastefully furnished chamber where a young girl—fifteen years of age, perhaps—lay propped up with a pile of diminutive pillows.

"Anabel, Anabel, my love, here are two doctors to see you," the old gentleman called softly.

The girl moved her fair head with a weary, peevish motion and whimpered softly in her sleep, but gave no further recognition of our presence.

"And what have been her symptoms, if you please, *Monsieur?*'' de Grandin asked as he rolled back the cuffs of his jacket and prepared to make an examination.

"Sleep," replied our host, "just sleep. Some time ago she suffered from influenza, lately she has been given to fits of protracted slumber from which I can not waken her. I fear she may have contracted sleeping sickness sir. I am told it sometimes follows influenza.''

"H'm.'' De Grandin passed his small, pliable hands rapidly over the girl's cheeks in the region of the ears, felt rapidly along her neck over the jugular vein, then raised a puzzled glance to me. "Have you some laudanum and aconite in your bag, Friend Trowbridge?'' he asked.

"There's some morphine," I answered, "and aconite; but no laudanum.''

"No matter," he waved his hand impatiently, bustling over to the medicine case and extracting two small phials from it. "No matter, this will do as well. Some water, if you please, *Monsieur*," he turned to the father, a medicine bottle in each hand.

"But, de Grandin"—I began, when a sudden kick from one of his slender, heavily-shod feet nearly broke my shin—"de Grandin, do you think that's the proper medication?" I finished lamely.

"Oh, *mais oui*, undoubtedly," he replied. "Nothing else would do in this case. Water, if you please, *Monsieur*," he repeated, again addressing the father.

I stared at him in ill-disguised amazement as he extracted a pellet from each of the bottles and quickly ground them to powder while the old gentleman filled a tumbler with water from the porcelain pitcher which stood on the chintz-draped wash-stand in the corner of the chamber. He was as familiar with the arrangement of my medicine case as I was, I knew, and knew that my phials were arranged by numbers instead of being labeled. Deliberately, I saw, he had passed over the morphine and aconite, and had chosen two bottles of plain, unmedicated sugar of milk pills. What his object was I had no idea, but I watched him measure out four teaspoonfuls of water, dissolve the powder in it, and pour the sham medication down the unconscious girl's throat.

"Good," he proclaimed as he washed the glass with meticulous care. "She will rest easily until the morning, *Monsieur*. When daylight comes we shall decide on further treatment. Will you now permit that we retire?" He bowed politely to the master of the house, who returned his courtesy and led us to a comfortably furnished room farther down the corridor.

"See here, de Grandin," I demanded when our host had wished us a pleasant good-night and closed the door upon us, "What was your idea in giving that child an impotent dose like that——?"

"S-s-sh!" he cut me short with a fierce whisper. "That young girl, *mon ami*, is no more suffering from encephalitis than you or I. There is no characteristic swelling of the face or neck, no diagnostic hardening of the jugular vein. Her temperature was a bit subnormal, it is true—but upon her breath I detected the odor of chloral hydrate. For some reason, good I hope, but bad I fear, she is drugged, and I thought it best to play the fool and pretend I believed the man's statements. *Pardieu,* the fool who knows himself no fool has an immense advantage over the fool who believes him one, my friend.''

''But——''

''But me no buts, Friend Trowbridge; remember how the door of this house opened with none to touch it, recall how it closed behind us in the same way, and observe this, if you will.'' Stepping softly, he crossed the room, pulled aside the chintz curtains at the window and tapped lightly on the frame which held the thick plate glass panes. *''Regardez vous,''* he ordered, tapping the frame a second time.

Like every other window I had seen in the house, this one was of the casement type, small panes of heavy glass being sunk into latticelike frames. Under de Grandin's directions I tapped the latter, and found them not painted wood, as I had supposed, but stoutly welded and bolted metal. Also, to my surprise, I found the turnbuckles for opening the casement were only dummies, the metal frames being actually securely bolted to the stone sills. To all intents, we were as firmly incarcerated as though serving a sentence in the state penitentiary.

''The door——'' I began, but he shook his head.

Obeying his gesture, I crossed the room and turned the handle lightly. It twisted under the pressure of my fingers, but, though we had heard no warning click of lock or bolt, the door itself was as firmly fastened as though nailed shut.

''Wh—why,'' I asked stupidly, ''what's it all mean, de Grandin?''

''Je ne sais quoi,'' he answered with a shrug, ''but one thing I know: I like not this house, Friend Trowbridge. I——''

Above the hissing of the rain against the windows and the howl of the sea-wind about the gables, there suddenly rose a scream, wire-edged with inarticulate terror, freighted with utter, transcendental anguish of body and soul.

"*Cordieu!*" He threw up his head like a hound hearing the call of the pack from far away. "Did you hear it, too, Friend Trowbridge?"

"Of course," I answered, every nerve in my body trembling in horripilation with the echo of the hopeless wail.

"*Pardieu,*" he repeated, "I like this house less than ever, now! Come, let us move this dresser before our door. It is safer that we sleep behind barricades this night, I think."

We blocked the door, and I was soon sound asleep.

"Trowbridge, Trowbridge, my friend"—de Grandin drove a sharp elbow into my ribs—"wake up, I beseech you. Name of a green goat, you lie like one dead, save for your so abominable snoring!"

"Eh?" I answered sleepily, thrusting myself deeper beneath the voluminous bedclothes. Despite the unusual occurrences of the night I was tired to the point of exhaustion, and fairly drunk with sleep.

"Up; arise, my friend," he ordered, shaking me excitedly. "The coast is clear, I think, and it is high time we did some exploring."

"Rats!" I scoffed, disinclined to leave my comfortable couch. "What's the use of wandering about a strange house to gratify a few unfounded suspicions? The girl might have been given a dose of chloral hydrate, but the chances are her father thought he was helping her when he gave it. As for these trick devices for opening and locking doors, the old man apparently lives here alone and has installed these mechanical aids to lessen his work. He has to hobble around with a cane, you know."

"Ah!" my companion assented sarcastically. "And that scream we heard, did he install that as an aid to his infirmities, also?"

"Perhaps the girl woke up with a nightmare," I hazarded, but he made an impatient gesture.

"Perhaps the moon is composed of green cheese,

also," he replied. "Up, up and dress; my friend. This house should be investigated while yet there is time. Attend me: But five minutes ago, through this very window, I did observe *Monsieur* our host, attired in a raincoat, depart from his own front door, and without his cane. *Parbleu*, he did skip as agilely as any boy, I assure you. Even now he is almost at the spot where we abandoned your automobile. What he intends doing there I know not. What I intend doing I know full well. Do you accompany me or not?"

"Oh, I suppose so," I agreed, crawling from the bed and slipping into my clothes. "How are you going to get past that locked door?"

He flashed me one of his sudden smiles, shooting the points of his little blond mustache upward like the horns of an inverted crescent. "Observe," he ordered, displaying a short length of thin wire. "In the days when woman's hair was still her crowning glory, what mighty deeds a lady could encompass with a hairpin! *Pardieu*, there was one little grisette in Paris who showed me some tricks in the days before the war! Regard me, if you please."

Deftly he thrust the pliable loop of wire into the keyhole, twisting it tentatively back and forth, at length pulling it out and regarding it carefully. *"Très bien,"* he muttered as he reached into an inside pocket, bringing out a heavier bit of wire.

"See," he displayed the finer wire, "with this I take an impression of that lock's tumblers, now"—quickly he bent the heavier wire to conform to the waved outline of the lighter loop—*"voilà,* I have a key!"

And he had. The lock gave readily to the pressure of his improvised key, and we stood in the long, dark hall, staring about us half curiously, half fearfully.

"This way, if you please," de Grandin ordered; "first we will look in upon *la jeunesse,* to see how it goes with her."

We walked on tiptoe down the corridor, entered the chamber where the girl lay, and approached the bed.

She was lying with her hands folded upon her breast in the manner of those composed for their final rest, her wide, periwinkle-blue eyes staring sightlessly before her, the short, tightly curled ringlets of her blond, bobbed hair surrounding her drawn, pallid face like a golden nimbus encircling the ivory features of a saint in some carved ikon.

My companion approached the bed softly, placing one hand on the girl's wrist with professional precision.

"Temperature low, pulse weak," he murmured, checking off her symptoms. "Complexion pale to the point of lividity,—ha, now for the eyes; sleeping, her pupils should have been contracted, while they should now be dilated—*Dieu de Dieu!* Trowbridge, my friend, come here.

"Look," he commanded, pointing to the apathetic girl's face. "Those eyes—*grand Dieu,* those eyes! It is sacrilege, nothing less."

I looked into the girl's face, then started back with a half-suppressed cry of horror. Asleep, as she had been when we first saw her, the child had been pretty to the point of loveliness. Her features were small and regular, clean-cut as those of a face in a cameo, the tendrils of her light-yellow hair had lent her a dainty, ethereal charm comparable to that of a Dresden china shepherdess. It had needed but the raising of her delicate, long-lashed eyelids to give her face the animation of some laughing sprite playing truant from fairyland.

Her lids were raised now, but the eyes they unveiled were no clear, joyous windows of a tranquil soul. Rather, they were the peepholes of a spirit in torment. The irises were a lovely shade of blue, it is true, but the optics themselves were things of horror. Rolling grotesquely to right and left, they peered futilely in opposite directions, lending to her sweet, pale face the half-ludicrous, wholly hideous expression of a bloating frog.

"Good heavens!" I exclaimed, turning from the deformed girl with a feeling of disgust akin to nausea; "What a terrible affliction!"

De Grandin made no reply, but bent over the girl's

still form, gazing intently at her malformed eyes. "It is not natural," he announced. "The muscles have been tampered with, and tampered with by someone who is a master hand at surgery. Will you get me your syringe and some strychnine, Friend Trowbridge? This poor one is still unconscious."

I hastened to our bedroom and returned with the hypodermic and stimulant, then stood beside him, watching eagerly, as he administered a strong injection.

The girl's narrow chest fluttered as the powerful drug took effect, and the pale lids dropped for a second over her repulsive eyes. Then, with a sob which was half moan, she attempted to raise herself on her elbow, fell back again, and, with apparent effort, gasped, "The mirror, let me have the mirror! Oh, tell me it isn't true; tell me it was a trick of some sort. Oh, the horrible thing I saw in the glass couldn't have been I. Was it?"

"*Tiens, ma petite,*" de Grandin replied, "but you speak in riddles. What is it you would know?"

"He—he"—the girl faltered weakly, forcing her trembling lips to frame the words—"that horrible old man showed me a mirror a little while ago and said the face in it was mine. Oh, it was horrible, horrible!"

"Eh? What is this?" de Grandin demanded on a rising note. " 'He'? 'Horrible old man'? Are you not his daughter? Is he not your father?"

"No," the girl gasped, so low her denial was scarcely audible. "I was driving home from Mackettsdale last—oh, I forget when it was, but it was at night—and my tires punctured. I—I think there must have been glass on the road, for the shoes were cut to ribbons. I saw the light in this home and came to ask for help. An old man—oh, I thought he was so nice and kind!—let me in and said he was all alone here and about to eat dinner, and asked me to join him. I ate some—some—oh, I don't remember what it was— and the next thing I knew he was standing by my bed, holding a mirror up to me and telling me it was my face I saw in the glass. Oh, please, *please*, tell me it

was some terrible trick he played on me. I'm not truly
hideous, am I?''

"Morbleu!" de Grandin muttered softly, tugging at
the ends of his mustache. "What is all this?"

To the girl he said: "But of course not. You are like
a flower, *Mademoiselle*. A little flower that dances in
the wind. You——''

"And my eyes, they aren't—they aren't"—she interrupted with piteous eagerness—"please tell me they
aren't——''

"Mais non, ma chère," he assured her. "Your eyes
are like the *pervenche* that mirrors the sky in springtime. They are——''

"Let—let me see the mirror, please," she interrupted
in an anxious whisper. "I'd like to see for myself, if
you—oh, I feel all weak inside——'' She lapsed back
against the pillow, her lids mercifully veiling the hideously distorted eyes and restoring her face to tranquil
beauty.

"Cordieu!" de Grandin breathed. "The chloral re-
asserted itself none too soon for Jules de Grandin's
comfort, Friend Trowbridge. Sooner would I have gone
to the rack than have shown that pitiful child her face
in a mirror.''

"But what's it all mean?" I asked. "She says she
came here, and——''

"And the rest remains for us to find out, I think,"
he replied evenly. "Come, we lose time, and to lose
time is to be caught, my friend.''

De Grandin led the way down the hall, peering eagerly into each door we passed in search of the owner's
chamber, but before his quest was satisfied he stopped
abruptly at the head of the stairs. "Observe, Friend
Trowbridge," he ordered, pointing a carefully mani-
cured forefinger to a pair of buttons, one white, one
black, set in the wall. "Unless I am more mistaken
than I think I am, we have here the key to the situation—or at least to the front door.''

He pushed vigorously at the white button, then ran
to the curve of the stairs to note the result.

Sure enough, the heavy door swung open on its hinges of cast bronze, letting gusts of rain drive into the lower hall.

"*Pardieu,*" he ejaculated, "we have here the open sesame; let us see if we possess the closing secret as well! Press the black button, Trowbridge, my friend, while I watch."

I did his bidding, and a delighted exclamation told me the door had closed.

"Now what?" I asked, joining him on the stairway.

"U'm," he pulled first one, then the other end of his diminutive mustache meditatively; "the house possesses its attractions, Friend Trowbridge, but I believe it would be well if we went out to observe what our friend, *le vieillard horrible,* does. I like not to have one who shows young girls their disfigured faces in mirrors near our conveyance."

Slipping into our raincoats we opened the door, taking care to place a wad of paper on the sill to prevent its closing tightly enough to latch, and scurried out into the storm.

As we left the shelter of the porch a shaft of indistinct light shone through the rain, as my car was swung from the highway and headed toward a depression to the left of the house.

"*Parbleu,* he is a thief, this one!" de Grandin exclaimed excitedly. "*Hola, Monsieur!*" He ran forward, swinging his arms like a pair of semaphores. "What sort of business is it you make with our *moteur?*"

The wailing of the storm tore the words from his lips and hurled them away, but the little Frenchman was not to be thwarted. "*Pardieu,*" he gasped, bending his head against the wind-driven rain, "I will stop the scoundrel if—*nom d'un coq,* he has done it!"

Even as he spoke the old man flung open the car's forward door and leaped, allowing the machine to go crashing down a low, steep embankment into a lake of slimy swamp-mud.

For a moment the vandal stood contemplating his

work, then burst into a peal of wild laughter more malignant than any profanity.

"*Parbleu,* robber, *Apache!* you shall laugh from the other side of your mouth!" de Grandin promised, as he made for the old man.

But the other seemed oblivious of our presence. Still chuckling at his work, he turned toward the house, stopped short as a sudden heavy gust of wind shook the trees along the roadway, then started forward with a yell of terror as a great branch, torn bodily from a towering oak tree came crashing toward the earth.

He might as well have attempted to dodge a meteorite. Like an arrow from the bow of divine justice, the great timber hurtled down, pinning his frail body to the ground like a worm beneath a laborer's brogan.

"Trowbridge, my friend," de Grandin announced matter-of-factly, "observe the evil effects of stealing motor cars."

We lifted the heavy bough from the prostrate man and turned him over on his back. De Grandin on one side, I on the other, we made a hasty examination, arriving at the same finding simultaneously. His spinal column was snapped like a pipestem.

"You have some last statement to make, *Monsieur?*" de Grandin asked curtly. "If so, you had best be about it, your time is short."

"Y—yes," the stricken man replied weakly. "I—I meant to kill you, for you might have hit upon my secret. As it is, you may publish it to the world, that all may know what it meant to offend a Marston. In my room you will find the documents. My—my pets—are—in—the—cellar. She—was—to—have—been—one—of—them." The pauses between his words became longer and longer, his voice grew weaker with each labored syllable. As he whispered the last sentence painfully there was a gurgling sound, and a tiny stream of blood welled up at the corner of his mouth. His narrow chest rose and fell once with a convulsive movement, then his jaw dropped limply. He was dead.

"Oh ho," de Grandin remarked, "it is a hemorrhage which finished him. A broken rib piercing his lung. U'm? I should have guessed it. Come, my friend, let us carry him to the house, then see what it was he meant by that talk of documents and pets. A pest upon the fellow for dying with his riddle half explained! Did he not know that Jules de Grandin can not resist the challenge of a riddle? *Parbleu,* we will solve this mystery, *Monsieur le Mort,* if we have to hold an autopsy to do so!''

"Oh, for heaven's sake, hush, de Grandin,'' I besought, shocked at his heartlessness. "The man is dead.''

"Ah bah!'' he returned scornfully. "Dead or not, did he not steal your motor car?''

We laid our gruesome burden on the hall couch and mounted the stairs to the second floor. With de Grandin in the lead we found the dead man's room and began a systematic search for the papers he had mentioned, almost with his last breath. After some time my companion unearthed a thick, leather-bound portfolio from the lower drawer of a beautiful old mahogany highboy, and spread its wide leaves open on the white-counterpaned bed.

"Ah,'' he drew forth several papers and held them to the light, "we begin to make the progress, Friend Trowbridge. What is this?''

He held out a newspaper clipping cracked from long folding and yellowed with age. It read:

Actress Jilts Surgeon's Crippled Son on Eve of Wedding

Declaring she could not stand the sight of his deformity, and that she had engaged herself to him only in a moment of thoughtless pity, Dora Lee, well-known variety actress, last night repudiated her promise to marry John Biersfield Marston, Jr., hopelessly crippled son of Dr. John Biersfield Marston, the well-known surgeon and expert osteologist. Neither the abandoned bridegroom nor his father could be seen by reporters from the *Planet* last night.

"Very good," de Grandin nodded, "we need go no farther with that account. A young woman, it would seem, once broke her promise to marry a cripple, and judging from this paper's date, that was in 1896. Here is another, what do you make of it?"

The clipping he handed me read as follows:

Surgeon's Son a Suicide

Still sitting in the wheel-chair from which he has not moved during his waking hours since he was hopelessly crippled while playing polo in England ten years ago, John Biersfield Marston, son of the famous surgeon of the same name, was found in his bedroom this morning by his valet. A rubber hose was connected with a gas jet, the other end being held in the young man's mouth.

Young Marston was jilted by Dora Lee, well-known vaudeville actress, on the day before the date set for their wedding, one month ago. He is reported to have been extremely low-spirited since his desertion by his fiancée.

Dr. Marston, the bereaved father, when seen by reporters from the *Planet* this morning, declared the actress was responsible for his son's death and announced his intention of holding her accountable. When asked if legal proceedings were contemplated, he declined further information.

"So?" de Grandin nodded shortly. "Now this one, if you please."

The third clipping was brief to the point of curtness:

Well-known Surgeon Retires

Dr. John Biersfield Marston, widely known throughout this section of the country as an expert in operations concerning the bones, has announced his intention of retiring from practice. His house has been sold, and he will move from the city.

"The record is clear so far," de Grandin asserted, studying the first clipping with raised eyebrows, "but—*morbleu,* my friend, look, look at this picture. This Dora Lee, of whom does she remind you? Eh?"

I took the clipping again and looked intently at the illustration of the article announcing young Marston's broken engagement. The woman in the picture was young and inclined to be overdressed in the voluminous, fluffy mode of the days before the Spanish-American War.

"U'm, no one whom I know——" I began, but halted abruptly as a sudden likeness struck me. Despite the towering pompadour arrangement of her blond hair and the unbecoming straw sailor hat above the coiffure, the woman in the picture bore a certain resemblance to the disfigured girl we had seen a half-hour before.

The Frenchman saw recognition dawn in my face, and nodded agreement. "But of course," he said. "Now, the question is, is this young girl whose eyes are so out of alinement a relative of this Dora Lee, or is the resemblance a coincidence, and if so, what lies behind it? *Hein?*"

"I don't know," I admitted, "but there must be some connection——"

"Connection? Of course there is a connection," de Grandin affirmed, rummaging deeper in the portfolio.

"A-a-ah! What is this? *Nom d'un nom,* Friend Trowbridge, I think I smell the daylight! Look!"

He held a full-page story from one of the sensational New York dailies before him, his eyes glued to the flowing type and crude, coarse-screened half-tones of half a dozen young women which composed the article.

"WHAT HAS BECOME OF THE MISSING GIRLS?" I read in bold-faced type across the top of the page.

"Are sinister, unseen hands reaching out from the darkness to seize our girls from palace and hovel, shop, stage and office?" the article asked rhetorically. "Where are Ellen Munro and Dorothy Sawyer and Phyllis Bouchet and three other lovely, light-haired girls who have walked into oblivion during the past year?"

I read to the end the sensational account of the girls' disappearances. The cases seemed fairly similar; each of the vanished young women had failed to return to her home and had never been accounted for in any manner, and in no instance, according to the newspaper, had there been any assignable reason for voluntary departure.

"*Parbleu,* but he was stupid, even for a journalist!" de Grandin asserted as I completed my inspection of the story. "Why, I wager even my good Friend Trowbridge has already noticed one important fact which this writer has treated as though it were as commonplace as the nose on his face."

"Sorry to disappoint you, old chap," I answered, "but it looks to me as though the reporter had covered the case from every possible angle."

"Ah? So?" he replied sarcastically. "*Morbleu,* we shall have to consult the oculist in your behalf when we return home, my friend. Look, look, I beseech you, upon the pictures of these so totally absent and unaccounted for young women, *cher ami,* and tell me if you do not observe a certain likeness among them, not only a resemblance to each other, but to that Mademoiselle Lee who jilted the son of Dr. Marston? Can you see it, now I have pointed it out?''

''No—wh—why, yes,—yes, of course!'' I responded, running my eye over the pictures accompanying the story. ''By the Lord Harry, de Grandin, you're right; you might almost say there is a family resemblance between these girls! You've put your finger on it, I do believe.''

''*Hélas,* no!'' he answered with a shrug. ''I have put my finger on nothing as yet, my friend. I reach, I grope, I feel about me like a blind man tormented by a crowd of naughty little boys, but nothing do the poor fingers of my mind encounter. Pah! Jules de Grandin, you are one great fool! Think, think, stupid one!''

He seated himself on the edge of the bed, cupping his face in his hands and leaning forward till his elbows rested on his knees.

Suddenly he sprang erect, one of his elfish smiles passing across his small, regular features. ''*Nom d'ua chat rouge,* my friend, I have it—I have it!'' he announced. ''The pets—the pets that old stealer of motor cars spoke of! They are in the basement! *Pardieu,* we will see those pets, *cher* Trowbridge; with our four collective eyes we will see them. Did not that so execrable stealer declare she was to have been one of them! Now, in the name of Satan and brimstone, whom could he have meant by 'she' if not that unfortunate child with eyes like *la grenouille?* Eh?''

''Why——'' I began, but he waved me forward.

''Come, come; let us go,'' he urged. ''I am impatient, I am restless, I am not to be restrained. We shall investigate and see for ourselves what sort of pets are kept by one who shows young girls their deformed faces in mirrors and—*parbleu!*—steals motor cars from my friends.''

Hurrying down the main stairway, we hunted about for the cellar entrance, finally located the door and holding above our heads a pair of candles from the hall, began descending a flight of rickety steps into a pitch-black basement, rock-walled and, judging by its damp, moldy odor, unfloored save by the bare, moist earth beneath the house.

"*Parbleu,* the dungeons of the château at Carcassonne are more cheerful than this," de Grandin commented as he paused at the stairs' foot, holding his candle aloft to make a better inspection of the dismal place.

I suppressed a shudder of mingled chill and apprehension as I stared at the blank stone walls, unpierced by windows or other openings of any sort, and made ready to retrace my steps. "Nothing here," I announced. "You can see that with half an eye. The place is as empty as——"

"Perhaps, Friend Trowbridge," he agreed, "but Jules de Grandin does not look with half an eye. He uses both eyes, and uses them more than once if his first glance does not prove sufficient. Behold that bit of wood on the earth yonder. What do you make of it?"

"U'm—a piece of flooring, maybe," I hazarded.

"Maybe yes, maybe no," he answered. "Let us see."

Crossing the cellar, he bent above the planks, then turned to me with a satisfied smile. "Flooring does not ordinarily have ring-bolts in it, my friend," he remarked, bending to seize the iron ring which was made fast to the boards by a stout staple.

"Ha!" As he heaved upward the planks came away from the black earth, disclosing a board-lined well about three feet square and of uncertain depth. An almost vertical ladder of two-by-four timbers led downward from the trap-door to the well's impenetrable blackness.

"*Allons,* we descend," he commented, turning about and setting his foot on the topmost rung of the ladder.

"Don't be a fool," I advised. "You don't know what's down there."

"True"—his head was level with the floor as he answered—"but I shall know, with luck, in a few moments. Do you come?"

I sighed with vexation as I prepared to follow him.

* * *

At the ladder's foot he paused, raising his candle and looking about inquiringly. Directly before us was a passageway through the earth, ceiled with heavy planks and shored up with timbers like the lateral workings of a primitive mine.

"Ah, the plot shows complications," he murmured, stepping briskly into the dark tunnel. "Do you come, Friend Trowbridge?"

I followed, wondering what manner of thing might be at the end of the black, musty passage, but nothing but fungus-grown timbers and walls of moist, black earth met my questing gaze.

De Grandin preceded me by some paces, and I suppose, we had gone fifteen feet through the passage when a gasp of mingled surprise and horror from my companion brought me beside him in two long strides. Fastened with nails to the timbers at each side of the tunnel were a number of white, glistening objects, objects which, because of their very familiarity, denied their identity to my wondering eyes. There was no mistaking the things; even a layman could not have failed to recognize them for what they were. I, as a physician, knew them even better. To the right of the passage hung fourteen perfectly articulated skeletons of human legs, complete from foot to ilium, gleaming white and ghostly in the flickering light of the candles.

"Good heavens!" I exclaimed.

"*Sang du diable!*" Jules de Grandin commented. "Behold what is there, my friend," he pointed to the opposite wall. Fourteen bony arms, complete from hand to shoulder-joint, hung pendulously from the tunnel's upright timbers.

"*Pardieu,*" de Grandin muttered, "I have known men who collected stuffed birds and dried insects; I have known those who stored away Egyptian mummies—even the skulls of men long dead—but never before have I seen a collection of arms and legs! *Parbleu,* he was *caduc*—mad as a hatter, this one, or I am much mistaken!"

"So these were his pets?" I answered. "Yes, the man was undoubtedly mad to keep such a collection, and in a place like this. Poor fellow——"

"*Nom d'un canon!*" de Grandin broke in; "what was that?"

From the darkness before us there came a queer, inarticulate sound, such as a man might make attempting to speak with a mouth half-filled with food, and, as though the noise had wakened an echo slumbering in the cavern, the sound was repeated, multiplied again and again till it resembled the babbling of half a dozen overgrown infants—or an equal number of full-grown imbeciles.

"Onward!" Responding to the challenge of the unknown like a warrior obeying the trumpet's call to charge, de Grandin dashed toward the strange noise, swung about, flashing his candle this side and that, then:

"*Nom de Dieu de nom de Dieu!*" he almost shrieked. "Look, Friend Trowbridge, look and say that you see what I see, or have I, too, gone mad?"

Lined up against the wall was a series of seven small wooden boxes, each with a door composed of upright slats before it, similar in construction to the coops in which country folk pen brooding hens—and no larger. In each of the hutches huddled an object the like of which I had never before seen, even in the terrors of nightmare.

The things had the torsos of human beings, though hideously shrunken from starvation and incrusted with scales of filth, but there all resemblance to mankind ceased. From shoulders and waist there twisted flaccid tentacles of unsupported flesh, the upper ones terminating in flat, paddlelike flippers which had some remote resemblance to hands, the lower ones ending in almost shapeless stubs which resembled feet only in that each had a fringe of five shriveled, unsupported protuberances of withered flesh.

On scrawny necks were balanced caricatures of faces, flat, noseless, chinless countenances with horrible crossed or divergent eyes, mouths widened almost beyond resemblance to buccal orifices, and—horror of horrors!—elongated, *split* tongues protruding several inches from the lips and wagging impotently in vain efforts to form words.

"Satan, thou art outdone!" de Grandin cried as he held his candle before a scrap of paper decorating one of the cages after the manner of a sign before an animal's den at the zoo. "Observe!" he ordered, pointing a shaking finger at the notice.

I looked, then recoiled, sick with horror. The paper bore the picture and name of Ellen Munro one of the girls mentioned as missing in the newspaper article we had found in the dead man's bedroom.

Beneath the photograph was scribbled in an irregular hand: "Paid 1-25-97."

Sick at heart we walked down the line of pens. Each was labeled with the picture of a young and pretty girl with the notation, "Paid," followed by a date. Every girl named as missing in the newspaper was represented in the cages.

Last of all, in a coop somewhat smaller than the rest, we found a body more terribly mutilated than any. This was marked with the photograph and name of Dora Lee. Beneath her name was the date of her "payment," written in bold red figures.

"Parbleu, what are we to do, my friend?" de Grandin asked in an hysterical whisper. "We can not return these poor ones to the world, that would be the worst form of cruelty; yet—yet I shrink from the act of mercy I know they would ask me to perform if they could speak."

"Let's go up," I begged. "We must think this thing over, de Grandin, and if I stay here any longer I shall faint."

"Bien," he agreed, and turned to follow me from the cavern of horrors.

"It is to consider," he began as we reached the upper hall once more. "If we give those so pitiful ones the stroke of mercy we are murderers before the law, yet what service could we render them by bringing them once more into the world? Our choice is a hard one, my friend.''

I nodded.

''*Morbleu*, but he was clever, that one,'' the Frenchman continued, half to me, half to himself. ''What a surgeon! Fourteen instances of Wyeth's amputation of the hip and as many more of the shoulder—and every patient lived, lived to suffer the tortures of that hell-hole down there! But it is marvelous! None but a madman could have done it.

''Bethink you, Friend Trowbridge. Think how the mighty man of medicine brooded over the suicide of his crippled son, meditating hatred and vengeance for the heartless woman who had jilted him. Then—snap! went his great mentality, and from hating one woman he fell to hating all, to plotting vengeance against the many for the sin of the one. And, *cordieu*, what a vengeance! How he must have laid his plans to secure his victims; how he must have worked to prepare that hell-under-the-earth to house those poor, broken bodies which were his handiwork, and how he must have drawn upon the great surgical skill which was his, even in his madness, to transform those once lovely ones into the visions of horror we have just beheld! Horror of horrors! To remove the bones and let the girls still live!''

He rose, pacing impatiently across the hall. ''What to do? What to do?'' he demanded, striking his open hands against his forehead.

I followed his nervous steps with my eyes, but my brain was too numbed by the hideous things I had just seen to be able to respond to his question.

I looked hopelessly past him at the angle of the wall by the great fireplace, rubbed my eyes and looked again. Slowly, but surely, the wall was declining from the perpendicular.

''De Grandin,'' I shouted, glad of some new phenomenon to command my thoughts, ''the wall—the wall's leaning!''

''Eh, the wall?'' he queried. ''*Pardieu*, yes! It is the rain; the foundations are undermined. Quick, quick, my friend! To the cellars, or those unfortunate ones are undone!''

We scrambled down the stairs leading to the basement, but already the earth floor was sopping with water. The well leading to the madman's subcellar was more than half full of bubbling, earthly ooze.

"Mary, have pity!" de Grandin exclaimed. "Like rats in a trap, they did die. God rest their tired souls"—he shrugged his shoulders as he turned to retrace his steps—"it is better so. Now, Friend Trowbridge, do you hasten aloft and bring down that young girl from the room above. We must run for it if we do not wish to be crushed under the falling timbers of this house of abominations!''

The storm had spent itself and a red, springtime sun was peeping over the horizon as de Grandin and I trudged up my front steps with the mutilated girl stumbling wearily between us.

"Put her to bed, my excellent one," de Grandin ordered Nora, my housekeeper, who came to meet us enveloped in righteous indignation and an outing flannel nightgown. *"Parbleu*, she has had many troubles!''

In the study, a glass of steaming whiskey and hot water in one hand, a vile-smelling French cigarette in the other, he faced me across the desk. "How was it you knew not that house, my friend?'' he demanded.

I grinned sheepishly. "I took the wrong turning at the detour," I explained, "and got on the Yerbysville Road. It's just recently been hard-surfaced, and I haven't used it for years because it was always impassable. Thinking we were on the Andover Pike all the while, I never connected the place with the old Olmsted mansion I'd seen hundreds of times from the road.''

"Ah, yes," he agreed, nodding thoughtfully, "a little turn from the right way, and—pouf!—what a distance we have to retrace.''

"Now, about the girl upstairs," I began, but he waved the question aside.

"The mad one had but begun his devil's work on her," he replied. "I, Jules de Grandin, will operate on her eyes and make them as straight as before, nor will I accept one penny for my work. Meantime, we must find her kindred and notify them she is safe and in good hands.

"And now"—he handed me his empty tumbler—"a little more whiskey, if you please, Friend Trowbridge."

CASEY AGONISTES

by Richard McKenna

You can't just plain die. You got to do it by the book.

That's how come I'm here in this TB ward with nine other recruits. Basic training to die.

You do it by stages. First a big ward, you walk around and go out and they call you mister. Then, if you got what it takes, a promotion to this isolation ward and they call you charles. You can't go nowhere, you meet the masks, and you get the feel of being dead.

Being dead is being weak and walled off. You hear car noises and see little doll-people down on the sidewalks, but when they come to visit you they wear white masks and nightgowns and talk past you in the wrong voices. They're scared you'll rub some off on them. You would, too, if you knew how.

Nobody ever visits me. I had practice being dead before I come here. Maybe that's how I got to be charles so quick.

It's easy, playing dead here. You eat your pills, make out to sleep in the quiet hours and drink your milk like a good little charles. You grin at their phony joshing about how healthy you look and feel. You all know better, but them's the rules.

Sick call is when they really make you know it. It's a parade—the head doctor and nurse, the floor nurse Mary Howard and two interns, all in masks and nightgowns. Mary pushes the wheeled rack with our fever charts on it. The doc is a tall skinhead with wooden eyes and pinchnose glasses. The head nurse is fat, with little pig eyes and a deep voice.

The doc can't see, hear, smell or touch you. He looks at your reflection in the chart and talks about you like you was real, but it's Mary that pulls down the cover and opens your pajama coat, and the interns poke and look and listen and tell the doc what they see and hear. He asks them questions for you to answer. You tell them how good you feel and they tell him. He ain't supposed to get contaminated.

Mary's small, dark and sweet and the head nurse gives her a bad time. One intern is small and dark like Mary, with soft black eyes and very gentle. The other one is pink and chubby.

The doc's voice is high and thin, like he ain't all there below decks. The head nurse snaps at Mary, snips at the interns, and puts a kind of dog wiggle in her voice when she talks to the doc.

I'm glad not to know what's under any of their masks, except maybe Mary's, because I can likely imagine better faces for them than God did. The head nurse makes rounds, writing the book. When she catches us out of line, like smoking or being up in a quiet hour, she gives Mary hell.

She gives us hell too, like we was babies. She kind of hints that if we ain't respectful to her and obey her rules maybe she won't let us die after all.

Christ, how I hate that hag! I hope I meet her in hell.

That's how it struck me, first day or two in isolation. I'd looked around for old shipmates, like a guy does, but didn't see any. On the third day one recognized me. I thought I knew that gravel voice, but even after he told me I couldn't hardly believe it was old Slop Chute Hewitt.

He was skin and bones and his blue eyes had a kind of puzzled look like I saw in them once year ago when a big limey sucker punched him in Nagasaki Joe's. When I remembered that, it made me know, all right.

He said glad to see me there and we both laughed. Some of the others shuffled over in striped bathrobes and all of a sudden I was in like Flynn, knowing Slop Chute. I found out they called the head doc Uncle Death. The fat nurse was Mama Death. The blond intern was Pink Waldo, the dark one Curly Waldo, and Mary was Mary. Knowing things like that is a kind of password.

They said Curly Waldo was sweet on Mary, but he was a poor Italian. Pink Waldo come of good family and was trying to beat him out. They were pulling for Curly Waldo.

When they left, Slop Chute and me talked over old times in China. I kept seeing him like he was on the *John D. Edwards*, sitting with a cup of coffee topside by the after fireroom hatch, while his snipes turned to down below. He wore bleached dungarees and shined shoes and he looked like a lord of the earth. His broad face and big belly. The way he stoked chow into himself in the guinea pullman—that's what give him his name. The way he took aboard beer and samshu in Kongmoon Happiness Garden. The way he swung the little ne-sans dancing in the hotels on Skibby Hill. Now . . . Godalmighty! It made me know.

But he still had the big jack-lantern grin.

"Remember little Connie that danced at the Palais?" he asked.

I remember her, half Portygee, cute as hell.

"You know, Charley, now I'm headed for scrap, the onliest one damn thing I'm sorry for is I didn't shack with her when I had the chance."

"She was nice," I said.

"She was green fire in the velvet, Charley. I had her a few times when I was on the *Monocacy*. She wanted to shack and I wouldn't never do it. Christ, Christ, I wish I did, now!"

"I ain't sorry for anything, that I can think of."

"You'll come to it, sailor. For every guy there's some one thing. Remember how Connie used to put her finger on her nose like a Jap girl?"

"Now, Mr. Noble, you mustn't keep arthur awake in quiet hour. Lie down yourself, please."

It was Mama Death, sneaked up on us.

''Now rest like a good boy, charles, and we'll have you home before you know it,'' she told me on her way out.

I thought a thought at her.

The ward had green-gray linoleum, high, narrow windows, a spar-color overhead, and five bunks on a side. My bunk was at one end next to the solarium. Slop Chute was across from me in the middle. Six of us was sailors, three soldiers, and there was one marine.

We got mucho sack time, training for the long sleep. The marine bunked next to me and I saw a lot of him.

He was a strange guy. Name of Carnahan, with a pointed nose and a short upper lip and a go-to-hell stare. He most always wore his radio earphones and he was all the time grinning and chuckling like he was in a private world from the rest of us.

It wasn't the program that made him grin, either, like I thought first. He'd do it even if some housewife was yapping about how to didify the dumplings. He carried on worst during sick call. Sometimes Uncle Death looked across almost like he could hear it direct.

I asked him about it and he put me off, but finally he told me. Seems he could hypnotize himself to see a big ape and then make the ape clown around. He told me I might could get to see it too. I wanted to try, so we did.

''He's there,'' Carnahan would say. ''Sag your eyes, look out the corners. He won't be plain at first.

''Just *expect* him, he'll come. Don't want him to do anything. You just *feel*. He'll do what's natural,'' he kept telling me.

I got where I could see the ape—Casey, Carnahan called him—in flashes. Then one day Mama Death was chewing out Mary and I saw him plain. He come up behind Mama and—I busted right out laughing.

He looked like a bowlegged man in an ape suit covered with red-brown hair. He grinned and made faces with a mouth full of big yellow teeth and he was furnished like John Keeno himself. I roared.

"Put on your phones so you'll have an excuse for laughing," Carnahan whispered. "Only you and me can see him, you know."

Fixing to be dead, you're ready for God knows what, but Casey was sure something.

"Hell, no, he ain't real," Carnahan said. "We ain't so real ourselves any more. That's why we can see him."

Carnahan told me okay to try and let Slop Chute in on it. It ended we cut the whole gang in, going slow so the masks wouldn't get suspicious.

It bothered Casey at first, us all looking at him. It was like we all had a string on him and he didn't know who to mind. He backed and filled and tacked and yawed all over the ward not able to steer himself. Only when Mama Death was there and Casey went after her, then it was like all the strings pulled the same way.

The more we watched him the plainer and stronger he got till finally he started being his own man. He came and went as he pleased and we never knew what he'd do next except that there'd be a laugh in it. Casey got more and more there for us, but he never made a sound.

He made a big difference. We all wore our earphones and giggled like idiots. Slop Chute wore his big sideways grin more often. Old Webster almost stopped griping.

There was a man filling in for a padre came to visitate us every week. Casey would sit on his knee and wiggle and drool, with one finger between those strong, yellow teeth. The man said the radio was a Godsend to us patient spirits in our hour of trial. He stopped coming.

Casey made a real show out of sick call. He kissed Mama Death smack on her mask, danced with her and bit her on the rump. He rode piggy back on Uncle Death. He even took a hand in Mary's romance.

One Waldo always went in on each side of a bunk to look, listen and feel for Uncle. Mary could go on either side. We kept count of whose side she picked and how close she stood to him. That's how we figured Pink Waldo was ahead.

Well, Casey started to shoo her gently in by Curly Waldo and then crowd her closer to him. And, you know, the count began to change in Curly's favor. Casey had something.

If no masks were around to bedevil, Casey would dance and turn handsprings. He made us all feel good.

Uncle Death smelled a rat and had the radio turned off during sick call and quiet hours. But he couldn't cut off Casey.

Something went wrong with Roby, the cheerful black boy next to Slop Chute. The masks were all upset about it and finally Mary come told him on the sly. He wasn't going to make it. They were going to flunk him back to the big ward and maybe back to the world.

Mary's good that way. We never see her face, of course, but I always imagine for her a mouth like Venus has, in that picture you see her standing in the shell.

When Roby had to go, he come around to each bunk and said goodbye. Casey stayed right behind him with his tongue stuck out. Roby kept looking around for Casey, but of course he couldn't see him.

He turned around, just before he left the ward, and all of a sudden Casey was back in the middle and scowling at him. Roby stood looking at Casey with the saddest face I ever saw him wear. Then Casey grinned and waved a hand. Roby grinned back and tears run down his black face. He waved and shoved off.

Casey took to sleeping in Roby's bunk till another recruit come in.

One day two masked orderlies loaded old Webster the whiner onto a go-to-Jesus cart and wheeled him off to X ray. They said. But later one came back and wouldn't look at us and pushed Webster's locker out and we knew. The masks had him in a quiet room for the graduation exercises.

They always done that, Slop Chute told me, so's not to hurt the morale of the guys not able to make the grade yet. Trouble was, when a guy went to X ray on a go-to-Jesus cart he never knew till he got back whether he was going to see the gang again.

Next morning when Uncle Death fell in for sick call, Casey come bouncing down the ward and hit him a haymaker plumb on the mask.

I swear the bald-headed bastard staggered. I know his glasses fell off and Pink Waldo caught them. He said something about a moment of vertigo, and made a quick job of sick call. Casey stayed right behind him and kicked his stern post every step he took.

Mary favored Curly Waldo's side that day without any help from Casey.

After that Mama Death really got ugly. She slob-bered loving care all over us to keep us from knowing what we was there for. We got baths and back rubs we didn't want. Quiet hour had to start on the dot and be really quiet. She was always reading Mary off in whis-pers, like she knew it bothered us.

Casey followed her around aping her duck waddle and poking her behind now and again. We laughed and she thought it was at her and I guess it was. So she got Uncle Death to order the routine temperatures taken rectally, which she knew we hated. We stopped laughing and she knocked off the rectal temperatures. It was a kind of unspoken agreement. Casey give her a worse time than ever, but we saved our laughing till she was gone.

Poor Slop Chute couldn't do anything about his big, lopsided grin that was louder than a belly laugh. Mama give him a real bad time. She arthured the hell out of him.

He was coming along first rate, had another hem-orrhage, and they started taking him to the clinic on a go-to-Jesus cart instead of in a chair. He was supposed to use ducks and a bedpan instead of going to the head, but he saved it up and after lights out we used to help him walk to the head. That made his reflection in the chart wrong and got him in deeper with Uncle Death.

I talked to him a lot, mostly about Connie. He said he dreamed about her pretty often now.

"I figure it means I'm near ready for the deep six, Charley."

"Figure you'll see Connie then?"

"No. Just hope I won't have to go on thinking about her then. I want it to be all night in and no reveille."

"Yeah," I said, "me too. What ever become of Connie?"

"I heard she ate poison right after the Reds took over Shanghai. I wonder if she ever dreamed about me?"

"I bet she did, Slop Chute," I said. "She likely used to wake up screaming and she ate the poison just to get rid of you."

He put on his big grin.

"You regret something, too, Charley. You find it yet?"

"Well, maybe," I said. "Once on a stormy night at sea on the *Black Hawk* I had a chance to push King Brody over the side. I'm sorry now I didn't."

"Just come to you?"

"Hell, no, it come to me three days later when he give me a week's restriction in Tsingtao. I been sorry ever since."

"No. It'll smell you out, Charley. You wait."

Casey was shadow boxing down the middle of the ward as I shuffled back to my bunk.

It must've been spring because the days were longer. One night, right after the nurse come through, Casey and Carnahan and me helped Slop Chute walk to the head. While he was there he had another hemorrhage.

Carnahan started for help but Casey got in the way and motioned him back and we knew Slop Chute didn't want it.

We pulled Slop Chute's pajama top off and steadied him. He went on his knees in front of the bowl and

the soft, bubbling cough went on for a long time. We
kept flushing it. Casey opened the door and went out
to keep away the nurse.

Finally it pretty well stopped. Slop Chute was too
weak to stand. We cleaned him up and I put my pajama top on him, and we stood him up. If Casey hadn't
took half the load, we'd a never got him back to his
bunk.

Godalmighty! I used to carry hundred-kilo sacks of
cement like they was nothing.

We went back and cleared up the head. I washed out
the pajama top and draped it on the radiator. I was in
a cold sweat and my face burned when I turned in.

Across the ward Casey was sitting like a statue beside Slop Chute's bunk.

Next day was Friday, because Pink Waldo made
some crack about fish to Curly Waldo when they
formed up for sick call. Mary moved closer to Curly
Waldo and gave Pink Waldo a cold look. That was
good.

Slop Chute looked waxy, and Uncle Death seemed
to see it because a gleam come into his wooden eyes.
Both Waldos listened all over Slop Chute and told uncle what they heard in their secret language. Uncle
nodded, and Casey thumbed his nose at him.

No doubt about it, the ways was greased for Slop
Chute. Mama Death come back soon as she could and
began to loosen the chocks. She slobbered arthurs all
over Slop Chute and flittered around like women do
when they smell a wedding. Casey give her extra special hell, and we all laughed right out and she hardly
noticed.

That afternoon two orderly-masks come with a go-
to-Jesus cart and wanted to take Slop Chute to X ray.
Casey climbed on the cart and scowled at them.

Slop Chute told 'em shove off, he wasn't going.

They got Mary and she told Slop Chute please go,
it was doctor's orders.

Sorry, no, he said.

"Please, for me, Slop Chute," she begged.

She knows our right names—that's one reason we

love her. But Slop Chute shook his head, and his big jaw bone stuck out.

Mary—she had to then—called Mama Death. Mama waddled in, and Casey spit in her mask.

"Now, arthur, what is this, arthur, you know we want to help you get well and go home, arthur," she arthured at Slop Chute. "Be a good boy now, arthur, and go along to the clinic."

She motioned the orderlies to pick him up anyway. Casey hit one in the mask and Slop Chute growled, "Sheer off, you bastards!"

The orderlies hesitated.

Mama's little eyes squinted and she wiggled her hands at them. "Let's not be naughty, arthur. Doctor knows best, arthur."

The orderlies looked at Slop Chute and at each other. Casey wrapped his arms and legs around Mama Death and began chewing on her neck. He seemed to mix right into her, someway, and she broke and run out of the ward.

She come right back, though, trailing Uncle Death. Casey met him at the door and beat hell out of him all the way to Slop Chute's bunk. Mama sent Mary for the chart, and Uncle Death studied Slop Chute's reflection for a minute. He looked pale and swayed a little from Casey's beating.

He turned toward Slop Chute and breathed in deep and Casey was on him again. Casey wrapped his arms and legs around him and chewed at his mask with those big yellow teeth. Casey's hair bristled and his eyes were red as the flames of hell.

Uncle Death staggered back across the ward and fetched up against Carnahan's bunk. The other masks were scared spitless, looking all around, kind of knowing.

Casey pulled away, and Uncle Death said maybe he was wrong, schedule it for tomorrow. All the masks left in a hurry except Mary. She went back to Slop Chute and took his hand.

"I'm sorry, Slop Chute," she whispered.

"Bless you, Connie," he said, and grinned. It was the last thing I ever heard him say.

Slop Chute went to sleep, and Casey sat beside his bunk. He motioned me off when I wanted to help Slop Chute to the head after lights out. I turned in and went to sleep.

I don't know what woke me. Casey was moving around fidgety-like, but of course not making a sound. I could hear the others stirring and whispering in the dark too.

Then I heard a muffled noise—the bubbling cough again, and spitting. Slop Chute was having another hemorrhage and he had his head under the blankets to hide the sound. Carnahan started to get up. Casey waved him down.

I saw a deeper shadow high in the dark over Slop Chute's bunk. It came down ever so gently and Casey would push it back up again. The muffled coughing went on.

Casey had a harder time pushing back the shadow. Finally he climbed on the bunk straddle of Slop Chute and kept a steady push against it.

The blackness came down anyway, little by little. Casey strained and shifted his footing. I could hear him grunt and hear his joints crack.

I was breathing forced draft with my heart like to pull off its bed bolts. I heard other bedsprings creaking. Somebody across from me whimpered low, but it was sure never Slop Chute that done it.

Casey went to his knees, his hands forced almost level with his head. He swung his head back and forth and I saw his lips curled back from the big teeth clenched tight together. . . . Then he had the blackness on his shoulders like the weight of the whole world.

Casey went down on hands and knees with his back arched like a bridge. Almost I thought I heard him grunt . . . and he gained a little.

Then the blackness settled heavier, and I heard Casey's tendons pull out and his bones snap. Casey and

Slop Chute disappeared under the blackness, and it overflowed from there over the whole bed . . . and more . . . and it seemed to fill the whole ward.

It wasn't like going to sleep, but I don't know anything it was like.

The mask's must've towed off Slop Chute's bulk in the night, because it was gone when I woke up.

So was Casey.

Casey didn't show up for sick call and I knew then how much he meant to me. With him around to fight back I didn't feel as dead as they wanted me to. Without him I felt deader than ever. I even almost liked Mama Death when she charlesed me.

Mary came on duty that morning with a diamond on her third finger and a brighter sparkle in her eye. It was a little diamond, but it was Curly Waldo's and it kind of made up for Slop Chute.

I wished Casey was there to see it. He would've danced all around her and kissed her nice, the way he often did. Casey loved Mary.

It was Saturday, I know, because Mama Death come in and told some of us we could be wheeled to a special church hooraw before breakfast next morning if we wanted. We said no thanks. But it was a hell of a Saturday without Casey. Sharkey Brown said it for all of us—"With Casey gone, this place is like a morgue again."

Not even Carnahan could call him up.

"Sometimes I think I feel him stir, and then again I ain't sure," he said. "It beats hell where he's went to."

Going to sleep that night was as much like dying as it could be for men already dead.

Music from far off woke me up when it was just getting light. I was going to try to cork off again, when I saw Carnahan was awake.

"Casey's around somewhere," he whispered.

"Where?" I asked, looking around. "I don't see him."

"I feel him," Carnahan said. "He's around."

The others began to wake up and look around. It was like the night Casey and Slop Chute went under. Then something moved in the solarium. . . .

It was Casey.

He come in the ward slow and bashful-like, jerking his head all around, with his eyes open wide, and looking scared we was going to throw something at him. He stopped in the middle of the ward.

"Yea, Casey!" Carnahan said in a low, clear voice.

Casey looked at him sharp.

"Yea, Casey!" we all said. "Come aboard, you hairy old bastard!"

Casey shook hands with himself over his head and went into his dance. He grinned . . . and I swear to God it was Slop Chute's big, lopsided grin he had on.

For the first time in my whole damn life I wanted to cry.

THE BODY-SNATCHER

by Robert Louis Stevenson

Every night in the year, four of us sat in the small parlour of the George at Debenham—the undertaker, and the landlord, and Fettes, and myself. Sometimes there would be more; but blow high, blow low, come rain or snow or frost, we four would be each planted in his own particular arm-chair. Fettes was an old drunken Scotchman, a man of education obviously, and a man of some property, since he lived in idleness. He had come to Debenham years ago, while still young, and by a mere continuance of living had grown to be an adopted townsman. His blue camlet cloak was a local antiquity, like the church-spire. His place in the parlour at the George, his absence from church, his old, crapulous, disreputable vices, were all things of course in Debenham. He had some vague Radical opinions and some fleeting infidelities, which he would now and again set forth and emphasise with tottering slaps upon the table. He drank rum—five glasses regularly every evening; and for the greater portion of his nightly visit to the George sat, with his glass in his right hand, in a state of melancholy alcoholic saturation. We called him the Doctor, for he was supposed to have some special knowledge of medicine, and had been known, upon a pinch, to set a fracture or reduce a dislocation; but beyond these slight particulars, we had no knowledge of his character and antecedents.

One dark winter night—it had struck nine some time before the landlord joined us—there was a sick man in the George, a great neighbouring proprietor suddenly struck down with apoplexy on his way to Parliament; and the great man's still greater London doctor had been telegraphed to his bedside. It was the first time that such a thing had happened in Debenham, for the railway was but newly open, and we were all proportionately moved by the occurrence.

"He's come," said the landlord, after he had filled and lighted his pipe.

"He?" said I. "Who?—not the doctor?"

"Himself," replied our host.

"What is his name?"

"Dr. Macfarlane," said the landlord.

Fettes was far through his third tumbler, stupidly fuddled, now nodding over, now staring mazily around him; but at the last word he seemed to awaken, and repeated the name "Macfarlane" twice, quietly enough the first time, but with sudden emotion at the second.

"Yes," said the landlord, "that's his name, Dr. Wolfe Macfarlane."

Fettes became instantly sober; his eyes awoke, his voice became clear, loud, and steady, his language forcible and earnest. We were all startled by the transformation, as if a man had risen from the dead.

"I beg your pardon," he said, "I am afraid I have not been paying much attention to your talk. Who is this Wolfe Macfarlane?" And then, when he had heard the landlord out, "It cannot be, it cannot be," he added; "and yet I would like well to see him face to face."

"Do you know him, Doctor?" asked the undertaker, with a gasp.

"God forbid!" was the reply. "And yet, the name is a strange one; it were too much to fancy two. Tell me, landlord, is he old?"

"Well," said the host, "he's not a young man, to be sure, and his hair is white; but he looks younger than you."

"He is older, though; years older. But," with a slap upon the table, "it's the rum you see in my face—rum and sin. This man, perhaps, may have an easy conscience and a good digestion. Conscience! Hear me speak. You would think I was some good, old decent Christian, would you not? But no, not I; I never canted. Voltaire might have canted if he'd stood in my shoes; but the brains''—with a rattling fillip on his bald head—''the brains were clear and active, and I saw and made no deductions.''

"If you know this doctor," I ventured to remark, after a somewhat awful pause, "I should gather that you do not share the landlord's good opinion."

Fettes paid no regard to me.

"Yes," he said, with sudden decision, "I must see him face to face."

There was another pause, and then a door was closed rather sharply on the first floor, and a step was heard upon the stair.

"That's the doctor," cried the landlord. "Look sharp, and you can catch him."

It was but two steps from the small parlour to the door of the old George Inn; the wide oak staircase landed almost in the street; there was room for a Turkey rug and nothing more between the threshold and the last round of the descent; but this little space was every evening brilliantly lit up, not only by the light upon the stair and the great signal-lamp below the sign, but by the warm radiance of the bar-room window. The George thus brightly advertised itself to passers-by in the cold street. Fettes walked steadily to the spot, and we, who were hanging behind, beheld the two men meet, as one of them had phrased it, face to face. Dr. Macfarlane was alert and vigorous. His white hair set off his pale and placid, although energetic, countenance. He was richly dressed in the finest of broadcloth and the whitest of linen, with a great gold watchchain, and studs and spectacles of the same precious material. He wore a broad-folded tie, white and speckled with lilac, and he carried on his arm a comfortable driving-coat of fur. There was no doubt but he became his years, breathing, as he did, of wealth and consideration; and it was a surprising contrast to see our parlour sot—bald, dirty, pimpled, and robed in his old camlet cloak—confront him at the bottom of the stairs.

"Macfarlane!" he said somewhat loudly, more like a herald than a friend.

The great doctor pulled up short on the fourth step, as though the familiarity of the address surprised and somewhat shocked his dignity.

"Toddy Macfarlane!" repeated Fettes.

The London man almost staggered. He stared for the swiftest of seconds at the man before him, glanced behind him with a sort of scare, and then in a startled whisper, "Fettes!" he said, "you!"

"Ay," said the other, "me! Did you think I was dead too? We are not so easy shut of our acquaintance."

"Hush, hush!" exclaimed the doctor. "Hush, hush! this meeting is so unexpected—I can see you are unmanned, I hardly knew you, I confess, at first; but I am overjoyed—overjoyed to have this opportunity. For the present it must be how-d'ye-do and good-bye in one, for my fly is waiting, and I must not fail the train; but you shall—let me see—yes—you shall give me your address, and you can count on early news of me. We must do something for you, Fettes. I fear you are out at elbows; but we must see to that for auld lang syne, as once we sang at suppers."

"Money!" cried Fettes; "money from you! The money that I had from you is lying where I cast it in the rain."

Dr. Macfarlane had talked himself into some measure of superiority and confidence, but the uncommon energy of this refusal cast him back into his first confusion.

A horrible, ugly look came and went across his almost venerable countenance. "My dear fellow," he said, "be it as you please; my last thought is to offend you. I would intrude on none. I will leave you my address, however——"

"I do not wish it—I do not wish to know the roof that shelters you," interrupted the other. "I heard your name; I feared it might be you; I wished to know if, after all, there were a God; I know now that there is none. Begone!''

He still stood in the middle of the rug, between the stair and doorway; and the great London physician, in order to escape, would be forced to step to one side. It was plain that he hesitated before the thought of this humiliation. White as he was, there was a dangerous glitter in his spectacles; but while he still paused uncertain, he became aware that the driver of his fly was peering in from the street at this unusual scene and caught a glimpse at the same time of our little body from the parlour, huddled by the corner of the bar. The presence of so many witnesses decided him at once to flee. He crouched together, brushing on the wainscot, and made a dart like a serpent, striking for the door. But his tribulation was not yet entirely at an end, for even as he was passing Fettes clutched him by the arm and these words came in a whisper, and yet painfully distinct, ''Have you seen it again?''

The great rich London doctor cried out aloud with a sharp, throttling cry; he dashed his questioner across the open space, and, with his hands over his head, fled out of the door like a detected thief. Before it had occurred to one of us to make a movement the fly was already rattling toward the station. The scene was over like a dream, but the dream had left proofs and traces of its passage. Next day the servant found the fine gold spectacles broken on the threshold, and that very night we were all standing breathless by the bar-room window, and Fettes at our side, sober, pale, and resolute in look.

''God protect us, Mr. Fettes!'' said the landlord, coming first into possession of his customary senses. ''What in the universe is all this? These are strange things you have been saying.''

Fettes turned toward us; he looked us each in succession in the face. ''See if you can hold your tongues,'' said he. ''That man Macfarlane is not safe to cross; those that have done so already have repented it too late.''

And then, without so much as finishing his third

glass, far less waiting for the other two, he bade us good-bye and went forth, under the lamp of the hotel, into the black night.

We three turned to our places in the parlour, with the big red fire and four clear candles; and as we recapitulated what had passed the first chill of our surprise soon changed into a glow of curiosity. We sat late; it was the latest session I have known in the old George. Each man, before we parted, had his theory that he was bound to prove; and none of us had any nearer business in this world than to track out the past of our condemned companion, and surprise the secret that he shared with the great London doctor. It is no great boast, but I believe I was a better hand at worming out a story than either of my fellows at the George; and perhaps there is now no other man alive who could narrate to you the following foul and unnatural events.

In his young days Fettes studied medicine in the schools of Edinburgh. He had talent of a kind, the talent that picks up swiftly what it hears and readily retails it for its own. He worked little at home; but he was civil, attentive, and intelligent in the presence of his masters. They soon picked him out as a lad who listened closely and remembered well; nay, strange as it seemed to me when I first heard it, he was in those days well favoured, and pleased by his exterior. There was, at that period, a certain extramural teacher of anatomy, whom I shall here designate by the letter K. His name was subsequently too well known. The man who bore it skulked through the streets of Edinburgh in disguise, while the mob that applauded at the execution of Burke called loudly for the blood of his employer. But Mr. K—— was then at the top of his vogue; he enjoyed a popularity due partly to his own talent and address, partly to the incapacity of his rival, the university professor. The students, at least, swore by his name, and Fettes believed himself, and was believed by others, to have laid the foundations of success when he had acquired the favour of this meteorically famous man. Mr. K—— was a *bon vivant* as well as an accomplished teacher; he liked a sly illusion no less than a careful preparation. In both capacities Fettes enjoyed and deserved his notice, and by the second year of his attendance he held the half-regular position of second demonstrator or subassistant in his class.

In this capacity, the charge of the theatre and lecture-room devolved in particular upon his shoulders. He had to answer for the cleanliness of the premises and the conduct of the other students, and it was as part of his duty to supply, receive, and divide the various subjects. It was with a view to this last—at that time very delicate—affair that he was lodged by Mr. K—— in the same wynd, and at last in the same building, with the dissecting-rooms. Here, after a night of turbulent pleasures, his hand still tottering, his sight still misty and confused, he would be called out of bed in the black hours before the winter dawn by the unclean and desperate interlops who supplied the table. He would open the door to these men, since infamous throughout the land. He would help them with their tragic burthen, pay them their sordid price, and remain alone, when they were gone, with the unfriendly relics of humanity. From such a scene he would return to snatch another hour or two of slumber, to repair the abuses of the night, and refresh himself for the labours of the day.

Few lads could have been more insensible to the impressions of a life thus passed among the ensigns of mortality. His mind was closed against all general considerations. He was incapable of interest in the fate and fortunes of another, the slave of his own desires and low ambitions. Cold, light, and selfish in the last resort, he had that modicum of prudence, miscalled morality, which keeps a man from inconvenient drunkenness or punishable theft. He coveted, besides, a measure of consideration from his masters and his fellow-pupils, and he had no desire to fail conspicuously in the external parts of life. Thus he made it his pleasure to gain some distinction in his studies, and day after day rendered unimpeachable eye-service to his employer, Mr. K——. For his day of work he indemnified himself by nights of roaring, blackguardly enjoyment; and when that balance had been struck, the organ that he called his conscience declared itself content.

The supply of subjects was a continual trouble to him as well as to his master. In that large and busy class, the raw material of the anatomists kept perpetually running out; and the business thus rendered necessary was not only unpleasant in itself, but threatened dangerous consequences to all who were concerned. It was the policy of Mr. K—— to ask no questions in his dealings with the trade. "They bring the body, and we pay the price," he used to say, dwelling on the alliteration—*"quid pro quo."* And, again, and somewhat profanely, "Ask no questions," he would tell his assistants, "for conscience' sake." There was no understanding that the subjects were provided by the crime of murder. Had that idea been broached to him in words, he would have recoiled in horror; but the lightness of his speech upon so grave a matter was, in itself, an offense against good manners, and a temptation to the men with whom he dealt. Fettes, for instance, had often remarked to himself upon the singular freshness of the bodies. He had been struck again and again by the hang-dog, abominable looks of the ruffians who came to him before the dawn; and putting things together clearly in his private thoughts, he perhaps attributed a meaning too immoral and too categorical to the unguarded counsels of his master. He understood his duty, in short, to have three branches: to take what was brought, to pay the price, and to avert the eye from any evidence of crime.

One November morning this policy of silence was put sharply to the test. He had been awake all night with a racking toothache—pacing his room like a caged beast or throwing himself in fury on his bed—and had fallen at last into that profound, uneasy slumber that so often follows on a night of pain, when he was awakened by the third or fourth angry repetition of the concerted signal. There was a thin, bright moonshine; it was bitter cold, windy, and frosty; the town had not yet awakened, but an indefinable stir already preluded the noise and business of the day. The ghouls had come later than usual, and they seemed more than usually eager to be gone. Fettes, sick with sleep, lighted them upstairs. He heard their grumbling Irish voices through a dream; and as they stripped the sack from their sad merchandise he leaned dozing, with his shoulder propped against the wall; he had to shake himself to find the men their money. As he did so his eyes lighted on the dead face. He started; he took two steps nearer, with the candle raised.

"God Almighty!" he cried. "That is Jane Galbraith!"

The men answered nothing, but they shuffled nearer the door.

"I know her, I tell you," he continued. "She was alive and hearty yesterday. It's impossible she can be dead; it's impossible you should have got this body fairly."

"Sure, sir, you're mistaken entirely," said one of the men.

But the other looked Fettes darkly in the eyes, and demanded the money on the spot.

It was impossible to misconceive the threat or to exaggerate the danger. The lad's heart failed him. He stammered some excuses, counted out the sum, and saw his hateful visitors depart. No sooner were they gone than he hastened to confirm his doubts. By a dozen unquestionable marks he identified the girl he had jested with the day before, He saw, with horror, marks upon her body that might well betoken violence. A panic seized him, and he took refuge in his room. There he reflected at length over the discovery that he had made; considered soberly the bearing of Mr. K——'s instructions and the danger to himself of interference in so serious a business, and at last, in sore perlexity, determined to wait for the advice of his immediate superior, the class assistant.

This was a young doctor, Wolfe Macfarlane, a high favourite among all the reckless students, clever, dissipated, and unscrupulous to the last degree. He had travelled and studied abroad. His manners were agreeable and a little forward. He was an authority on the stage, skilful on the ice or the links with skate or golfclub; he dressed with nice audacity, and, to put the finishing touch upon his glory, he kept a gig and a strong trotting-horse. With Fettes he was on terms of intimacy; indeed, their relative positions called for some community of life; and when subjects were scarce the pair would drive far into the country in Macfarlane's gig, visit and desecrate some lonely graveyard, and return before dawn with their booty to the door of the dissecting-room.

On that particular morning Macfarlane arrived somewhat earlier than his wont. Fettes heard him, and met him on the stairs, told him his story, and showed him the cause of his alarm. Macfarlane examined the marks on her body.

"Yes," he said with a nod, "it looks fishy."

"Well, what should I do?" asked Fettes.

"Do?" repeated the other. "Do you want to do anything? Least said soonest mended, I should say."

"Some one else might recognise her," objected Fettes. "She was as well known as the Castle Rock."

"We'll hope not," said Macfarlane, "and if anybody does—well, you didn't, don't you see, and there's an end. The fact is, this has been going on too long. Stir up the mud, and you'll get K—— into the most unholy trouble; you'll be in a shocking box yourself. So will I, if you come to that. I should like to know how any one of us would look, or what the devil we should have to say for ourselves, in any Christian witness-box. For me, you know there's one thing certain—that, practically speaking, all our subjects have been murdered."

"Macfarlane!" cried Fettes.

"Come now!" sneered the other. "As if you hadn't suspected it yourself!"

"Suspecting is one thing——"

"And proof another. Yes, I know; and I'm as sorry as you are this should have come here," tapping the body with his cane. "The next best thing for me is not to recognise it; and," he added coolly, "I don't. You may, if you please. I don't dictate, but I think a man of the world would do as I do; and I may add, I fancy that is what K—— would look for at our hands. The question is, Why did he choose us two for his assistants? And I answer, because he didn't want old wives."

This was the tone of all others to affect the mind of a lad like Fettes. He agreed to imitate Macfarlane. The body of the unfortunate girl was duly dissected, and no one remarked or appeared to recognise her.

One afternoon, when his day's work was over, Fettes dropped into a popular tavern and found Macfarlane sitting with a stranger. This was a small man, very pale and dark, with coal-black eyes. The cut of his features gave a promise of intellect and refinement which was but feebly realised in his manners, for he proved, upon a nearer acquaintance, coarse, vulgar, and stupid. He exercised, however, a very remarkable control over Macfarlane; issued orders like the Great Bashaw; became inflamed at the least discussion or delay, and commented rudely on the servility with which he was obeyed. This most offensive person took a fancy to Fettes on the spot, plied him with drinks, and honoured him with unusual confidences on his past career. If a tenth part of what he confessed were true, he was a very loathsome rogue; and the lad's vanity was tickled by the attention of so experienced a man.

"I'm a pretty bad fellow myself," the stranger remarked, "but Macfarlane is the boy—Toddy Macfarlane I call him. Toddy, order your friend another glass." Or it might be, "Toddy, you jump up and shut the door." "Toddy hates me," he said again. "Oh, yes, Toddy, you do!"

"Don't you call me that confounded name," growled Macfarlane.

"Hear him! Did you ever see the lads play knife? He would like to do that all over my body," remarked the stranger.

"We medicals have a better way than that," said

Fettes. "When we dislike a dead friend of ours, we dissect him."

Macfarlane looked up sharply, as though this jest were scarcely to his mind.

The afternoon passed. Gray, for that was the stranger's name, invited Fettes to join them at dinner, ordered a feast so sumptuous that the tavern was thrown in commotion, and when all was done commanded Macfarlane to settle the bill. It was late before they separated; the man Gray was incapably drunk. Macfarlane, sobered by his fury, chewed the cud of the money he had been forced to squander and the slights he had been obliged to swallow. Fettes, with various liquors singing in his head, returned home with devious footsteps and a mind entirely in abeyance. Next day Macfarlane was absent from the class, and Fettes smiled to himself as he imagined him still squiring the intolerable Gray from tavern to tavern. As soon as the hour of liberty had struck he posted from place to place in quest of his last night's companions. He could find them, however, nowhere; so returned early to his rooms, went early to bed, and slept the sleep of the just.

At four in the morning he was awakened by the well-known signal. Descending to the door, he was filled with astonishment to find Macfarlane with his gig, and in the gig one of those long and ghastly packages with which he was so well acquainted.

"What?" he cried. "Have you been out alone? How did you manage?"

But Macfarlane silenced him roughly, bidding him turn to business. When they had got the body upstairs and laid it on the table, Macfarlane made at first as if he were going away. Then he paused and seemed to hesitate; and then, "You had better look at the face," said he, in tones of some constraint. "You had better," he repeated, as Fettes only stared at him in wonder.

"But where, and how, and when did you come by it?" cried the other.

"Look at the face," was the only answer.

Fettes was staggered; strange doubt assailed him. He looked from the young doctor to the body, and then back again. At last, with a start, he did as he was bidden. He had almost expected the sight that met his eyes, and yet the shock was cruel. To see, fixed in the rigidity of death and naked on that coarse layer of sackcloth, the man whom he had left well clad and full of meat and sin upon the threshold of a tavern, awoke, even in the thoughtless Fettes, some of the terrors of the conscience. It was a *cras tibi* which re-echoed in his soul, that two whom he had known should have come to lie upon these icy tables. Yet these were only secondary thoughts. His first concern regarded Wolfe. Unprepared for a challenge so momentous, he knew not how to look his comrade in the face. He durst not meet his eye, and he had neither words nor voice at his command.

It was Macfarlane himself who made the first advance. He came up quietly behind and laid his hand gently but firmly on the other's shoulder.

"Richardson," said he, "may have the head."

Now Richardson was a student who had long been anxious for that portion of the human subject to dissect. There was no answer, and the murderer resumed: "Talking of business, you must pay me; your accounts, you see, must tally."

Fettes found a voice, the ghost of his own: "Pay you!" he cried. "Pay you for that?"

"Why, yes, of course you must. By all means and on every possible account, you must," returned the other. "I dare not give it for nothing, you dare not take it for nothing; it would compromise us both. This is another case like Jane Galbraith's. The more things are wrong the more we must act as if all were right. Where does old K—— keep his money?"

"There," answered Fettes hoarsely, pointing to a cupboard in the corner.

"Give me the key, then," said the other, calmly, holding out his hand.

There was an instant's hesitation, and the die was cast. Macfarlane could not suppress a nervous twitch,

the infinitesimal mark of an immense relief, as he felt
the key between his fingers. He opened the cupboard,
brought out pen and ink and a paper-book that stood
in one compartment, and separated from the funds in
a drawer a sum suitable to the occasion.

"Now, look, here," he said, "there is the payment
made—first proof of your good faith: first step to your
security. You have now to clinch it by a second. Enter
the payment in your book, and then you for your part
may defy the devil."

The next few seconds were for Fettes an agony of
thought; but in balancing his terrors it was the most
immediate that triumphed. Any future difficulty
seemed almost welcome if he could avoid a present
quarrel with Macfarlane. He set down the candle which
he had been carrying all this time, and with a steady
hand entered the date, the nature, and the amount of
the transaction.

"And now," said Macfarlane, "it's only fair that
you should pocket the lucre. I've had my share already. By the bye, when a man of the world falls into
a bit of luck, has a few shillings extra in his pocket—
I'm ashamed to speak of it, but there's a rule of conduct in the case. No treating, no purchase of expensive
classbooks, no squaring of old debts; borrow, don't
lend."

"Macfarlane," began Fettes, still somewhat
hoarsely, "I have put my neck in a halter to oblige
you."

"To oblige me?" cried Wolfe. "Oh, come! You did,
as near as I can see the matter, what you downright
had to do in self-defence. Suppose I got into trouble,
where would you be? This second little matter flows
clearly from the first. Mr. Gray is the continuation of
Miss Galbraith. You can't begin and then stop. If you
begin, you must keep on beginning; that's the truth.
No rest for the wicked."

A horrible sense of blackness and the treachery of
fate seized hold upon the soul of the unhappy student.

"My God!" he cried, "but what have I done? and
when did I begin? To be made a class assistant—in the

name of reason, where's the harm in that? Service
wanted the position: Service might have got it. Would
he have been where *I* am now?''

"My dear fellow," said Macfarlane, "what a boy
you are! What harm *has* come to you? What harm *can*
come to you if you hold your tongue? Why, man, do
you know what this life is? There are two squads of
us—the lions and the lambs. If you're a lamb, you'll
come to lie upon these tables like Gray or Jane Galbraith; if you're a lion, you'll live and drive a horse
like me, like K——, like all the world with any wit or
courage. You're staggered at the first. But look at
K——! My dear fellow, you're clever, you have pluck. I
like you, and K—— likes you. You were born to lead
the hunt; and I tell you, on my honour and my experience of life, three days from now you'll laugh at all
these scarecrows like a high-school boy at a farce.''

And with that Macfarlane took his departure and
drove off up the wynd in his gig to get under cover
before daylight. Fettes was thus left alone with his
regrets. He saw the miserable peril in which he stood
involved. He saw, with inexpressible dismay, that there
was no limit to his weakness, and that, from concession to concession, he had fallen from the arbiter of
Macfarlane's destiny to his paid and helpless accomplice. He would have given the world to have been a
little braver at the time, but it did not occur to him
that he might still be brave. The secret of Jane Galbraith and the cursed entry in the daybook closed his
mouth.

Hours passed; the class began to arrive; the members of the unhappy Gray were dealt out to one and to
another, and received without remark. Richardson was
made happy with the head; and before the hour of freedom rang Fettes trembled with exultation to perceive
how far they had already gone toward safety.

For two days he continued to watch, with increasing
joy, the dreadful process of disguise.

On the third day Macfarlane made his appearance.
He had been ill, he said; but he made up for lost time
by the energy with which he directed the students. To

Richardson in particular he extended the most valuable assistance and advice, and that student, encouraged by the praise of the demonstrator, burned high with ambitious hopes, and saw the medal already in his grasp.

Before the week was out Macfarlane's prophecy had been fulfilled. Fettes had outlived his terrors and had forgotten his baseness. He began to plume himself upon his courage, and had so arranged the story in his mind that he could look back on these events with an unhealthy pride. Of his accomplice he saw but little. They met, of course, in the business of the class; they received their orders together from Mr. K——. At times they had a word or two in private, and Macfarlane was from first to last particularly kind and jovial. But it was plain that he avoided any reference to their common secret; and even when Fettes whispered to him that he had cast in his lot with the lions and forsworn the lambs, he only signed to him smilingly to hold his peace.

At length an occasion arose which threw the pair once more into a closer union. Mr. K—— was again short of subjects; pupils were eager, and it was a part of this teacher's pretensions to be always well supplied. At the same time there came the news of a burial in the rustic graveyard of Glencorse. Time has little changed the place in question. It stood then, as now, upon a crossroad, out of call of human habitations, and buried fathom deep in the foliage of six cedar trees. The cries of the sheep upon the neighbouring hills, the streamlets upon either hand, one loudly singing among pebbles, the other dripping furtively from pond to pond, the stir of the wind in mountainous old flowering chestnuts, and once in seven days the voice of the bell and the old tunes of the precentor, were the only sounds that disturbed the silence around the rural church. The Resurrection Man—to use a by-name of the period—was not to be deterred by any of the sanctities of customary piety. It was part of his trade to despise and desecrate the scrolls and trumpets of old tombs, the paths worn by the feet of worshippers and mourners, and the offerings and the inscriptions of bereaved affection. To rustic neighbourhoods, where love is more than commonly tenacious, and where some bonds of blood or fellowship unite the entire society of a parish, the body-snatcher, far from being repelled by natural respect, was attracted by the ease and safety of the task. To bodies that had been laid in earth, in joyful expectation of a far different awakening, there came that hasty, lamp-lit, terror-haunted resurrection of the spade and mattock. The coffin was forced, the cerements torn, and the melancholy relics, clad in sackcloth, after being rattled for hours on moonless by-ways, were at length exposed to uttermost indignities before a class of gaping boys.

Somewhat as two vultures may swoop upon a dying lamb, Fettes and Macfarlane were to be let loose upon a grave in that green and quiet resting-place. The wife of a farmer, a woman who had lived for sixty years, and been known for nothing but good butter and a godly conversation, was to be rooted from her grave at midnight and carried, dead and naked, to that far-away city that she had always honoured with her Sunday's best; the place beside her family was to be empty till the crack of doom; her innocent and almost venerable members to be exposed to that last curiosity of the anatomist.

Late one afternoon the pair set forth, well wrapped in cloaks and furnished with a formidable bottle. It rained without remission—a cold, dense, lashing rain. Now and again there blew a puff of wind, but these sheets of falling water kept it down. Bottle and all, it was a sad and silent drive as far as Penicuik, where they were to spend the evening. They stopped once, to hide their implements in a thick bush not far from the churchyard, and once again at the Fisher's Tryst, to have a toast before the kitchen fire and vary their nips of whiskey with a glass of ale. When they reached their journey's end the gig was housed, the horse was fed and comforted, and the two young doctors in a private room sat down to the best dinner and the best wine the house afforded. The lights, the fire, the beating rain upon the window, the cold, incongruous work that lay before them, added zest to their enjoyment of the meal. With every glass their cordiality increased. Soon Macfarlane handed a little pile of gold to his companion.

"A compliment," he said. "Between friends these little d——d accommodations ought to fly like pipe-lights."

Fettes pocketed the money, and applauded the sentiment to the echo. "You are a philosopher," he cried. "I was an ass till I knew you. You and K—— between you, by the Lord Harry! but you'll make a man of me."

"Of course, we shall," applauded Macfarlane. "A man? I tell you, it required a man to back me up the other morning. There are some big, brawling, forty-year-old cowards who would have turned sick at the look of the d——d thing; but not you—you kept your head. I watched you."

"Well, and why not?" Fettes thus vaunted himself. "It was no affair of mine. There was nothing to gain on the one side but disturbance, and on the other I could count on your gratitude, don't you see?" And he slapped his pocket till the gold pieces rang.

Macfarlane somehow felt a certain touch of alarm at these unpleasant words. He may have regretted that he had taught his young companion so successfully, but he had no time to interfere, for the other noisily continued in this boastful strain:

"The great thing is not to be afraid. Now, between you and me, I don't want to hang—that's practical; but for all cant, Macfarlane, I was born with a contempt. Hell, God, Devil, right, wrong, sin, crime, and all the old gallery of curiosities—they may frighten boys, but men of the world, like you and me, despise them. Here's to the memory of Gray!"

It was by this time growing somewhat late. The gig, according to order, was brought round to the door with both lamps brightly shining, and the young men had to pay their bill and take the road. They announced that they were bound for Peebles, and drove in that direction till they were clear of the last houses of the town; then, extinguishing the lamps, returned upon their course, and followed a by-road toward Glencorse. There was no sound but that of their own passage, and the incessant, strident pouring of the rain. It was pitch dark; here and there a white gate or a white stone in the wall guided them for a short space across the night; but for the most part it was at a foot pace, and almost groping, that they picked their way through that resonant blackness to their solemn and isolated destination. In the sunken woods that traverse the neighbourhood of the burying ground the last glimmer failed them, and it became necessary to kindle a match and reillumine one of the lanterns of the gig. Thus, under the dripping trees, and environed by huge and moving shadows, they reached the scene of their unhallowed labours.

They were both experienced in such affairs, and powerful with the spade; and they had scarce been twenty minutes at their task before they were rewarded by a dull rattle on the coffin lid. At the same moment Macfarlane, having hurt his hand upon a stone, flung it carelessly above his head. The grave, in which they now stood almost to the shoulders, was close to the edge of the plateau of the graveyard; and the gig lamp had been propped, the better to illuminate their labours, against a tree, and on the immediate verge of the steep bank descending to the stream. Chance had taken a sure aim with the stone. Then came a clang of broken glass, night fell upon them; sounds alternately dull and ringing announced the bounding of the lantern down the bank, and its occasional collision with the trees. A stone or two, which it had dislodged in its descent, rattled behind it into the profundities of the glen; and then silence, like night, resumed its sway; and they might bend their hearing to its utmost pitch, but naught was to be heard except the rain, now marching to the wind, now steadily falling over miles of open country.

They were so nearly at an end of their abhorred task that they judged it wisest to complete it in the dark. The coffin was exhumed and broken open; the body inserted in the dripping sack and carried between them to the gig; one mounted to keep it in its place, and the other, taking the horse by the mouth, groped along by wall and bush until they reached the wider road by the Fisher's Tryst. Here was a faint, diffused radiancy, which they hailed like daylight; by that they pushed the horse to a good pace and began to rattle along merrily in the direction of the town.

They had both been wetted to the skin during their operations, and now, as the gig jumped among the deep ruts, the thing that stood propped between them fell now upon one and now upon the other. At every repetition of the horrid contact each instinctively repelled it with the greater haste; and the process, natural although it was, began to tell upon the nerves of the companions. Macfarlane made some ill-favoured jest about the farmer's wife, but it came hollowly from his lips, and was allowed to drop in silence. Still their unnatural burthen bumped from side to side; and now the head would be laid, as if in confidence, upon their shoulders, and now the drenching sack-cloth would flap icily about their faces. A creeping chill began to possess the soul of Fettes. He peered at the bundle, and it seemed somehow larger than at first. All over the country-side, and from every degree of distance, the farm dogs accompanied their passage with tragic ululations; and it grew and grew upon his mind that some unnatural miracle had been accomplished, that some nameless change had befallen the dead body, and that it was in fear of their unholy burthen that the dogs were howling.

"For God's sake," said he, making a great effort to arrive at speech, "for God's sake, let's have a light!"

Seemingly Macfarlane was affected in the same direction; for, though he made no reply, he stopped the horse, passed the reins to his companion, got down, and proceeded to kindle the remaining lamp. They had by that time got no farther than the cross-road down to Auchenclinny. The rain still poured as though the deluge were returning, and it was no easy matter to make a light in such a world of wet and darkness.

When at last the flickering blue flame had been transferred to the wick and began to expand and clarify, and shed a wide circle of misty brightness around the gig, it became possible for the two young men to see each other and the thing they had along with them. The rain had moulded the rough sacking to the outlines of the body underneath; the head was distinct from the trunk, the shoulders plainly modelled; something at once spectral and human riveted their eyes upon the ghastly comrade of their drive.

For some time Macfarlane stood motionless, holding up the lamp. A nameless dread was swathed, like a wet sheet, about the body, and tightened the white skin upon the face of Fettes; a fear that was meaningless, a horror of what could not be, kept mounting to his brain. Another beat of the watch, and he had spoken. But his comrade forestalled him.

"That is not a woman," said Macfarlane, in a hushed voice.

"It was a woman when we put her in," whispered Fettes.

"Hold that lamp," said the other. "I must see her face."

And as Fettes took the lamp his companion untied the fastenings of the sack and drew down the cover from the head. The light fell very clear upon the dark, well-moulded features and smooth-shaven cheeks of a too familiar countenance, often beheld in dreams of both of these young men. A wild yell rang up into the night; each leaped from his own side into the roadway; the lamp fell, broke, and was extinguished; and the horse, terrified by this unusual commotion, bounded and went off toward Edinburgh at a gallop, bearing along with it, sole occupant of the gig, the body of the dead and long-dissected Gray.

THE AUTOPSY

by Michael Shea

Dr. Winters stepped out of the tiny Greyhound station and into the midnight street that smelled of pines. The station's window showed the only light, save for a luminous clockface several doors down and a little neon beer logo two blocks farther on. He could hear a river. It ran deep in a gorge west of town, but the town was only a few streets wide and a mile or so long, and the current's blurred roar was distinct, like the noise of a ghost river running between the banks of dark shop windows. When he had walked a short distance, Dr. Winters set his suitcase down, pocketed his hands, and looked at the stars—thick as cobblestones in the black gulf.

"A mountain hamlet—a mining town," he said. "Stars. No moon. We are in Bailey."

He was talking to his cancer. It was in his stomach. Since learning of it, he had developed this habit of wry communion with it. He meant to show courtesy to this uninvited guest, Death. It would not find him churlish, for that would make its victory absolute. Except, of course, that its victory would *be* absolute, with or without his ironies.

He picked up his suitcase and walked on. The starlight made faint mirrors of the windows' blackness and showed him the man who passed: lizard-lean, white-haired (at fifty-seven), a man traveling on death's business, carrying his own death in him, and even bearing death's wardrobe in his suitcase. For this was filled—aside from his medical kit and some scant necessities—with mortuary bags. The sheriff had told him on the phone of the improvisations that presently enveloped the corpses, and so the doctor had packed these, laying them in his case with bitter amusement, checking the last one's breadth against his chest before the mirror, as a woman will gauge a dress before donning it, and telling his cancer:

"Oh, yes, that's plenty roomy enough for both of us!"

The case was heavy, and he stopped frequently to rest and scan the sky. What a night's work to do, probing pungent, soulless filth, eyes earthward, beneath such a ceiling of stars! It had taken five days to dig the ten men out. The autumnal equinox had passed, but the weather here had been uniformly hot. And warmer still, no doubt, so deep in the earth.

He entered the courthouse by a side door. His heels knocked on the linoleum corridor. A door at the end of it, on which was lettered NATE CRAVEN, COUNTY SHERIFF, opened well before he reached it, and his friend stepped out to meet him.

"Dammit, Carl, you're *still* so thin they could use you for a whip. Gimme that. You're in too good a shape already. You don't need the exercise."

The case hung weightless from the sheriff's hand, imparting no tilt at all to his bull shoulders. Despite his implied self-derogation, he was only moderately paunched for a man his age and size. He had a rough-hewn face, and the bulk of brow, nose, and jaw made his greenish eyes look small until one engaged them and felt the snap and penetration of their intelligence. In the office he half filled two cups from a coffee urn and topped both off with bourbon from a bottle in his desk. When they had finished these, they had finished trading news of mutual friends. The sheriff mixed another round and sipped from his, in a silence clearly prefatory to the work at hand.

"They talk about rough justice," he said. "I've sure seen it now. One of those . . . patients of yours that you'll be working on? He was a killer. Christ, 'killer' doesn't half say it. A killer's the least of what he was.

The blast killing *him*, that was the justice part. Those other nine, they were the rough. And it just galls the hell out of me, Carl! If that kiss-ass boss of yours has his way, the rough won't even stop with their being dead! There won't even be any compensation for their survivors! Tell me—has he broke his back yet? I mean, touching his toes for Fordham Mutual?''

"You refer, I take it, to the estimable Coroner Waddleton of Fordham County." Dr. Winters paused to sip his drink. With a delicate flaring of his nostrils he communicated all the disgust, contempt, and amusement he had felt in his four years as pathologist in Waddleton's office. The sheriff laughed.

"Clear pictures seldom emerge from anything the coroner says," the doctor continued. "He took your name in vain. Vigorously and repeatedly. These expressions formed his opening remarks. He then developed the theme of our office's strict responsibility to the letter of the law, and of the workmen's compensation law in particular. Death benefits accrue only to the dependents of decedents whose deaths arise *out of the course* of their employment, not merely *in* the course of it. Victims of a maniacal assault, though they die on the job, are by no means necessarily compensable under the law. We then contemplated the tragic injustice of an insurance company—*any* insurance company—having to pay benefits to unentitled persons, solely through the laxity and incompetence of investigating officers. Your name came up again, and Coroner Waddleton subjected it to further abuse. Fordham Mutual, campaign contributor or not, is certainly a major insurance company and is therefore entitled to the same fair treatment that all such companies deserve."

Craven uttered a bark of wrathful mirth and spat expertly into his wastebasket. "Ah, the impartial public servant! What's seven widows and sixteen dependent children, next to Fordham Mutual?" He drained his cup and sighed. "I'll tell you what, Carl. We've been five days digging those men out and the last two days sifting half that mountain for explosive traces, with those insurance investigators hanging on our elbows, and the most they could say was that there was 'strong presumptive evidence' of a bomb. Well, I don't budge for that because I don't have to. Waddleton can shove his 'extraordinary circumstances.' If you don't find anything in those bodies, then that's all the autopsy there is to it, and they get buried right here where their families want 'em.''

The doctor was smiling at his friend. He finished his cup and spoke with his previous wry detachment, as if the sheriff had not interrupted his narrative.

''The honorable coroner then spoke with remarkable volubility on the subject of Autopsy Consent forms and the malicious subversion of private citizens by vested officers of the law. He had, as it happened, a sheaf of such forms on his desk, all signed, all with a rider clause typed in above the signatures. A cogent paragraph. It had, among its other qualities, the property of turning the coroner's face purple when he read it aloud. He read it aloud to me three times. It appeared that the survivors' consent was contingent on two conditions: that the autopsy be performed *in locum mortis,* that is to say in Bailey, and that only if the coroner's pathologist found concrete evidence of homicide should the decedents be subject either to removal from Bailey or to further necropsy. It was well written. I remember wondering who wrote it.''

The sheriff nodded musingly. He took Dr. Winters's empty cup, set it by his own, filled both two-thirds with bourbon, and added a splash of coffee to the doctor's. The two friends exchanged a level stare, rather like poker players in the clinch. The sheriff regarded his cup, sipped from it.

''In locum mortis. What-all does that mean exactly?''

'' 'In the place of death.' ''

''Oh. Freshen that up for you?''

''I've just started it, thank you.''

Both men laughed, paused, and laughed again, some might have said immoderately.

''He all but told me that I *had* to find something to

compel a second autopsy,'' the doctor said at length. ''He would have sold his soul—or taken out a second mortgage on it—for a mobile X-ray unit. He's right, of course. If those bodies have trapped any bomb fragments, that would be the surest and quickest way of finding them. It still amazes me your Dr. Parsons could let his X-ray go unfixed for so long.''

''He sets bones, stitches wounds, writes prescriptions, and sends anything tricky down the mountain. Just barely manages that. Drunks don't get much done.''

''He's gotten that bad?''

''He hangs on and no more. Waddleton was right there, not deputizing him pathologist. I doubt he could find a cannonball in a dead rat. I wouldn't say it where it could hurt him, as long as he's still managing, but everyone here knows it. His patients sort of look after *him* half the time. But Waddleton would have sent you, no matter who was here. Nothing but his best for party contributors like Fordham Mutual.''

The doctor looked at his hands and shrugged. ''So. There's a killer in the batch. Was there a bomb?''

Slowly the sheriff planted his elbows on the desk and pressed his hands against his temples, as if the question had raised a turbulence of memories. For the first time the doctor—half hearkening throughout to the never-quite-muted stirrings of the death within him—saw his friend's exhaustion: the tremor of hand, the bruised look under the eyes.

''When I've told you what we have, I guess you'll end up assuming what I do about it. But I think assuming is as far as any of us will get with this one. It's one of those nightmare specials, Carl. The ones no one ever does get to the bottom of.

''All right, then. About two months ago, we had a man disappear—Ronald Hanley. Mine worker, rock-steady, family man. He didn't come home one night, and we never found a trace of him. OK, that happens sometimes. About a week later, the lady that ran the laundromat, Sharon Starker, *she* disappeared, no trace. We got edgy then. I made an announcement on the local radio about a possible weirdo at large, spelled out special precautions everybody should take. We put both our squad cars on the night beat, and by day we set to work knocking on every door in town collecting alibis for the two times of disappearance.

"No good. Maybe you're fooled by this uniform and think I'm a law officer, protector of the people, and all that? A natural mistake. A lot of people were fooled. In less than seven weeks, six people vanished, just like that. Me and my deputies might as well have stayed in bed round the clock, for all the good we did." The sheriff drained his cup.

"Anyway, at last we got lucky. Don't get me wrong now. We didn't go all hog-wild and actually prevent a crime or anything. But we *did* find a body—except it wasn't the body of any of the seven people that had disappeared. We'd taken to combing the woods nearest town, with temporary deputies from the miners to help. Well, one of those boys was out there with us last week. It was hot—like it's been for a while now—and it was real quiet. He heard this buzzing noise and looked around for it, and he saw a beeswarm up in the crotch of a tree. Except he was smart enough to know that that's not usual around here—beehives. So it wasn't bees. It was bluebottle flies, a goddamned big cloud of them, all over a bundle that was wrapped in a tarp."

The sheriff studied his knuckles. He had, in his eventful life, occasionally met men literate enough to understand his last name and rash enough to be openly amused by it, and the knuckles—scarred knobs—were eloquent of his reactions. He looked back into his old friend's eyes.

"We got that thing down and unwrapped it. Billy Lee Davis, one of my deputies, he was in Viet Nam, been near some bad, bad things and held on. Billy Lee blew his lunch all over the ground when we unwrapped that thing. It was a man. Some of a man. We knew he'd stood six-two because all the bones were there, and he'd probably weighed between two fifteen and two twenty-five, but he folded up no bigger than a big-size laundry package. Still had his face, both shoulders, and the left arm, but all the rest was clean. It wasn't animal work. It was knife work, all the edges neat as butcher cuts. Except butchered meat, even when you drain it all you can, will bleed a good deal afterwards, and there wasn't one goddamned drop of blood on the tarp, nor in that meat. It was just as pale as fish meat.''

Deep in his body's center, the doctor's cancer touched him. Not a ravening attack—it sank one fang of pain, questioningly, into new untasted flesh, probing the scope for its appetite there. He disguised his tremor with a shake of the head.

''A cache, then.''

The sheriff nodded. ''Like you might keep a pot roast in the icebox for making lunches. I took some pictures of his face, then we put him back and erased our traces. Two of the miners I'd deputized did a lot of hunting, were woods-smart. So I left them on the first watch. We worked out positions and cover for them, and drove back.

''We got right on tracing him, sent out descriptions to every town within a hundred miles. He was no one I'd ever seen in Bailey, nor anyone else either, it began to look like, after we'd combed the town all day with the photos. Then, out of the blue, Billy Lee Davis smacks himself on the forehead and says, ''Sheriff, *I* seen this man somewhere in town, and not long ago!''

''He'd been shook all day since throwing up, and then all of a sudden he just snapped to. Was dead sure. Except he couldn't remember where or when. We went over and over it, and he tried and tried. It got to where I wanted to grab him by the ankles and hang him upside down and shake him till it dropped out of him. But it was no damn use. Just after dark we went back to that tree—we'd worked out a place to hide the cars and a route to it through the woods. When we were close, we walkie-talkied the men we'd left for an all-clear to come up. No answer at all. And when we got there, all that was left of our trap was the tree. No body, no tarp, no Special Assistant Deputies. Nothing.''

This time Dr. Winters poured the coffee and bourbon. ''Too much coffee,'' the sheriff muttered, but drank anyway. ''Part of me wanted to chew nails and break necks. And part of me was scared shitless. When we got back, I got on the radio station again and made an emergency broadcast and then had the man at the station rebroadcast it every hour. Told everyone to do everything in groups of three, to stay together at night in threes at least, to go out little as possible, keep armed and keep checking up on each other. It had such a damn-fool sound to it, but just pairing-up was no protection if half of one of those pairs was the killer. I sent our corpse's picture out statewide, I deputized more men and put them on the streets to beef up the night patrol.

''It was next morning that things broke. The sheriff of Rakehell called—he's over in the next county. He said our corpse looked a lot like a man named Abel Dougherty, a mill-hand with Con Wood over there. I left Billy Lee in charge and drove right out.

''This Dougherty had a cripple older sister he always checked back to by phone whenever he left town for long, a habit no one knew about, probably embarrassed him. Sheriff Peck there only found out about it when the woman called him, said her brother'd been four days gone for vacation and not rung her once. He'd hardly had her report for an hour when he got the picture I sent out, and recognized it. And *I* hadn't been in his office more than ten minutes when Billy Lee called me there. He'd remembered.

''When he'd seen Dougherty was the Sunday night three days before we found him. Where he'd seen him was the Trucker's Tavern outside the north end of town. The man had made a stir by being jolly drunk and latching onto a miner who was drinking there, man named Joe Allen, who'd started at the mine about two months back. Dougherty kept telling him that he wasn't Joe Allen, but Dougherty's old buddy named Sykes that had worked with him at Con Wood for a coon's age, and what the hell kind of joke was this, come have a beer old buddy and tell me why you took off so sudden and what the hell you been doing with yourself.

"Allen took it laughing. Dougherty'd clap him on the shoulder, Allen'd clap him right back and make every kind of joke about it, say, 'Give this man another beer, I'm standing in for a long-lost friend of his.' Dougherty was so big and loud and stubborn, Billy Lee was worried about a fight starting, and he wasn't the only one worried. But this Joe Allen was a natural good ol' boy, handled it perfect. We'd checked him out weeks back along with everyone else, and he was real popular with the other miners. Finally Dougherty swore he was going to take him on to another bar to help celebrate the vacation Dougherty was starting out on. Joe Allen got up grinning, said goddamn it, he couldn't accommodate Dougherty by being this fellow Sykes, but he could sure as hell have a glass with any serious drinking man that was treating. He went out with him, and gave everyone a wink as he left, to the general satisfaction of the audience."

Craven paused. Dr. Winters met his eyes and knew his thought, two images: the jolly wink that roused the room to laughter, and the thing in the tarp aboil with bright blue flies.

"It was plain enough for me," the sheriff said. "I told Billy Lee to search Allen's room at the Skettles' boardinghouse and then go straight to the mine and take him. We could fine-polish things once we had him. Since I was already in Rakehell, I saw to some of the loose ends before I started back. I went with Sheriff Peck down to Con Wood, and we found a picture of Eddie Sykes in the personnel files. I'd seen Joe Allen often enough, and it was his picture in that file.

"We found out Sykes had lived alone, was an on-again, off-again worker, private in his comings and goings, and hadn't been around for a while. But one of the sawyers there could be pretty sure of when Sykes left Rakehell because he'd gone to Sykes's cabin the morning after a big meteor shower they had out there about nine weeks back, since some thought the shower might have reached the ground, and not far from Sykes's side of the mountain. He wasn't in that morning, and the sawyer hadn't seen him since.

"After all those weeks, it was sewed up just like that. Within another hour I was almost back in Bailey, had the pedal to the metal, and was barely three miles out of town, when it all blew to shit. I *heard* it blow, I was that close to collaring him. I tell you, Carl, I felt . . . like a *bullet*. I was going to rip right through this Sykes, this goddamned cannibal monster. . . .

"We had to reconstruct what happened. Billy Lee got impatient and went after him alone, but luckily he radioed Travis—my other deputy—first. Travis was on the mountain dragnetting around that tree for clues, but he happened to be near his car when Billy Lee called him. He said he'd just been through Allen's room and had got something really odd. It was a sphere, half again big as a basketball, heavy, made of something that wasn't metal or glass but was a little like both. He could half-see into it, and it looked to be full of some kind of circuitry and components. He hadn't found anything else unusual. He was going to take this thing along with him, and go after Allen now. He told Travis to get up to the mine for backup. He'd be there first and should already have Allen by the time Travis arrived.

"Tierney, the shift boss up there, had an assistant that told us the rest. Billy Lee parked behind the offices where the men in the yard wouldn't see the car. He went upstairs to arrange the arrest with Tierney. They got half a dozen men together. Just as they came out of the building, they saw Allen take off running from the squad car. He had the sphere under his arm.

"The whole compound's fenced in, and Tierney'd already phoned to have all the gates shut. Allen zigged and zagged some but caught on quick to the trap. The sphere slowed him, but he still had a good lead. He hesitated a minute and then ran straight for the main shaft. A cage was just going down with a crew, and he risked every bone in him jumping down after it, but he got safe on top. By the time they got to the switches, the cage was down to the second level, and Allen and the crew had got out Tierney got it back up. Billy Lee ordered the rest back to get weapons and follow, and him and Tierney rode the cage right back down. And about two minutes later half the god-damned mine blew up.''

The sheriff stopped as if cut off, his lips parted to say more, his eyes registering for perhaps the hundredth time his amazement that there was no more, that the weeks of death and mystification ended here, with this split-second recapitulation: more death, more answerless dark, sealing all.

''Nate.''

''What.''

''Wrap it up and go to bed. I don't need your help. You're dead on your feet.''

''I'm not on my feet. And I'm coming along.''

''Give me a picture of the victims' position relative to the blast. I'm going to work, and you're going to bed.''

The sheriff shook his head absently. ''They're mining in shrinkage stopes. The adits—levels—branch off lateral from the vertical shaft. From one level they hollow out overhand up to the one above. Scoop out big chambers and let most of the broken rock stay inside so they can stand on the heaps to cut the ceiling higher. They leave sections of support wall between stopes, and those men were buried several stopes in from the shaft. The cave-in killed *them*. The mountain just folded them up in their own hill of tailings. No kind of fragments reached them. I'm dead sure. The only ones they *found* were of some standard charges that the main blast set off, and those didn't even get close. The big one blew out where the adit joined the shaft, right where, and right when, Billy Lee and Tierney got out of the cage. And there is *nothing* left there, Carl. No sphere, no cage, no Tierney, no Billy Lee Davis. Just rock blown fine as flour.''

Dr. Winters nodded and, after a moment, stood up. ''Come on, Nate. I've got to get started. I'll be lucky to have even a few of them done before morning. Drop me off and go to sleep, till then at least. You'll still be there to witness most of the work.''

The sheriff rose, took up the doctor's suitcase, and led him out of the office without a word, concession in his silence.

The patrol car was behind the building. The doctor saw a crueler beauty in the stars than he had an hour before. They got in, and Craven swung them out onto the empty street. The doctor opened the window and hearkened, but the motor's surge drowned out the river sound. Before the thrust of their headlights, ranks of old-fashioned parking meters sprouted shadows tall across the sidewalks, shadows that shrank and were cut down by the lights' passage. The sheriff said:

"All those extra dead. For nothing! Not even to . . . *feed* him! If it *was* a bomb, and he made it, he'd know how powerful it was. He wouldn't try some stupid escape stunt with it. And how did he even know that globe was there? We worked it out that Allen was just ending a shift, but he wasn't even up out of the ground before Billy Lee'd parked out of sight from the shaft.''

"Let it rest, Nate. I want to hear more, but after you've slept. I know you. All the photos will be there, and the report complete, all the evidence neatly boxed and carefully described. When I've looked things over, I'll know exactly how to proceed by myself.''

Bailey had neither hospital nor morgue, and the bodies were in a defunct ice-plant on the edge of town. A generator had been brought down from the mine, lighting improvised, and the refrigeration system reactivated. Dr. Parsons's office, and the tiny examining room that served the sheriff's station in place of a morgue, had furnished this makeshift with all the equipment that Dr. Winters would need beyond what he carried with him. A quarter-mile outside the main body of the town, they drew up to it. Tree-flanked, unneighbored by any other structure, it was a double building; the smaller half—the office—was illuminated. The bodies would be in the big windowless refrigerator segment. Craven pulled up beside a second squad car parked near the office door. A short rake-thin man wearing a large white stetson got out of the car and came over. Craven rolled down his window.

"Trav. This here's Dr. Winters."

" 'Lo, Nate. Dr. Winters. Everything's shipshape inside. Felt more comfortable out here. Last of those newshounds left two hours ago."

"They sure do hang on. You take off now, Trav. Get some sleep and be back at sunup. What temperature we getting?"

The pale stetson, far clearer in the starlight than the shadow-face beneath it, wagged dubiously. "Thirty-six. She won't get lower—some kind of leak."

"That should be cold enough," the doctor said.

Travis drove off, and the sheriff unlocked the padlock on the office door. Waiting behind him, Dr. Winters heard the river again—a cold balm, a whisper of freedom—and overlying this, the stutter and soft snarl of the generator behind the building, a gnawing, remorseless sound that somehow fed the obscure anguish that the other soothed. They went in.

The preparations had been thoughtful and complete. "You can wheel 'em out of the fridge on this and do the examining in here," the sheriff said, indicating a table and a gurney. "You should find all the gear you need on this big table here, and you can write up your reports on that desk. The phone's not hooked up—there's a pay phone at the last gas station if you have to call me."

The doctor nodded, checking over the material on the larger table: scalpels, postmortem and cartilage knives, intestine scissors, rib shears, forceps, probes, mallet and chisels, a blade saw and electric bone saw, scale, jars for specimens, needles and suture, sterilizer, gloves. . . . Beside this array were a few boxes and envelopes with descriptive sheets attached, containing the photographs and such evidentiary objects as had been found associated with the bodies.

"Excellent," he muttered.

"The overhead light's fluorescent, full spectrum or

whatever they call it. Better for colors. There's a pint of decent bourbon in that top desk drawer. Ready to look at 'em?''

"Yes.''

The sheriff unbarred and slid back the big metal door to the refrigeration chamber. Icy tainted air boiled out of the doorway. The light within was dimmer than that provided in the office—a yellow gloom wherein ten oblong heaps lay on trestles.

The two stood silent for a time, their stillness a kind of unpremeditated homage paid the eternal mystery at its threshold. As if the cold room were in fact a shrine, the doctor found a peculiar awe in the row of veiled forms. The awful unison of their dying, the titan's grave that had been made for them, conferred on them a stern authority, Death's Chosen Ones. His stomach hurt, and he found he had his hand pressed to his abdomen. He glanced at Craven and was relieved to see that his friend, staring wearily at the bodies, had missed the gesture.

"Nate. Help me uncover them.''

Starting at opposite ends of the row, they stripped the tarps off and piled them in a corner. Both were brusque now, not pausing over the revelation of the swelled, pulpy faces—most three-lipped with the gaseous burgeoning of their tongues—and the fat, livid hands sprouting from the filthy sleeves. But at one of the bodies Craven stopped. The doctor saw him look, and his mouth twist. Then he flung the tarp on the heap and moved to the next trestle.

When they came out, Dr. Winters took out the bottle and glasses Craven had put in the desk, and they had a drink together. The sheriff made as if he would speak, but shook his head and sighed.

"I *will* get some sleep, Carl. I'm getting crazy thoughts with this thing.'' The doctor wanted to ask those thoughts. Instead he laid a hand on his friend's shoulder.

"Go home, Sheriff Craven. Take off the badge and lie down. The dead won't run off on you. We'll all still be here in the morning.''

* * *

When the sound of the patrol car faded, the doctor stood listening to the generator's growl and the silence of the dead, resurgent now. Both the sound and the silence seemed to mock him. The afterecho of his last words made him uneasy. He said to his cancer:

"What about it, dear colleague? We *will* still be here tomorrow? All of us?"

He smiled, but felt an odd discomfort, as if he had ventured a jest in company and roused a hostile silence. He went to the refrigerator door, rolled it back, and viewed the corpses in their ordered rank, with their strange tribunal air. "What, sirs?" he murmured. "Do you judge me? Just who is to examine whom tonight, if I may ask?"

He went back into the office, where his first step was to examine the photographs made by the sheriff in order to see how the dead had lain at their uncovering. The earth had seized them with terrible suddenness. Some crouched, some partly stood, others sprawled in crazy free-fall postures. Each successive photo showed more of the jumble as the shovels continued their work between shots. The doctor studied them closely, noting the identifications inked on the bodies as they came completely into view.

One man, Roger Willet, had died some yards from the main cluster. It appeared he had just straggled into the stope from the adit at the moment of the explosion. He should thus have received, more directly than any of the others, the shock waves of the blast. If bomb fragments were to be found in any of the corpses, Mr. Willet's seemed likeliest to contain them. Dr. Winters pulled on a pair of surgical gloves.

Willet lay at one end of the line of trestles. He wore a thermal shirt and overalls that were strikingly new beneath the filth of burial. Their tough fabrics jarred with the fabric of his flesh—blue, swollen, seeming easily torn or burst, like ripe fruit. In life Willet had grease-combed his hair. Now it was a sculpture of dust, spikes and whorls shaped by the head's last grindings against the mountain that clenched it.

Rigor had come and gone—Willet rolled laxly onto the gurney. As the doctor wheeled him past the others, he felt a slight self-consciousness. The sense of some judgment flowing from the dead assembly—unlike most such vagrant fantasies—had an odd tenacity in him. This stubborn unease began to irritate him with himself, and he moved more briskly.

He put Willet on the examining table and cut the clothes off him with shears, storing the pieces in an evidence box. The overalls were soiled with agonal waste expulsions. The doctor stared a moment with unwilling pity at his naked subject.

"You won't ride down to Fordham in any case," he said to the corpse. "Not unless I find something pretty damned obvious." He pulled his gloves tighter and arranged his implements.

Waddleton had said more to him than he had reported to the sheriff. The doctor was to find, and forcefully to record that he had found, strong "indicators" absolutely requiring the decedents' removal to Fordham for X-ray and an exhaustive second postmortem. The doctor's continued employment with the Coroner's Office depended entirely on his compliance in this. He had received this stipulation with a silence Waddleton had not thought it necessary to break. His present resolution was all but made at that moment. Let the obvious be taken as such. If the others showed as plainly as Willet did the external signs of death by asphyxiation, they would receive no more than a thorough external exam. Willet he would examine internally as well, merely to establish in depth for this one what should appear obvious in all. Otherwise, only when the external exam revealed a clearly anomalous feature—and clear and suggestive it must be—would he look deeper.

He rinsed the caked hair in a basin, poured the sediment into a flask and labeled it. Starting with the scalp, he began a minute scrutiny of the body's surfaces, recording his observations as he went.

The characteristic signs of asphyxial death were evident, despite the complicating effects of autolysis and putrefaction. The eyeballs' bulge and the tongue's protrusion were, by now, as much due to gas pressure as to the mode of death, but the latter organ was clamped between locked teeth, leaving little doubt as to that mode. The coloration of degenerative change—a greenish-yellow tint, a darkening and mapping-out of superficial veins—was marked, but not sufficient to obscure the blue of cyanosis on the face and neck, nor the pinpoint hemorrhages freckling neck, chest, and shoulders. From the mouth and nose the doctor scraped matter he was confident was the blood-tinged mucous typically ejected in the airless agony.

He began to find a kind of comedy in his work. What a buffoon death made of a man! A blue pop-eyed three-lipped thing. And there was himself, his curious solicitous intimacy with this clownish carrion. Excuse me, Mr. Willet, while I probe this laceration. What do you feel when I do this? Nothing? Nothing at all? Fine, now what about these nails? Split them clawing at the earth, did you? Yes. A nice bloodblister under this thumbnail, I see—got it on the job a few days before your accident, no doubt? Remarkable calluses here, still quite tough . . .

The doctor looked for an unanalytic moment at the hands—puffed dark paws, gestureless, having renounced all touch and grasp. He felt the wastage of the man concentrated in the hands. The painful futility of the body's fine articulation when it is seen in death—this poignancy he had long learned not to acknowledge when he worked. But now he let it move him a little. This Roger Willet, plodding to his work one afternoon, had suddenly been scrapped, crushed to a nonfunctional heap of perishable materials. It simply happened that his life had chanced to move too close to the passage of a more powerful life, one of those inexorable and hungry lives that leave human wreckage—known or undiscovered—in their wakes. Bad luck, Mr. Willet. Naturally, we feel very sorry about this. But this Joe Allen, your co-worker. Apparently he was some sort of . . . cannibal. It's complicated. We don't understand it all. But the fact is we have to dismantle you now to a certain extent. There's really no hope of your using these parts of yourself again, I'm afraid. Ready now?

The doctor proceeded to the internal exam with a vague eagerness for Willet's fragmentation, for the disarticulation of that sadness in his natural form. He grasped Willet by the jaw and took up the postmortem knife. He sank its point beneath the chin and began the long, gently sawing incision that opened Willet from throat to groin.

In the painstaking separation of the body's laminae Dr. Winters found absorption and pleasure. And yet throughout he felt, marginal but insistent, the movement of a stream of irrelevant images. These were of the building that contained him, and of the night containing it. As from outside, he saw the plant—bleached planks, iron roofing—and the trees crowding it, all in starlight, a ghost-town image. And he saw the refrigerator vault beyond the wall as from within, feeling the stillness of murdered men in a cold yellow light. And at length a question formed itself, darting in and out of the weave of his concentration as the images did: Why did he still feel, like some stir of the air, that sense of mute vigilance surrounding his action, furtively touching his nerves with its inquiry as he worked? He shrugged, overtly angry now. Who else was attending but Death? Wasn't he Death's hireling, and this Death's place? Then let the master look on.

Peeling back Willet's cover of hemorrhage-stippled skin, Dr. Winters read the corpse with an increasing dispassion, a mortuary text. He confined his inspection to the lungs and mediastinum and found there unequivocal testimony to Willet's asphyxial death. The pleurae of the lungs exhibited the expected ecchymoses—bruised spots in the glassy enveloping membrane. Beneath, the polyhedral surface lobules of the lungs themselves were bubbled and blistered—the expected interstitial emphysema. The lungs, on section, were intensely and bloodily congested. The left half of the heart he found contracted and empty, while the right was overdistended and engorged with dark blood, as were the large veins of the upper mediastinum. It was a classic picture of death by suffocation, and at length the doctor, with needle and suture, closed up the text again.

He returned the corpse to the gurney and draped one of his mortuary bags over it in the manner of a shroud. When he had help in the morning, he would weigh the bodies on a platform scale the office contained and afterward bag them properly. He came to the refrigerator door, and hesitated. He stared at the door, not moving, not understanding why.

Run. Get out. Now.

The thought was his own, but it came to him so urgently he turned around as if someone behind him had spoken. Across the room a thin man in smock and gloves, his eyes shadows, glared at the doctor from the black windows. Behind the man was a shrouded cart, behind that, a wide metal door.

Quietly, wonderingly, the doctor asked, "Run from what?" The eyeless man in the glass was still half-crouched, afraid.

Then, a moment later, the man straightened, threw back his head, and laughed. The doctor walked to the desk and sat down shoulder to shoulder with him. He pulled out the bottle and they had a drink together, regarding each other with identical bemused smiles. Then the doctor said, "Let me pour you another. You need it, old fellow. It makes a man himself again."

Nevertheless his reentry of the vault was difficult, toilsome, each step seeming to require a new summoning of the will to move. In the freezing half-light all movement felt like defiance. His body lagged behind his craving to be quick, to be done with this molestation of the gathered dead. He returned Willet to his pallet and took his neighbor. The name on the tag wired to his boot was Ed Moses. Dr. Winters wheeled him back to the office and closed the big door behind him.

With Moses his work gained momentum. He expected to perform no further internal necropsies. He thought of his employer, rejoicing now in his seeming-submission to Waddleton's ultimatum. The impact would be dire. He pictured the coroner in shock, a sheaf of Pathologist's Reports in one hand, and smiled.

Waddleton could probably make a plausible case for incomplete examination. Still, a pathologist's discretionary powers were not well-defined. Many good ones would approve the adequacy of the doctor's method, given his working conditions. The inevitable litigation with a coalition of compensation claimants would be strenuous and protracted. Win or lose, Waddleton's venal devotion to the insurance company's interest would be abundantly displayed. Further, immediately on his dismissal the doctor would formally disclose its occult cause to the press. A libel action would ensue that he would have as little cause to fear as he had to fear his firing. Both his savings and the lawsuit would long outlast his life.

Externally, Ed Moses exhibited a condition as typically asphyxial as Willet's had been, with no slightest mark of fragment entry. The doctor finished his report and returned Moses to the vault, his movements brisk and precise. His unease was all but gone. That queasy stirring of the air—had he really felt it? It had been, perhaps, some new reverberation of the death at work in him, a psychic shudder of response to the cancer's stealthy probing for his life. He brought out the body next to Moses in the line.

Walter Lou Jackson was big, six feet two inches from heel to crown, and would surely weigh out at more than two hundred pounds. He had writhed mightily against his million-ton coffin with an agonal strength that had torn his face and hands. Death had mauled him like a lion. The doctor set to work.

His hands were fully themselves now—fleet, exact, intricately testing the corpse's character as other fingers might explore a keyboard for its latent melodies. And the doctor watched them with an old pleasure, one of the few that had never failed him, his mind at one remove from their busy intelligence. All the hard deaths! A worldful of them, time without end. Lives wrenched kicking from their snug meat-frames. Walter Lou Jackson had died very hard. Joe Allen brought this on you, Mr. Jackson. We think it was part of his attempt to escape the law.

But what a botched flight! The unreason of it—more than baffling—was eerie in its colossal futility. Beyond question, Allen had been cunning. A ghoul with a psychopath's social finesse. A good old boy who could make a tavernful of men laugh with delight while he cut his victim from their midst, make them applaud his exit with the prey, who stepped jovially into the darkness with murder at his side clapping him on the shoulder. Intelligent, certainly; with a strange technical sophistication as well, suggested by the sphere. Then what of the lunacy yet more strongly suggested by the same object? In the sphere was concentrated all the lethal mystery of Bailey's long nightmare.

Why the explosion? Its location implied an ambush for Allen's pursuers, a purposeful detonation. Had he aimed at a limited cave-in from which he schemed some inconceivable escape? Folly enough in this—far more if, as seemed sure, Allen had made the bomb himself, for then he would have to know its power was grossly inordinate to the need.

But if it was not a bomb, had a different function and only incidentally an explosive potential, Allen might underestimate the blast. It appeared the object was somehow remotely monitored by him, for the timing of events showed he had gone straight for it the instant he emerged from the shaft—shunned the bus waiting to take his shift back to town and made a beeline across the compound for a patrol car that was hidden from his view by the office building. This suggested something more complex than a mere explosive device, something, perhaps, whose destruction was itself more Allen's aim than the explosion produced thereby.

The fact that he risked the sphere's retrieval at all pointed to this interpretation. For the moment he sensed its presence at the mine, he must have guessed that the murder investigation had led to its discovery and removal from his room. But then, knowing himself already liable to the extreme penalty, why should Allen go to such lengths to recapture evidence incriminatory of a lesser offense, possession of an explosive device?

Then grant that the sphere was something more, something instrumental to his murders that could guarantee a conviction he might otherwise evade. Still, his gambit made no sense. Since the sphere—and thus the lawmen he could assume to have taken it—was already at the mine office, he must expect the compound to be sealed at any moment. Meanwhile, the gate was open, escape into the mountains a strong possibility for a man capable of stalking and destroying two experienced and well-armed woodsmen lying in ambush for him. Why had he all but ensured his capture to weaken a case against himself that his escape would have rendered irrelevant? Dr. Winters watched as his own fingers, like a hunting pack round a covert, converged on a small puncture wound below Walter Lou Jackson's xiphoid process, between the eighth ribs.

His left hand touched its borders, the fingers' inquiry quick and tender. The right hand introduced a probe, and both together eased it into the wound. It was rarely fruitful to use a probe on corpses this decayed; the track of the wound would more properly be examined by section. But an inexplicable sense of urgency had taken hold of him. Gently, with infinite pains not to pierce in the softened tissues an artifactual track of his own, he inched the probe in. It moved unobstructed deep into the body, curving upward through the diaphragm toward the heart. The doctor's own heart accelerated. He watched his hands move to record the observation, watched them pause, watched them return to their survey of the corpse, leaving pen and page untouched.

External inspection revealed no further anomaly. All else he observed the doctor recorded faithfully, wondering throughout at the distress he felt. When he had finished, he understood it. Its cause was not the discovery of an entry wound that might bolster Waddleton's case. For the find had, within moments, revealed to him that, should he encounter anything he thought to be a mark of fragment penetration, he was going to ignore it. The damage Joe Allen had done was going to end here, with this last grand slaughter, and would not extend to the impoverishment of his victims' survivors. His mind was now made up: for Jackson and the remaining seven, the external exams would be officially recorded as contraindicating the need for any internal exam.

No, the doctor's unease as he finished Jackson's external—as he wrote up his report and signed it—had a different source. His problem was that he did not believe the puncture in Jackson's thorax *was* a mark of fragment entry. He disbelieved this, and had no idea why he did so. Nor had he any idea why, once again, he felt afraid. He sealed the report. Jackson was now officially accounted for and done with. Then Dr. Winters took up the post-mortem knife and returned to the corpse.

First the long sawing slice, unzipping the mortal overcoat. Next, two great square flaps of flesh reflected, scrolled laterally to the armpits' line, disrobing the chest: one hand grasping the flap's skirt, the other sweeping beneath it with the knife, flensing through the glassy tissue that joined it to the chest wall, and shaving all muscles from their anchorages to bone and cartilage beneath. Then the dismantling of the strongbox within. Rib shears—so frank and forward a tool, like a gardener's. The steel beak bit through each rib's gristle anchor to the sternum's centerplate. At the sternum's crownpiece the collarbones' ends were knifed, pried, and sprung free from their sockets. The coffer unhasped, unhinged, a knife teased beneath the lid and levered it off.

Some minutes later the doctor straightened up and stepped back from his subject. He moved almost drunkenly, and his age seemed scored more deeply in his face. With loathing haste he stripped his gloves off. He went to the desk, sat down, and poured another drink. If there was something like horror in his face, there was also a hardening in his mouth's line and the muscles of his jaw. He spoke to his glass: "So be it, your Excellency. Something new for your humble servant. Testing my nerve?"

Jackson's pericardium, the shapely capsule containing his heart, should have been all but hidden between the big blood-fat loaves of his lungs. The doctor had found it fully exposed, the lungs flanking it wrinkled lumps less than a third their natural bulk. Not only they, but the left heart and the superior mediastinal veins—all the regions that should have been grossly engorged with blood—were utterly drained of it.

The doctor swallowed his drink and got out the photographs again. He found that Jackson had died on his stomach across the body of another worker, with the upper part of a third trapped between them. Neither these two subjacent corpses nor the surrounding earth showed any stain of a blood loss that must have amounted to two liters.

Possibly the pictures, by some trick of shadow, had failed to pick it up. He turned to the Investigator's Report, where Craven would surely have mentioned any significant amounts of bloody earth uncovered during the disinterment. The sheriff recorded nothing of the kind. Dr. Winters returned to the pictures.

Ronald Pollock, Jackson's most intimate associate in the grave, had died on his back, beneath and slightly askew of Jackson, placing most of their torsos in contact, save where the head and shoulder of the third interposed. It seemed inconceivable Pollock's clothing should lack any trace of such massive drainage from a death mate thus embraced.

The doctor rose abruptly, pulled on fresh gloves, and returned to Jackson. His hands showed a more brutal speed now, closing the great incision temporarily with a few widely spaced sutures. He replaced him in the vault and brought out Pollock, striding, heaving hard at the dead shapes in the shifting of them thrusting always—so it seemed to him—just a step ahead of urgent thoughts he did not want to have, deformities that whispered at his back, emitting faint, chill gusts of putrid breath. He shook his head—denying, delaying—and pushed the new corpse onto the worktable. The scissors undressed Pollock in greedy bites.

But at length, when he had scanned each scrap of fabric and found nothing like the stain of blood, he came to rest again, relinquishing that simplest, desired resolution he had made such haste to reach. He stood at the instrument table, not seeing it, submitting to the approach of the half-formed things at his mind's periphery.

The revelation of Jackson's shriveled lungs had been more than a shock. He had felt a stab of panic too, in fact that same curiously explicit terror of this place that had urged him to flee earlier. He acknowledged now that the germ of that quickly suppressed terror had been a premonition of this failure to find any trace of the missing blood. Whence the premonition? It had to do with a problem he had steadfastly refused to consider: the mechanics of so complete a drainage of the lungs' densely reticulated vascular structure. Could the earth's crude pressure by itself work so thoroughly, given only a single vent both slender and strangely curved? And then the photograph he had studied. It frightened him now to recall the image—some covert meaning stirred with it, struggling to be seen. Dr. Winters picked the probe up from the table and turned again to the corpse. As surely and exactly as if he had already ascertained the wound's presence, he leaned forward and touched it: a small, neat puncture, just beneath the xiphoid process. He introduced the probe. The wound received it deeply, in a familiar direction.

The doctor went to the desk and took up the photograph again. Pollock's and Jackson's wounded areas were not in contact. The third man's head was sandwiched between their bodies at just that point. He searched out another picture, in which this third man was more central, and found his name inked in below his image: Joe Allen.

Dreamingly, Dr. Winters went to the wide metal door, shoved it aside, entered the vault. He did not search, but went straight to the trestle where Sheriff

Craven had paused some hours before. He found the same name on its tag.

The body, beneath decay's spurious obesity, was trim and well-muscled. The face was square-cut, shelf-browed, with a vulpine nose skewed by an old fracture. The swollen tongue lay behind the teeth, and the bulge of decomposition did not obscure what the man's initial impact must have been—handsome and open, his now-waxen black eyes sly and convivial. Say, good buddy, got a minute? I see you comin' on the swing shift every day, don't I? Yeah, Joe Allen. Look, I know it's late, you want to get home, tell the wife you ain't been in there drinkin' since you got off, right? Oh, yeah, I hear that. But his damn disappearance thing's got me so edgy, and I'd swear to God just as I was coming here I seen someone moving around back of that frame house up the street. See how the trees thin out a little down back of the yard, where the moonlight gets in? That's right. Well, I got me this little popper here. Oh, yeah, that's a beauty, we'll have it covered between us. I knew I could spot a man ready for some trouble—couldn't find a patrol car anywhere on the street. Yeah, just down in here now, to that clump of pine. Step careful, you can barely see. That's right. . . .

The doctor's face ran with sweat. He turned on his heel and walked out of the vault, heaving the door shut behind him. In the office's greater warmth he felt the perspiration soaking his shirt under the smock. His stomach rasped with steady oscillations of pain, but he scarcely attended it. He went to Pollock and seized up the postmortem knife.

The work was done with surreal speed, the laminae of flesh and bone recoiling smoothly beneath his desperate but unerring hands, until the thoracic cavity lay exposed, and in it, the vampire-stricken lungs, two gnarled lumps of gray tissue.

He searched no deeper, knowing what the heart and veins would show. He returned to sit at the desk, weakly drooping, the knife, forgotten, still in his left hand. He looked at his reflection in the window, and it seemed his thoughts originated with that fainter, more tenuous Dr. Winters hanging like a ghost outside.

What was this world he lived in? Surely, in a lifetime, he had not begun to guess. To feed in such a way! There was horror enough in this alone. But to feed thus *in his own grave*. How had he accomplished it—leaving aside how he had fought suffocation long enough to do anything at all? How was it to be comprehended, a greed that raged so hotly it would glut itself at the very threshold of its own destruction? That last feast was surely in his stomach still.

Dr. Winters looked at the photograph, at Allen's head snugged into the others' middles like a hungry suckling nuzzling to the sow. Then he looked at the knife in his hand. The hand felt empty of all technique. Its one impulse was to slash, cleave, obliterate the remains of this gluttonous thing, this Joe Allen. He must do this, or flee it utterly. There was no course between. He did not move.

"I *will* examine him," said the ghost in the glass, and did not move. Inside the refrigeration vault, there was a slight noise.

No. It had been some hitch in the generator's murmur. Nothing in there could move. There was another noise, a brief friction against the vault's inner wall. The two old men shook their heads at one another. A catch clicked, and the metal door slid open. Behind the staring image of his own amazement, the doctor saw that a filthy shape stood in the doorway and raised its arms toward him in a gesture of supplication. The doctor turned in his chair. From the shape came a whistling groan, the decayed fragment of a human voice.

Pleadingly, Joe Allen worked his jaw and spread his purple hands. As if speech were a maggot struggling to emerge from his mouth, the blue tumescent face toiled, the huge tongue wallowed helplessly between the viscid lips.

The doctor reached for the telephone, lifted the receiver. Its deadness to his ear meant nothing—he could not have spoken. The thing confronting him, with each least movement that it made, destroyed the very frame of sanity in which words might have meaning, reduced the world itself around him to a waste of dark and silence, a starlit ruin where already, everywhere, the alien and unimaginable was awakening to its new dominion. The corpse raised and reached out one hand as if to stay him—turned, and walked toward the instrument table. Its legs were leaden, it rocked its shoulders like a swimmer, fighting to make its passage through gravity's dense medium. It reached the table and grasped it exhaustedly. The doctor found himself on his feet, crouched slightly, weightlessly still. The knife in his hand was the only part of himself he clearly felt, and it was like a tongue of fire, a crematory flame. Joe Allen's corpse thrust one hand among the instruments. The thick fingers, with a queer simian ineptitude, brought up a scalpel. Both hands clasped the little handle and plunged the blade between the lips, as a thirsty child might a Popsicle, then jerked it out again, slashing the tongue. Turbid fluid splashed down to the floor. The jaw worked stiffly, the mouth brought out words in a wet ragged hiss:

"Please. Help me. Trapped in *this*." One dead hand struck the dead chest. "Starving."

"What are you?"

"Traveler. Not of Earth."

"An eater of human flesh. A drinker of human blood."

"No. No. Hiding only. Am small. Shape hideous to you. Feared death."

"You brought death." The doctor spoke with the calm of perfect disbelief, himself as incredible to him as the thing he spoke with. It shook its head, the dull, popped eyes glaring with an agony of thwarted expression.

"Killed none. Hid in this. Hid in this not to be killed. Five days now. Drowning in decay. Free me. Please."

"No. You have come to feed on us, you are not hiding in fear. We are your food, your meat and drink.

You fed on those two men within your grave. *Their* grave. For you, a delay. In fact, a diversion that has ended the hunt for you.''

"No! No! Used men already dead. For me, five days, starvation. Even less. Fed only from need. Horrible necessity!''

The spoiled vocal instrument made a mangled gasp of the last word—an inhuman snake-pit noise the doctor felt as a cold flicker of ophidian tongues within his ears—while the dead arms moved in a sodden approximation of the body language that swears truth.

"No,'' the doctor said. "You killed them all. Including your . . . tool—this man. *What are you?*'' Panic erupted in the question that he tried to bury by answering himself instantly. "Resolute, yes. That surely. You used death for an escape route. You need no oxygen perhaps.''

"Extracted more than my need from gasses of decay. A lesser component of our metabolism.''

The voice was gaining distinctness, developing makeshifts for tones lost in the agonal rupturing of the valves and stops of speech, more effectively wrestling vowel and consonant from the putrid tongue and lips. At the same time the body's crudity of movement did not quite obscure a subtle, incessant experimentation. Fingers flexed and stirred, testing the give of tendons, groping the palm for old points of purchase and counterpressure there. The knees, with cautious repetitions, assessed the new limits of their articulation.

"What was the sphere?''

"My ship. Its destruction our first duty facing discovery.'' (Fear touched the doctor, like a slug climbing his neck; he had seen, as it spoke, a sharp spastic activity of the tongue, a pleating and shrinkage of its bulk as at the tug of some inward adjustment.) "No chance to reenter. Leaving this body takes far too long. Not even time to set it for destruct—must extrude a cilium, chemical key to broach hull shield. In shaft was my only chance to halt my host.''

Though the dead mask hung expressionless, conveyed no irony, the thing's articulacy grew uncannily—each word more smoothly shaped, nuances of tone creeping into its speech. Its right arm tested its wrist as it spoke, and the scalpel the hand still held cut white sparks from the air, while the word *host* seemed itself a little razor-cut, an almost teasing abandonment of fiction preliminary to attack.

But the doctor found that fear had gone from him. The impossibility with which he conversed, and was about to struggle, was working in him an overwhelming amplification of his life's long helpless rage at death. He found his parochial pity for Earth alone stretched to the transstellar scope this traveler commanded, to the whole cosmic trash yard with its bulldozed multitudes of corpses; galactic wheels of carnage—stars, planets with their most majestic generations—all trash, cracked bones and foul rags that pooled, settled, reconcatenated in futile symmetries gravid with new multitudes of briefly animate trash.

And this, standing before him now, was the death it was given him particularly to deal—his mite was being called in by the universal Treasury of Death, and Dr. Winters found himself, an old healer, on fire to pay. His own, more lethal, blade tugged at his hand with its own sharp appetite. He felt entirely the Examiner once more, knew the precise cuts he would make, swiftly and without error. *Very soon now,* he thought and coolly probed for some further insight before its onslaught:

"Why must your ship be destroyed, even at the cost of your host's life?"

"We must not be understood."

"The livestock must not understand what is devouring them."

"Yes, Doctor. Not all at once. But one by one. You will understand what is devouring you. That is essential to my feast."

The doctor shook his head. "You are in your grave already, Traveler. That body will be your coffin. You will be buried in it a second time, for all time."

The thing came one step nearer and opened its mouth. The flabby throat wrestled as with speech, but what sprang out was a slender white filament, more than whip-fast. Dr. Winters saw only the first flicker of its eruption, and then his brain nova-ed, thinning out at light-speed to a white nullity.

When the doctor came to himself, it was in fact to a part of himself only. Before he had opened his eyes he found that his wakened mind had repossessed proprioceptively only a bizarre truncation of his body. His head, neck, left shoulder, arm, and hand declared themselves—the rest was silence.

When he opened his eyes, he found that he lay supine on the gurney, and naked. Something propped his head. A strap bound his left elbow to the gurney's edge, a strap he could feel. His chest was also anchored by a strap, and this he could not feel. Indeed, save for its active remnant, his entire body might have been bound in a block of ice, so numb was it, and so powerless was he to compel the slightest movement from the least part of it.

The room was empty, but from the open door of the vault there came slight sounds: the creak and soft frictions of heavy tarpaulin shifted to accommodate some business involving small clicking and kissing noises.

Tears of fury filled the doctor's eyes. Clenching his one fist at the starry engine of creation that he could not see, he ground his teeth and whispered in the hot breath of strangled weeping:

"Take it back, this dirty little shred of life! I throw it off gladly like the filth it is." The slow knock of boot soles loudened from within the vault, and he turned his head. From the vault door Joe Allen's corpse approached him.

It moved with new energy, though its gait was grotesque, a ducking, hitching progress, jerky with circumventions of decayed muscle, while above this galvanized, struggling frame, the bruise-colored face hung inanimate, an image of detachment. With terrible clarity the thing was revealed for what it was—a damaged hand-puppet vigorously worked from within. And when that frozen face was brought to hang above the doctor, the reeking hands, with the light, solicitous touch of friends at sickbeds, rested on his naked thigh.

The absence of sensation made the touch more dreadful than if felt. It showed him that the nightmare he still desperately denied at heart had annexed his body while he—holding head and arm free—had already more than half-drowned in its mortal paralysis. There, from his chest on down, lay his nightmare part, a nothingness freely possessed by an unspeakability. The corpse said:

"Rotten blood. Thin nourishment. I had only one hour alone before you came. I fed from my neighbor to my left—barely had strength to extend a siphon. Fed from the right while you worked. Tricky going—you are alert. I expected Dr. Parsons. The energy needs of animating this"—one hand left the doctor's thigh and smote the dusty overalls—"and of host-transfer, very high. Once I have you synapsed, I will be near starvation again."

A sequence of unbearable images unfolded in the doctor's mind, even as the robot carrion turned from the gurney and walked to the instrument table: the sheriff's arrival just after dawn, alone of course, since Craven always took thought for his deputies' rest and because on this errand he would want privacy to consider any indiscretion on behalf of the miners' survivors that the situation might call for; Craven's finding his old friend, supine and alarmingly weak; his hurrying over, his leaning near. Then, somewhat later, a police car containing a rack of still wet bones might plunge off the highway above some deep spot in the gorge.

The corpse took an evidence box from the table and put the scalpel in it. Then it turned and retrieved the mortuary knife from the floor and put that in as well, saying as it did so, without turning, "The sheriff will come in the morning. You spoke like close friends. He will probably come alone."

The coincidence with his thoughts had to be accident, but the intent to terrify and appall him was clear. The tone and timing of that patched-up voice were unmistakably deliberate—sly probes that sought his anguish specifically, sought his mind's personal center. He watched the corpse—over at the table—dipping an apish but accurate hand and plucking up rib shears, scissors, clamps, adding all to the box. He stared, momentarily emptied by shock of all but the will to know finally the full extent of the horror that had appropriated his life. Joe Allen's body carried the box to the worktable beside the gurney, and the expressionless eyes met the doctor's.

"I have gambled. A grave gamble. But now I have won. At risk of personal discovery we are obliged to disconnect, contract, hide as well as possible in the host-body. Suicide in effect. I disregarded situational imperatives, despite starvation before disinterment and subsequent autopsy being all but certain. I caught up with the crew, tackled Pollock and Jackson microseconds before the blast. I computed five days' survival from this cache. I could disconnect at limit of my strength to do so, but otherwise I would chance autopsy, knowing the doctor was an alcoholic incompetent. And now see my gain. You are a prize host. Through you I can feed with near impunity even when killing is too dangerous. Safe meals are delivered to you still warm."

The corpse had painstakingly aligned the gurney parallel to the worktable but offset, the table's foot extending past the gurney's, and separated from it by a distance somewhat less than the reach of Joe Allen's right arm. Now the dead hands distributed the implements along the right edge of the table, save for the scissors and the box. These the corpse took to the table's foot, where it set down the box and slid the scissors's jaws round one strap of its overalls. It began to speak again, and as it did, the scissors dismembered its cerements in unhesitating strokes.

"The cut must be medical, forensically right, though a smaller one is easier. I must be careful of the pectoral muscles or these arms will not convey me. I am no larva anymore—over fifteen hundred grams."

To ease the nightmare's suffocating pressure, to

thrust out some flicker of his own will against its en-
gulfment, the doctor flung a question, his voice more
cracked than the other's now was:

"Why is my arm free?"

"The last, fine neural splicing needs a sensory-
motor standard, to perfect my brain's fit to yours.
Lacking this eye-hand coordinating check, only a much
coarser control of the host's characteristic motor patterns is possible. This done, I flush out the paralytic,
unbind us, and we are free together."

The grave-clothes had fallen in a puzzle of fragments, and the cadaver stood naked, its dark gas-
rounded contours making it seem some sleek marine
creature, ruddered with the black-veined gas-distended
sex. Again the voice had teased for his fear, had uttered the last word with a savoring protraction, and
now the doctor's cup of anguish brimmed over; horror
and outrage wrenched his spirit in brutal alternation
as if trying to tear it naked from its captive frame. He
rolled his head in this deadlock, his mouth beginning
to split with the slow birth of a mind-emptying outcry.

The corpse watched this, giving a single nod that
might have been approbation. Then it mounted the
worktable and, with the concentrated caution of some
practiced convalescent reentering his bed, lay on its
back. The dead eyes again sought the living and found
the doctor staring back, grinning insanely.

"Clever corpse!" the doctor cried. "Clever, carnivorous corpse! Able alien! Please don't think I'm crit-
icizing. Who am I to criticize? A mere arm and
shoulder, a talking head, just a small piece of a pathologist. But I'm confused." He paused, savoring the
monster's attentive silence and his own buoyancy in
the hysterical levity that had unexpectedly liberated
him. "You're going to use your puppet there to pluck
you out of itself and put you on me. But once he's
pulled you from your driver's seat, won't he go dead,
so to speak, and drop you? You could get a nasty
knock. Why not set a plank between the tables—the
puppet opens the door, and you scuttle, ooze, lurch,
flop, slither, as the case may be, across the bridge. No

messy spills. And in any case, isn't this an odd, rather clumsy way to get around among your cattle? Shouldn't you at least carry your own scalpels when you travel? There's always the risk you'll run across that one host in a million that isn't carrying one with him.''

He knew his gibes would be answered to his own despair. He exulted, but solely in the momentary bafflement of the predator—in having, for just a moment, mocked its gloating assurance to silence and marred its feast.

Its right hand picked up the postmortem knife beside it, and the left wedged a roll of gauze beneath Allen's neck, lifting the throat to a more prominent arch. The mouth told the ceiling:

''We retain larval form till entry of the host. As larvae we have locomotor structures, and sense buds usable outside our ships' sensory amplifiers. I waited coiled round Joe Allen's bed leg till night, entered by his mouth as he slept.'' Allen's hand lifted the knife, held it high above the dull, quick eyes, turning it in the light. ''Once lodged, we have three instars to adult form,'' the voice continued absently—the knife might have been a mirror from which the corpse read its features. ''Larvally we have only a sketch of our full neural tap. Our metamorphosis is cued and determined by the host's endosomatic ecology. I matured in three days.'' Allen's wrist flexed, tipping the knife's point downmost. ''Most supreme adaptations are purchased at the cost of inessential capacities.'' The elbow pronated and slowly flexed, hooking the knife bodyward. ''Our hosts are all sentients, ecodominants, are already carrying the baggage of coping structures for the planetary environment we find them in. Limbs, sensory portals''—the fist planted the fang of its tool under the chin, tilted it and rode it smoothly down the throat, the voice proceeding unmarred from under the furrow that the steel ploughed—''somatic envelopes, instrumentalities''—down the sternum, diaphragm, abdomen the stainless blade painted its stripe of gaping, muddy tissue—''with a host's brain we inherit all these, the mastery of any planet, netted in its dominant's cerebral nexus. Thus our genetic codings are now all but disencumbered of such provisions.''

So swiftly that the doctor flinched, Joe Allen's hand slashed four lateral cuts from the great wound's axis. The seeming butchery left two flawlessly drawn thoracic flaps cleanly outlined. The left hand raised the left flap's hem, and the right coaxed the knife into the aperture, deepening it with small stabs and slices. The posture was a man's who searches a breast pocket, with the dead eyes studying the slow recoil of flesh. The voice, when it resumed, had geared up to an intenser pitch:

"Galactically, the chordate nerve/brain paradigm abounds, and the neural labyrinth is our dominion. Are we to make plank bridges and worm across them to our food? Are cockroaches greater than we for having legs to run up walls and antennae to grope their way? All the quaint, hinged crutches that life sports! The stilts, fins, fans, springs, stalks, flippers, and feathers, all in turn so variously terminating in hooks, clamps, suckers, scissors, forks, or little cages of digits! And besides all the gadgets it concocts for wrestling through its worlds, it is all knobbed, whiskered, crested, plumed, vented, spiked, or measeled over with perceptual gear for combing pittances of noise or color from the environing plentitude."

Invincibly calm and sure, the hands traded tool and tasks. The right flap eased back, revealing ropes of ingeniously spared muscle while promising a genuine appearance once sutured back in place. Helplessly the doctor felt his delirious defiance bleed away and a bleak fascination rebind him.

"We are the taps and relays that share the host's aggregate of afferent nerve-impulse precisely at its nodes of integration. We are the brains that peruse these integrations, integrate them with our existing banks of the host-specific data, and, lastly, let their consequences flow down the motor pathway—either the consequences they seek spontaneously, or those we wish to graft upon them. We are besides a streamlined alimentary/circulatory system and a reproductive apparatus. And more than this we need not be.''

The corpse had spread its bloody vest, and the feculent hands now took up the rib shears. The voice's sinister coloration of pitch and stress grew yet more marked—the phrases slid from the tongue with a cobra's seeking sway, winding their liquid rhythms round the doctor till a gap in his resistance should let them pour through to slaughter the little courage left him.

''For in this form we have inhabited the densest brainweb of three hundred races, lain intricately snug within them like thriving vine on trelliswork. We've looked out from too many variously windowed masks to regret our own vestigial senses. None read their worlds definitively. Far better then our nomad's range and choice than an unvarying tenancy of one poor set of structures. Far better to slip on as we do whole living beings and wear at once all of their limbs and organs, memories and powers—wear all these as tightly congruent to our wills as a glove is to the hand that fills it.''

The shears clipped through the gristle, stolid, bloody jaws monotonously feeding, stopping short of the sternoclavicular joint in the manubrium where the muscles of the pectoral girdle have an important anchorage.

''No consciousness of the chordate type that we have found has been impermeable to our finesse—no dendritic pattern so elaborate we could not read its stitchwork and thread ourselves to match, precisely map its each synaptic seam till we could loosen it and retailor all to suit ourselves. We have strutted costumed in the bodies of planetary autarchs, venerable manikins of moral fashion, but cut of the universal cloth: the weave of fleet electric filaments of experience that we easily reshuttled to the warp of our wishes. Whereafter— newly hemmed and gathered—their living fabric hung obedient to our bias, investing us with honor and influence unlimited.''

The tricky verbal melody, through the corpse's deft, unfaltering self-dismemberment—the sheer neuromuscular orchestration of the compound activity—struck

Dr. Winters with the detached enthrallment great keyboard performers could bring him. He glimpsed the alien's perspective—a Gulliver waiting in a Brobdingnagian grave, then marshaling a dead giant against a living, like a dwarf in a huge mechanical crane, feverishly programming combat on a battery of levers and pedals, waiting for the robot arms' enactments, the remote, titanic impact of the foes—and he marveled, filled with a bleak wonder at life's infinite strategy and plasticity. Joe Allen's hands reached into his half-opened abdominal cavity, reached deep below the uncut anterior muscle that was exposed by the shallow, spurious incision of the epidermis, till by external measure they were extended far enough to be touching his thighs. The voice was still as the forearms advertised a delicate rummaging with the buried fingers. The shoulders drew back. As the steady withdrawal brought the wrists into view, the dead legs tremored and quaked with diffuse spasms.

"You called your kind our food and drink, Doctor. If you were merely that, an elementary usurpation of your motor tracts alone would satisfy us, give us perfect cattle-control—for what rarest word or subtlest behavior is more than a flurry of varied muscles? That trifling skill was ours long ago. It is not mere blood that feeds this lust I feel now to tenant you, this craving for an intimacy that years will not stale. My truest feast lies in compelling you to feed in that way. It lies in the utter deformation of your will this will involve. Had gross nourishment been my prime need, then my grave-mates—Pollock and Jackson—could have eked out two weeks of life for me or more. But I scorned a cowardly parsimony in the face of death. I reinvested more than half the energy that their blood gave me in fabricating chemicals to keep their brains alive, and fluid-bathed with oxygenated nutriment."

The corpse reached into its gaping abdomen, and out of its cloven groin the smeared hands pulled two long skeins of silvery filament. The material looked like masses of nerve fiber, tough and scintillant—for the weave of it glittered with a slight incessant movement of each single thread. These nerve skeins were contracting. They thickened into two swollen nodes, while at the same time the corpse's legs tremored and faintly twitched, as the bright vermiculate roots of the parasite withdrew from within Allen's musculature. When the nodes lay fully contracted—the doctor could just see their tips within the abdomen—then the legs lay still as death.

"I had accessory neural taps only to spare, but I could access much memory, and all of their cognitive responses, and having in my banks all the organ of Corti's electrochemical conversions of English words, I could whisper anything to them directly into the eighth cranial nerve. Those are our true feast, Doctor, such bodiless electric storms of impotent cognition as I tickled up in those two little bone globes. I was forced to drain them just before disinterment, but they lived till then and understood everything—*everything* I did to them."

When the voice paused, the dead and living eyes were locked together. They remained so a moment, and then the dead face smiled.

It recapitulated all the horror of Allen's first resurrection—this waking of expressive soul in that purple death mask. And it was a demon-soul the doctor saw awaken: the smile was barbed with fine, sharp hooks of cruelty at the corners of the mouth, while the barbed eyes beamed fond, languorous anticipation of his pain. Remotely, Dr. Winters heard the flat sound of his own voice asking:

"And Joe Allen?"

"Oh, yes, Doctor. He is with us now, has been throughout. I grieve to abandon so rare a host! He is a true hermit-philosopher, well-read in four languages. He is writing a translation of Marcus Aurelius—he was, I mean, in his free time. . . ."

Long minutes succeeded of the voice accompanying the surreal self-autopsy, but the doctor lay resigned, emptied of reactive power. Still, the full understanding of his fate reverberated in his mind as the parasite sketched his future for him in that borrowed voice.

And it did not stop haunting Winters, the sense of what a *virtuoso* this entity was, how flawlessly this mass of neural fibers played the tricky instrument of human speech. As flawlessly as it had puppeteered the corpse's face into that ghastly smile. And with the same artistic aim: to waken, to amplify, to ripen its host-to-be's outrage and horror. The voice, with ever more melody and gloating verve, sent waves of realization through the doctor, amplifications of the Unspeakable.

The parasite's race had traced and tapped the complex interface between the cortical integration of sense input and the neural output governing response. It had interposed its brain between, sharing consciousness while solely commanding the pathways of reaction. The host, the bottled personality, was mute and limbless for any least expression of its own will, while hellishly articulate and agile in the service of the parasite's. It was the host's own hands that bound and wrenched the life half out of his prey, his own loins that experienced the repeated orgasms crowning his other despoliations of their bodies. And when they lay, bound and shrieking still, ready for the consummation, it was his own strength that hauled the smoking entrails from them, and his own intimate tongue and guzzling mouth he plunged into the rank, palpitating feast.

And the doctor had glimpses of the racial history that underlay the aliens' predatory present. Glimpses of a dispassionate, inquiring breed so advanced in the analysis of its own mental fabric that, through scientific commitment and genetic self-sculpting, it had come to embody its own model of perfected consciousness. It had grown streamlined to permit its entry of other beings and its direct acquisition of their experiential worlds. All strictest scholarship at first, until there matured in the disembodied scholars their long-germinal and now blazing, jealous hatred for all "lesser" minds rooted and clothed in the soil and sunlight of solid, particular worlds. The parasite spoke of the "cerebral music," the "symphonies of agonized paradox'' that were its invasion's chief plunder. The doctor felt the truth behind this grandiloquence: the parasite's actual harvest from the systematic violation of encoffined personalities was the experience of a barren supremacy of means over lives more primitive, perhaps, but vastly wealthier in the vividness and passionate concern with which life for them was imbued.

The corpse had reached into its thorax and with its dead hands aided the parasite's retraction of its upper-body root system. More and more of its livid mass had gone dead, until only its head and the arm nearer the doctor remained animate, while the silvery worming mass grew in its bleeding abdominal nest.

Then Joe Allen's face grinned, and his hand hoisted up the nude, regathered parasite from his sundered gut and held it for the doctor to view—his tenant-to-be. Winters saw that from the squirming mass of nerve cord one thick filament still draped down, remaining anchored in the canyoned chest toward the upper spine. This, he understood, would be the remote-control line by which it could work at a distance the crane of its old host's body, transferring itself to Winters by means of a giant apparatus it no longer inhabited. This, he knew, was his last moment. Before his own personal horror should begin, and engulf him, he squarely met the corpse's eyes and said:

"Goodbye, Joe Allen. Eddie Sykes, I mean. I hope he gave you strength, the Golden Marcus. I love him too. You are guiltless. Peace be with you at the last."

The demon smile stayed fixed, but, effortlessly, Winters looked through it to the real eyes, those of the encoffined man. Tormented eyes foreseeing death, and craving it. The grinning corpse reached out its viscid cargo—a seething, rippling, multinodular lump that completely filled the erstwhile logger's roomy palm. It reached this across and laid it on the doctor's groin. He watched the hand set the bright medusa's head—his new self—on his own skin, but felt nothing.

He watched the dead hand return to the table, take up the scalpel, reach back over, and make a twelve-inch incision up his abdomen, along his spinal axis. It was a deep, slow cut—now sectioning, just straight down through the abdominal wall—and it proceeded in the eerie, utter absence of physical sensation. The moment this was done, the fiber that had stayed anchored in the corpse snapped free, whipped back across the gap, and rejoined the main body that now squirmed toward the incision, its port of entry.

The corpse collapsed. Emptied of all innervating energy, it sagged slack and flaccid, of course. Or had it. . . ? Why was it. . . ? That nearer arm was *supinated*. Both elbow and wrist at the full upturned twist. The palm lay open, offering. *The scalpel still lay in the palm.*

Simple death would have dropped the arm earthward, it would now hang slack. With a blaze, like a nova of light, Winters understood. The man, Sykes, had—for a microsecond before his end—repossessed himself. Had flung a dying impulse of *his* will down through his rotten, fading muscles and had managed a single independent gesture in the narrow interval between the demon's departure and his own death. He had clutched the scalpel and flung out his arm, locking the joints as life left him.

It rekindled Winters's own will, lit a fire of rage and vengefulness. He had caught hope from his predecessor.

How precariously the scalpel lay on the loosened fingers! The slightest tremor would unfix the arm's joints, it would fall and hang and drop the scalpel down farther than Hell's deepest recess from his grasp. And he could see that the scalpel was just—only just—in the reach of his fingers at his forearm's fullest stretch from the bound elbow. The horror crouched on him and, even now slowly feeding its trunk line into his groin incision, at first stopped the doctor's hand with a pang of terror. Then he reminded himself that, until implanted, the enemy was a senseless mass, bristling with plugs, with input jacks for senses, but, until installed in the physical amplifiers of eyes and ears, an utterly deaf, blind monad that waited in a perfect solipsism between two captive sensory envelopes.

He saw his straining fingers above the bright tool of freedom, thought with an insane smile of God and Adam on the Sistine ceiling, and then, with a life span of surgeon's fine control, plucked up the scalpel. The arm fell and hung.

"Sleep," the doctor said. "Sleep revenged."

But he found his retaliation harshly reined-in by the alien's careful provisions. His elbow had been fixed with his upper arm almost at right angles to his body's long axis; his forearm could reach his hand inward and present it closely to the face, suiting the parasite's need of an eye-hand coordinative check, but could not, even with the scalpel's added reach, bring its point within four inches of his groin. Steadily the parasite fed in its tapline. It would usurp motor control in three or four minutes at most, to judge by the time its extrication from Allen had taken.

Frantically the doctor bent his wrist inward to its limit, trying to pick through the strap where it crossed his inner elbow. Sufficient pressure was impossible, and the hold so awkward that even feeble attempts threatened the loss of the scalpel. Smoothly the root of alien control sank into him. It was a defenseless thing of jelly against which he lay lethally armed, and he was still doomed—a preview of all his thrall's impotence-to-be.

But of course there was a way. Not to survive. But to escape, and to have vengeance. For a moment he stared at his captor, hardening his mettle in the blaze of hate it lit in him. Then, swiftly, he determined the order of his moves, and begun.

He reached the scalpel to his neck and opened his superior thyroid vein—his inkwell. He laid the scalpel by his ear, dipped his finger in his blood, and began to write on the metal surface of the gurney, beginning by his thigh and moving toward his armpit. Oddly, the incision of his neck, though this was muscularly awake, had been painless, which gave him hopes that raised his courage for what remained to do.

When he had done the message read:

PARASITE
CUT ME
TILL FIND
1500 GM NERVE
FIBER

He wanted to write goodbye to his friend, but the alien had begun to pay out smaller auxiliary filaments collaterally with the main one, and all now lay in speed.

He took up the scalpel, rolled his head to the left, and plunged the blade deep in his ear.

Miracle! Last accidental mercy! It was painless. Some procedural, highly specific anesthetic was in effect. With careful plunges, he obliterated the right inner ear and then thrust silence, with equal thoroughness, into the left. The slashing of the vocal cords followed, then the tendons in the back of the neck that hold it erect. He wished he were free to unstring knees and elbows too, but it could not be. But blinded, deaf, with centers of balance lost, with only rough motor control—all these conditions should fetter the alien's escape, should it in the first place manage the reanimation of a bloodless corpse in which it had not yet achieved a fine-tuned interweave. Before he extinguished his eyes, he paused, the scalpel poised above his face, and blinked them to clear his aim of tears. The right, then the left, both retinas meticulously carved away, the yolk of vision quite scooped out of them. The scalpel's last task, once it had tilted the head sideways to guide the blood flow absolutely clear of possible effacement of the message, was to slash the external carotid artery.

When this was done, the old man sighed with relief and laid his scalpel down. Even as he did so, he felt the deep inward prickle of an alien energy—something that flared, crackled, flared, *groped for*, but did not quite find its purchase. And inwardly, as the doctor sank toward sleep—cerebrally, as a voiceless man must speak—he spoke to the parasite these carefully chosen words:

"Welcome to your new house. I'm afraid there's been some vandalism—the lights don't work, and the plumbing has a very bad leak. There are some other things wrong as well—the neighborhood is perhaps a little *too* quiet, and you may find it hard to get around very easily. But it's been a lovely home to me for fifty-seven years, and somehow I think you'll stay. . . ."

The face, turned toward the body of Joe Allen, seemed to weep scarlet tears, but its last movement before death was to smile.

BACK TO THE BEAST

by Manly Wade Wellman

(From the Smith City Mirror, June 26, 1927)

Police are searching today for Dr. J. E. Lawlor, well-known physician and scientist, following a report from his secretary, James Brock, that he had disappeared from his home at 2100 Van Ness Avenue.

According to Brock, Dr. Lawlor locked himself into his private laboratory twelve days ago, ordering his servants not to disturb him, and to send food down by means of a dumbwaiter. As he had followed this plan several times before while working on experiments, Brock complied with his request. The time set was ten days and when there had been no response from the laboratory during the two days following the elapse of this period, Brock feared some accident and, with the help of George Dmitri, Dr. Lawlor's cook, and Emil Bonner, his chauffeur, he forced the door this morning and found that the doctor was gone.

A weird angle is added to the incident by the dead body of a large ape which Brock found in a corner of the disordered laboratory. Although Dr. Lawlor was known to be interested in natural history and to have conducted several experiments with animals recently, Brock stated that he was sure the ape was not in the laboratory when it was closed twelve days ago. The table was covered with papers, which have been turned over to the police.

Brock, Dmitri and Bonner are held for questioning by Chief of Police John Walton.

Dr. Lawlor has no immediate family. A brother, Stanley Lawlor, of Topeka, Kansas, has been notified.

(From the Smith City Mirror, June 28, 1927)

Attempts to determine the species of the ape found dead in the laboratory of Dr. J. E. Lawlor, who disappeared last Saturday, were unsuccessful when Professor F. W. Baylor, head of the natural science department of the state university, said today that he had never seen such a creature before.

"There are eight kinds of anthropoid apes known to science," said Professor Baylor, "but this ape belongs to none of them. It has some of the characteristics of several, but resembles no single kind greatly. It is either a freak or of a species unknown until now."

Professor Baylor has ordered the animal embalmed and intends to send it to fellow-students of natural history in Chicago.

(From the Smith City Mirror, June 29, 1927)

James Brock, private secretary of Dr. J. E. Lawlor, 2100 Van Ness Avenue, was placed under arrest today to face charges of kidnaping and possibly murder of his employer last Saturday.

The arrest took place following the reading of papers purporting to be a journal of an experiment performed by the doctor, which Brock turned over to the police upon his employer's disappearance. Brock had been held for questioning, but was given his liberty Saturday.

The contents of the journal were not made public, but Chief John Walton described them as "preposterous and unbelievable, a forgery by Brock to cover a very evident crime."

(Extracts from the papers given to police by James Brock as the journal of Dr. James Everett Lawlor)

June 15—All is in readiness for my experiment—the final step in my great work that will afford scientists a true glimpse of how man appeared in the dim past. The narrow persons who refuse to believe in evolution will be forced to see the truth, for we will confront them, not with theories, but with proofs.

I have material now that would fill a great book—notes telling how I first discovered the combination of elements that induces deterioration and of my experiments with it, first on the lowest forms of life, then on more complex animals, with surprizing and enlightening results. Years have been consumed in this study, but soon they will be paid for when I reveal what I have learned.

The elements for the two serums, products of nearly a lifetime of labor and observation, are at hand. One serum is the deteriorator, which when properly mingled and administered will make vital changes in the organs and tissues of an animal, changes which finally result in giving it the appearance of its ancestors untold ages ago. This change can be arrested by the administration of the counter-agent, which will restore the transformed creature to its former condition.

I do not suppose that any person less determined or less scientific in mind than I would dare perform this experiment upon himself; but after all, it is as safe as such a thing can be. I have studied its effects and powers too much and too long to go wrong now, and I know that I shall not be mentally incapable of handling it. The change is physiological, not psychological. Foretelling the course of the whole process is a mere matter of rationalization.

As I plan it, I will let the deteriorator work in my blood for five days, then the counter-agent for five days, to make sure that the effects of the experiment are completely dissipated. Thus I expect to see in my mirror what my ancestors were like five thousand centuries ago, and then return to the body and semblance of Dr. Lawlor, all within two weeks at the least.

I have locked my door for ten days. Brock, a sound, sensible fellow who obeys my orders without questioning, will see to it that I am undisturbed. And after this private experiment, I shall present my findings to my fellow-scientists as the proof of their theories. Who can say that my name shall not be numbered with those of the great evolutionists?

June 16—For twenty-four hours I have had the serum in my blood. With what care I compounded it and injected it into the vein of my arm, you may well imagine. The effects were noticeable at once. My blood flowed faster and for a few moments I felt strangely light-headed, as if I had been drinking. This latter feeling passed away and I perspired freely, but felt no unpleasant sensations. Throughout the day I have taken notes on the progress of the experiments, and tonight my mirror shows me that it is a success.

The change in my appearance has not been so great as I expected, but it is very evident. I am florid and ruddy where I have generally been pale. I am far more robust and all over my body my hair has grown out, especially on the breast and shoulders and outsides of the arms—a strange condition for me, always smooth-skinned and of late years partly bald. I never felt better physically in my life, and I look, not the fine-drawn and slender scientist, but a full-bodied, really splendid savage.

In excess of well-being and in joy at the certain fulfilment of my expectations, I danced and leaped up and down this evening. Then, a little ashamed of myself, I sat down to write.

June 17—The effects of the serum are more pronounced today. Where yesterday I was but a primitive man, still decidedly human, I am today a man with a pronounced bestial look. My forehead has receded, my jaw is heavy, with sharp-pointed teeth. The change works in me every moment; I can feel it in my flesh and bones. Among other things, I am positively shaggy. The hair makes my clothes a discomfort and I have them completely off.

I am never weary of watching my body as it changes almost before my very eyes. It is especially interesting to see how springy and flexible my joints have become, and how my feet have a tendency to turn their palms inward. This is because of the great toe, which is beginning to stand out from the others like a thumb; excellent proof that our ancestors were tree-dwellers and could get a grip with their feet.

June 18—When I awoke on my cot this morning, my first glance was toward the mirror. I was unable to recognize myself, unable to recognize even the thing I had been last night. In the broad, coarse face, with flat nose, splay nostrils, little beady eyes under beetling brows, wide mouth and brutal jaws, in the hairy, hulking body, there was no reminder of what had once been Dr. Lawlor. Some scholars would be frightened at the speed and effectiveness with which the serum has worked, but I can think of nothing save the triumph to science.

I am stooped considerably and stand unsteadily on my legs; not that they are not strong, but the tendency of my feet to turn inward has increased, so that I walk for the most part on the outer edges. Their prehensile powers are developed, too, and they can pick up objects quite easily.

It is also interesting to note that my mental processes have not changed one whit—I can think as clearly and as deeply as ever. As I predicted, the serum does not affect the brain tissues; or, if it does, it does not keep them from functioning properly.

I have been hungry all day. The food Brock sent to me was not sufficient, especially as regards meat, and I must send up a note with the empty dishes for him to increase the amount.

June 19—This part of the experiment will stop tomorrow, for I shall then mix and administer the counter-agent.

Tonight I see myself to be an eery creature, half beast, half man. I am hard put to it to walk without supporting myself on the table and the backs of the chairs. So must our ancestors have looked when they swung down from the trees to achieve their first adventures on the ground and to conquer the world.

These five days, what with the many notes I have taken, will provide a fitting climax for the scientific book that I contemplate. How it will astound the world! What honors and distinctions may descend upon me! Fame is mine, certainly; fortune, if I wish it, may follow.

So good-night and good-bye, my primitive self yonder in the mirror. Tomorrow I shall commence the journey back to the appearance of Dr. Lawlor, that I may immortalize you in all your fascinating grotesqueness.

June 20—How could I—oh, how could I not provide against this? With all the machinery of my experimentation evidently flawless, I must forget a single item— an item maddeningly simple, maddeningly obvious, and yet a thing that has proved my undoing.

Let me remain sane for a moment and marshal the incidents as they occurred. There is not much to tell. This morning I went to my shelf of chemicals for the ingredients to compound into the counteracting serum. My hands, which of course had become clumsy and primitive, seemed to have trouble in picking up the little vials, but this did not worry me as I began the combining of my materials. Two of them I mixed in a graduated glass and then reached for a pipette to administer the third.

But my unsteady manipulation did not allow the proper proportion to flow in. I released a drop too much, and though there was a corresponding effervescence, I could see that the mixture was a failure. I poured it out and tried again, with the same result. With growing uneasiness I made a third attempt, and again my clumsy hands failed me.

Too late, I realized that the mingling of the elements in the proper proportions and manner had been a task that required all the delicacy of a skilled chemist. My hands, no longer the deft, steady hands of Dr. Lawlor, were those of a sub-human creature and as such not equal to the feat!

Horrible, horrible! I moaned aloud when I realized what had happened and what would follow. Without the counter-agent I could not neutralize, or even halt, the progress of the deteriorator. Down I must go, back along the road up which the human race has struggled for untold centuries!

Again and again I desperately tried to mix the dose, until I had used up all my materials. Once or twice I thought that I had approximated the proper mingling, but when I injected it, there was no effect.

I sit here tonight, a rung farther toward the beast from whence we sprang, instead of on the road back toward man. Like one lowered into a well, I see above me a circle of light growing smaller and dimmer as I descend into darkness and horror! What shall I do?

[From this point forward, the journal is written in an almost unintelligible scrawl.]

June 24—For three days I have not written. I have not slept and have eaten only when the pangs of hunger roused me from my half-trance of misery. Horror has closed over my head like water.

At first I searched frantically for more materials for the counter-agent, literally wrecking my laboratory, but to no avail. I had used it all in trying to mix the saving dose three days ago.

Today was to have been the last day of my experiment. Perhaps the servants will force the lock if I do not come out. And then?

I could never make them understand. I have no more power of speech than any other beast, for a beast I have surely become. I can not bear to look in the mirror, for I see only a dark, hairy form, hunched over the table, a pencil clutched in its paw. And that is I, James Lawlor! What wonder that I border on the edge of insanity?

Let whoever reads these words take warning from my plight. Do not meddle with the scheme of things as nature has planned—delve not into her mysterious past. I have done that, and it was my complete and dreadful undoing. If it had not come in this way it would have come in another, I do not doubt for a moment.

June 25—Morning. I have not budged from the chair where I sat to write last evening. I heard Brock's voice outside the door, asking me if I was coming out. I dared not make a sound in reply, and he went away.

Is existence bearable in such a condition? Even now, the sliding back into lower and lower form continues. It will not be long before I am no longer even the ape-thing I appear. Perhaps the serum will carry me back through the ages until I am the slimy sea-crawler from which all life had its beginning. Oh, God! . . .

And as if in answer to that name, comes the memory of what still remains in a drawer of my table. Arsenic—not an easy death, but a quick one. So shall I die, for if ever a creature was justified in taking its own life, that creature is myself.

I will leave this journal as an account of what has happened, and as a warning to others. The formulas for my serums and all that pertains to them I will destroy. Never shall another scientist meet with my fate if I can order it otherwise. There, the papers are flaming in the grate. Now for the arsenic—so much, in a glass of water—farewell!

[Here the journal ends.]

THE INCALLING

by M. John Harrison

The incalling was held somewhere in that warren of
defeated streets which lies between Camden Road and
St. Pancras, where the old men cough and spit their
way under the railway arches every evening to exercise
their dogs among the discarded fish-and-chip papers.
Clerk had made a great point of punctuality and then
failed to give me precise directions. I don't think he
expected me to turn up at all. He had reached some
crux only partly visible to the outsider, and his life
was terribly muddled—a book was long overdue, he
had been evicted suddenly from his furnished flat in
Harrow, he had a sense of impending middle age which
he obviously felt he couldn't face without company of
some sort; and beneath all this was something deeper
which he hinted at constantly but refused to unveil. A
publisher has a limited vocabulary of responses to such
a situation; to show him that I knew my responsibili-
ties I took him frequently to the pubs and restaurants
of Great Portland Street—where he inevitably ate little, seemed nervous, and instead of discussing the
work in progress murmured almost inaudibly of Frazer
and Blavatsky, or his quarrels with G——, and where,
among the turned heads and plump shoulders of lunch-
ing secretaries, his thin white acne'd face hovered like
the ghost of a child starved to death. I was curious; he
sensed this, and made energetic efforts to draw me in.
He was lonely; I wanted to help, of course, if I could,
but not from so intimate a distance; and lately our
meetings had become memorable as a series of com-

ically protracted farewells on station platforms and embarrassed, hasty protestations of friendship made through the windows of departing taxicabs.

Anyway: I went to Camden that night not because I had any interest in the proceedings, but because I felt sorry for him, because lunches aren't enough, and because he was one of those people who can't seem to enjoy their follies without a sense of complicity. I would have accompanied him with equal enthusiasm to the Soho backstreet of his choice. Thanks to an unexplained delay on the North London Line I arrived shortly after the thing was due to begin, with no idea of exactly where it was to take place.

I found myself in a short empty crescent at one end of which stood a shuttered greengrocery—the pavement in front of it stacked with broken wooden boxes and some spoiled foreign fruit filling the cool air with a thick, yeasty odour while feral pigeons pecked about on the flagstones in the flailing light—and at the other the secondhand clothes shop owned by Clerk's mentor, a woman of uncertain nationality who called herself Mrs. Sprake. This was a dim, oppressive cubbyhole with a cracked wardrobe mirror propped up against one wall, where faded tea-gowns hung limp and vacant behind the wire screened windows like the inmates of a political prison for women. Before the war it had been a 'corner cafe'; faded glass panels above the door advertised vanished soft drinks, and its atmosphere still felt etiolated as if from passage over gas burners on foggy November nights. Here I had to ask directions from the boy behind the counter, a fat-legged ten or eleven-year-old in short grey trousers who I imagined then to be Mrs. Sprake's son—although now I'm not sure if their relationship could ever have been described so simply.

He was sucking something as I entered, and stooped quickly to take it out of his mouth, as if he were afraid whoever had come in might confiscate it. Over his shoulder I could see down a narrow passage to where a small television screen flickered silently and greyly in the gloom. A dog was moving about in another room. Dusty clothing pressed in from all sides, touching my wrists. When I told him why I was there he stared into the mirror and said uninterestedly, "It's the fourth house down." His voice was peculiarly mature for his clothing and his prepubescent, sidling eyes. There was aniseed on his breath, and whatever he had been eating had left a brownish deposit in the downy hairs at the corner of his mouth. "Mr. Clerk invited me," I explained, "but I forgot the way." He shrugged slightly, and his hand moved behind the counter, but he said nothing more, and I doubted if he had even taken any notice of the name. As I turned to go he had transferred his gaze to the distant television and, with a motion too quick to follow, had reclaimed his tidbit and was chewing again.

On the way out I brushed against a stiff peach-coloured bodice covered with green sequins, to be startled by a sudden smell of the empty dance hall—some American perfume, faded and innocent; and beneath it, like a memory of the disingenuous festivals of a post-war Saturday night, the quick thin bitterness of ancient perspiration.

Much of the crescent was untenanted. In company with the surrounding streets it had been built as a genteel transit camp and matured as a ghetto. Now it was a long declining dream. I stood at the door of Mrs. Sprake's house, staring at the cracked flags, the forgotten net curtains bunched and sagging like dirty ectoplasm, the tilted first floor balconies with their strange repetitive wrought-iron figures, and wondering if it might not be better to leave now before anyone had time to answer the bell. All the other doors were boarded up. Old paint hung like shredded wallpaper from the inner curve of an arched window. Across the road one whole building was missing from the terrace—fireplaces and outlines of extinct rooms clung to the walls of the flanking houses. I could telephone Clerk in the morning and tell him I hadn't been able to find the place; but it was too late now to go in search of a cinema, and too early for anything else;

besides, the boy had seen me, and if I left I should look a fool.

Clerk himself opened the door, but not before I had heard footsteps approach, pause and recede, then a woman's voice saying clearly, "We don't normally encouarge gatherings," and, "He must come in, of course," on a rising, partly interrogative note.

His white face tilted out at me from the darkness of the hall, like the head of some long-necked animal thrust unexpectedly round the door. He looked tired and a little ill. Warmer air seemed to flow out past him, and for a second I was whirled along the sensory interface of outdoors and in, the one reeking of pulpy exotic fruit, the other of aniseed and dusty hessian, rushing together like incompatible ocean currents. The light of a single low-wattage lamp yellowed a passage-way made narrow by piled tea-chests and bales of folded clothing, out of which the staircase, uncarpeted but thick with chocolate brown paint, ascended into a deeper gloom. It appeared to be a mere annex of the shop, and smelt so similar that I wondered if the chewing boy had somehow got ahead of me.

"Oh, hello Austin," said Clerk. He blinked. "For a moment I thought you were someone else."

I was relieved to see him, but not for long. It was plain he'd made some sort of gaffe by inviting me and was regretting it. "You're late," he told me nervously; he said that I should "try and fit myself in"; we had a ridiculous whispered misunderstanding over who should go first along the cramped hall. Finally he hurried me through into a small front parlour with bare white walls, where in preparation for the ceremony all the furniture had been shoved away from the centre of the room, exposing about ten square feet of freshly scrubbed unvarnished floorboards. On one side of the hall door were two ordinary wooden dining chairs, a spindly table between them draped with the same greyish imitation lace that hung before the window. Pushed up against the facing wall there was a two-seat sofa covered in fawn PVC material, marked about the arms by a cat or other small animal. A second door, opposite the window, led off into a kitchen, from which came the sound of water being run into a sink. On the sofa, still and ill-determined in the poor light, sat Alice Sprake.

Clerk introduced her proprietorially as "the daughter of the house", becoming animated when he addressed her; she said nothing. She was eighteen or twenty years old and only her eyes, brown and unemotional, recalled her relationship to the boy in the clothes shop. She was vague. Although she looked levelly enough at me, I hardly felt the touch of her hand.

"I expect you're tired of waiting, are you?" I said brightly. Both of them ignored me, so I sat down. A small thickset woman wearing the perpetual mourning of the Greek Cypriot widow came through the scullery door. She was a little under middle age, but moved slowly as though her legs pained her; her face was thickly powdered in a strange lifeless orange colour; the sound of her breathing was quite plain in the room. She had under her arm one of those cheap religious pictures you see gathering dust in Catholic shop-windows, and this she proceeded to hang—with what seemed a great deal of effort—on a nail above the sofa. It was a Gethsemane, in the most lurid stereoscopic greys and greens. For a while I couldn't understand what was wrong with it; then I saw that it was upside down, the feeble soon-to-be-martyred face swimming out of it loose-mouthed and emotionally spent, staring into the room like a drowned man in a restaurant fish-tank.

"There," she said thickly. "That is that." She slumped on the sofa beside the girl, to stare exhaustedly at a spot on the wall above my head.

The silence drew out interminably. Clerk and I sat on the hard chairs; Alice Sprake and her mother sat on the sofa; nobody spoke, nothing was done. After a few minutes of this I realised that Clerk was staring so avidly at the girl that his eyes were watering. I couldn't see what absorbed him so. She belonged in some shop window herself, her flat adolescent face prim in the confinement of a gilt frame, the whole musculature immobile and stylised, the profile very slightly concave, the mouth so small and secretive. She had a dreamy manner certainly (which appeared at times to extend into an actual vagueness of physical presence—one might come into a room, I sensed, and spend ten minutes there before realising she was in it); but it was the unattractive fake dreaminess of the convent girl and the mass production madonna, the self-contemplatory lassitude of pubertal iron deficiency. I changed my opinion of Clerk's motives; then changed it back again, out of charity. He was oblivious. I felt like a voyeur. None of us after all understand our own motives. Mrs. Sprake, meanwhile, twitched her feet—she sat sprawled back, hands limp at her sides—and seemed to be perfectly occupied with the wall. I tried to see through the grey net curtains. It was dark now in the street, but no lamps had come on. Someone walked slowly and heavily under the window, dragging footsteps close enough to be in the room. Clerk adjusted his spectacles, coughed. The drowned man mouthed at us from the iridescent gloom of his fishtank. I couldn't bear it. "Er, why must the picture be upside down?" I said. "I suppose there's some particular significance to that?"

Clerk stared at me like a betrayed dog. The streetlights came on, filling the place with a dull orange glare.

Both women got up at once and left, Mrs. Sprake going into the scullery, where she unlatched the back door, Alice into the hall. I heard retreating footsteps on the stairs, then the sound of someone coming in from the garden. The chewing boy put his head round the scullery door and gazed at the icon. Mrs. Sprake reappeared standing on tiptoe behind him, looked straight at me and said, "You must kip silent, you understand? Kip very quiet." She cuffed the boy's ear. "You eat too much of that. There will be none left, and then what will you do?" And to me again, with what I thought must be pride, "My children are very good children, Mr. Austing, very, very good. They do

all their poor mother can't.'' The boy smiled at me
with a mixture of shyness and impudence. He shifted
his tidbit from one side of his open mouth to the other,
letting it pause for an instant on his stained tongue so
I could almost see it. ''Fetch the chalk then,'' he said,
watching me closely. He had no vestige of her Medi-
terranean accent. The ghost of aniseed whispered from
his mouth and reached into the corners of the room.
''It can be done, Mr. Clerk,'' called Mrs. Sprake from
the kitchen. ''It has not been done for fifteen hundred
of years, but my children are clever children.'' Clerk
looked dazed now that the girl had gone. He blinked
at the boy. ''Shut up and give me the chalk,'' said the
boy.

He knelt down on the scrubbed floor and stared up
at the icon, licking the half-inch or so of green chalk
she had brought him. Suddenly he put it wholly in his
mouth. When it came back it was pasty and covered
with spittle, and the aniseed reek in the room had re-
doubled. He quickly used it to draw a large and irregular circle on the floor, shuffling along backwards on
his haunches and dragging the hand with chalk in it
along behind him. When he had completed this he sat
in the middle of the circle for a second, his eyes vacant. Then he popped the chalk back into his mouth
and seemed to swallow it entirely.

He got up stiffly and perched on the arm of the sofa,
stretching his legs and grinning. One of his shoelaces
had come undone. He caught my eye, made a little
motion of the head to implicate me in some irony directed at Clerk, who had taken off his horn-rims,
folded them carefully away, and was yearning toward
the hall door with watery eyes. When I refused to join
in, he shrugged and laughed quietly.

The door opened and back came Alice Sprake, to
be trapped on Clerk's adhesive gaze like a small grey
fly.

She went straight to the centre of the green chalk
circle and stood there, one leg relaxed, the other stiffened to take her weight. She had dressed in some sort
of complicated muslin shift, the drooping skirts of

which revealed the lower part of her thighs. Her legs were short and plump, inexpertly shaved. Her feet were bare, the soles grubby. She brought with her faint odours of dust and perspiration; the decayed echo of *fin-de-siècle* water sprites and eurhythmical entertainments. She faced the boy as if waiting for a cue. The boy chewed and raised his hand. In the scullery Mrs. Sprake switched on a small portable gramophone, which began to play an aimless, thready piece for violin and flute. With a shuffle and slap of bare feet on bare boards, Alice Sprake started to dance about in the chalk circle, her fixed and tranquil face now turned to Clerk, now to the reversed icon, now to the chewing boy. It was harmless at first. She waved her arms, trailing ectoplasmic fans of muslin in the peculiar light. She was a very poor dancer. Clerk had put his horn rims back on; they followed her every movement, sodium light flashing from their lenses as he turned his head. Mrs. Sprake leant on the doorframe with her arms folded, nodding to herself. The chewing boy let himself slide to the floor; back against the sofa, he drew one knee up to his chest, clasped it, and rocked himself to and fro. I coughed unhappily behind my hand, wondering how much Clerk had paid, and wishing I'd never seen him in my life.

But there was something wrong with the record player, and the music diminished steadily into a low, distant groan; the boy grew rigid (orange twilight limned his clenched jaw), while his mother let her arms fall to her sides, allowed all interest to leave her eyes; Clerk's expression became strained with greed. And abruptly Alice Sprake had ceased to be a village hall *danseuse* from some vanished Edwardian summer-twilight rehearsal, awkwardly pirouetting, heartbreakingly inept and weary, and was fluttering in what might have been real panic round and round in a circle, impaled and fluttering there on Clerk's stare, awash in the lurid glare beneath that drowned green man. The boy coughed painfully. Through clenched teeth he said, "Now, Mr. Clerk!" His mother jerked awake and reached out her arm. Bleak white light flooded the room from an unshaded two hundred watt fitment in the ceiling. The drowned man leapt stereoscopically from his frame into the space above the sofa, caught open-mouthed in that act of unspeakable despair. The music ended, or became inaudible. Clerk scrambled to his feet and stepped into the circle. Alice Sprake made a strange writhing motion and pulled off her shift.

She began to trudge along the chalk line, round and round, compliant and bovine, Clerk not far behind, his eyes locked in that peculiar spasm of unsexual greed, fixed on her thick white back and low, pear-shaped buttocks. There was gooseflesh on her thighs, the light had bleached her pubic hair to a pathetic grey-ish tuft. Her degradation, it seemed to me, was complete: as was that of everybody else in the room. Her feet scraped interminably, and Clerk's scraped after. Round and round they went.

"Fucking hell, Clerk," I said. "You must be mad."

I got up, meaning to wait for him outside—or perhaps not even to wait, or ever see him again. Mrs. Sprake had vanished, but her son had now joined the endless shuffling procession in the centre of the room. As Clerk followed the girl, he followed Clerk. His jaw were rigid and he had forgotten his titbit. An unending trickle of brown fluid was running out of the corner of his mouth. I slammed the front door and stood on the cooling pavement. My hands were shaking, but to this day I honestly believe it was out of fury. Clerk came out after about an hour, wiping his mouth as if he'd been ill. I don't know why I waited. Neither of us apologised for our behaviour. We went in silence down the High Street, past the alcoholics muttering behind locked news-stands, past the ticket office and down the moaning escalator, to be sucked into the echoing passages, the hot zones and sudden cold winds of the Camden Underground, to breathe the thin dingy air of two separate carriages on the same train (and for all I know to read, with the same sensation of time suspended and an endless life under the earth, the same life-insurance posters and No Smoking signs). We made no plans to meet again. I thought he seemed depressed and fearful, but that may have been a moral judgement.

Why he was indulging himself in so shabby a farce I couldn't conceive: but it was plain that none of his problems would be solved by encouraging it, so I sent a letter to the agency which represented him, reminding them that his book was due (indeed, long overdue), that our contract had been, if anything, overly generous as to completion dates, that we hoped he would soon see his way clear, and so on. I had given him up, or so I told myself, but I had my assistant sign it. A couple of days later they wrote to tell me that he had changed his address and they were having trouble getting hold of him.

As for the Sprakes, I couldn't think of them as having much existence at all outside the strained and grubby events of that evening. I imagined them as spending most of their time in a sort of dull stupor—immobile on a third-floor landing, looking mechanically down into a back garden full of rusty wheels, hard-packed earth and willow herb; silent and still behind the till of the second-hand clothes shop, eyes unfocused. I knew of course that they must get around the world somehow—shop for food, hurry along under the black rains of Camden to a launderette, do the things ordinary people do—but saw them only as withdrawn and barely human, lying perpetually but indifferently in wait for the credulous.

A langorous, unthinking contract exists between charlatan and victim, an understanding of which both are deeply aware. It didn't occur to me that there might be anything more to Clerk's obsession than the occasional reaffirmation of this covenant—until, about a month after the Incalling and out of an impulse I didn't understand, I found myself spying on him down by Charing Cross Pier.

It was a squally afternoon on the Victoria Embankment, one of those afternoons that wraps you one minute in a clinging mist of rain and the next surprises you with the pale lucid airs, the clarity and the depth of vision of quite another kind of day. The long arcs of Waterloo Bridge sprang out white and tense against the heavy blues and greys of the distant City. The river was agitated, high but falling under a cloudy sky. Gulls swirled in low fat circles over something in the water. The wind blew from Parliament, smelling of rain and fried food, and I was huddled in the shadow of the Gilbert memorial, waiting for a bus. A pleasure boat docked, a crowd developed on the covered gangways of the pier behind me—camera bags swinging, flapping nylon waterproofs, American and Japanese voices—and there he was, his white face unhealthy and out of place among all the tanned ones, his thin shoulders hunched and splotched with rain. He came up the oily black duckboards tearing his ticket in half and staring anxiously about him. I suppose I should have gone up to him and said hello; instead I turned my head away and pretended to be studying the plump complacent features of Frampton's bronze Gilbert, hoping to be taken for a sightseer.

I don't know why I did it. Something stealthy in his manner found an echo in my own. He was obviously waiting for someone; out of the corner of my eye I saw him go up to the confectionery kiosk by the railway bridge and stand there, glancing frequently back at the still-emptying boat as it wallowed at the pier.

A moment later Alice Sprake materialised at the head of the gangway and turned right towards Cleopatra's Needle.

She passed not six inches away from me, her hair blowing out from under a damp headscarf. She had on a dove grey suit with a long skirt and puffed sleeves which had once belonged to a much older woman. Hurrying along the wide empty pavement under the lamp standards with their iron fish and strings of fairy lights, she looked like the ghost of a Victorian afternoon; and as she went, the band in Embankment Gardens struck up the march from Lincke's 'Father Rhine'. Clerk, too, passed close by me, his face a white smear between the sodden, turned-up points of his collar and his eyes so occupied with Alice Sprake I might have been a mile away. His trousers were soaked, his cheap shoes waterlogged, and he seemed to be shuddering with cold. He looked more ill than I had ever seen him. I think she was unaware of what was going on. He kept fifteen yards behind her, and when she showed signs of stopping or slowing became suddenly interested in a balk of rotting timber bobbing far out in the river. She vanished for a second or two then reappeared on the waterstair of the Needle. Rain blew round Clerk's dark lonely figure. When she left the stair and crossed the road, he drifted after her. The dripping trees of the gardens shook briefly in the wind then closed over them.

I watched all this without surprise, feeling as detached as a man trying to follow, without benefit of commentary and through the condensation on a television dealer's window, the announcement of some foreign war: then, suddenly depressed, went over to the Charing Cross underground station and bought a ticket to Camden Town.

There, the sky was high, and for a moment at least, clear. If a wind blew down from Hampstead, it was a benign one; and as the old men dragged their dogs from intersection to intersection, the pavements were drying out. The blue-painted frontage of Mrs. Sprake's shop looked shabby but less malicious in the watery light. No-one moved in the street or behind the counter; the clothes were only old clothes; and the smell of spoiled fruit drifting down the crescent from the greengrocer's made me quite hungry as I loitered on a nearby corner. I had been there for perhaps three quarters of an hour when Alice Sprake came into view, walking more quickly now and carrying a plastic Marks & Spencer's bag. She closed the door of the shop firmly behind her; a face appeared briefly at an upper window; emptiness seemed to grip the place more tightly than before.

A little later, Clerk hurried up and took station in the street. He shuffled his feet; settled his raincoat closer about him; bent his long neck this way and that like a disturbed waterfowl. His gaze switched from tilted balcony to empty shop, then back again. I think he had begun to follow the girl about the real world (the world, that is, outside this strained liberty and grubby constraints of the ritual) long before this incident took place. I found myself furious with him—with his miserable damp trouser legs, cracked suede shoes all cardboard and dye, his face like melting floor-wax—and not a little disgusted with myself. The smell of spoilt fruit plugged my throat. It was coming on to rain in heavy, isolated spots. I strode off down the crescent as though my anger alone might be sufficient to end the episode—reluctant for some reason to leave even as I wondered impatiently why on earth I had wasted my time, and not caring much if he saw me.

Nothing ended, however. I simply got lost among the unfamiliar backstreets beside Regent's Canal. I could find neither the tube station nor the North London Line; not even the High Street. I blundered on to the canal towpath, and, with the dull green water full of greedy little fish on one side and the high decaying walls of a goods yard on the other, convinced myself I was walking toward Islington, not Camden at all. I had to go further out of my way to get off it again. I didn't want to get into the brick wastes east of York Way. The cloudbase lowered and the wind whipped across the lock basins, picking at the tethers of the crumbling boats and the plumage of a few miserable-looking ducks. Concrete steps rescued me finally, but now it was teeming with rain. I glimpsed from a distance the curious Greek shops of Pratt Street and lost them again almost immediately. Then, wandering past the urns and stone draperies of a Victorian cemetery that had been turned into some sort of park—empty yellow swings, a child's roundabout gravely turning, sleepy alcoholics muttering the spirit's language from the benches—I caught a whiff of rotten fruit.

I was back at the end of the crescent. The light seemed to be fading already. I had lost an hour. Clerk still stood patiently at his corner, like a tethered animal with its fur plastered down by the rain. Water streamed from his uplifted face. I thought I detected movement at an upper window—but Clerk's eyes were as vacant as the shop, and he seemed preoccupied by something else. It occurred to me that he wasn't strictly 'watching' anything: rather, it was as if he had got as close to some object as he possibly could, and was content just to be bobbing about at the interface until such time as he was able to penetrate it. Whatever it was, I left him there. A couple of streets away, I knew, the evening rush hour was beginning on a main road full of illuminated shop signs, tyres hissing through the wet. I turned to it thankfully, feeling sympathetic (or so I described it to myself) and intrusive, willing to leave him to it without further comment, voiced or otherwise. I was, perhaps, simply relieved at having found someone familiar, if not comforting, among all those doomed wet streets.

I was some yards along the pavement when he said suddenly and clearly, "Leave me alone Austin. I know what you're up to."

When I looked back, astonished, he hadn't moved. The rain humiliated him and he stared on, that indefinable expression of need and illness pulling his face slowly out of shape, flesh into putty, into water and chaos.

A few days later September set in like an infection. The air throbbed, and in less than a day grew thick and humid; by the next morning the traffic was piling it up and pushing it down Fitzroy Street into the Square, where it died before we had a chance to breathe it. When Tottenham Court Road became sticky and intolerable after ten a.m., and my office untenable after eleven, I gave up and went to Scotland for a three week break. I didn't expect Clerk's dreary entanglements to follow me as far as the Buchaille Etive Mor, but the day I was due to leave I got a sour letter from him, and they did.

It was a peculiar letter, complicated, full of hidden accusations and reproofs. He was muddled, spoke of an illness—although he wasn't specific—and quoted extensively, for some reason I couldn't follow, from *Gerontion*. He made no reference to the Sprakes but went into detail about the 'insulting' letter he presumed had originated in my office, going on to attack his agent quite bitterly for forwarding it; and he left me in no doubt as to where our 'late' friendship stood. At least he had done some work—his completed manuscript came under separate covers. The agency rang me up that afternoon to ask me if I'd heard from him. "He won't answer the phone, and he's ignoring everything but cheques," they said, and seemed a bit hurt that he'd sent the book direct. Realising that I was about to be embroiled again, this time in some silly professional squabble, I left the whole thing with my assistant. "If they ring again, get them to try a registered letter," I told him. "I'm not Clerk's keeper." But it had begun to look as if I was, and he only grinned cynically. "There can't be much wrong with him if he's cashing his bloody cheques."

So I spent a good part of my holiday trying to forget Eliot's eerie

> We have not reached conclusion, when I
> Stiffen in a rented house.

and when I got back, found Clerk's manuscript still cluttering up the office.

"You should have a look at that," said my assistant maliciously. "They won't typeset from that, I didn't really know what to do with it. It hasn't even got a title."

I sighed and took it home that night and couldn't read more than a couple of pages—the typescript was scrawled all over with illegible corrections in a peculiar brownish ink, and I couldn't tell whether it was a novel disguised as a memoir or a diary disguised as a novel.

"I'll have to go and see him about it, I suppose."

"More fool you."

Clerk now lived somewhere in the bedsitter belt of Tufnell Park. Fool or not, I caught a bus over there, the manuscript under my arm in a box meant for fools-cap typing paper. It was shortly before dusk at the end of a protracted, airless day: my sinuses ached, and the evening wind curling between the rows of tall shabby houses was no relief—it stirred briefly, nuzzling at the gutters where it found only the dust and heat of a month past, then settled down like an exhausted dog. Five or six bellpushes were tacked up by the outer door. I worked them in turn but no-one answered. A few withered geraniums rustled uneasily in a second floor window box. I pushed the door and it opened. In some places we're all ghosts. I swam aimlessly about in the heat of the hall, knocking and getting no response. Up on the first floor landing a woman stood in a patch of yellow light and folded her arms to watch me pass; in the room behind her was a television, and a child calling out in thin excitement.

Clerk lived right at the top of the stairs where the heat was thickest, in three unconnected rooms. I tapped experimentally on each open door in turn. "Clerk?" Empty jam jars glimmered from the kitchen shelves, the wallpaper bulged sadly in the corner above the sink, and on the table was a note saying, "Milk, bread, catfood, bacon," the last two items heavily underlined and the writing not Clerk's. A lavatory flushed distantly as I went into what seemed to be his study, where everything had an untouched, dusty look. "Clerk?" Bills and letters were strewn over the cracked pink linoleum, a pathetic and personal detritus of final demands which I tried furiously to ignore; it was too intimate a perspective—all along he had forced me to see too much of himself, he had protected himself in no way. "Clerk!" I called. From his desk—if he ever sat at it—he had a view of the walled garden far below, choked like an ancient pool with elder and *Colutea arborescens* and filling up steadily with the coming night. It was very quiet.

"Clerk?"

He had come silently up the stairs while I poked about among his things and was now standing at the window of the bedsitting room, peering round the cur-

tain into the street. I fidgeted in the doorway, holding
the manuscript in front of me like a fool. "Clerk?"
He knew perfectly well that I was there but he wanted
me to see that the street was more important. Between
us the room stretched dim and bleak: a bed with its
top cover pulled back, some things arranged on top of
a chest of drawers, books and magazines stacked hap-
hazardly along the skirting boards. He had done nothing to make the place comfortable. A suitcase stood
in the middle of the floor as if he'd simply left it there
the day he moved in.

"I rang the bell," I said, "but nobody came."

He stared harder into the street.

"So you made yourself at home anyway," he said.
He shivered suddenly and jerked the curtains closed.
"You've got a bloody nerve, Austin, following me
around—" On the verge of developing this he shrugged
and only repeated, "A bloody nerve," then sat down
tiredly on the bed, looking at his hands, the vile
cabbage-rose wallpaper, anything but me. With the
curtains drawn the room became much larger and
vaguer, filling up with vinegar-coloured gloom. I could
hardly see him. "What do you want, then?" he asked,
apparently surprised to find me still there. "I'm on my
own all bloody day, then people come just when I don't
want to be bothered with them."

I should have left him to it, abandoned him to the
cabbage roses, 'Milk, bread, catfood,' and the *Psychic
News,* and gone home. Instead I held the manuscript
up like a charm or entry permit and went into the
gloom where he waited for me. He had become a spectre of himself. His miserable, aggressive face bobbed
about above the bed, a tethered white balloon, what
flesh remained to it clinging like lumps of yellow plas-
ticine at the cheekbone and jaw, the temples sunken,
the whites of the eyes mucous and protuberant. He was
wearing the bottom half of a pair of striped pyjamas,
his stomach bulging out over the drawcord like some
atrocious pregnancy while the rest of his body seemed
reduced, temporary, all skin and bone. If the pursuit
of Alice Sprake from Charing Cross to Camden had

sickened him, where had he followed her since, and how far, to make him look like this? I was filled equally with repugnance and compassion, and in fighting both only made myself seem mealy mouthed and foolish.

"Look," I admitted, "you're not at all well, and I realise this is inconvenient. But we really ought to discuss this book. It could be really fine, I'm sure, if we just clarify a few things, a really fine book." This was rubbish, of course, and I could hear my assistant laughing sardonically somewhere in the more honest places of my skull. Not that I imagined Clerk would swallow it, but a publisher has his duties—and I had some idea of cheering him up, I suppose, as an easy solution to my own embarrassment. "Why don't you get back into bed and take it easy while I make some coffee or something? Then we can thrash it out—"

He laughed quietly to himself, whether at my expense or his own I wasn't sure.

"Suit yourself Austin. Make as much coffee as you like. I'm going to sleep. You're a patronising bastard but I'm sure you know that already."

I dropped the manuscript on the end of the bed, preparing to walk out and wash my hands of him. But it was something of a victory to have got him to talk to me at all, and somehow I found myself in the kitchen, pottering about among the dirty cups and staring out into the garden as I waited for the water to boil. I had to put money in the gas. There was an extraordinary staleness in the air, as if no-one had lived there for years, and I wondered if he'd cooked himself anything to eat that day, or even the day before. Milk, bread and catfood, but the milk was off, the cat gone, and the bread mouldy: and down in the garden twilight piling up among the elder boughs. I heard him moving about in the bedsitting room, muttering to himself. "You don't mind black coffee?" I called. When I got back with the tray I found him sitting up in bed. He had taken the manuscript out of its box and scattered it all over the room.

"Go on Austin," he taunted, "be reasonable about

that. Perhaps we could have some tea next, eh?'' He had tried to tear the thing in half before throwing it about, but his only success had been to crumple a few sheets at either end. I put the tray down and went round on my knees picking pages up at random while he stared at me with dislike and misery. I had the felling, there in the half-dark full of his desperation and my feebleness, that his head and neck had become detached somehow from his shoulders and were weaving independently about over the bed, sick and lost. "I don't want your coffee. I don't want your advice. I won't make any changes, Austin, so forget it. Take the bloody thing as it is or leave it there on the floor. Just get out, that's all."

"Clerk, you're ill—"

I thought he was going to hit me. The tray went over with a crash, spraying hot coffee over my legs. He struggled to his feet, and, wearing a great tangle of bed linen like a cloak, came half-running half-falling toward me, arms outstretched and fingers hooked— only to turn aside at the last instant and head for the window, where he writhed his shoulders free of the dirty topsheet and Dutch blanket, tore the curtains completely off their runners and stared into the street as if his life depended on the next thing he saw, shaking and sweating and shouting "Fuck off!" over and over again.

"Christ, Clerk—"

"—off, fuck off, fuck off, fuck off, fuck—"

I pushed him aside. It was dark, and the sodium lamps had flared up like a forgotten war. Ten or fifteen yards away across the road, shadowy in the disastrous orange glare, his face turned up to study the window and his jaws moving firmly and rhythmically from side to side, Mrs. Sprake's son sat kicking his heels on a low garden wall. Dark shrubbery moved behind him. He looked straight at me, I thought, and nodded. The room was silent. Coffee dribbled down my calf, sticky and cooling. Beside me, Clerk had closed his eyes and was resting his forehead against the window pane. I felt his hip tremble suddenly against me, but I couldn't get my eyes off the boy in the street.

"Is this what's making you ill?" I asked. "Being mixed up with this spiritual stuff?" I had some mad idea that they might be drugging or blackmailing him.

Clerk groaned. "What on earth are you talking about, Austin," he said wearily. He let himself slide to the floor. Kneeling amid the debris of his book, holding on to the window frame, he made an odd gurgling noise. He turned his head away. At first I thought he was laughing. Then I realised he was being sick. He panted and coughed, his thin shoulders heaving.

"I've got cancer, you bloody fool," he said. "I've had it for two years. The Sprakes are my only hope—so just go away now, will you?"

I left him there, wiping his mouth on a sheet of the manuscript and staring vacantly ahead as if he were dead already, and rushed out of the place. I was choking with nausea, self-disgust, and an anger I could barely contain. The woman on the landing was waiting for me, arms still folded.

"He's poorly is he, doctor?" she said, "I thought so," and shook her head slowly. "I hope it's not catching—"

She stood in my way while, above, Clerk sobbed dryly. I knew he was staring out of the window again, eyes wide in that swollen papier-mâché puppet's face.

"Excuse me," I said.

But when I got to the doorstep the chewing boy was nowhere to be seen. I ran across the road and looked into the bushes, which were still moving. It was the wind. I stood there for a moment. Tufnell Park was like a grave. I could hear faint, running footsteps a street away. At least I had the advantage of knowing where the child would go.

It's hard to say what made me so angry. Perhaps it was that Clerk should have to relinquish the world clutching only memories of that grubby little ceremony; that his despair should bequeath him in the end only endless puzzling images of the waste land between Camden and King's Cross, with its tottering houses and its old men spitting in corners full of ancient dust each grain of which has begun as dog-dirt or vomit or decayed food; that he could be promised only the fakery of sodium light, the deadly curve of the crescent and the far off buzz of traffic beyond Mrs. Sprake's second-hand clothes shop. I couldn't quite separate compassion and personal outrage, and I don't suppose I ever shall. I went after the boy because I couldn't bear to think of a dying man made confused and hateful by charlatans—and, again, to silence a part of me which understood this: where human sympathy is absent it can't easily be replaced by lunch in Great Portland Street.

He got home before me, of course, and by the time I reached the crescent it was deserted but for the eternal reek of smashed fruit (and behind that something old, foggy, a smell which belonged to the same street, certainly, but in an unfamiliar time). I went to the house first and banged loudly on the door, but there was no reply. I shouted, but all that achieved was echoes, "Mrs. Sprake! Mrs. Sprake!" racing away over acres of railway sidings, dull canal water and decaying squares, until I had a vision of my cries travelling perfect and undiminished all the way to Islington, as if the whole universe were suddenly dark, uninhabited, and sensitive to the slightest sound. After a minute or two of this I tried tapping on the front room window instead. Then I put my eye to a gap in the net curtain.

Mrs. Sprake was in there, sprawled heavily on the sofa with the light turned off, arms limp at her sides. She had rolled her skirt up to her waist and her stockings down to her knees. On the wall in front of her hung the same cheap icon she had employed for the Incalling—had her eyes been open, they would have been focused on it. Perhaps they were focused on it anyway. The doomed man yearned down at her from his showcase, but her face was slack and expressionless. Beneath the horrible orange powder and soft, pitted skin lay an ignorance and indifference so intense as to seem avid, an abrogation, a vacancy, and a

frightening weariness. I stared in astonishment at her
exposed belly and thick white thighs; then rapped the
window so hard it cracked under my knuckles. At the
sound of this she opened her eyes suddenly and peered
in my direction; her lips moved exhaustedly, like those
of a sick fish. I was terrified I might somehow discover
exactly what I had interrupted. I shouted "Open up!"
or something equally useless, but moved off hurriedly
down the street before she had a chance to comply.

In the dim grey wash of light from a forty watt bulb
inside, I fought briefly with the door of the shop; it
gave only to my full weight, and then so suddenly that
I went down heavily on one knee over the threshold.

Nobody was there. From the passage behind the
counter, where the air was lax and hot, issued a smell
of time, dust and artificial flowers (then, worked
through that like a live thread, the distant familiar stink
of the boy); and the television still flickered silently
in its back room, as if nobody had bothered to turn it
off since my last visit. "Hello?" I went through and
stood there in the fitful pewter glow, rubbing my
bruised leg. If I put my ear close to the television I
could hear it whisper, "So far we have managed to
avoid this." "I know you're here!" I called. I knew
nothing. Except for Mrs. Sprake at her inexplicable
devotions the universe was still uninhabited—dolorous,
scoured, yet waiting to respond instantly to some
crude signal I couldn't give—I felt abandoned to it,
left for dead. I drifted toward the staircase in the corner, then up it, the heat pressing against my chest like
a firm dry hand.

The whole top floor, knocked into one large room
and all but one of its windows bricked up twenty or
thirty years before, had been given over to him. The
furniture was a clutter of the rickety stuff you can find
any day in the junk shops toward Chalk Farm; a bed,
a dresser, some bentwood chairs. On the dresser was
a pile of what looked like grey feathers, and pushed
away in one corner were some stuffed animals mounted
on bits of wood. It all looked dreary and neglected—
uninhabited, and yet at the same time as if he spent

most of his life there. He was squatting on the bare
floor watching me intently, his pudgy hands on his
knees. "There's nothing for you here, Mr. Austin,"
he said. "Why don't you go home?"

"You don't know what I came for. Besides, I'd rather
speak to whoever's responsible for you—your mother,
if you can wake her up."

He moved his jaws once, mechanically.

"You're horrified, Mr. Austin, and who can blame
you? It was immaterial to you what Clerk did with his
life. Now you find you can't ignore him any longer,
and you care what he does with his death. Good!" In
front of him on a low occasional table he had arranged
a fragment of mirror, two ordinary white candles, and
an old bottle dug up from some Victorian towpath: all
positioned so that when he looked into the glass the
twin unsteady flames underlit his face without themselves being reflected. "Good! It's never too late to
find compassion—" And he smiled suddenly, rubbing
his hands on his knees— "You're safe! *You* need nothing we have here!" The bottle contained a few inches
of cloudy preservative. Floating in that was something
which looked like a thick, contorted black root. It was
corked, but even so every fibre of the grey floorboards
and white plaster, every bit of furniture, had soaked
up the reek of aniseed—now they gave it back into the
air like a fog, to fill the mouth and coat every delicate
membrane of the nose. "Later you may discover your
compassion is not as pure as you imagine, or your rage
for justice; but for the moment . . . We're all revolted
by illness, Mr. Austin, revolted and frightened . . .
There's no reason on Earth to feel ashamed of that!"

For a moment he gave his attention to the little altar,
and when he spoke again his voice was thoughtful and
cold.

"I know exactly why you're here, you see. You came
for reassurance. In any case it was useless to bother.
Go home now."

I went over to the window, but it wouldn't open.
Outside was that absorbent, sodium-lit vacancy,
stretching all the way to Islington. If I concentrated, I

could hear something that might have been traffic on
Camden High Street. I tried breathing deeply to accli-
matise myself to the stink, but that only made me feel
worse. "I'm not leaving here until I know what you
promised him," I said, "and what your mother
charged him for it. It's a grubby fraud and I'll have it
stopped—"

"Leave the window alone!" He swivelled round ir-
ritably, his pudgy legs suddenly shooting out in front
of him. He stood up and came rapidly across the room.
"My mother is shit, Mr. Austin, under my feet. Why
do you keep going on about her? I give her this—"
And he writhed the fingers of his right hand. He stared
up at me. "Why don't you go home?" he said sav-
agely. "I don't want you here. Clerk? Clerk is shit
too—" He shrugged. "What do I care? We gave him
nothing he didn't want. He's a tinkerer."

Nothing moved in the street.

"Christ," I said softly, "you little brat, you."

I tried to catch hold of his shoulder, but somehow
my hand made no contact. He twisted from under it
and ran off a few steps. When he turned back his face
was as I'd first seen it, blank and uninterested, hardly
even self-involved. "Fucking cunt pig," he said distinctly, without any human emphasis. He began chewing rapidly. "Fucking cunt pig." He went and sat
down in front of his altar, hunching his shoulders and
gazing into the mirror. The whole room forgot me and
filled up with silence. He laughed, then coughed urgently. "The window, Mr. Austin!" he hissed. He
seemed to be having some sort of choking fit. "Go
on!"

I stared down into that hopeless little landscape of
death, at the blistered paint, the gaps between the
houses and the ancient rubbish in the gutters. Nothing.
Then Alice Sprake walked sedately into view on the
other side of the street, with Clerk drifting along in
her wake like a dead waterfowl. She was wearing the
same dove grey skirt I had seen on the Embankment,
and her prim adolescent features were dreamy, secretive. He had put his raincoat on but was otherwise as

I had seen him an hour before—and down from its hem poked his long scrawny legs in their striped pyjama trousers. His feet were bare. I watched her draw him along behind her at a steadily increasing pace toward St. Pancras. They never once looked up. He was very close to her as they were sucked out of sight, but she didn't seem to know he was there, or sense in any way his white awful face bobbing loosely about over her shoulder, his gaping pain and greed. In a moment the universe was uninhabited again and they were pulled deep into it toward some crux of railway lines and dark water.

Behind me the chewing boy stretched his arms and scuffed his feet. He yawned. "You see?" he said. "Go home now, Mr. Austin," he added, almost kindly. "There's nothing you can do for him. You never could."

I went across to him and kicked the table over. The mirror broke: the bottle fell on the floor and came uncorked: the candles tumbled end over end through the brown and stinking air. I bent down and hit him while he sat there, as hard as I could on the left cheek.

"Speak like a child," I said.

He rolled about in the mess spilled from the bottle, making a high, thin chuckling sound, then lay there grinning up at me. His head rolled to one side, he let his mouth fall open and brown fluid gushed down his chin. He chewed and chewed.

"Yes, sir?" he enquired. "Do you want to buy something or sell something? My mother isn't available presently for buying, but I am allowed to sell. We buy and sell all kinds of garments, sir—"

I ran out after Clerk and the girl but I never caught up with them.

Clerk died perhaps two months later, somewhere in the black end of a rainy November; slipping over the edge of a pulmonary complication at two in the morning, that hour which erodes all determination and wears the confused substance to a stub. The cancer had eaten his insides entirely away, but he was trying to correct the manuscript of the novel which finally appeared last week as *The World Reversed* (a title suggested by my assistant). We discovered the following pencilled against the opening sentences of Chapter Eight: "When the dead look back, if they look back on us at all, they do so without rancour or pity, sadness or any sense of the waste of it. They crumble too soon and become too much a minute part of events to have any more involvement with us, and waste quickly away like footmarks on an oily pavement in October. This I know, though not from personal experience. Yet their evaporation is continual, they boil up continually around us, we inhale them as we go, and each resultant outward breath impregnates the soft brick of the city like smoke, dampens every blown newspaper, and as a curious acidic moisture loosens the pigeon dung on the ledges above . . ." There is more, but the handwriting is difficult to interpret.

On the night he died, or it may have been a couple of nights later, I had this dream—

I was walking along the grass verge of some provincial road, one of those roads which always seem empty and bleak, the hedges crusted at their roots with a thin grey mud thrown up by the wheels of passing vehicles, the fields on either side empty of livestock yet cropped short, the isolated houses unlit and shut up; a landscape apparently untenanted but showing signs of a continual invisible use. It was dark, but not night. Light had been bleached out of the still air and drained from all objects so that although there was no reversal of contrast the scene had about it the feel of a photographic negative. Walking beside me in her dove grey suit, her head bowed and prim, her expression at once placid and secretive, was Mrs. Sprake's daughter, Alice. Why I should have been so close to her, whether there was any feeling between us, I can't say. It seems unlike me. Her bovine calm had repelled me—and still does—when awake; but we cannot be responsible for what we feel in dreams. What is clear is that I felt a sense of unease on her behalf, and turned continually

to stare backward at the distant figure which followed
us.

"We should have a pleasant time," she said. Awake,
I cannot imagine this: but I remember it clearly.

"You had better go ahead of me," I told her, and
we walked like that for some minutes, in single file,
while our pursuer remained a mote of energy in the
middle distance, trotting doggedly along but seeming
to make no headway. After a little while we were
drawn into the outskirts of a small dull manufacturing
town, along a protracted, gently curving dual carriage-
way, lined with the semi-detached houses and recessed
shopfronts of some postwar ribbon development.
Through the gaps in the houses I glimpsed the vacant
cinders of a transport cafe car park, puddled and luminous; then a scrapyard full of bluish moonlight, and
a canal, and a crematorium in a muddy park. There
was no wind or noise. I imagined the road falling into
darkness behind us as we went, each traffic intersection, each garage with its peculiar rusted petrol pumps
and abandoned forecourt dissolving into the vacuum
through which our pursuer flailed his way, panting and
groaning as he fought his own dissolution. When I
looked again, he was no closer. I began to drag Alice
Sprake along nonetheless, urging her on with "We
must hurry," and "Please do hurry."

These was no relief to be had from the vast silent
space beyond the thin crust of buildings. It was uninhabited and smelt faintly of burnt rubber and ancient
summer dust, it was a magnetic emptiness which had
drawn us there simply for the sake of being there. Ages
seemed to pass. If there were echoes of our quickening
pace, they came back transmuted from that vacancy
which is the source of everything, and we did not recognise them. Eventually it became plain that the
curving road was merely an enormous circle, and all
that part of it we had already walked only a few degrees of arc. Later still, the scrapyard passed again,
the distant sports fields and crematorium, the cinders
and the puddled forecourts and the hanging signs.
Within the circle and without it were only acres of

unemotional darkness, dragging at the footsteps of old men and invalids, sifting down to end as dust in gutters at windy corners, absorbent of all effort, all anxiety, all movement except that of the desperate creature behind us. I glanced back to make sure that he remained in the middle distance, held there by his very effort to progress—

I glanced back and he was at my heels, his face was Clerk's, looming white and pasty like melting floor wax over my shoulder an inch from my own, bobbing and weaving on the end of that pale rubbery stalk. His eyes were huge and avid, full of terror, his huge mouth vomited brown fluid, an abscess of misery and desire so close I knew it must burst and drench me. At the instant of touching, between the cup and the lip, that bleak image of the provinces flew apart and faded, as if he had brought with him landscapes of his own, a thin envelope of relics to insulate against the vacuum. Late taxicabs and mid-day restaurants formed briefly around us only to evaporate and give way to the Sprakes' front room, the watery, quivering purlieus of Embankment Gardens and finally the cracked pink linoleum, the walled garden, the cabbage roses, the milk, bread and catfood of his rented grave in Tufnell Park, the thinning atmosphere of self-disgust which had sustained him in desolation. "I'm on my own all bloody day," he whispered. "My bloody day—" I winced away, afraid of some infinite prolongation of our last, hopeless meeting; yet in that moment felt whatever substance he now had left to him dissolve: and like smoke sucked from some distant corner of the room toward the hearth he was drawn through me and into Alice Sprake, who waited on the green chalk line, bovine and compliant, all grey degraded gooseflesh and grubby feet, one ill-shaved leg stiffened to take her weight. She made no attempt to move at the moment of penetration, and he was absorbed. I woke up sweating in a pale grey dawn with a faint, remote sound of shunting engines dying in my skull, and stayed at home that day.

I give this for what it is worth: as a completion,

perhaps. But if you take it as such you must remember that it is a personal one, and I draw nothing from it in the way of conclusions. I never knew what the In-calling was supposed to achieve—or even whether what I witnessed in Camden represented failure or success. Clerk had said that the Sprakes were his last hope: on the evidence, their crude urban magic doesn't seem to have done him much good. He is, after all, dead. Perhaps it would have worked better elsewhere in Europe, where they still have some small link with older traditions. My own part in it, if I can be said to have had one, I would prefer to forget.

THE CASE OF
LADY SANNOX

by A. Conan Doyle

The relations between Douglas Stone and the notorious Lady Sannox were very well known both among the fashionable circles of which she was a brilliant member, and the scientific bodies which numbered him among their most illustrious *confrères*. There was naturally, therefore, a very widespread interest when it was announced one morning that the lady had absolutely and for ever taken the veil, and that the world would see her no more. When, at the very tail of this rumour, there came the assurance that the celebrated operating surgeon, the man of steel nerves, had been found in the morning by his valet, seated on one side of his bed, smiling pleasantly upon the universe, with both legs jammed into one side of his breeches and his great brain about as valuable as a cap full or porridge, the matter was strong enough to give quite a little thrill of interest to folk who had never hoped that their jaded nerves were capable of such a sensation.

Douglas Stone in his prime was one of the most remarkable men in England. Indeed, he could hardly be said to have ever reached his prime, for he was but nine-and-thirty at the time of this little incident. Those who knew him best were aware that, famous as he was as a surgeon, he might have succeeded with even greater rapidity in any of a dozen lines of life. He could have cut his way to fame as a soldier, struggled to it as an explorer, bullied for it in the courts, or built

it out of stone and iron as an engineer. He was born
to be great, for he could plan what another man dare
not do, and he could do what another man dare not
plan. In surgery none could follow him. His nerve, his
judgment, his intuition, were things apart. Again and
again his knife cut away death, but grazed the very
springs of life in doing it, until his assistants were as
while as the patient. His energy, his audacity, his full-
blooded self-confidence—does not the memory of
them still linger to the south of Marylebone Road and
the north of Oxford Street?

His vices were as magnificent as his virtues, and
infinitely more picturesque. Large as was his income,
and it was the third largest of all professional men in
London, it was far beneath the luxury of his living.
Deep in his complex nature lay a rich vein of sensu-
alism, at the sport of which he placed all the prizes of
his life. The eye, the ear, the touch, the palate—all
were his masters. The bouquet of old vintages, the
scent of rare exotics, the curves and tints of the dain-
tiest potteries of Europe—it was to these that the quick-
running stream of gold was transformed. And then
there came his sudden mad passion for Lady Sannox,
when a single interview with two challenging glances
and a whispered word set him ablaze. She was the
loveliest woman in London, and the only one to him.
He was one of the handsomest men in London, but
not the only one to her. She had a liking for new experiences, and was gracious to most men who wooed
her. It may have been cause or it may have been effect
that Lord Sannox looked fifty, though he was but six-
and-thirty.

He was a quiet, silent, neutral-tinted man, this lord,
with thin lips and heavy eyelids, much given to gar-
dening, and full of home-like habits. He had at one
time been fond of acting, had even rented a theatre in
London, and on its boards had first seen Miss Marion
Dawson, to whom he had offered his hand, his title,
and the third of a county. Since his marriage this early
hobby had become distasteful to him. Even in private
theatricals it was no longer possible to persuade him

to exercise the talent which he had often shown that he possessed. He was happier with a spud and a watering-can among his orchids and chrysanthemums.

It was quite an interesting problem whether he was absolutely devoid of sense, or miserably wanting in spirit. Did he know his lady's ways and condone them, or was he a mere blind, doting fool? It was a point to be discussed over the teacups in snug little drawing-rooms, or with the aid of a cigar in the bow windows of clubs. Bitter and plain were the comments among men upon his conduct. There was but one who had a good word to say for him, and he was the most silent member in the smoking-room. He had seen him break in a horse at the university, and it seemed to have left an impression upon his mind.

But when Douglas Stone became the favorite, all doubts as to Lord Sannox's knowledge or ignorance were set for ever at rest. There was no subterfuge about Stone. In his high-handed, impetuous fashion, he set all caution and discretion at defiance. The scandal became notorious. A learned body intimated that his name had been struck from the list of its vice-presidents. Two friends implored him to consider his professional credit. He cursed them all three, and spent forty guineas on a bangle to take with him to the lady. He was at her house every evening, and she drove in his carriage in the afternoons. There was not an attempt on either side to conceal their relations; but there came at last a little incident to interrupt them.

It was a dismal winter's night, very cold and gusty, with the wind whooping in the chimneys and blustering against the window-panes. A thin spatter of rain tinkled on the glass with each fresh sough of the gale, drowning for the instant the dull gurgle and drip from the eaves. Douglas Stone had finished his dinner, and sat by his fire in the study, a glass of rich port upon the malachite table at his elbow. As he raised it to his lips, he held it up against the lamplight, and watched with the eye of a connoisseur the tiny scales of beeswing which floated in its rich ruby depths. The fire, as it spurted up, threw fitful lights upon his bold, clear-cut face, with its widely-opened grey eyes, its thick and yet firm lips, and the deep, square jaw, which had something Roman in its strength and its animalism. He smiled from time to time as he nestled back in his luxurious chair. Indeed, he had a right to feel well pleased, for, against the advice of six colleagues, he had performed an operation that day of which only two cases were on record, and the result had been brilliant beyond all expectation. No other man in London would have had the daring to plan, or the skill to execute, such a heroic measure.

But he had promised Lady Sannox to see her that evening and it was already half-past eight. His hand was outstretched to the bell to order the carriage when he heard the dull thud of the knocker. An instant later there was the shuffling of feet in the hall, and the sharp closing of a door.

"A patient to see you, sir, in the consulting-room," said the butler.

"About himself?"

"No, sir; I think he wants you to go out."

"It is too late," cried Douglas Stone peevishly. "I won't go."

"This is his card, sir."

The butler presented it upon the gold salver which had been given to his master by the wife of a Prime Minister.

" 'Hamil Ali, Smyrna.' Hum! The fellow is a Turk, I suppose."

"Yes, sir. He seems as if he came from abroad, sir. And he's in a terrible way."

"Tut, tut! I have an engagement. I must go somewhere else. But I'll see him. Show him in here, Pim."

A few moments later the butler swung open the door and ushered in a small and decrepit man, who walked with a bent back and with the forward push of the face and blink of the eyes which goes with extreme short sight. His face was swarthy, and his hair and beard of the deepest black. In one hand he held a turban of white muslin striped with red, in the other a small chamois leather bag.

"Good-evening," said Douglas Stone, when the butler had closed the door. "You speak English, I presume?"

"Yes, sir. I am from Asia Minor, but I speak English when I speak slow."

"You wanted me to go out, I understand?"

"Yes, sir. I wanted very much that you should see my wife."

"I could come in the morning, but I have an engagement which prevents me from seeing your wife to-night."

The Turk's answer was a singular one. He pulled the string which closed the mouth of the chamois leather bag, and poured a flood of gold on to the table.

"There are one hundred pounds there," said he, "and I promise you that it will not take you an hour. I have a cab ready at the door."

Douglas Stone glanced at his watch. An hour would not make it too late to visit Lady Sannox. He had been there later. And the fee was an extraordinarily high one. He had been pressed by his creditors lately, and he could not afford to let such a chance pass. He would go.

"What is the case?" he asked.

"Oh, it is so sad a one! So sad a one! You have not, perhaps, heard of the daggers of the Almohades?"

"Never."

"Ah, they are Eastern daggers of a great age and of a singular shape, with the hilt like what you call a stirrup. I am a curiosity dealer, you understand, and that is why I have come to England from Smyrna, but next week I go back once more. Many things I brought with me, and I have a few things left, but among them, to my sorrow, is one of these daggers."

"You will remember that I have an appointment, sir," said the surgeon, with some irritation. "Pray confine yourself to the necessary details."

"You will see that it is necessary. To-day my wife fell down in a faint in the room in which I keep my wares, and she cut her lower lip upon this cursed dagger of Almohades."

"I see," said Douglas Stone, rising. "And you wish me to dress the wound?"

"No, no, it is worse than that."

"What then?"

"These daggers are poisoned."

"Poisoned!"

"Yes, and there is no man, East or West, who can tell now what is the poison or what the cure. But all that is known I know, for my father was in this trade before me, and we have had much to do with these poisoned weapons."

"What are the symptoms?"

"Deep sleep, and death in thirty hours."

"And you say there is no cure. Why then should you pay me this considerable fee?"

"No drug can cure, but the knife may."

"And how?"

"The poison is slow of absorption. It remains for hours in the wound."

"Washing, then, might cleanse it?"

"No more than in a snake-bite. It is too subtle and too deadly."

"Excision of the wound, then?"

"That is it. If it be on the finger, take the finger off. So said my father always. But think of where this wound is, and that it is my wife. It is dreadful!"

But familiarity with such grim matters may take the finer edge from a man's sympathy. To Douglas Stone this was already an interesting case, and he brushed aside as irrelevant the feeble objections of the husband.

"It appears to be that or nothing," said he brusquely. "It is better to lose a lip than a life."

"Ah, yes, I know that you are right. Well, well, it is kismet, and must be faced. I have the cab, and you will come with me and do this thing."

Douglas Stone took his case of bistouries from a drawer, and placed it with a roll of bandage and a compress of lint in his pocket. He must waste no more time if he were to see Lady Sannox.

"I am ready," said he, pulling on his overcoat.

"Will you take a glass of wine before you go out into this cold air?"

His visitor shrank away, with a protesting hand upraised.

"You forget that I am a Mussulman, and a true follower of the Prophet," said he. "But tell me what is the bottle of green glass which you have placed in your pocket?"

"It is chloroform."

"Ah, that also is forbidden to us. It is a spirit, and we make no use of such things."

"What! You would allow your wife to go through an operation without an anæsthetic?"

"Ah! she will feel nothing, poor soul. The deep sleep has already come on, which is the first working of the poison. And then I have given her of our Smyrna opium. Come, sir, for already an hour has passed."

As they stepped out into the darkness, a sheet of rain was driven in upon their faces, and the hall lamp, which dangled from the arm of a marble caryatid, went out with a fluff. Pim, the butler, pushed the heavy door to, straining hard with his shoulder against the wind, while the two men groped their way towards the yellow glare which showed where the cab was waiting. An instant later they were rattling upon their journey.

"Is it far?" asked Douglas Stone.

"Oh, no. We have a very little quiet place off the Euston Road."

The surgeon pressed the spring of his repeater and listened to the little tings which told him the hour. It was a quarter past nine. He calculated the distances, and the short time which it would take him to perform so trivial an operation. He ought to reach Lady Sannox by ten o'clock. Through the fogged windows he saw the blurred gas-lamps dancing past, with occasionally the broader glare of a shop front. The rain was pelting and rattling upon the leathern top of the carriage, and the wheels swashed as they rolled through puddle and mud. Opposite to him the white headgear of his companion gleamed faintly through the obscurity. The surgeon felt in his pockets and arranged his needles, his ligatures and his safety-pins, that no time might be wasted when they arrived. He chafed with impatience and drummed his foot upon the floor.

But the cab slowed down at last and pulled up. In an instant Douglas Stone was out, and the Smyrna merchant's toe was at his very heel.

"You can wait," said he to the driver.

It was a mean-looking house in a narrow and sordid street. The surgeon, who knew his London well, cast a swift glance into the shadows, but there was nothing distinctive—no shop, no movement, nothing but a double line of dull, flat-faced houses, a double stretch of wet flagstones which gleamed in the lamplight, and a double rush of water in the gutters which swirled and gurgled towards the sewer gratings. The door which faced them was blotched and discoloured, and a faint light in the fan pane above it served to show the dust and the grime which covered it. Above, in one of the bedroom windows, there was a dull yellow glimmer. The merchant knocked loudly, and, as he turned his dark face towards the light, Douglas Stone could see that it was contracted with anxiety. A bolt was drawn, and an elderly woman with a taper stood in the doorway, shielding the thin flame with her gnarled hand.

"Is all well?" gasped the merchant.

"She is as you left her, sir."

"She has not spoken?"

"No; she is in a deep sleep."

The merchant closed the door, and Douglas Stone walked down the narrow passage, glancing about him in some surprise as he did so. There was no oilcloth, no mat, no hat-rack. Deep grey dust and heavy festoons of cobwebs met his eyes everywhere. Following the old woman up the winding stair, his firm footfall echoed harshly through the silent house. There was no carpet.

The bedroom was on the second landing. Douglas Stone followed the old nurse into it, with the merchant at his heels. Here, at least, there was furniture and to spare. The floor was littered and the corners piled with

Turkish cabinets, inlaid tables, coats of chain mail, strange pipes, and grotesque weapons. A single small lamp stood upon a bracket on the wall. Douglas Stone took it down, and picking his way among the lumber, walked over to a couch in the corner, on which lay a woman dressed in the Turkish fashion, with yashmak and veil. The lower part of the face was exposed, and the surgeon saw a jagged cut which zigzagged along the border of the under lip.

"You will forgive the yashmak," said the Turk. "You know our views about woman in the East."

But the surgeon was not thinking about the yashmak. This was no longer a woman to him. It was a case. He stooped and examined the wound carefully.

"There are no signs of irritation," said he. "We might delay the operation until local symptoms develop."

The husband wrung his hands in incontrollable agitation.

"Oh! sir, sir!" he cried. "Do not trifle. You do not know. It is deadly. I know, and I give you my assurance that an operation is absolutely necessary. Only the knife can save her."

"And yet I am inclined to wait," said Douglas Stone.

"That is enough!" the Turk cried, angrily. "Every minute is of importance, and I cannot stand here and see my wife allowed to sink. It only remains for me to give you my thanks for having come, and to call in some other surgeon before it is too late."

Douglas Stone hesitated. To refund that hundred pounds was no pleasant matter. But of course if he left the case he must return the money. And if the Turk were right and the woman died, his position before a coroner might be an embarrassing one.

"You have had personal experience of this poison?" he asked.

"I have."

"And you assure me that an operation is needful."

"I swear it by all that I hold sacred."

"The disfigurement will be frightful."

"I can understand that the mouth will not be a pretty one to kiss."

Douglas Stone turned fiercely upon the man. The speech was a brutal one. But the Turk has his own fashion of talk and of thought, and there was no time for wrangling. Douglas Stone drew a bistoury from his case, opened it and felt the keen straight edge with his forefinger. Then he held the lamp closer to the bed. Two dark eyes were gazing up at him through the slit in the yashmak. They were all iris, and the pupil was hardly to be seen.

"You have given her a very heavy dose of opium."

"Yes, she has had a good dose."

He glanced again at the dark eyes which looked straight at his own. They were dull and lustreless, but, even as he gazed, a little shifting sparkle came into them, and the lips quivered.

"She is not absolutely unconscious," said he.

"Would it not be well to use the knife while it would be painless?"

The same thought had crossed the surgeon's mind. He grasped the wounded lip with his forceps, and with two swift cuts he took out a broad V-shaped piece. The woman sprang up on the couch with a dreadful gurgling scream. Her covering was torn from her face. It was a face that he knew. In spite of that protruding upper lip and that slobber of blood, it was a face that he knew. She kept on putting her hand up to the gap and screaming. Douglas Stone sat down at the foot of the couch with his knife and his forceps. The room was whirling round, and he had felt something go like a ripping seam behind his ear. A bystander would have said that his face was the more ghastly of the two. As in a dream, or as if he had been looking at something at the play, he was conscious that the Turk's hair and beard lay upon the table, and that Lord Sannox was leaning against the wall with his hand to his side, laughing silently. The screams had died away now, and the dreadful head had dropped back again upon the pillow, but Douglas Stone still sat motionless, and Lord Sannox still chuckled quietly to himself.

"It was really very necessary for Marion, this operation," said he, "not physically, but morally, you know, morally."

Douglas Stone stepped forwards and began to play with the fringe of the coverlet. His knife tinkled down upon the ground, but he still held the forceps and something more.

"I had long intended to make a little example," said Lord Sannox, suavely. "Your note of Wednesday miscarried, and I have it here in my pocket-book. I took some pains in carrying out my idea. The wound, by the way, was from nothing more dangerous than my signet ring."

He glanced keenly at his silent companion, and cocked the small revolver which he held in his coat pocket. But Douglas Stone was still picking at the coverlet.

"You see you have kept your appointment after all," said Lord Sannox.

And at that Douglas Stone began to laugh. He laughed long and loudly. But Lord Sannox did not laugh now. Something like fear sharpened and hardened his features. He walked from the room, and he walked on tiptoe. The old woman was waiting outside.

"Attend to your mistress when she awakes," said Lord Sannox.

Then he went down to the street. The cab was at the door, and the driver raised his hand to his hat.

"John," said Lord Sannox, "you will take the doctor home first. He will want leading downstairs, I think. Tell his butler that he has been taken ill at a case."

"Very good, sir."

"Then you can take Lady Sannox home."

"And how about yourself, sir?"

"Oh, my address for the next few months will be Hotel di Roma, Venice. Just see that the letters are sent on. And tell Stevens to exhibit all the purple chrysanthemums next Monday and to wire me the result."

THE NEEDLE MEN

by George R. R. Martin

Living in Uptown, Jerry had seen a lot of things never dreamt of in places like Forest Park and Wilmette. But he had learned to mind his own business as well, so it was no wonder that he hardly thought twice about the guy with the needle until he bumped into the cops on the steps of his building.

He hadn't really seen anything suspicious, after all. It was a Friday night when it happened, and Jerry had been down on Rush Street, checking out the action at some singles bars, with a notable lack of success. He'd had a few Michelobs too many and was close to getting sloshed, so when the cute brunette he'd been talking to went off with someone else, he made up his mind to call it a night. He rode the el back to Argyle, staring pensively out at the weathered sooty brick and grey windows of the buildings near the tracks, blinking whenever blue-white sparks came crackling off the third rail to etch hard, intense shadows on the tenement walls.

From the Argyle el stop it was a short walk to the six-flat where Jerry shared an apartment with three roommates. Even at midnight, Argyle was lively; country music blasted out the open doors of redneck bars, dim female silhouettes writhed in the windows of the strip joints, the 24-hour coffee shops were open and crowded. Jerry had to step over one derelict, passed out in front of a grocery store. A second sidled up to him by the drugstore, mumbling something in a raspy boozy voice, but he shied off when Jerry threw him a look. It was that kind of neighborhood. "Yeasty," Jerry liked to call it; hillbillies and Hispanics and blacks and a lot of Orientals, pushed together cheek-to-jowl and hating every minute of it. On the other side of Sheridan, along Marine Drive, the highrises stood, full of young marrieds and singles. Respectability was kind of nibbling at the edges of the area, chewing up the old overcrowded tenements and spitting out renovated condos, but Jerry figured the process of digestion would take a long long time.

In the meantime, rents were cheap, at least by Chicago standards. Jerry was a struggling free-lance journalist, so cheap mattered. Besides, he figured he needed to see the seamy side of life, seething and bubbling, and Uptown had plenty of that.

The shortest way from the el to his building cut through an alley just on the far side of Sheridan, and brought him up the back stairs. The alley was dark, but that had long since stopped bothering him; you only had to look at him to know Jerry wasn't worth mugging. So that Friday night he ducked into the alley, as he had a thousand times before, and that was where he saw the guy with the hypo.

There wasn't much to it. The guy was shutting the trunk of his car, a battered old black Javelin, just as Jerry came around the corner and started towards the rickety wooden staircase at the back of his six-flat. Jerry didn't see him very well, and didn't try. Just a white guy, youngish, with a little dark moustache, wearing one of those sports coats with leather patches at the elbows. He and Jerry traded a brief, wary glance, the way two strangers will when they meet in an alley in Uptown, and then the guy started around the car to the driver's side. As he did, he slid something into this jacket pocket, and Jerry glimpsed it briefly; a hypodermic needle. He thought nothing of it. The neighborhood was full of junkies.

As he climbed wearily up the stairs to the back door of his third floor apartment, he heard the car growl and turn over below him, and the headlights speared out and lit up the alley for a few moments. Jerry was pleased. He was just drunk enough so he was having difficulty getting his key into the lock, and the light helped. "A-*ha*," he said, pushing it in and turning. By the time the door closed behind him, the Javelin was gone.

Jerry didn't give the incident another thought until the night the cops arrived.

It was near dusk. He'd eaten at a Siamese restaurant down south of Lawrence and was walking back, savoring the coolness of the evening. Coming up from the south like he was brought him to the front of his building, but long before he got there he saw there was commotion. A cop car was sitting right outside his door, a crowd had gathered around the steps, and two cops were trying to calm down some crazy lady. When he got closer, he saw that the crazy lady was Mrs. Monroe, the black woman who lived in 2-East with an army of kids.

Jerry pushed through the crowd and walked right up. Mrs. Monroe was crying, and trying to say something, but nothing sensible was coming out. One of the cops, a fat one with a red face, scowled at Jerry when he approached. "*Hey,*" he barked.

"I live here," Jerry said. "What's going on?"

"It's none of your concern," said the beer-bellied cop. "Her kid run off, is all. Now get on by if you're going in. We'll handle her."

Jerry shrugged, looked curiously at the sobbing Mrs. Monroe, and went on through the front door. Like all the other six-flats on the block, his had a tiled entry hall, mailboxes and doorbells on the walls, a second door barring the way to the stairs. You needed a key or a buzz from upstairs to get past that one. Between the two doors, watching the scene on the steps, were a couple of his neighbors. The Gumbo Granny was in her rocker. She and the old wicker chair with its faded flowered cushion came crawling out of 1-East every morning, and she sat there until dark, rocking and watching the street and rocking and smoking her pipe and rocking and holding incoherent conversations with whoever entered or left the building. Jerry nodded, but he knew better than to try to talk to her.

But the girl from 2-West was also standing there, and that was a different matter. She was a short, attractive blonde, about 25 or so. She'd only moved in about a month ago, with a couple of female roommates. He had the vague impression they were grad students at Northwestern, or something like that. The rest of them were pretty plain, but the blonde had a cute smile and a nice ass. She was standing casually by the door, wearing a white turtleneck sweater and a pair of tight jeans, listening to the argument outside. Jerry took out his key and hesitated. This seemed like a perfect opportunity to get to know her. "Do you know what happened?" he asked her, nodding towards Mrs. Monroe and the cops.

She turned and brushed a strand of hair from her eyes. Her hair was very long and very straight and very blonde, just the way Jerry liked it. "One of her kids is missing," she said. "The oldest one, I think."

"Chollie," Jerry said. That was what everyone called him. He was a slight, well-mannered kid, always dribbling a basketball around the block, though Jerry had never seen him actually play the game. He was about sixteen, he thought; shy, maybe a little simple-minded. "Do they know what happened to him?"

"The police think it's just a runaway," she said. "That's what the fat one said, anyway. That was what set her off. They aren't very concerned. He hasn't been gone very long, I guess."

"How long is that?"

"She said she sent him out around eleven last Friday, to get some milk. No one has seen him since."

"Tough," said Jerry, shaking his head. "Chollie didn't strike me like the sort to run away. He was always so quiet. I hope nothing happened to him."

"Well, the police told her that no bodies of that description have turned up, anyway."

"Thank God for that much," Jerry said.

"Dey ain't gone to be no body," said the Gumbo

Granny, rocking back and forth and sucking on her pipe.

"Excuse me?" the blonde said.

Jerry had to stifle a groan. It was always a mistake to speak to the Gumbo Granny. Once you acknowledged her, she got going, and once she got going she didn't stop. She was an old, *old* black woman, a tiny little monkey of a woman with dry, wrinkled brown skin and pink palms. She was nearly bald, and she had a pink spot around her left eye, a patch of pinkness in the middle of that wizened old face. It made her look a little bit like a dog Jerry remembered from the *Our Gang* comedies he'd watched as a kid, only with the colors switched around. She was half-senile and didn't make sense most of the time, and even when she did you couldn't always understand her, since she talked funny. Evidently she'd come up from New Orleans at some point, though she'd lived in the building as long as anyone could remember. It was on account of New Orleans that the younger people in the building started calling her the Gumbo Granny. There was no name on her mailbox, but then she never got any mail.

When the blonde spoke to her, the Gumbo Granny took the pipe out of her mouth and rocked slowly back and forth, nodding to herself. "He's gone, lawdy, lawdy. He's gone. I tells 'em and I tells 'em, but dey don't lissen." She shook her small head, and rocked.

"Did you see something?" the blonde asked, frowning. "Do you know where the boy's gone?"

Jerry started to tell her not to pay attention to the old woman, that she was crazy as a loon, but before he could the Gumbo Granny was off again. "Yessum, I knows, I knows. I tells 'em, yessum. Won't get me out in dem streets at night, no, no, lawdy. Ain't findin' no body, no, no." She nodded to herself, her old tired eyes all wrinkled up and wise. "Dey got him, yessum, dey got ol' Chollie. I tells 'em, but dey don't lissen. Dey got him."

"Who?" said the blonde.

The Gumbo Granny peered around warily, as if to make sure there was no one lurking in the shadows beneath the stairs, and then she leaned forward in her rocker and whispered, "Dem needle mens got him." She nodded, satisfied, and settled back in her chair again, sucking on her pipe as she rocked and creaked, rocked and creaked. Outside the police had finally stopped the flow of Mrs. Monroe's tears, and they were talking quietly now. The crowd of spectators on the sidewalk had begun to drift away in search of other, livelier diversions. It was clear that not much was going to come of this one.

"The needle men," said Jerry, curious despite himself. He'd probably regret asking, he thought, but he heard himself say, "Who are the needle men?"

The Gumbo Granny smiled conspiratorially. "We had 'um down in New Orleans, yessuh, yessuh. Dey's tricky, dem needle mens, I knows all dey ways, you don't see me goin' out at night, nosuh, nosuh. Dey's hidin' out dere, awaitin', and dey got needles, dem big *loooong* kind long as you arm, and all sharp, with stuffs on 'em, yessuh, stuffs. Dey jump out at you, dey do, and poke you with dem needles, and you's done, lawdy, you's never seen again. Ain't findin' no body, not when dem needle mens gets you." She cackled.

The blonde from 2-West smiled. "A morbid thought," she said drily.

"Needle men," said Jerry. "She's crazy." The Gumbo Granny rocked away as if she never heard him. He and the blonde traded sympathetic smiles, the kind that say let's-indulge-the-pitiful-old-thing. "Why would these needle men stab Mrs. Monroe's boy?" the blonde asked. "Are they ghosts?"

"Lawdy, no. No, no, no. Don't you know nothin'?" The old woman rocked and clucked. "You's so young, don't know nothin' though, nothin'. I tells 'em, but they don't lissen. Dem needle mens ain't no ha'nts. Dey's from Charity."

"Charity?"

"Hospital, yessum, yessum. Charity Hospital. It's bodies dey wants, bodies, fo' de students to cut up on, so dey creeps out with dem *loooong* needles with de stuffs on de end, and dey stabs the black folks and drags 'em back. Nobody misses no po' black folks, nosuh. I seen 'em hidin' in de bushes, hidin' in de alleys, dem needle mens with dem needles, but dey ain't a-gettin' me. My daddy learned me, yessuh, and I knows 'em, yes I do. Chollie wouldn't lissen, but I tells 'em, I knows. Knowed 'em down in New Orleans when I was just a littlest girl, knowed how to spy 'em then. Knows 'em up here too, yes I do. Ain't gone get ol' me with dem needles, drag me off fo' dem practice doctuhs to cut up on.''

She rocked and smoked away. Outside the fat policeman was questioning Mrs. Monroe and filling out a form.

"He'll come back, I bet,'' Jerry said, with a glance through the door. "Maybe there was a fight or something, but Chollie was a good kid.''

The blonde shrugged.

"My name is Jerry McCulloch, by the way,'' he said, smiling. "I'm a writer. Live in 3-West.''

"Hi,'' she said, returning his smile. She was awfully pretty. He loved her hair. "I'm Kris. Kris Shelby''

"You're downstairs of us, right? With a couple of other girls?''

She nodded. "It's a long way from school, but the rent is low enough to make up for the el fares, and the apartment is bigger than anything we could have gotten near campus. Tuition is so high these days, you have to do all sorts of things to make ends meet.'' She wrinkled her nose. "Like living in this neighborhood, even.''

Jerry nodded with sympathy.

"What do you write?'' Kris asked. She had nice green eyes, he noticed. Very cool and alert.

"Anything they'll pay me for,'' he said with practiced modesty. "I sold a piece to the *Tribune* magazine once, on the abandoned coal tunnels beneath the Loop. There's a whole honeycomb of them, haven't been used for years. Maybe you read it?'' Kris shook her head. "Well, it's not important. I do just odds and ends, really. Right now I'm working on a piece I'm hoping to sell to the *Reader.* Who knows?'' He shrugged. "What about you?''

"What about me?'' Kris said, lightly. She smiled.

Jerry stammered, and restrained an urge to ask about her hometown or her major. That was the kind of inane talk that always got him spurned down on Rush Street. He decided not to come on too strong. He looked at his watch. "Hey, I got to go,'' he said. "Glad we met. Now if it gets too loud upstairs, you'll know who to bitch at.''

She nodded. "See you around,'' she said, turning her attention back to the street.

Jerry started up the stairs. At the first landing, he turned back and called down to her, "Hey, Kris.'' When she looked up, he said, "Watch out for them needle men!'' She smiled and nodded, and Jerry was feeling very good as he bounded up the stairs to the third floor. Harold and his latest true love were in the living room, listening to the stereo and making out on the couch. Alan was watching some old movie on the tube in his room. "How was that restaurant?'' he called out when Jerry passed.

"Not bad.'' Jerry leaned through the open door. "I met that blonde from downstairs. Kris.''

"Nice,'' said Alan.

"Yeah,'' Jerry said, grinning. He went back to the kitchen to get himself a beer. The light in the fridge was burned out, and he hadn't bothered flicking on the overhead, so he found himself fumbling around in back. Finally he found a Bud.

He yanked off the tab there in the darkened kitchen, and was just lifting the can to his lips when a car went past in the alley down below. All Jerry could see was the wash of its lights against the back of the buildings across the way, a dim, moving reflection.

That was when he finally remembered the guy with the needle.

He had a restless night. It was all so silly. The junkie in the leather-patched sports coat and the Gumbo

Granny's needle men and Chollie Monroe had nothing to do with one another, that was obvious. Even so, it made Jerry feel strange. It *had* been Friday night, after all. He frowned and drank another Bud and went to bed.

He tossed and turned for more than an hour, his water bed sloshing softly underneath him every time he moved. Finally he drifted off to sleep. When he woke again, it was the middle of the night, and the apartment was dark and dead and quiet. A cool breeze was blowing in the open window, and the rippling curtains threw long shadows across his bed. Jerry stirred groggily and moved to shut the window a bit, and there he was, standing outside the window, a man in a sports coat with leather patches at the elbows. He had a dead white face, and he was smiling a terrible thin smile. As Jerry watched, his arm came through the open window. He was holding a long slender needle.

Jerry screamed, and wrenched away, and all of a sudden he was tangled in his sheets on the floor, and Harold was standing in the doorway in his jockey shorts, saying, "Hey, you okay?"

"He's coming in the window," Jerry said breathlessly, from the floor.

Harold glanced at the open window, where the curtains twisted lazily in the breeze. "You moron," he said. "We're on the third floor."

Everybody had a big laugh about Jerry's nightmare the next morning, when they were all bumping into one another trying to make breakfast. Everybody but Jerry, that is. He just scowled at them and drank his coffee, and then he went off to the Post Office to check his box. You had to have a Post Office box in this neighborhood, the way the mail was always getting ripped off.

He went down the front stairs, expecting that he'd have to listen to the Gumbo Granny spin more wild stories about deranged needle men. Fortunately she wasn't there; her rocker was in the entryway, but she wasn't in it. Jerry blessed his good fortune and went on by.

He was sitting in a booth at the coffee shop on Lawrence, sorting through his mail and waiting for a cheese omelette, when it suddenly hit him how odd that was. All the years he'd lived in that building he'd never seen the Gumbo Granny's rocker without the Gumbo Granny. In the morning she brought it out with her. In the evening she took it in with her. In between they were always there, rocking. Always.

A kind of shiver went through him. "No," he said aloud.

"What do mean *no?*" the waitress said. She was standing there with his cheese omelette in hand. "This is what you ordered, buster."

"Uh, yeah," said Jerry, abashed. "I didn't mean you."

The waitress looked at him strangely, set down his order, and walked off.

"No," Jerry repeated, picking up his fork.

But that evening, when he returned to the apartment, the rocker was still there. Empty. Jerry ignored it.

The next day he came and went by the back stairs. He tried not to think about the rocker, The Gumbo Granny, needle men, or anything like that. He was down in the Loop all day, and after dark he went drinking for a couple of hours, but it was no use. He couldn't even concentrate on the women around him. He kept staring into his beer and seeing that empty rocker.

When he came up the alley near to midnight, he saw something even more chilling. Parked in the shadows across from his building was an old, battered black Javelin. Half-drunk as he was, it startled him. He stopped in his tracks and stared at it. It was empty. Jerry looked around warily. Seeing no one, he approached the car. The trunk was locked.

He retreated upstairs, and went to bed. "No," he said loudly to himself, in the privacy of his bedroom.

But before he went to sleep, he closed and locked his window.

The following morning he had to force himself to go out at all. He felt ridiculously nervous, with the rocker in front and the Javelin in back, but finally he laughed and said, "This is absurd," and went down the front way.

The Gumbo Granny's rocker was still in the entry-way, still vacant. And now Jerry noticed something else as well. The old lady's pipe was lying on the tiles next to the rocker, in a smear of black ash.

He was standing there by the mailboxes, looking at it, when Kris came down. "Hi, Jerry," she said. "You're leaning against my mailbox."

He moved aside. "Uh," he said, as Kris got out her mail, "have you seen her lately? In the last couple days?"

"Who?" said Kris.

"Her. The old lady. The Gumbo Granny."

Kris looked at the rocker and wrinkled her nose. "No, I don't think so. Why?"

"She never leaves her rocker there like that. Never. She's always in it. But it's been there for three days now. I haven't seen her once in all that time."

Kris brushed back a fallen strand of hair, and smiled mischievously. "Maybe the needle men got her," she said. She opened the inner door and started back up-stairs, but when Jerry did not move she looked back at him. "Jerry," she asked, "is anything wrong?"

"No," he said quickly. "No, nothing." If he told her half of the crazy stuff going through his head, he knew, he'd *never* get anywhere with her.

Kris shrugged and went upstairs.

The police made him hold for ten minutes and trans-ferred him four times before he finally got connected with someone willing to talk to him. "I'm trying to get some information, officer," Jerry said. "I'm a re-porter, and I need some figures on the number of dis-appearances from the Uptown area. Not killings, just cases where somebody vanished, with no body or anything, you understand?''

''What kind of time period you asking about? This week? This month? All year? You'll have to be more precise.''

''Oh, hell, I don't know. This month, say. Can you get me the figures?''

''A lot of people vanish. Kids run off to New York or L.A. or God knows where, men skip out on alimony and child support, people duck collection agencies. We can't begin to keep track of 'em all, let alone find 'em. Not if they don't want to be found. What do you want this for, anyway?''

''It's a story I'm working on,'' Jerry said. ''I'm a reporter.''

''Yeah?'' The voice sounded suspicious. ''Who you with?''

''I'm kind of freelancing.''

''I see,'' the policeman said. ''Well, you better come downtown and talk to someone else. You got to be accredited, you know. We don't give out information to every joker who calls up and says he's from the press.''

A kid vanished earlier this week. Charlie Monroe, Chollie they called him. Can you tell me if he's been found?''

''What business is it of yours? You family or something?''

Jerry didn't reply.

''Look, I can't help you. You better come downtown.'' Click.

Jerry hung up, frowning.

The rocker and pipe were gone the next morning, but somehow that failed to make Jerry feel any better. He knocked on the door of 1-East, a little warily, but still hoping that the Gumbo Granny herself would come scuffling to the door to tell him she'd been sick. He would have settled for a relative, telling him that she'd died. But there was no answer.

He spent the day at his typewriter, working on an

assignment he'd pulled from the features editor of a neighborhood weekly, but he wasn't able to work up much enthusiasm about the gyros-pizza war for the stomachs of North Side singles. It was such a stupid story, anyway. Now if these damned needle men were only real, and he could prove it, expose them—*that* would be a story worth doing. Better even than his tunnels under the Loop. It could even get him a staff writer job someplace. At the very least it was a certain sale.

Jerry pushed his typewriter away from him and sat thinking. The typewriter was an electric. It kept humming, like it was impatient, rushing him. He turned it off.

Then he found his notebook and took the el up to Evanston, to check out the library at Northwestern.

That night Jerry returned in a fever. He'd filled twelve pages of his notebook in his close, careful script. He was so full with the story he felt he just *had* to talk to someone before he went nuts. But Alan was off somewhere, no telling when he'd be back, and Steve was still out of town. Harold was in his bedroom, but the door was closed, and when Jerry put his ear to it he heard thumping and low moans. Harold wouldn't like being interrupted. Besides, he was still giving Jerry a hard time over that nightmare. No sense giving him more ammunition.

"Damn," he said. He glanced at his notebook again. Then he said, "What the hell," and went down to the second floor.

One of the roommates answered the door, a heavy, bovine sort with mousy brown hair and bad acne. "Kris is studying for a big test," she told him. "She won't want to be disturbed." She sniffed. "Her class standing is low enough as is."

"Never mind that," Jerry said, "I have to talk to her." He insisted until he was let into the apartment. The other roommate was in a corner of the darkened living room, studying under a tensor lamp. She looked up at him vaguely from behind coke-bottle glasses while the pudgy one went to fetch Kris.

"Hi," Kris said. "What's the matter?"

"I want to tell you something," he said. "Come on, I'll buy you a drink."

Across Sheridan was a small bar patronized by the Marine Drive crowd, about the only place in the immediate vicinity where you could drink without listening to country music or worrying about knife fights. A bouncer kept out the derelicts, the rednecks, and other undesirables. He gave Jerry a long glance, but finally passed them when Kris smiled at him. Jerry led her to a small table by the window, ordered a pitcher of dark beer and a couple of shrimp cocktails, and opened his notebook.

"They were *real*," he said in an excited whisper.

"Who?" Kris asked. "No, wait. I bet I know. The needle men."

Jerry nodded. "I was working all day, reading old books about life in New Orleans, folklore, looking over some newspaper microfilms. Nothing was ever proved about these needle men, but there were stories. For years and years, from the turn of the century or earlier well into the twenties. It was a black superstition, especially. If it was a superstition. They preyed on blacks, you see, because they were all so poor, and nobody much cared whether a few of them vanished or not. The police just laughed at the needle men stories, but the blacks passed the warnings along, word of mouth. It was just like the Gumbo Granny said. They were supposed to be medical students. They carried these long needles, tipped with poison or anaesthetic, something like that, and they skulked around in alleys and parks and such. Just a scratch from one of those needles was supposed to be enough. The victim would go under in seconds, and other needle men would come and cart him off to Charity Hospital or the medical schools, wherever cadavers were needed for demonstration and dissection. Later on, a lot of blacks wouldn't go to movies, because the needle men liked to operate inside of theaters. They'd come and sit behind you, you see, and push their needles through the back of your seat. A little prick in the small of the back, that's all it would take. Then they'd carry you out like you were drunk or sick, and you'd never be seen again. No bodies to be found, of course.''

Kris speared a tiny shrimp with her toothpick, dipped it in cocktail sauce, and nibbled at it delicately, a pinky stuck out. Her hair fell around her shoulders in a gorgeous honey-colored cascade, lit by dim reflections from the lights above the bar. But her green eyes regarded him skeptically, and for a moment Jerry thought he'd blown it for good with his talk of the needle men. She was going to laugh, or shrug him off as a crackpot, or . . . he wasn't sure.

Instead she finished the shrimp, drank a bit of her beer, and said, ''Well, it's an interesting story. Colorful. You can probably make an article out of it.''

''Exactly what I'm going to do!'' Jerry said.

''It'll have to be a kind of historical feature for some New Orleans magazine, though,'' she said. ''You know, quaint old bogey men.''

''No, no,'' Jerry said. ''You don't understand. That's just the background. I'm going to bring all up to date, work in the modern stuff. Here and now. In Chicago.''

Kris ate another shrimp and smiled. ''That kind of story you might sell to the *Enquirer,* but nowhere else. Don't you think you're being silly?''

''No!'' Jerry said stoutly.

''You really think these needle men exist? Not only in New Orleans around the turn of the century, but here and now, today, in Chicago? Is that what you think? And they carried off Chollie Monroe to provide some medical school with an experimental cadaver?'' She shook her head, smiling. ''You don't look like the sort of person to go off the deep end.''

Jerry flushed. ''It's not just Chollie,'' he insisted. ''They got the Gumbo Granny, too. They had to. She knew all about them, you see. And there's more. Listen to me.'' He told her all about the guy with the hypodermic needle, and the black Javelin.

Kris listened to him politely enough, sipping her beer and nibbling on shrimp, but when he had finished she did not look convinced. "A sports coat with leather patches, you say? I think I've seen him in the alley too. I know I've seen the car. But that doesn't mean anything. He probably lives in one of the other buildings around here. What's so mysterious about that? There's a white Mustang back there a lot too. It belongs to my roommate." She wrinkled her nose. "The hypodermic—well, maybe he is a junkie. Or a doctor. I don't know. Either one is more likely than being a needle man, don't you think?"

"Even so," Jerry said, confused, "what about the Gumbo Granny?"

"Ah," said Kris, smiling, "that I happen to know about. I mentioned it to my roommate, Sheila, after I saw you by the mailboxes. The old lady had a stroke, Jerry. That's all. Just a stroke. The day after that fuss with the Monroe boy. She was out there in the morning, rocking, and she had her attack. Someone found her, called the hospital, the ambulance came and carted her away. Of course they wouldn't think to remove the rocker. So it stayed there, for days and days."

"It's gone now."

Kris smiled. "You know this neighborhood as well as I do. It finally got stolen, obviously. *You* put a perfectly good piece of furniture down there, and see how long it stays around."

Jerry sat back and shut his notebook. Suddenly he felt very confused. Kris was making a lot of sense, and his story was disintegrating around him. "What hospital is she in?" he asked.

"How should I know?" Kris said.

"Well," said Jerry. "Maybe you're right. I ought to check it out, though. This story could really make me." He brightened. "I know, I can call around to all the hospitals, until I find her."

"Asking for the Gumbo Granny?" Kris said. She smiled. "The staffs will love you. And won't you feel foolish when you find her?"

"Yes," Jerry admitted, ruefully. He tasted his beer. The head was gone, faded while they'd talked. "Still, it's worth doing. I mean, what if she *isn't* in a hospital? Then I'd be right, maybe." He scratched his head. "Your roommate saw an ambulance take the old lady away, right? They said she'd had a stoke?"

"Right."

"Well, what if one of these needle men came in, gave her an injection. She was too old to resist. She'd go under like *that*." He snapped his fingers. "And then, what would be simpler than to pull right up with an ambulance, and carry out the old lady in broad daylight. She had no relatives, like poor Chollie. Who could object? If the needle men are med students, the ambulance drivers are probably in with them, right? Certainly they could get an ambulance easy enough."

Kris laughed and shook her head. "Oh, come on. Listen to yourself, Jerry. You're kind of cute, and I thought you were bright, but you're talking like a real paranoid. The Gumbo Granny had nothing on you!" She leaned across the table and took his hand. "Listen to me," she said, giving him a small, affectionate squeeze. "All this theorizing is bad enough, but your whole motive is crazy. Contraband corpses for medical schools? Body snatching? Come *on*. That stuff might have been great in the days of Burke and Hare, maybe even in 19th century New Orleans, but today? Are these needle men part of the faculties of the med schools, or do they just drive up, lift the bodies out of the trunks of their car, and dicker with the professors? I'm sure medical schools can get bodies in simpler ways, don't you think?"

Jerry grinned at her. "It so happens," he said, squeezing her hand back, and delighted by the warmth of it, "that I thought of that. It puzzled me for a bit too, but finally I figured it all out. It will be in my article."

"Yes?" Kris said, patiently.

"Transplants," Jerry said proudly.

She raised an eyebrow.

"No, really," he said. "Think about it. The old

needle men, they just wanted bodies, like the old lady said. For the teaching hospitals and med schools. They needed 'em for dissection and weren't choosy about how they got them. Today, of course, that demand isn't there, and there are channels and procedures and such. But still, the needle men are out there. *Why*, I asked myself. Why, for transplants. Just watch late night TV sometime, you see all those public service spots, donate your kidneys here, leave your eyes there. You go to get a driver's license and they try to sign you up as an organ donor. Really, the demand is there. A lot of people need kidneys and livers and stuff, and there aren't enough to go around. You figure some rich people would be willing to pay almost anything to live, right? So there's got to be a black market in body parts, even if no one writes about it. The needle men. Only now they just put their victims to sleep instead of killing them, you see. The bodies get taken somewhere, still alive, and cut up for transplants. I bet there's money in it. A *lot* of money.''

''And Uptown is full of these needle men?'' Kris said.

''What better place? Today when I got off the el, a guy was lying passed out on the stairs. If some other guy had been helping him off, I never would have looked twice. We got so many runaways and such the police don't even count 'em. I know. I called them. There's gang wars, there's race trouble between the Orientals and the hillbillies and the blacks, there's fights in the bars most nights. Illegal aliens are working everywhere, nobody's got any records on them but their employers, and if one of them vanishes—well, he just got caught by immigration, or skipped town. Down in the all-black ghettoes, maybe a white needle man would stand out, like they used to in New Orleans. But Uptown is so damn mixed that nobody stands out. Think about it. This is prime territory.''

Kris let go of his hand and poured them both more beer. ''Drink up,'' she said, ''I've got to get back and study. I can see there is no dissuading you from this. You've got every crazy detail worked out, don't you?''

"It's not crazy," Jerry said. "At least I don't think it is."

You can't prove a word of any of it, Jerry."

"Not now," Jerry said, "but I'll get proof, one way or the other.

This story will make a real name for me, I'm not about to let it slip through my fingers. The needle men don't know I'm on to them. I'm going to start checking up on runaways and disappearances, that kind of thing. And I'm going to watch that damn Javelin real carefully. From my back stairs, I can see the whole alley. I'll buy binoculars. And a gun. Yes. I'd better start carrying a gun."

"You start wandering the alley with binoculars and a gun and the police will be locking *you* up, not your needle men. Don't you think you're taking this folk tale a little too . . ." She stopped. "Oh my God," she said, looking out the window.

Jerry looked out too. Across the street was another tavern, a rough noisy place Jerry had never dared enter. Two men had just come out of it. A white man in a corduroy jacket with leather patches on the elbows was helping a black youth into a waiting car. The black seemed to be drunk or unconscious. The car, Jerry noted, was a black Javelin.

"Oh, it's just coincidence," Kris said, but her voice sounded as if even she no longer believed it. She licked her lips. "He's just drunk. There are a thousand explanations."

"We'd better get back," Jerry said. "The needle men are out tonight." He paid the bill and ushered Kris out of there. In the alley, every shadow seemed to hold a smiling shape with a long, long needle, but they hurried past and up the back stairs, and nothing leaped out at them. Both of them were breathing hard when they reached Kris' landing. From the stairs, Jerry tried to tell himself.

He put his arms around her and bent to kiss her, hoping she'd permit it. Her enthusiasm took him by surprise. When they finally broke apart, Kris was studying him from those wide, green eyes. "Oh, damn you," she said. "It's silly, but now you've got me seeing needle men everywhere." She wrinkled her nose. "I hate to admit it, but I'm frightened."

Jerry stood dumbfounded, not knowing what to say.

"I don't know how to ask this," Kris said. "Will you stay the night? With me? It'd make me sleep easier."

Jerry tried to keep from grinning. "Oh, sure," he said. "Me too."

"Thanks," Kris said. She turned and unlocked the door. Her apartment had the same layout as his own, but it was a lot neater. Better furnished, too. She and her roommates did a lot better than him. Kris didn't let him admire the decor, however. She led him straight to the bedroom, oddly enough the one right below his own.

Books were strewn all over the bed. She gathered them up and set them on a nightstand, then turned and touched the light switch. A dimmer. Illumination went down to a soft glow, and Kris turned to him with a smile. "Naked fear makes me horny," she said. "What are you waiting for?"

"Uh," said Jerry. He grinned. "Sure." Then it was a race to get undressed, and they tumbled into bed together laughing.

Afterwards, Jerry felt better than he had for years; a girl like Kris, a story like the needle men. Things were really coming together for him. He said as much to her, as she nestled up against him and he stroked her soft, fine hair.

"Ummmm," she said, raising her head. "The needle men. Did you have to mention them again? I'd managed to forget about them for a few moments." She laughed. "It all seems silly now. Are you really going through with it?"

"Of course," he said, wounded.

She sighed. "Good luck," she said. She kissed his chest lightly, and her hand started doing interesting things lower down. 'Can you stay the whole night, or will your roommates call the police? Maybe you should go up and tell them where you are. We don't want them thinking you've been carried off by the needle men.'' She giggled.

"They don't know anything about the needle men,'' Jerry said, "and they don't care where I spend my nights. We're not that close. You know how it is sometimes.'' He smiled. "I'll stay. Hell, I'll move in if you want me.''

I'll have to think about that one,'' Kris said. She sat up suddenly, and climbed out of bed. "Excuse,'' she said.

"Hey, where you going?'' Jerry asked.

"The little girl's room,'' she said. "Don't worry. I'll be back.'' She padded to the door, nude. Even in the vague, dim light, she was lovely. Her long hair moved behind her as she walked.

She was gone a long time. Jerry got restless. For a moment, he even felt afraid. He thought he heard a door open and close somewhere, and he had a sudden vision of the needle man, creeping up the back stairs with his long, sharp needle in hand, jimmying the lock, stealing down the hall, slowly, quietly. He could be out there right now, white-faced, grinning, needle poised and ready for Kris to emerge from the bathroom. Or maybe he'd already gotten her, maybe she was lying at his feet even now, and he was about to open the door and come in for Jerry too.

"God,'' Jerry said. He was giving himself the shivers. He shifted in bed, saw Kris' books stacked up on the nightstand, picked up one on impulse. It was hard to read anything in the dim light, but if it would take his mind off the needle men it was worth the eyestrain.

He flipped through a few pages, frowned, flipped, stared. "Oh,'' he said, in a small whimper. "Oh, no. No.''

That was when the door opened. They were standing there, all of them, Kris and her roommates, smiling. Kris had the needle. "You never asked me my major, Jerry,'' she said. "I'm in med school, second year. You'd be amazed at how expensive it is.'' She shrugged and came towards him.

THE SHIFTING GROWTH

by Edgar Jepson
and John Gawsworth

"Come at once. Must operate for me. Great chance probably. Race special, Lincoln, King's Cross 9.30. Don't fail. Clavering."

That was the wire, plus punctuation, I read for the second time, as that special carried me out of London.

It was a bit puzzling. I knew that Clavering would put himself out more than a little to help me, for we had been close pals all the five years we walked St. Thomas's, and he knew that the fee for an operation in Lincoln would be very useful to a recent settler in Harley Street. But what did he mean by "Great chance probably"? Was the patient a county swell, who would be the beginning of a valuable connection in the North? Hardly likely: the North has its own surgeons. But if it didn't mean that, what on earth could it mean?

I cudgelled my brains for an explanation, and then it struck me that since I should know at twelve o'clock, I was rather wasting my time bothering about it at nine-thirty, and I turned to my *Times* and the conversation of the five racing enthusiasts in the carriage with me.

Everything gives way to a race special, and we ran into Lincoln three minutes after the hour. Clavering was there, and directly we had struggled to one another through the jostling stream of race-goers, I saw that he was under the weather—badly under the weather.

"Talk when we get to the house," he said, and we shoved through the crowd to his car.

The house, the perfect house for the country doctor, early nineteenth century, and in the main street, had belonged to his father and grandfather, both doctors before him, and it was about as old-world inside as it was out. He was in such a state that he took me straight to the surgery—a bit old-fashioned, but with all the fittings of the newest, and plunged into the case, but mixing a whisky-and-soda for me as he did so.

"It's my girl," he said, and there was a bit of a choke in his voice which impressed me, for there had never been anything soft about him that I had noticed, "Sylvia Bard, swimming champion of the South of France, the girl I'm engaged to—and that won't be for long—unless the operation works out all right. It's beaten us, the case has, and there isn't a good man in the North who hasn't seen her."

And then he pulled himself together and gave me the details clearly enough. Miss Bard had always been healthy, scarcely had a day's illness since the measles of her childhood, played a good game of golf and tennis, and even played hockey for the county. At the end of the last hockey season she had gone with her people to the Riviera to train, and about six weeks after her return the trouble had begun.

It was abdominal.

She had been all the quicker to notice it, because she had always enjoyed such good health. The trouble had been slight enough at first, and it had grown serious slowly. But neither he nor the men he had called into consultation had been able to diagnose it. They had, of course, tried every treatment they could think of. It had yielded to none of them.

Then he said: "Did you ever see or hear of a growth that shifted?" It was almost a cry of anguish.

"I did not. A growth couldn't shift," I said, with absolute certainty.

"But this one does. Just look at these X-ray photographs."

He pulled open a drawer and took out a whole packet of them, and we looked through them together.

They were incredible.

There was the growth all right—in the colon—a growth with what looked like adhesions, and as Clavering said, rather like the blob in the advertisement of Stephens' blue-black ink, and like no other growth ever X-rayed: at any rate, none I had ever seen. But in hardly any two of the photographs was it in the same place!

It was unbelievable; in some of the photographs it looked to have moved a good eight inches.

"But hang it all! Why didn't you operate?" I cried.

"Operate! We did operate! Dowling operated, and there isn't a better man in the North. But when he opened up the gut—the growth wasn't there, and he couldn't find it!"

I looked at him.

"And that's why I sent for you—to operate again. And I'm afraid we've let it go too long—that she won't stand it—the first time was bad enough. But you're the quickest hand with a knife I've ever seen, and you may just get it done in time."

"Well—well," I said softly. "And you wired: 'Great chance probably.' "

"You're made in the North, if you bring it off," he said dully.

"It sounds as if I ought to be. Lead me to it!"

"She's all ready to move straight into the theatre—at the hospital," he said. "No use not having the best conditions."

"Right. And I should like a sandwich. Hurried over my breakfast. It's steadying, you know."

"And that's ready, too," said Clavering.

I ate the sandwich, and in ten minutes I was drawing on my steaming rubber gloves in the operating theatre of the hospital, and they wheeled the patient in, as dismal a wreck of a pretty girl as I have ever set eyes on.

"But this is a case of starvation!" I said.

"I know, that's what it looks like," said Clavering dully. "But it can't be."

"Then you'd better try a blood transfusion the moment I've finished," I snapped, and I began my examination.

The growth jumped at your eyes in that emaciated abdomen, and I pressed it. The response to the pressure was odd, a kind of twisting, muscular response. I had never know a growth respond like that before. I nodded to the anæsthetist, and he got to work, and devilish little anæsthetic he had to use before the poor girl was under.

It was my turn, and I had made up my mind about one thing: I was going to find that growth when I opened up. I ran a needle through it and moored it to the spot. It was sensitive: the surface of the abdomen above it fairly rippled.

I picked up my instruments—as a rule I start with three, the one I'm using and a couple between my fingers, for speed's sake—and got to work. I made a longer incision than I usually do, nearly the whole length of the growth, for it still seemed to be rippling, and opened up the colon on to a black-and-red spongy mass, dragging at the needle which held it fast.

And from the middle of that seething sponge there stared up at me two set, unwinking eyes.

An octopus!

In an operation one is prepared for anything; but I admit that those eyes—for a second I thought they were a devil's—jarred me badly. But at the same moment it flashed on me that the brute was tugging away at the needle with the full tension of all its suckers set against the walls of the gut, and if the needle gave, it would not be much use my having found the growth. In the next ten seconds I must have ploughed the knife through and through that writhing sponge fifty times.

The writhing stopped.

I took forceps and drew it out. It came smoothly and easily: not a sucker held. I never thought you could kill the brutes so quickly.

"There's your growth!" I said, and I dropped it into the basin.

Uncompressed, it looked as if it would have filled a drain-pipe, and split the colon of an ox. And the eyes were still staring, stupidly.

Clavering retched. But then he was under the weather, and it did look nasty.

I had the gut washed out and sewn up inside of ten minutes—the quickest abdominal I ever did—or anybody else.

Sylvia Bard recovered—a long job. But I should say that she is about as strong as ever she was. At any rate, she is married to Clavering.

"Great chance probably?" I should think so! The octopus was in every big paper in England next morning and all over the world before night, and of course I have never looked back.

But oh, if it hadn't occurred to me to moor the growth to the gut before I began to operate!

CAMPS

Jack Dann

As Stephen lies in bed, he can think only of pain.

He imagines it as sharp and blue. After receiving an injection of Demerol, he enters pain's cold regions as an explorer, an objective visitor. It is a country of ice and glass, monochromatic plains and valleys filled with wash blue shards of ice, crystal pyramids and pinnacles, squares, oblongs, and all manner of polyhedron—block upon block of painted blue pain.

Although it is mid-afternoon, Stephen pretends it is dark. His eyes are tightly closed, but the daylight pouring into the room from two large windows intrudes as a dull red field extending infinitely behind his eyelids.

"Josie," he asks through cotton mouth, "aren't I due for another shot?" Josie is crisp and fresh and large in her starched white uniform. Her peaked nurse's cap is pinned to her mouse brown hair.

"I've just given you an injection, it will take effect soon." Josie strokes his hand, and he dreams of ice.

"Bring me some ice," he whispers.

"If I bring you a bowl of ice, you'll only spill it again."

"Bring me some ice . . ." By touching the ice cubes, by turning them in his hand like a gambler favoring his dice, he can transport himself into the beautiful blue country. Later, the ice will melt, and he will spill the bowl. The shock of cold and pain will awaken him.

Stephen believes that he is dying, and he has re-

solved to die properly. Each visit to the cold country
brings him closer to death; and death, he has learned,
is only a slow walk through icefields. He has come to
appreciate the complete lack of warmth and the beautifully etched face of his magical country.

But he is connected to the bright, flat world of the
hospital by plastic tubes—one breathes cold oxygen
into his left nostril; another passes into his right nostril and down his throat to his stomach; one feeds him
intravenously, another draws his urine.

"Here's your ice," Josie says. "But mind you, don't
spill it." She places the small bowl on his tray table
and wheels the table close to him. She has a musky
odor of perspiration and perfume; Stephen is reminded of old women and college girls.

"Sleep now, sweet boy."

Without opening his eyes, Stephen reaches out and
places his hand on the ice.

"Come now, Stephen, wake up. Dr. Volk is here to
see you."

Stephen feels the cool touch of Josie's hand, and he
opens his eyes to see the doctor standing beside him.
The doctor has a gaunt long face and thinning brown
hair; he is dressed in a wrinkled green suit.

"Now we'll check the dressing, Stephen," he says
as he tears away a gauze bandage on Stephen's abdomen.

Stephen feels the pain, but he is removed from it.
His only wish is to return to the blue dreamlands. He
watches the doctor peel off the neat crosshatchings of
gauze. A terrible stink fills the room.

Josie stands well away from the bed.

"Now we'll check your drains." The doctor pulls a
long drainage tube out of Stephen's abdomen, irrigates
and disinfects the wound, inserts a new drain, and re-
peats the process by pulling out another tube just below the rib cage.

Stephen imagines that he is swimming out of the
room. He tries to cross the hazy border into cooler
regions, but it is difficult to concentrate. He has only

a half-hour at most before the Demerol will wear off. Already, the pain is coming closer, and he will not be due for another injection until the night nurse comes on duty. But the night nurse will not give him an injection without an argument. She will tell him to fight the pain.

But he cannot fight without a shot.

"Tomorrow we'll take that oxygen tube out of your nose," the doctor says, but his voice seems far away, and Stephen wonders what he is talking about.

He reaches for the bowl of ice, but cannot find it.

"Josie, you've taken my ice."

"I took the ice away when the doctor came. Why don't you try to watch a bit of television with me; Soupy Sales is on."

"Just bring me some ice," Stephen says. "I want to rest a bit." He can feel the sharp edges of pain breaking through the gauzy wraps of Demerol.

"I love you, Josie," he says sleepily as she places a fresh bowl of ice on his tray.

As Stephen wanders through his ice blue dreamworld, he sees a rectangle of blinding white light. It looks like a doorway into an adjoining world of brightness. He has glimpsed it before on previous Demerol highs. A coal-dark doorway stands beside the bright one.

He walks toward the portals, passes through white-blue cornfields.

Time is growing short. The drug cannot stretch it much longer. Stephen knows that he has to choose either the bright doorway or the dark, one or the other. He does not even consider turning around, for he has dreamed that the ice and glass and cold blue gemstones have melted behind him.

It makes no difference to Stephen which doorway he chooses. On impulse he steps into blazing, searing whiteness.

Suddenly he is in a cramped world of people and sound.

The boxcar's doors were flung open. Stephen was

being pushed out of the cramped boxcar that stank of sweat, feces and urine. Several people had died in the car, and added their stink of death to the already fetid air.

"Carla, stay close to me," shouted a man beside Stephen. He had been separated from his wife by a young woman who pushed between them, as she tried to return to the dark safety of the boxcar.

SS men in black, dirty uniforms were everywhere. They kicked and pummeled everyone within reach. Alsatian guard dogs snapped and barked. Stephen was bitten by one of the snarling dogs. A woman beside him was being kicked by soldiers. And they were all being methodically herded past a high barbed-wire fence. Beside the fence was a wall.

Stephen looked around for an escape route, but he was surrounded by other prisoners, who were pressing against him. Soldiers were shooting indiscriminately into the crowd, shooting women and children alike.

The man who had shouted to his wife was shot.

"Sholom, help me, help me," screamed a scrawny young woman whose skin was as yellow and pimpled as chicken flesh.

And Stephen understood that *he* was Sholom. He was a Jew in this burning, stinking world, and this woman, somehow, meant something to him. He felt the yellow star sewn on the breast of his filthy jacket. He grimaced uncontrollably. The strangest thoughts were passing through his mind, remembrances of another childhood: morning prayers with his father and rich uncle, large breakfasts on Saturdays, the sounds of his mother and father quietly making love in the next room, *yortzeit* candles burning in the living room, his brother reciting the "four questions" at the Passover table.

He touched the star again and remembered the Nazi's facetious euphemism for it: *Pour le Semite*.

He wanted to strike out, to kill the Nazis, to fight and die. But he found himself marching with the others, as if he had no will of his own. He felt that he was cut in half. He had two selves now; one watched the other. One self wanted to fight. The other was numbed; it cared only for itself. It was determined to survive.

Stephen looked around for the woman who had called out to him. She was nowhere to be seen.

Behind him were railroad tracks, electrified wire, and the conical tower and main gate of the camp. Ahead was a pitted road littered with corpses and their belongings. Rifles were being fired and a heavy, sickly sweet odor was everywhere. Stephen gagged, others vomited. It was the overwhelming stench of death, of rotting and burning flesh. Black clouds hung above the camp, and flames spurted from the tall chimneys of ugly buildings, as if from infernal machines.

Stephen walked onward; he was numb, unable to fight or even talk. Everything that happened around him was impossible, the stuff of dreams.

The prisoners were ordered to halt, and the soldiers began to separate those who would be burned from those who would be worked to death. Old men and women and young children were pulled out of the crowd. Some were beaten and killed immediately while the others looked on in disbelief. Stephen looked on, as if it was of no concern to him. Everything was unreal, dreamlike. He did not belong here.

The new prisoners looked like *Musselmänner*, the walking dead. Those who became ill, or were beaten or starved before they could "wake up" to the reality of the camps became *Musselmänner*. *Musselmänner* could not think or feel. They shuffled around, already dead in spirit, until a guard or disease or cold or starvation killed them.

"Keep marching," shouted a guard, as Stephen stopped before an emaciated old man crawling on the ground. "You'll look like him soon enough."

Suddenly, as if waking from one dream and finding himself in another, Stephen remembered that the chicken-skinned girl was his wife. He remembered their life together, their children and crowded flat. He remembered the birthmark on her leg, her scent, her hungry love-making. He had once fought another boy over her.

His glands opened up with fear and shame; he had ignored her screams for help.

He stopped and turned, faced the other group. "Fruma," he shouted, then started to run.

A guard struck him in the chest with the butt of his rifle, and Stephen fell into darkness.

He spills the icewater again and awakens with a scream.

"It's my fault," Josie says, as she peels back the sheets. "I should have taken the bowl away from you. But you fight me."

Stephen lives with the pain again. He imagines that a tiny fire is burning in his abdomen, slowly consuming him. He stares at the television high on the wall and watches Soupy Sales.

As Josie changes the plastic sac containing his intravenous saline solution, an orderly pushes a cart into the room and asks Stephen if he wants a print for his wall.

"Would you like me to choose something for you?" Josie asks.

Stephen shakes his head and asks the orderly to show him all the prints. Most of them are familiar still-lifes and pastorals, but one catches his attention. It is a painting of a wheat field. Although the sky looks ominously dark, the wheat is brightly rendered in great broad strokes. A path cuts through the field and crows fly overhead.

"That one," Stephen says. "Put that one up."

After the orderly hangs the print and leaves, Josie asks Stephen why he chose that particular painting.

"I like Van Gogh," he says dreamily, as he tries to detect a rhythm in the surges of abdominal pain. But he is not nauseated, just gaseous.

"Any particular reason why you like Van Gogh?" asks Josie. "He's my favorite artist, too."

"I didn't say he was my favorite," Stephen says, and Josie pouts, an expression which does not fit her prematurely lined face. Stephen closes his eyes, glimpses the cold country, and says, "I like the painting because it's so bright that it's almost frightening. And the road going through the field"—he opens his eyes—"doesn't go anywhere. It just ends in the field. And the crows are flying around like vultures."

"Most people see it as just a pretty picture," Josie says.

"What's it called?"

" 'Wheatfields with Blackbirds.' "

"Sensible. My stomach hurts, Josie. Help me turn over on my side." Josie helps him onto his left side, plumps up his pillows, and inserts a short tube into his rectum to relieve the gas. "I also like the painting with the large stars that all look out of focus," Stephen says. "What's it called?"

" 'Starry Night.' "

"That's scary, too," Stephen says. Josie takes his blood pressure, makes a notation on his chart, then sits down beside him and holds his hand. "I remember something," he says. "Something just—" He jumps as he remembers, and pain shoots through his distended stomach. Josie shushes him, checks the intravenous needle, and asks him what he remembers.

But the memory of the dream recedes as the pain grows sharper. "I hurt all the fucking time, Josie," he says, changing position. Josie removes the rectal tube before he is on his back.

"Don't use such language, I don't like to hear it. I know you have a lot of pain," she says, her voice softening.

'Time for a shot."

"No, honey, not for some time. You'll just have to bear with it."

Stephen remembers his dream again. He is afraid of it. His breath is short and his heart feels as if it is beating in his throat, but he recounts the entire dream to Josie.

He does not notice that her face has lost its color.

"It's only a dream, Stephen. Probably something you studied in history."

"But it was so real, not like a dream at all."

"That's enough!" Josie says.

"I'm sorry I upset you. Don't be angry."

"I'm *not* angry."

"I'm sorry," he says, fighting the pain, squeezing Josie's hand tightly. "Didn't you tell me that you were in the Second World War?"

Josie is composed once again. "Yes, I did, but I'm surprised you remembered. You were very sick. I was a nurse overseas, spent most of the war in England. But I was one of the first servicewomen to go into any of the concentration camps."

Stephen drifts with the pain; he appears to be asleep.

"You must have studied very hard," Josie whispers to him. Her hand is shaking just a bit.

It is twelve o'clock and his room is death quiet. The sharp shadows seem to be the hardest objects in the room. The fluorescents burn steadily in the hall outside.

Stephen looks out into the hallway, but he can see only the far white wall. He waits for his night nurse to appear: it is time for his injection. A young nurse passes by his doorway. Stephen imagines that she is a cardboard ship sailing through the corridors.

He presses the buzzer, which is attached by a clip to his pillow. The night nurse will take her time, he tells himself. He remembers arguing with her. Angrily, he presses the buzzer again.

Across the hall, a man begins to scream, and there is a shuffle of nurses into his room. The screaming turns into begging and whining. Although Stephen has never seen the man in the opposite room, he has come to hate him. Like Stephen, he has something wrong with his stomach, but he cannot suffer well. He can only beg and cry, try to make deals with the nurses, doctors, God and angels. Stephen cannot muster any pity for this man.

The night nurse finally comes into the room, says, "You have to try to get along without this," and gives him an injection of Demerol.

"Why does the man across the hall scream so?" Stephen asks, but the nurse is already edging out of the room.

"Because he's in pain."

"So am I," Stephen says in a loud voice. "But I can keep it to myself."

"Then stop buzzing me constantly for an injection. That man across the hall has had half of his stomach removed. He's got something to scream about."

So have I, Stephen thinks; but the nurse disappears before he can tell her. He tries to imagine what the man across the hall looks like. He thinks of him as being bald and small, an ancient baby. Stephen tries to feel sorry for the man, but his incessant whining disgusts him.

The drug takes effect; the screams recede as he hurtles through the dark corridors of a dream. The cold country is dark, for Stephen cannot persuade his night nurse to bring him some ice. Once again, he sees two entrances. As the world melts behind him, he steps into the coal-black doorway.

In the darkness he hears an alarm, a bone-jarring clangor.

He could smell the combined stink of men pressed closely together. They were all lying upon two badly constructed wooden shelves. The floor was dirt; the smell of urine never left the barracks.

"Wake up," said a man Stephen knew as Viktor. "If the guard finds you in bed, you'll be beaten again."

Stephen moaned, still wrapped in dreams. "Wake up, wake up," he mumbled to himself. He would have a few more minutes before the guard arrived with the dogs. At the very thought of dogs, Stephen felt revulsion. He had once been bitten in the face by a large dog.

He opened his eyes, yet he was still half-asleep, exhausted. You are in a death camp, he said to himself. You must wake up. You must fight by waking up. Or you will die in your sleep. Shaking uncontrollably, he said, "Do you want to end up in the oven; perhaps you will be lucky today and live."

As he lowered his legs to the floor; he felt the sores open on the soles of his feet. He wondered who would die today and shrugged. It was his third week in the camp. Impossibly, against all odds, he had survived. Most of those he had known in the train had either died or become *Musselmänner*. If it was not for Viktor, he, too, would have become a *Musselmänner*. He had a breakdown and wanted to die. He babbled in English. But Viktor talked him out of death, shared his portion of food with him, and taught him the new rules of life.

"Like everyone else who survives, I count myself first, second and third—then I try to do what I can for someone else," Viktor had said.

"I will survive," Stephen repeated to himself, as the guards opened the door, stepped into the room, and began to shout. Their dogs growled and snapped but heeled beside them. The guards looked sleepy; one did not wear a cap, and his red hair was tousled.

Perhaps he spent the night with one of the whores, Stephen thought. Perhaps today would not be so bad . . .

And so begins the morning ritual: Josie enters Stephen's room at quarter to eight, fusses with the chart attached to the footboard of his bed, pads about aimlessly, and finally goes to the bathroom. She returns, her stiff uniform making swishing sounds. Stephen can feel her standing over the bed and staring at him. But he does not open his eyes. He waits a beat.

She turns away, then drops the bedpan. Yesterday it was the metal ashtray; day before that, she bumped into the bedstand.

"Good morning, darling, it's a beautiful day," she says, then walks across the room to the windows. She parts the faded orange drapes and opens the blinds.

"How do you feel today?"

"Okay, I guess."

Josie takes his pulse and asks, "Did Mr. Gregory stop in to say hello last night?"

"Yes,"Stephen says. "He's teaching me how to play gin rummy. What's wrong with him?"

"He's very sick."

"I can see that; has he got cancer?"

"I don't know," says Josie, as she tidies up his night table.

"You're lying again," Stephen says, but she ignores him. After a time, he says, "His girl friend was in to see me last night. I bet his wife will be in today."

"Shut your mouth about that," Josie says. "Let's get you out of that bed so I can change the sheets."

Stephen sits in the chair all morning. He is getting well but is still very weak. Just before lunchtime, the orderly wheels his cart into the room and asks Stephen if he would like to replace the print hanging on the wall.

"I've seen them all," Stephen says. "I'll keep the one I have." Stephen does not grow tired of the Van Gogh painting; sometimes, the crows seem to have changed position.

"Maybe you'll like this one," the orderly says as he pulls out a cardboard print of Van Gogh's "Starry Night." It is a study of a village nestled in the hills, dressed in shadows. But everything seems to be boiling and writhing as in a fever dream. A cypress tree in the foreground looks like a black flame, and the vertiginous sky is filled with great blurry stars. It is a drunkard's dream. The orderly smiles.

"So you did have it," Stephen says.

"No, I traded some other pictures for it. They had a copy in the West Wing."

Stephen watches him hang it, thanks him, and waits for him to leave. Then he gets up and examines the painting carefully. He touches the raised facsimile brushstrokes and turns toward Josie, feeling an odd sensation in his groin. He looks at her, as if seeing her for the first time. She has an overly full mouth which curves downward at the corners when she smiles. She is not a pretty woman—too fat, he thinks.

"Dance with me," he says, as he waves his arms

and takes a step forward, conscious of the pain in his stomach.

"You're too sick to be dancing just yet," but she laughs at him and bends her knees in a mock plié.

She has small breasts for such a large woman, Stephen thinks. Feeling suddenly dizzy, he takes a step toward the bed. He feels himself slip to the floor, feels Josie's hair brushing against his face, dreams that he's all wet from her tongue, feels her arms around him, squeezing, then feels the weight of her body pressing down on him, crushing him. . . .

He wakes up in bed, catheterized. He has an intravenous needle in his left wrist, and it is difficult to swallow, for he has a tube down his throat.

He groans, tries to move.

"Quiet, Stephen," Josie says, stroking his hand.

"What happened?" he mumbles. He can only remember being dizzy.

"You've had a slight setback, so just rest. The doctor had to collapse your lung; you must lie very still."

"Josie, I love you," he whispers, but he is too far away to be heard. He wonders how many hours or days have passed. He looks toward the window. It is dark, and there is no one in the room.

He presses the buzzer attached to his pillow and remembers a dream. . . .

"You must fight," Viktor said.

It was dark, all the other men were asleep, and the barracks was filled with snoring and snorting. Stephen wished they could all die, choke on their own breath. It would be an act of mercy.

"Why fight?" Stephen asked, and he pointed toward the greasy window, beyond which were the ovens that smoked day and night. He made a fluttering gesture with his hand—smoke rising.

"You must fight, you must live, living is everything. It is the only thing that makes sense here."

"We're all going to die, anyway," Stephen whispered. "Just like your sister . . . and my wife."

''No, Sholom, we're going to live. The others may die, but we're going to live. You must believe that.''

Stephen understood that Viktor was desperately trying to convince himself to live. He felt sorry for Viktor; there could be no sensible rationale for living in a place like this.

Stephen grinned, tasted blood from the corner of his mouth, and said, ''So we'll live through the night, maybe.''

And maybe tomorrow, he thought. He would play the game of survival a little longer.

He wondered if Viktor would be alive tomorrow. He smiled and thought: If Viktor dies, then I will have to take his place and convince others to live. For an instant, he hoped Viktor would die so that he could take his place.

The alarm sounded. It was three o'clock in the morning, time to begin the day.

This morning Stephen was on his feet before the guards could unlock the door.

''Wake up,'' Josie says, gently tapping his arm. ''Come on, wake up.''

Stephen hears her voice as an echo. He imagines that he has been flung into a long tunnel; he hears air whistling in his ears but cannot see anything.

''Whassimatter?'' he asks. His mouth feels as if it is stuffed with cotton; his lips are dry and cracked. He is suddenly angry at Josie and the plastic tubes that hold him in his bed as if he was a latter-day Gulliver. He wants to pull out the tubes, smash the bags filled with saline, tear away his bandages.

''You were speaking German,'' Josie says. ''Did you know that?''

''Can I have some ice?''

''No,'' Josie says impatiently. ''You spilled again, you're all wet.''

''. . . for my mouth, dry . . .''

''Do you remember speaking German, honey. I have to know.''

"Don't remember, bring ice, I'll try to think about it."

As Josie leaves to get him some ice, he tries to remember his dream.

"Here, now, just suck on the ice." She gives him a little hill of crushed ice on the end of a spoon.

"Why did you wake me up, Josie?" The layers of dream are beginning to slough off. As the Demerol works out of his system, he has to concentrate on fighting the burning ache in his stomach.

"You were speaking German. Where did you learn to speak like that?"

Stephen tries to remember what he said. He cannot speak any German, only a bit of classroom French. He looks down at his legs (he has thrown off the sheet) and notices, for the first time, that his legs are as thin as his arms. "My God, Josie, how could I have lost so much weight?"

"You lost about forty pounds, but don't worry, you'll gain it all back. You're on the road to recovery now. Please, try to remember your dream."

"I can't, Josie! I just can't seem to get ahold of it."

"Try."

"Why is it so important to you?"

"You weren't speaking college German, darling. You were speaking slang. You spoke in a patois that I haven't heard since the forties."

Stephen feels a chill slowly creep up his spine. "What did I say?"

Josie waits a beat, then says, "You talked about dying."

"Josie?"

"Yes," she says, pulling at her fingernail.

"When is the pain going to stop?"

"It will be over soon." She gives him another spoonful of ice. "You kept repeating the name Viktor in your sleep. Can you remember anything about him?"

Viktor, Viktor, deep-set blue eyes, balding head and broken nose, called himself a Galitzianer. Saved my life. "I remember," Stephen says. "His name is Viktor Shmone. He is in all my dreams now."

Josie exhales sharply.

"Does that mean anything to you?" Stephen asks anxiously.

"I once knew a man from one of the camps." She speaks very slowly and precisely. "His name was Viktor Shmone. I took care of him. He was one of the few people left alive in the camp after the Germans fled." She reaches for her purse, which she keeps on Stephen's night table, and fumbles an old, torn photograph out of a plastic slipcase.

As Stephen examines the photograph, he begins to sob. A thinner and much younger Josie is standing beside Viktor and two other emaciated-looking men. "Then I'm not dreaming," he says, "and I'm going to die. That's what it means." He begins to shake, just as he did in his dream, and, without thinking, he makes the gesture of rising smoke to Josie. He begins to laugh.

"Stop that," Josie says, raising her hand to slap him. Then she embraces him and says, "Don't cry, darling, it's only a dream. Somehow, you're dreaming the past."

"Why?" Stephen asks, still shaking.

"Maybe you're dreaming because of me, because we're so close. In some ways, I think you know me better than anyone else, better than any man, no doubt. You might be dreaming for a reason; maybe I can help you."

"I'm afraid, Josie."

She comforts him and says, "Now tell me everything you can remember about the dreams."

He is exhausted. As he recounts his dreams to her, he sees the bright doorway again. He feels himself being sucked into it. "Josie," he says, "I must stay awake, don't want to sleep, dream. . . ."

Josie's face is pulled tight as a mask; she is crying.

Stephen reaches out to her, slips into the bright doorway, into another dream.

* * *

It was a cold cloudless morning. Hundreds of prisoners were working in the quarries; each work gang came from a different barracks. Most of the gangs were made up of *Musselmänner,* the faceless majority of the camp. They moved like automatons, lifting and carrying the great stones to the numbered carts, which would have to be pushed down the tracks.

Stephen was drenched with sweat. He had a fever and was afraid that he had contracted typhus. An epidemic had broken out in the camp last week. Every morning several doctors arrived with the guards. Those who were too sick to stand up were taken away to be gassed or experimented upon in the hospital.

Although Stephen could barely stand, he forced himself to keep moving. He tried to focus all his attention on what he was doing. He made a ritual of bending over, choosing a stone of certain size, lifting it, carrying it to the nearest cart, and then taking the same number of steps back to his dig.

A *Musselmänn* fell to the ground, but Stephen made no effort to help him. When he could help someone in a little way, he would, but he would not stick his neck out for a *Musselmänn.* Yet something niggled at Stephen. He remembered a photograph in which Viktor and this *Musselmänn* were standing with a man and a woman he did not recognize. But Stephen could not remember where he had ever seen such a photograph.

"Hey, you," shouted a guard. "Take the one on the ground to the cart."

Stephen nodded to the guard and began to drag the *Musselmänn* away.

"Who's the new patient down the hall?" Stephen asks as he eats a bit of cereal from the breakfast tray Josie has placed before him. He is feeling much better now; his fever is down, and the tubes, catheter and intravenous needle have been removed. He can even walk around a bit.

"How did you find out about that?" Josie asks.

"You were talking to Mr. Gregory's nurse. Do you think I'm dead already? I can still hear."

Josie laughs and takes a sip of Stephen's tea. "You're far from dead! In fact, today is a red-letter day; you're going to take your first shower. What do you think about that?"

"I'm not well enough yet," he says, worried that he will have to leave the hospital before he is ready.

"Well, Dr. Volk thinks differently, and his word is law."

"Tell me about the new patient."

"They brought in a man last night who drank two quarts of motor oil; he's on the dialysis machine."

"Will he make it?"

"No, I don't think so; there's too much poison in his system."

We should all die, Stephen thinks. It would be an act of mercy. He glimpses the camp.

"Stephen!"

He jumped, then awakens.

"You've had a good night's sleep; you don't need to nap. Let's get you into that shower and have it done with." Josie pushes the tray table away from the bed. "Come on, I have your bathrobe right here."

Stephen puts on his bathrobe, and they walk down the hall to the showers. There are three empty shower stalls, a bench and a whirlpool bath. As Stephen takes off his bathrobe, Josie adjusts the water pressure and temperature in the corner stall.

"What's the matter?" Stephen asks, after stepping into the shower. Josie stands in front of the shower stall and holds his towel, but she will not look at him. "Come on," he says, "you've seen me naked before."

"That was different."

"How?" He touches a hard, ugly scab that has formed over one of the wounds on his abdomen.

"When you were very sick, I washed you in bed, as if you were a baby. Now it's different." She looks down at the wet tile floor, as if she is lost in thought.

"Well, I think it's silly," he says. "Come on, it's hard to talk to someone who's looking the other way.

I could break my neck in here and you'd be staring down at the fucking floor.''

"I've asked you not to use that word," she says in a very low voice.

"Do my eyes still look yellowish?''

She looks directly at his face and says, "No, they look fine."

Stephen suddenly feels faint, then nauseated; he has been standing too long. As he leans against the cold shower wall, he remembers his last dream. He is back in the quarry. He can smell the perspiration of the men around him, feel the sun baking him, draining his strength. It is so bright. . . .

He finds himself sitting on the bench and staring at the light on the opposite wall. I've got typhus, he thinks, then realizes that he is in the hospital. Josie is beside him.

"I'm sorry," he says.

"I shouldn't have let you stand so long; it was my fault.''

"I remembered another dream." He begins to shake, and Josie puts her arms around him.

"It's all right now, tell Josie about your dream.''

She's an old, fat woman, Stephen thinks. As he describes the dream, his shaking subsides.

"Do you know the man's name?" Josie asks. "The one the guard ordered you to drag away.''

"No," Stephen says. "He was a *Musselmänn,* yet I thought there was something familiar about him. In my dream I remembered the photograph you showed me. He was in it.''

"What will happen to him?''

"The guards will give him to the doctors for experimentation. If they don't want him, he'll be gassed.''

"You must not let that happen," Josie says, holding him tightly.

"Why?'' asks Stephen, afraid that he will fall into the dreams again.

"If he was one of the men you saw in the photograph, you must not let him die. Your dreams must fit the past.''

"I'm afraid."

"It will be all right, baby," Josie says, clinging to him. She is shaking and breathing heavily.

Stephen feels himself getting an erection. He calms her, presses his face against hers, and touches her breasts. She tells him to stop, but does not push him away.

"I love you," he says as he slips his hand under her starched skirt. He feels awkward and foolish and warm.

"This is wrong," she whispers.

As Stephen kisses her and feels her thick tongue in his mouth, he begins to dream. . . .

Stephen stopped to rest for a few seconds. The *Musselmänn* was dead weight. I cannot go on, Stephen thought; but he bent down, grabbed the *Musselmänn* by his coat, and dragged him toward the cart. He glimpsed the cart, which was filled with the sick and dead and exhausted; it looked no different than a carload of corpses marked for a mass grave.

A long, gray cloud covered the sun, then passed, drawing shadows across gutted hills.

On impulse, Stephen dragged the *Musselmänn* into a gully behind several chalky rocks. Why am I doing this? he asked himself. If I'm caught, I'll be ash in the ovens, too. He remembered what Viktor had told him: "You must think of yourself all the time, or you'll be no help to anyone else."

The *Musselmänn* groaned, then raised his arm. His face was gray with dust and his eyes were glazed.

"You must lie still," Stephen whispered. "Do not make a sound. I've hidden you from the guards, but if they hear you, we'll all be punished. One sound from you and you're dead. You must fight to live, you're in a death camp, you must fight so you can tell of this later."

"I have no family, they're all—"

Stephen clapped his hand over the man's mouth and whispered, "Fight, don't talk. Wake up, you cannot survive the death camp by sleeping."

The man nodded, and Stephen climbed out of the gully. He helped two men carry a large stone to a nearby cart.

"What are you doing?" shouted a guard.

"I left my place to help these men with this stone; now I'll go back where I was."

"What the hell are you trying to do?" Viktor asked.

Stephen felt as if he was burning up with fever. He wiped the sweat from his eyes, but everything was still blurry.

"You're sick, too. You'll be lucky if you last the day."

"I'll last," Stephen said, "But I want you to help me get him back to the camp."

"I won't risk it, not for a *Musselmänn*. He's already dead, leave him."

"Like you left me?"

Before the guard could take notice, they began to work. Although Viktor was older than Stephen, he was stronger. He worked hard every day and never caught the diseases that daily reduced the barracks' numbers. Stephen had a touch of death, as Viktor called it, and was often sick.

They worked until dusk, when the sun's oblique rays caught the dust from the quarries and turned it into veils and scrims. Even the guards sensed that this was a quiet time, for they would congregate together and talk in hushed voices.

"Come, now, help me," Stephen whispered to Viktor. "I've been doing that all day," Viktor said. "I'll have enough trouble getting you back to the camp, much less carry this *Musselmänn*.

"We can't leave him."

"Why are you so preoccupied with this *Musselmänn*? Even if we can get him back to the camp, his chances are nothing. I know, I've seen enough, I know who has a chance to survive."

"You're wrong this time," Stephen said. He was dizzy and it was difficult to stand. The odds are I won't last the night, and Viktor knows it, he told himself.

"I had a dream that if this man dies, I'll die, too. I just feel it."

"Here we learn to trust our dreams," Viktor said. "They make as much sense as this. . . ." He made the gesture of rising smoke and gazed toward the ovens, which were spewing fire and black ash.

The western portion of the sky was yellow, but over the ovens it was red and purple and dark blue. Although it horrified Stephen to consider it, there was a macabre beauty here. If he survived, he would never forget these sense impressions, which were stronger than anything he had ever experienced before. Being so close to death, he was, perhaps for the first time, really living. In the camp, one did not even consider suicide. One grasped for every moment, sucked at life like an infant, lived as if there was no future.

The guards shouted at the prisoners to form a column; it was time to march back to the barracks.

While the others milled about, Stephen and Viktor lifted the *Musselmänn* out of the gully. Everyone nearby tried to distract the guards. When the march began, Stephen and Viktor held the *Musselmänn* between them, for he could barely stand.

"Come on, dead one, carry your weight," Viktor said. "Are you so dead that you cannot hear me? Are you as dead as the rest of your family?" The *musselmänn* groaned and dragged his legs. Viktor kicked him. "You'll walk or we'll leave you here for the guards to find."

"Let him be," Stephen said.

"Are you dead or do you have a name?" Viktor continued.

"Berek," croaked the *Musselmänn*. "I am not dead."

"Then we have a fine bunk for you," Viktor said. "You can smell the stink of the sick for another night before the guards make a selection." Viktor made the gesture of smoke rising.

Stephen stared at the barracks ahead. They seemed to waver as the heat rose from the ground. He counted every step. He would drop soon, he could not go on, could not carry the *Musselmänn*.

He began to mumble in English.

"So you're speaking American again," Viktor said.

Stephen shook himself awake, placed one foot before the other.

"Dreaming of an American lover?"

"I don't know English and I have no American lover."

"Then who is this Josie you keep talking about in your sleep. . . ?"

"Why were you screaming?" Josie asks, as she washes his face with a cold washcloth.

"I don't remember screaming," Stephen says. He discovers a fever blister on his lip. Expecting to find an intravenous needle in his wrist, he raises his arm.

"You don't need an IV," Josie says. "You just have a bit of a fever. Dr. Volk has prescribed some new medication for it."

"What time is it?" Stephen stares at the whorls in the ceiling.

"Almost three P.M. I'll be going off soon."

"Then I've slept most of the day away," Stephen says, feeling something crawling inside him. He worries that his dreams still have a hold on him. "Am I having another relapse?"

"You'll do fine," Josie says.

"I should be fine now. I don't want to dream anymore."

"Did you dream again, do you remember anything?"

"I dreamed that I saved the *Musselmänn*," Stephen says.

"What was his name?" asks Josie.

"Berek, I think. Is that the man you knew?"

Josie nods and Stephen smiles at her. "Maybe that's the end of the dreams," he says, but she does not respond. He asks to see the photograph again.

"Not just now," Josie says.

"But I have to see it. I want to see if I can recognize myself. . . ."

Stephen dreamed he was dead, but it was only the fever. Viktor sat beside him on the floor and watched the others. The sick were moaning and crying; they slept on the cramped platform, as if proximity to one another could insure a few more hours of life. Wan moonlight seemed to fill the barracks.

Stephen awakened, feverish. "I'm burning up," he whispered to Viktor.

"Well," Viktor said, "you've got your *Musselmänn*. If he lives, you live. That's what you said, isn't it?"

"I don't remember, I just knew that I couldn't let him die."

"You'd better go back to sleep, you'll need your strength. Or we may have to carry *you*, tomorrow."

Stephen tried to sleep, but the fever was making lights and spots before his eyes. When he finally fell asleep, he dreamed of a dark country filled with gemstones and great quarries of ice and glass.

"What?" Stephen asked, as he sat up suddenly, awakened from damp black dreams. He looked around and saw that everyone was watching Berek, who was sitting under the window at the far end of the room.

Berek was singing the *Kol Nidre* very softly. It was the Yom Kippur prayer, which was sung on the most holy of days. He repeated the prayer three times, and then once again in a louder voice. The others responded, intoned the prayer as a recitative. Viktor was crying quietly, and Stephen imagined that the holy spirit animated Berek. Surely, he told himself, that face and those pale unseeing eyes were those of a dead man. He remembered the story of the golem, shuddered, found himself singing and pulsing with fever.

When the prayer was over, Berek fell back into his fever trance. The others became silent, then slept. But there was something new in the barracks with them tonight, a palpable exultation. Stephen looked around

at the sleepers and thought: We're surviving, more
dead than alive, but surviving. . . .

"You were right about that *Musselmänn*," Viktor
whispered. "It's good that we saved him."

"Perhaps we should sit with him," Stephen said.
"He's alone." But Viktor was already asleep; and Stephen was suddenly afraid that if he sat beside Berek,
he would be consumed by his holy fire.

As Stephen fell through sleep and dreams, his face
burned with fever.

Again he wakes up screaming.

"Josie," he says, "I can remember the dream, but
there's something else, something I can't see, something terrible. . . ."

"Not to worry," Josie says, "it's the fever." But
she looks worried, and Stephen is sure that she knows
something he does not.

"Tell me what happened to Viktor and Berek," Stephen says. He presses his hands together to stop them
from shaking.

"They lived, just as you are going to live and have
a good life."

Stephen calms down and tells her his dream.

"So you see," she says, "you're even dreaming
about surviving."

"I'm burning up."

"Dr. Volk says you're doing very well." Josie sits
beside him, and he watches the fever patterns shift
behind his closed eyelids.

"Tell me what happens next, Josie."

"You're going to get well."

"There's something else. . . ."

"Shush, now, there's nothing else." She pauses,
then says, "Mr. Gregory is supposed to visit you tonight. He's getting around a bit; he's been back and
forth all day in his wheelchair. He tells me that you
two have made some sort of a deal about dividing up
all the nurses."

Stephen smiles, opens his eyes, and says, "It was
Gregory's idea. Tell me what's wrong with him."

"All right, he has cancer, but he doesn't know it, and you must keep it a secret. They cut the nerve in his leg because the pain was so bad. He's quite comfortable now, but, remember, you can't repeat what I've told you."

"Is he going to live?" Stephen asks. "He's told me about all the new projects he's planning. So I guess he's expecting to get out of here."

"He's not going to live very long, and the doctor didn't want to break his spirit."

"I think he should be told."

"That's not your decision to make, nor mine."

"Am I going to die, Josie?"

"No!" she says, touching his arm to reassure him.

"How do I know that's the truth?"

"Because I say so, and I couldn't look you straight in the eye and tell you if it wasn't true. I should have known it would be a mistake to tell you about Mr. Gregory."

"You did right," Stephen says. "I won't mention it again. Now that I know, I feel better." He feels drowsy again.

"Do you think you're up to seeing him tonight?"

Stephen nods, although he is bone-tired. As he falls asleep, the fever patterns begin to dissolve, leaving a bright field. With a start, he opens his eyes: he has touched the edge of another dream.

"What happened to the man across the hall, the one who was always screaming?"

"He's left the ward," Josie says. "Mr. Gregory had better hurry, if he wants to play cards with you before dinner. They're going to bring the trays up soon."

"You mean he died, don't you."

"Yes, if you must know, he died. But *you're* going to live."

There is a crashing noise in the hallway. Someone shouts, and Josie runs to the door.

Stephen tries to stay awake, but he is being pulled back into the cold country.

"Mr. Gregory fell trying to get into his wheelchair by himself," Josie says. "He should have waited for his nurse, but she was out of the room and he wanted to visit you.''

But Stephen does not hear a word she says.

There were rumors that the camp was going to be liberated. It was late, but no one was asleep. The shadows in the barracks seemed larger tonight.

''It's better for us if the Allies don't come,'' Viktor said to Stephen.

''Why do you say that?''

''Haven't you noticed that the ovens are going day and night? The Nazis are in a hurry.''

''I'm going to try to sleep,'' Stephen said.

''Look around you, even the *Musselmänner* are agitated,'' Viktor said. ''Animals become nervous before the slaughter. I've worked with animals. People are not so different.''

''Shut up and let me sleep,'' Stephen said, and he dreamed that he could hear the crackling of distant gunfire.

''Attention,'' shouted the guards as they stepped into the barracks. There were more guards than usual, and each one had two Alsatian dogs. ''Come on, form a line. Hurry.''

''They're going to kill us,'' Viktor said, ''then they'll evacuate the camp and save themselves.''

The guards marched the prisoners toward the north section of the camp. Although it was still dark, it was hot and humid, without a trace of the usual morning chill. The ovens belched fire and turned the sky aglow. Everyone was quiet, for there was nothing to be done. The guards were nervous and would cut down anyone who uttered a sound, as an example for the rest.

The booming of big guns could be heard in the distance. If I'm going to die, Stephen thought, I might as well go now and take a Nazi with me. Suddenly, all of his buried fear, aggression and revulsion surfaced; his face became hot and his heart felt as if it was pumping in his throat. But Stephen argued with himself. There was always a chance. He had once heard of some women who were waiting in line for the ovens; for no apparent reason the guards sent them back to their barracks. Anything could happen. There was always a chance. But to attack a guard would mean certain death.

The guns became louder. Stephen could not be sure, but he thought the noise was coming from the west. The thought passed through his mind that everyone would be better off dead. That would stop all the guns and screaming voices, the clenched fists and wildly beating hearts. The Nazis should kill everyone, and then themselves, as a favor to humanity.

The guards stopped the prisoners in an open field surrounded on three sides by forestland. Sunrise was moments away; purple black clouds drifted across the sky, touched by gray in the east. It promised to be a hot, gritty day.

Half-Step Walter, a Judenrat sympathizer who worked for the guards, handed out shovel heads to everyone.

"He's worse than the Nazis," Viktor said to Stephen.

"The Judenrat thinks he will live," said Berek, "but he will die like a Jew with the rest of us."

"Now, when it's too late, the *Musselmänn* regains consciousness," Viktor said.

"Hurry," shouted the guards, "or you'll die now. As long as you dig, you'll live."

Stephen hunkered down on his knees and began to dig with the shovel head.

"Do you think we might escape?" Berek whined.

"Shut up and dig," Stephen said. "There is no escape, just stay alive as long as you can. Stop whining, are you becoming a *Musselmänn* again?" Stephen noticed that other prisoners were gathering up twigs and branches. So the Nazis plan to cover us up, he thought.

"That's enough," shouted a guard. "Put your shovels down in front of you and stand a line."

The prisoners stood shoulder to shoulder along the edge of the mass grave. Stephen stood between Viktor and Berek. Someone screamed and ran and was shot immediately.

I don't want to see trees or guards or my friends, Stephen thought as he stared into the sun. I only want to see the sun, let it burn out my eyes, fill up my head with light. He was shaking uncontrollably, quaking with fear.

Guns were booming in the background.

Maybe the guards won't kill us, Stephen thought, even as he heard the crack-crack of their rifles. Men were screaming and begging for life. Stephen turned his head, only to see someone's face blown away.

Screaming, tasting vomit in his mouth, Stephen fell backward, pulling Viktor and Berek into the grave with him.

Darkness, Stephen thought. His eyes were open, yet it was dark, I must be dead, this must be death. . . .

He could barely move. Corpses can't move, he thought! Something brushed against his face; he stuck out his tongue, felt something spongy. It tasted bitter. Lifting first one arm and then the other, Stephen moved some branches away. Above, he could see a few dim stars; the clouds were lit like lanterns by a quarter moon.

He touched the body beside him; it moved. That must be Viktor, he thought. "Viktor, are you alive, say something if you're alive." Stephen whispered, as if in fear of disturbing the dead.

Viktor groaned and said, "Yes, I'm alive, and so is Berek."

"And the others?"

"All dead. Can't you smell the stink? You, at least, were unconscious all day."

"They can't *all* be dead," Stephen said, then he began to cry.

"Shut up," Viktor said, touching Stephen's face to comfort him. "We're alive, that's something. They could have fired a volley into the pit."

"I thought I was dead," Berek said. He was a shadow among shadows.

"Why are we still here?" Stephen asked.

"We stayed in here because it is safe," Viktor said.

"But they're all dead," Stephen whispered, amazed that there could be speech and reason inside a grave.

"Do you think it's safe to leave now?" Berek asked Viktor.

"Perhaps. I think the killing has stopped. By now the Americans or English or whoever they are have taken over the camp. I heard gunfire and screaming. I think it's best to wait a while longer."

"Here?" asked Stephen. "Among the dead?"

"It's best to be safe."

It was late afternoon when they climbed out of the grave. The air was thick with flies. Stephen could see bodies sprawled in awkward positions beneath the coverings of twigs and branches. "How can I live when all the others are dead?" he asked himself aloud.

"You live, that's all," answered Viktor.

They kept close to the forest and worked their way back toward the camp.

"Look there," Viktor said, motioning Stephen and Berek to take cover. Stephen could see trucks moving toward the camp compound.

"Americans," whispered Berek.

"No need to whisper now," Stephen said. "We're safe."

"Guards could be hiding anywhere," Viktor said. "I haven't slept in the grave to be shot now."

They walked into the camp through a large break in the barbed-wire fence, which had been hit by an artillery shell. When they reached the compound, they found nurses, doctors, and army personnel bustling about.

"You speak English," Viktor said to Stephen, as they walked past several quonsets. "Maybe you can speak for us."

"I told you, I can't speak English."

"But I've heard you!"

"Wait," shouted an American army nurse. "You fellows are going the wrong way." She was stocky and spoke perfect German. "You must check in at the hospital; it's back that way."

"No," said Berek, shaking his head. "I won't go in there."

"There's no need to be afraid now," she said. "You're free. Come along, I'll take you to the hospital."

Something familiar about her, Stephen thought. He felt dizzy and everything turned gray.

"Josie," he murmured, as he fell to the ground.

"What is it?" Josie asks. "Everything is all right, Josie is here."

"Josie," Stephen mumbles.

"You're all right."

"How can I live when they're all dead?" he asks.

"It was a dream," she says as she wipes the sweat from his forehead. "You see, your fever has broken, you're getting well."

"Did you know about the grave?"

"It's all over now, forget the dream."

"Did you know?"

"Yes," Josie says. "Viktor told me how he survived the grave, but that was so long ago, before you were even born. Dr. Volk tells me you'll be going home soon."

"I don't want to leave, I want to stay with you."

"Stop that talk, you've got a whole life ahead of you. Soon, you'll forget all about this, and you'll forget me, too."

"Josie," Stephen asks, "let me see that old photograph again. Just one last time."

"Remember, this is the last time," she says as she hands him the faded photograph.

He recognizes Viktor and Berek, but the young man standing between them is not Stephen. "That's not me," he says, certain that he will never return to the camp.

Yet the shots still echo in his mind.

HERBERT WEST— REANIMATOR

by H. P. Lovecraft

I. *From the Dark*

Of Herbert West, who was my friend in college and in after life, I can speak only with extreme terror. This terror is not due altogether to the sinister manner of his recent disappearance, but was engendered by the whole nature of his life-work, and first gained its acute form more than seventeen years ago, when we were in the third year of our course at the Miskatonic University Medical School in Arkham. While he was with me, the wonder and diabolism of his experiments fascinated me utterly, and I was his closest companion. Now that he is gone and the spell is broken, the actual fear is greater. Memories and possibilities are ever more hideous than realities.

The first horrible incident of our acquaintance was the greatest shock I ever experienced, and it is only with reluctance that I repeat it. As I have said, it happened when we were in the medical school, where West had already made himself notorious through his wild theories on the nature of death and the possibility of overcoming it artificially. His views, which were widely ridiculed by the faculty and by his fellow-students, hinged on the essentially mechanistic nature of life; and concerned means for operating the organic machinery of mankind by calculated chemical action after the failure of natural processes. In his experiments with various animating solutions he had killed and treated immense numbers of rabbits, guinea-pigs, cats, dogs, and monkeys, till he had become the prime nuisance of the college. Several times he had actually obtained signs of life in animals supposedly dead; in many cases violent signs; but he soon saw that the perfection of his process, if indeed possible, would necessarily involve a lifetime of research. It likewise became clear that, since the same solution never worked alike on different organic species, he would require human subjects for further and more specialised progress. It was here that he first came into conflict with the college authorities, and was debarred from future experiments by no less a dignitary than the dean of the medical school himself—the learned and benevolent Dr. Allan Halsey, whose work in behalf of the stricken is recalled by every old resident of Arkham.

I had always been exceptionally tolerant of West's pursuits, and we frequently discussed his theories, whose ramifications and corollaries were almost infinite. Holding with Haeckel that all life is a chemical and physical process, and that the so-called "soul" is a myth, my friend believed that artificial reanimation of the dead can depend only on the condition of the tissues; and that unless actual decomposition has set in, a corpse fully equipped with organs may with suitable measures be set going again in the peculiar fashion known as life. That the psychic or intellectual life might be impaired by the slight deterioration of sensitive brain-cells which even a short period of death would be apt to cause, West fully realised. It had at first been his hope to find a reagent which would restore vitality before the actual advent of death, and only repeated failures on animals has shewn him that the natural and artificial life-motions were incompatible. He then sought extreme freshness in his specimens, injecting his solutions into the blood immediately after the extinction of life. It was this circumstance which made the professors so carelessly sceptical, for they felt that true death had not occurred in any case. They did not stop to view the matter closely and reasoningly.

It was not long after the faculty had interdicted his work that West confided to me his resolution to get fresh human bodies in some manner, and continue in secret the experiments he could no longer perform openly. To hear him discussing ways and means was rather ghastly, for at the college we had never procured anatomical specimens ourselves. Whenever the morgue proved inadequate, two local negroes attended to this matter, and they were seldom questioned. West was then a small, slender, spectacled youth with delicate features, yellow hair, pale blue eyes, and a soft voice, and it was uncanny to hear him dwelling on the relative merits of Christchurch Cemetery and the potter's field. We finally decided on the potter's field, because practically every body in Christchurch was embalmed; a thing of course ruinous to West's researches.

I was by this time his active and enthralled assistant, and helped him make all his decisions, not only concerning the sources of bodies but concerning a suitable place for our loathsome work. It was I who thought of the deserted Chapman farmhouse beyond Meadow Hill, where we fitted up on the ground floor an operating room and a laboratory, each with dark curtains to conceal our midnight doings. The place was far from any road, and in sight of no other house, yet precautions were none the less necessary; since rumours of strange lights, started by chance nocturnal roamers, would soon bring disaster on our enterprise. It was agreed to call the whole thing a chemical laboratory if discovery should occur. Gradually we equipped our sinister haunt of science with materials either purchased in Boston or quietly borrowed from the college—materials carefully made unrecognisable save to expert eyes—and provided spades and picks for the many burials we should have to make in the cellar. At the college we used an incinerator, but the apparatus was too costly for our unauthorised laboratory. Bodies were always a nuisance—even the small guinea-pig bodies from the slight clandestine experiments in West's room at the boarding-house.

We followed the local death-notices like ghouls, for our specimens demanded particular qualities. What we wanted were corpses interred soon after death and without artificial preservation; preferably free from malforming disease, and certainly with all organs present. Accident victims were our best hope. Not for many weeks did we hear of anything suitable; though we talked with morgue and hospital authorities, ostensibly in the college's interest, as often as we could without exciting suspicion. We found that the college had first choice in every case, so that it might be necessary to remain in Arkham during the summer, when only the limited summer-school classes were held. In the end, though, luck favoured us; for one day we heard of an almost ideal case in the potter's field; a brawny young workman drowned only the morning before in Sumner's Pond, and buried at the town's expense without delay or embalming. That afternoon we found the new grave, and determined to begin work soon after midnight.

It was a repulsive task that we undertook in the black small hours, even though we lacked at that time the special horror of graveyards which later experiences brought to us. We carried spades and oil dark lanterns, for although electric torches were then manufactured, they were not as satisfactory as the tungsten contrivances of today. The process of unearthing was slow and sordid—it might have been gruesomely poetical if we had been artists instead of scientists—and we were glad when our spades struck wood. When the pine box was fully uncovered West scrambled down and removed the lid, dragging out and propping up the contents. I reached down and hauled the contents out of the grave, and then both toiled hard to restore the spot to its former appearance. The affair made us rather nervous, especially the stiff form and vacant face of our first trophy, but we managed to remove all traces of our visit. When we had patted down the last shovelful of earth we put the specimen in a canvas sack and set out for the old Chapman place beyond Meadow Hill.

On an improvised dissecting-table in the old farm-house, by the light of a powerful acetylene lamp, the specimen was not very spectral looking. It had been a sturdy and apparently unimaginative youth of wholesome plebeian type—large-framed, grey-eyed, and brown-haired—a sound animal without psychological subtleties, and probably having vital processes of the simplest and healthiest sort. Now, with the eyes closed, it looked more asleep than dead; though the expert test of my friend soon left no doubt on that score. We had at last what West had always longed for—a real dead man of the ideal kind, ready for the solution as prepared according to the most careful calculations and theories for human use. The tension on our part became very great. We knew that there was scarcely a chance for anything like complete success, and could not avoid hideous fears at possible grotesque results of partial animation. Especially were we apprehensive concerning the mind and impulses of the creature, since in the space following death some of the more delicate cerebral cells might well have suffered deterioration. I, myself, still held some curious notions about the traditional ''soul'' of man, and felt an awe at the secrets that might be told by one returning from the dead. I wondered what sights this placid youth might have seen in inaccessible spheres, and what he could relate if fully restored to life. But my wonder was not overwhelming, since for the most part I shared the materialism of my friend. He was calmer than I as he forced a large quantity of his fluid into a vein of the body's arm, immediately binding the incision securely.

The waiting was gruesome, but West never faltered. Every now and then he applied his stethoscope to the specimen, and bore the negative results philosophically. After about three-quarters of an hour without the least sign of life he disappointedly pronounced the solution inadequate, but determined to make the most of his opportunity and try one change in the formula before disposing of his ghastly prize. We had that afternoon dug a grave in the cellar, and would have to fill it by dawn—for although we had fixed a lock on the house we wished to shun even the remotest risk of a ghoulish discovery. Besides, the body would not be even approximately fresh the next night. So taking the solitary acetylene lamp into the adjacent laboratory, we left our silent guest on the slab in the dark, and bent every energy to the mixing of a new solution; the weighing and measuring supervised by West with an almost fanatical care.

The awful event was very sudden, and wholly unexpected. I was pouring something from one test-tube to another, and West was busy over the alcohol blast-lamp which had to answer for a Bunsen burner in this gasless edifice, when from the pitch-black room we had left there burst the most appalling and daemoniac succession of cries that either of us had ever heard. Not more unutterable could have been the chaos of hellish sound if the pit itself had opened to release the agony of the damned, for in one inconceivable cacophony was centred all the supernal terror and unnatural despair of animate nature. Human it could not have been—it is not in man to make such sounds—and without a thought of our late employment or its possible discovery both West and I leaped to the nearest window like stricken animals; overturning tubes, lamp, and retorts, and vaulting madly into the starred abyss of the rural night. I think we screamed ourselves as we stumbled frantically toward the town, though as we reached the outskirts we put on a semblance of restraint—just enough to seem like belated revellers staggering home from a debauch.

We did not separate, but managed to get to West's room, where we whispered with the gas up until dawn. By then we had calmed ourselves a little with rational theories and plans for investigation, so that we could sleep through the day—classes being disregarded. But that evening two items in the paper, wholly unrelated, made it again impossible for us to sleep. The old deserted Chapman house had inexplicably burned to an amorphous heap of ashes; that we could understand because of the upset lamp. Also, an attempt had been made to disturb a new grave in the potter's field, as if by futile and spadeless clawing at the earth. That we could not understand, for we had patted down the mould very carefully.

And for seventeen years after that West would look frequently over his shoulder, and complain of fancied footsteps behind him. Now he had disappeared.

II. *The Plague-Daemon*

I shall never forget that hideous summer sixteen years ago, when like a noxious afrite from the halls of Eblis typhoid stalked leeringly through Arkham. It is by that satanic scourge that most recall the year, for truly terror brooded with bat-wings over the piles of coffins in the tombs of Christchurch Cemetery; yet for me there is a greater horror in that time—a horror known to me alone now that Herbert West has disappeared.

West and I were doing post-graduate work in summer classes at the medical school of Miskatonic University, and my friend had attained a wide notoriety because of his experiments leading toward the revivification of the dead. After the scientific slaughter of uncounted small animals the freakish work had ostensibly stopped by order of our sceptical dean, Dr. Allan Halsey; though West had continued to perform certain secret tests in his dingy boarding-house room, and had on one terrible and unforgettable occasion taken a human body from its grave in the potter's field to a deserted farmhouse beyond Meadow Hill.

I was with him on that odious occasion, and saw him inject into the still veins the elixir which he thought would to some extent restore life's chemical and physical processes. It had ended horribly—in a delirium of fear which we gradually came to attribute to our own overwrought nerves—and West had never afterward been able to shake off a maddening sensation of being haunted and hunted. The body had not been quite fresh enough; it is obvious that to restore normal mental attributes a body must be very fresh indeed; and the burning of the old house had prevented us from burying the thing. It would have been better if we could have known it was underground.

After that experience West had dropped his researches for some time; but as the zeal of the born scientist slowly returned, he again became importunate with the college faculty, pleading for the use of the dissecting-room and of fresh human specimens for the work he regarded as so overwhelmingly important. His pleas, however, were wholly in vain; for the decision of Dr. Halsey was inflexible, and the other professors all endorsed the verdict of their leader. In the radical theory of reanimation they saw nothing but the immature vagaries of a youthful enthusiast whose slight form, yellow hair, spectacled blue eyes, and soft voice gave no hint of the supernormal—almost diabolical—power of the cold brain within. I can see him now as he was then—and I shiver. He grew sterner of face, but never elderly. And now Sefton Asylum has had the mishap and West has vanished.

West clashed disagreeably with Dr. Halsey near the end of our last undergraduate term in a wordy dispute that did less credit to him than to the kindly dean in point of courtesy. He felt that he was needlessly and irrationally retarded in a supremely great work; a work which he could of course conduct to suit himself in later years, but which he wished to begin while still possessed of the exceptional facilities of the university. That the tradition-bound elders should ignore his singular results on animals, and persist in their denial of the possibility of reanimation, was inexpressibly disgusting and almost incomprehensible to a youth of West's logical temperament. Only greater maturity could help him understand the chronic mental limitations of the "professor-doctor" type—the product of generations of pathetic Puritanism; kindly, conscientious, and sometimes gentle and amiable, yet always narrow, intolerant, custom-ridden, and lacking in perspective. Age has more charity for these incomplete

yet high-souled characters, whose worst real vice is
timidity, and who are ultimately punished by general
ridicule for their intellectual sins—sins like Ptolema-
ism, Calvinism, anti-Darwinism, anti-Nietzscheism,
and every sort of Sabbatarianism and sumptuary leg-
islation. West, young despite his marvellous scientific
acquirements, had scant patience with good Dr. Halsey and his erudite colleagues; and nursed an increasing resentment, coupled with a desire to prove his
theories to these obtuse worthies in some striking and
dramatic fashion. Like most youths, he indulged in
elaborate day-dreams of revenge, triumph, and final
magnanimous forgiveness.

And then had come the scourge, grinning and lethal,
from the nightmare caverns of Tartarus. West and I
had graduated about the time of its beginning, but had
remained for additional work at the summer school,
so that we were in Arkham when it broke with full
daemoniac fury upon the town. Though not as yet li-
censed physicians, we now had our degrees, and were
pressed frantically into public service as the numbers
of the stricken grew. The situation was almost past
management, and deaths ensued too frequently for the
local undertakers fully to handle. Burials without embalming were made in rapid succession, and even the
Christchurch Cemetery receiving tomb was crammed
with coffins of the unembalmed dead. This circumstance was not without effect on West, who thought
often of the irony of the situation—so many fresh specimens, yet none for his persecuted researches! We were
frightfully overworked, and the terrific mental and
nervous strain made my friend brood morbidly.

But West's gentle enemies were no less harassed with
prostrating duties. College had all but closed, and
every doctor of the medical faculty was helping to fight
the typhoid plague. Dr. Halsey in particular had distinguished himself in sacrificing service, applying his
extreme skill with whole-hearted energy to cases which
many others shunned because of danger or apparent
hopelessness. Before a month was over the fearless
dean had become a popular hero, though he seemed

unconscious of his fame as he struggled to keep from
collapsing with physical fatigue and nervous exhaustion. West could not withhold admiration for the for-
titude of his foe, but because of this was even more
determined to prove to him the truth of his amazing
doctrines. Taking advantage of the disorganisation of
both college work and municipal health regulations,
he managed to get a recently deceased body smuggled
into the university dissecting-room one night, and in
my presence injected a new modification of his solution. The thing actually opened its eyes, but only stared
at the ceiling with a look of soul-petrifying horror before collapsing into an inertness from which nothing
could rouse it. West said it was not fresh enough—the
hot summer air does not favour corpses. That time we
were almost caught before we incinerated the thing,
and West doubted the advisability of repeating his daring misuse of the college laboratory.

The peak of the epidemic was reached in August.
West and I were almost dead, and Dr. Halsey did die
on the 14th. The students all attended the hasty funeral
on the 15th, and bought an impressive wreath, though
the latter was quite overshadowed by the tributes sent
by wealthy Arkham citizens and by the municipality
itself. It was almost a public affair, for the dean had
surely been a public benefactor. After the entombment
we were all somewhat depressed, and spent the afternoon at the bar of the Commercial House; where West,
though shaken by the death of his chief opponent,
chilled the rest of us with references to his notorious
theories. Most of the students went home, or to various duties, as the evening advanced; but West per-
suaded me to aid him in "making a night of it." West's
landlady saw us arrive at his room about two in the
morning, with a third man between us; and told her
husband that we had all evidently dined and wined
rather well.

Apparently this acidulous matron was right; for
about 3 a.m. the whole house was aroused by cries
coming from West's room, where when they broke
down the door they found the two of us unconscious

on the blood-stained carpet, beaten, scratched, and mauled, and with the broken remnants of West's bottles and instruments around us. Only an open window told what had become of our assailant, and many wondered how he himself had fared after the terrific leap from the second story to the lawn which he must have made. There were some strange garments in the room, but West upon regaining consciousness said they did not belong to the stranger, but were specimens collected for bacteriological analysis in the course of investigations on the transmission of germ diseases. He ordered them burnt as soon as possible in the capacious fireplace. To the police we both declared ignorance of our late companion's identity. He was, West nervously said, a congenial stranger whom he had met at some downtown bar of uncertain location. We had all been rather jovial, and West and I did not wish to have our pugnacious companion hunted down.

That same night saw the beginning of the second Arkham horror—the horror that to me eclipsed the plague itself. Christchurch Cemetery was the scene of a terrible killing; a watchman having been clawed to death in a manner not only too hideous for description, but raising a doubt as to the human agency of the deed. The victim had been seen alive considerably after midnight—the dawn revealed the unutterable thing. The manager of a circus at the neighbouring town of Bolton was questioned, but he swore that no beast had at any time escaped from its cage. Those who found the body noted a trail of blood leading to the receiving tomb, where a small pool of red lay on the concrete just outside the gate. A fainter trail led away toward the woods, but it soon gave out.

The next night devils danced on the roofs of Arkham, and unnatural madness howled in the wind. Through the fevered town had crept a curse which some said was greater than the plague, and which some whispered was the embodied daemon-soul of the plague itself. Eight houses were entered by a nameless thing which strewed red death in its wake—in all, seventeen maimed and shapeless remnants of bodies were left behind by the voiceless, sadistic monster that crept abroad. A few persons had half seen it in the dark, and said it was white and like a malformed ape or anthropomorphic fiend. It had not left behind quite all that it had attacked, for sometimes it had been hungry. The number it had killed was fourteen; three of the bodies had been in stricken homes and had not been alive.

On the third night frantic bands of searchers, led by the police, captured it in a house on Crane Street near the Miskatonic campus. They had organised the quest with care, keeping in touch by means of volunteer telephone stations, and when someone in the college district had reported hearing a scratching at a shuttered window, the net was quickly spread. On account of the general alarm and precautions, there were only two more victims, and the capture was effected without major casualties. The thing was finally stopped by a bullet, though not a fatal one, and was rushed to the local hospital amidst universal excitement and loathing.

For it had been a man. This much was clear despite the nauseous eyes, the voiceless simianism, and the daemoniac savagery. They dressed its wound and carted it to the asylum at Sefton, where it beat its head against the walls of a padded cell for sixteen years—until the recent mishap, when it escaped under circumstances that few like to mention. What had most disgusted the searchers of Arkham was the thing they noticed when the monster's face was cleaned—the mocking, unbelievable resemblance to a learned and self-sacrificing martyr who had been entombed but three days before—the late Dr. Allan Halsey, public benefactor and dean of the medical school of Miskatonic University.

To the vanished Herbert West and to me the disgust and horror were supreme. I shudder tonight as I think of it; shudder even more than I did that morning when West muttered through his bandages,

"Damn it, it wasn't *quite* fresh enough!"

III. *Six Shots by Moonlight*

It is uncommon to fire all six shots of a revolver with great suddenness when one would probably be sufficient, but many things in the life of Herbert West were uncommon. It is, for instance, not often that a young physician leaving college is obliged to conceal the principles which guide his selection of a home and office, yet that was the case with Herbert West. When he and I obtained our degrees at the medical school of Miskatonic University, and sought to relieve our poverty by setting up as general practitioners, we took great care not to say that we chose our house because it was fairly well isolated, and as near as possible to the potter's field.

Reticence such as this is seldom without a cause, nor indeed was ours; for our requirements were those resulting from a life-work distinctly unpopular. Outwardly we were doctors only, but beneath the surface were aims of far greater and more terrible moment— for the essence of Herbert West's existence was a quest amid black and forbidden realms of the unknown, in which he hoped to uncover the secret of life and restore to perpetual animation the graveyard's cold clay. Such a quest demands strange materials, among them fresh human bodies; and in order to keep supplied with these indispensable things one must live quietly and not far from a place of informal interment.

West and I had met in college, and I had been the only one to sympathise with his hideous experiments. Gradually I had come to be his inseparable assistant, and now that we were out of college we had to keep together. It was not easy to find a good opening for two doctors in a company, but finally the influence of the university secured us a practice in Bolton—a factory town near Arkham, the seat of the college. The Bolton Worsted Mills are the largest in the Miskatonic Valley, and their polyglot employees are never popular as patients with the local physicians. We chose our house with the greatest care, seizing at last on a rather run-down cottage near the end of Pond Street; five numbers from the closest neighbour, and separated from the local potter's field by only a stretch of meadow land, bisected by a narrow neck of the rather dense forest which lies to the north. The distance was greater than we wished, but we could get no nearer house without going on the other side of the field, wholly out of the factory district. We were not much displeased, however, since there were no people between us and our sinister source of supplies. The walk was a trifle long, but we could haul our silent specimens undisturbed.

Our practice was surprisingly large from the very first—large enough to please most young doctors, and large enough to prove a bore and a burden to students whose real interest lay elsewhere. The mill-hands were of somewhat turbulent inclinations; and besides their many natural needs, their frequent clashes and stabbing affrays gave us plenty to do. But what actually absorbed our minds was the secret laboratory we had fitted up in the cellar—the laboratory with the long table under the electric lights, where in the small hours of the morning we often injected West's various solutions into the veins of the things we dragged from the potter's field. West was experimenting madly to find something which would start man's vital motions anew after they had been stopped by the thing we call death, but had encountered the most ghastly obstacles. The solution had to be differently compounded for difference types—what would serve for guinea-pigs would not serve for human beings, and different human specimens required large modifications.

The bodies had to be exceedingly fresh, or the slight decomposition of brain tissue would render perfect reanimation impossible. Indeed, the greatest problem was to get them fresh enough—West had had horrible experiences during his secret college researches with corpses of doubtful vintage. The results of partial or imperfect animation were much more hideous than were the total failures, and we both held fearsome recollections of such things. Ever since our first daemoniac session in the deserted farmhouse on Meadow Hill in Arkham, we had felt a brooding menace; and West, though a calm, blond, blue-eyed scientific automaton in most respects, often confessed to a shuddering sensation of stealthy pursuit. He half felt that he was followed—a psychological delusion of shaken nerves, enhanced by the undeniably disturbing fact that at least one of our reanimated specimens was still alive—a frightful carnivorous thing in a padded cell at Sefton. Then there was another—our first—whose exact fate we had never learned.

We had fair luck with specimens in Bolton—much better than in Arkham. We had not been settled a week before we got an accident victim on the very night of burial, and made it open its eyes with an amazingly rational expression before the solution failed. It had lost an arm—if it had been a perfect body we might have succeeded better. Between then and the next January we secured three more; one total failure, one case of marked muscular motion, and one rather shivery thing—it rose of itself and uttered a sound. Then came a period when luck was poor; interments fell off, and those that did occur were of specimens either too diseased or too maimed for use. We kept track of all the deaths and their circumstances with systematic care.

One March night, however, we unexpectedly obtained a specimen which did not come from the potter's field. In Bolton the prevailing spirit of Puritanism had outlawed the sport of boxing—with the usual result. Surreptitious and ill-conducted bouts among the mill-workers were common, and occasionally professional talent of low grade was imported. This late winter night there had been such a match; evidently with disastrous results, since two timorous Poles had come to us with incoherently whispered entreaties to attend to a very secret and desperate case. We followed them to an abandoned barn, where the remnants of a crowd of frightened foreigners were watching a silent black form on the floor.

The match had been between Kid O'Brien—a lubberly and now quaking youth with a most un-Hibernian

hooked nose—and Buck Robinson, "The Harlem
Smoke". The negro had been knocked out, and a moment's examination shewed us that he would perma-
nently remain so. He was a loathsome, gorilla-like
thing, with abnormally long arms which I could not
help calling fore legs, and a face that conjured up
thoughts of unspeakable Congo secrets and tom-tom
poundings under an eerie moon. The body must have
looked even worse in life—but the world holds many
ugly things. Fear was upon the whole pitiful crowd,
for they did not know what the law would exact of them
if the affair were not hushed up; and they were grateful
when West, in spite of my involuntary shudders, offered to get rid of the thing quietly—for a purpose I
knew too well.

There was bright moonlight over the snowless landscape, but we dressed the thing and carried it home
between us through the deserted streets and meadows,
as we had carried a similar thing one horrible night in
Arkham. We approached the house from the field in
the rear, took the specimen in the back door and down
the cellar stairs, and prepared it for the usual experiment. Our fear of the police was absurdly great, though
we had timed our trip to avoid the solitary patrolman
of that section.

The result was wearily anticlimactic. Ghastly as our
prize appeared, it was wholly unresponsive to every
solution we injected in its black arm; solutions prepared from experience with white specimens only. So
as the hour grew dangerously near to dawn, we did as
we had done with the others—dragged the thing across
the meadows to the neck of the woods near the potter's
field, and buried it there in the best sort of grave the
frozen ground would furnish. The grave was not very
deep, but fully as good as that of the previous specimen—the thing which had risen of itself and uttered a
sound. In the light of our dark lanterns we carefully
covered it with leaves and dead vines, fairly certain
that the police would never find it in a forest so dim
and dense.

The next day I was increasingly apprehensive about

the police, for a patient brought rumours of a suspected fight and death. West had still another source of worry, for he had been called in the afternoon to a case which ended very threateningly. An Italian woman had become hysterical over her missing child—a lad of five who had strayed off early in the morning and failed to appear for dinner—and had developed symptoms highly alarming in view of an always weak heart. It was a very foolish hysteria, for the boy had often run away before; but Italian peasants are exceedingly superstitious, and this woman seemed as much harassed by omens as by facts. About seven o'clock in the evening she had died, and her frantic husband had made a frightful scene in his efforts to kill West, whom he wildly blamed for not saving her life. Friends had held him when he drew a stiletto, but West departed amidst his inhuman shrieks, curses, and oaths of vengeance. In his latest affliction the fellow seemed to have forgotten his child, who was still missing as the night advanced. There was some talk of searching the woods, but most of the family's friends were busy with the dead woman and the screaming man. Altogether, the nervous strain upon West must have been tremendous. Thoughts of the police and of the mad Italian both weighed heavily.

We retired about eleven, but I did not sleep well. Bolton had a surprisingly good police force for so small a town, and I could not help fearing the mess which would ensue if the affair of the night before were ever tracked down. It might mean the end of all our local work—and perhaps prison for both West and me. I did not like those rumours of a fight which were floating about. After the clock had struck three the moon shone in my eyes, but I turned over without rising to pull down the shade. Then came the steady rattling at the back door.

I lay still and somewhat dazed, but before long heard West's rap on my door. He was clad in dressing-gown and slippers, and had in his hands a revolver and an electric flashlight. From the revolver I knew that he was thinking more of the crazed Italian than of the police.

"We'd better both go," he whispered. "It wouldn't do not to answer it anyway, and it may be a patient—it would be like one of those fools to try the back door."

So we both went down the stairs on tiptoe, with a fear partly justified and partly that which comes only from the soul of the weird small hours. The rattling continued, growing somewhat louder. When we reached the door I cautiously unbolted it and threw it open, and as the moon streamed revealingly down on the form silhouetted there, West did a peculiar thing. Despite the obvious danger of attracting notice and bringing down on our heads the dreaded police investigation—a thing which after all was mercifully averted by the relative isolation of our cottage—my friend suddenly, excitedly, and unnecessarily emptied all six chambers of his revolver into the nocturnal visitor.

For that visitor was neither Italian nor policeman. Looming hideously against the spectral moon was a gigantic misshapen thing not to be imagined save in nightmares—a glassy-eyed, ink-black apparition nearly on all fours, covered with bits of mould, leaves, and vines, foul with caked blood, and having between its glistening teeth a snow-white, terrible, cylindrical object terminating in a tiny hand.

IV. *The Scream of the Dead*

The scream of a dead man gave to me that acute and added horror of Dr. Herbert West which harassed the latter years of our companionship. It is natural that such a thing as a dead man's scream should give horror, for it is obviously not a pleasing or ordinary occurrence; but I was used to similar experiences, hence suffered on this occasion only because of a particular circumstance. And, as I have implied, it was not of the dead man himself that I became afraid.

Herbert West, whose associate and assistant I was, possessed scientific interests far beyond the usual routine of a village physician. That was why, when establishing his practice in Bolton, he had chosen an isolated house near the potter's field. Briefly and brutally stated, West's sole absorbing interest was a secret study of the phenomena of life and its cessation, leading toward the reanimation of the dead through injections of an excitant solution. For this ghastly experimenting it was necessary to have a constant supply of very fresh human bodies; very fresh because even the least decay hopelessly damaged the brain structure, and human because we found that the solution had to be compounded differently for different types of organisms. Scores of rabbits and guinea-pigs had been killed and treated, but their trail was a blind one. West had never fully succeeded because he had never been able to secure a corpse sufficiently fresh. What he wanted were bodies from which vitality had only just departed; bodies with every cell intact and capable of receiving again the impulse toward that mode of motion called life. There was hope that this second and artificial life might be made perpetual by repetitions of the injection, but we had learned that an ordinary natural life would not respond to the action. To establish the artificial motion, natural life must be extinct—the specimens must be very fresh, but genuinely dead.

The awesome quest had begun when West and I were students at the Miskatonic University Medical School in Arkham, vividly conscious for the first time of the thoroughly mechanical nature of life. That was seven years before, but West looked scarcely a day older now—he was small, blond, clean-shaven, soft-voiced, and spectacled, with only an occasional flash of a cold blue eye to tell of the hardening and growing fanaticism of his character under the pressure of his terrible investigations. Our experiences had often been hideous in the extreme; the results of defective reanimation, when lumps of graveyard clay had been galvanised into morbid, unnatural, and brainless motion by various modifications of the vital solution.

One thing had uttered a nerve-shattering scream; another had risen violently, beaten us both to unconsciousness, and run amuck in a shocking way before it could be placed behind asylum bars; still another, a loathsome African monstrosity, had clawed out of its shallow grave and done a deed—West had had to shoot that object. We could not get bodies fresh enough to shew any trace of reason when reanimated, so had perforce created nameless horrors. It was disturbing to think that one, perhaps two, of our monsters still lived—that thought haunted us shadowingly, till finally West disappeared under frightful circumstances. But at the time of the scream in the cellar laboratory of the isolated Bolton cottage, our fears were subordinate to our anxiety for extremely fresh specimens. West was more avid than I, so that it almost seemed to me that he looked half-covetously at any very healthy living physique.

It was in July, 1910, that the bad luck regarding specimens began to turn. I had been on a long visit to my parents in Illinois, and upon my return found West in a state of singular elation. He had, he told me excitedly, in all likelihood solved the problem of freshness through an approach from an entirely new angle—that of artificial preservation. I had known that he was working on a new and highly unusual embalming compound, and was not surprised that it had turned out well; but until he explained the details I was rather puzzled as to how such a compound could help in our work, since the objectionable staleness of the specimens was largely due to delay occurring before we secured them. This, I now saw, West had clearly recognised; creating his embalming compound for future rather than immediate use, and trusting to fate to supply again some very recent and unburied corpse, as it had years before when we obtained the negro killed in the Bolton prize-fight. At last fate had been kind, so that on this occasion there lay in the secret cellar laboratory a corpse whose decay could not by any possibility have begun. What would happen on reanimation, and whether we could hope for a revival of mind and reason, West did not venture to predict. The experiment would be a landmark in our studies, and he had saved the new body for my return, so that both might share the spectacle in accustomed fashion.

West told me how he had obtained the specimen. It had been a vigorous man; a well-dressed stranger just off the train on his way to transact some business with the Bolton Worsted Mills. The walk through the town had been long, and by the time the traveller paused at our cottage to ask the way to the factories his heart had become greatly overtaxed. He had refused a stimulant, and had suddenly dropped dead only a moment later. The body, as might be expected, seemed to West a heaven-sent gift. In his brief conversation the stranger had made it clear that he was unknown in Bolton, and a search of his pockets subsequently revealed to him to be one Robert Leavitt of St. Louis, apparently without a family to make instant inquiries about his disappearance. If this man could not be restored to life, no one would know of our experiment. We buried our materials in a dense strip of woods between the house and the potter's field. If, on the other hand, he could be restored, our fame would be brilliantly and perpetually established. So without delay West had injected into the body's wrist the compound which would hold it fresh for use after my arrival. The matter of the presumably weak heart, which to my mind imperilled the success of our experiment, did not appear to trouble West extensively. He hoped at last to obtain what he had never obtained before—a rekindled spark of reason and perhaps a normal, living creature.

So on the night of July 18, 1910, Herbert West and I stood in the cellar laboratory and gazed at a white, silent figure beneath the dazzling arc-light. The embalming compound had worked uncannily well, for as I stared fascinatedly at the sturdy frame which had lain two weeks without stiffening I was moved to seek West's assurance that the thing was really dead. This assurance he gave readily enough; reminding me that the reanimating solution was never used without careful tests as to life; since it could have no effect if any of the original vitality were present. As West proceeded to take preliminary steps, I was impressed by the vast intricacy of the new experiment; an intricacy so vast that he could trust no hand less delicate than his own. Forbidding me to touch the body, he first injected a drug in the wrist just beside the place his needle had punctured when injecting the embalming compound. This, he said, was to neutralise the compound and release the system to a normal relaxation so that the reanimating solution might freely work when injected. Slightly later, when a change and a gentle tremor seemed to affect the dead limbs, West stuffed a pillow-like object violently over the twitching face, not withdrawing it until the corpse appeared quiet and ready for our attempt at reanimation. The pale enthusiast now applied some last perfunctory tests for absolute lifelessness, withdrew satisfied, and finally injected into the left arm an accurately measured amount of the vital elixir, prepared during the afternoon with a greater care than we had used since college days, when our feats were new and groping. I cannot express the wild, breathless suspense with which we waited for results on this first really fresh specimen—the first we could reasonably expect to open its lips in rational speech, perhaps to tell of what it had seen beyond the unfathomable abyss.

West was a materialist, believing in no soul and attributing all the working of consciousness to bodily phenomena; consequently he looked for no revelation of hideous secrets from gulfs and caverns beyond death's barrier. I did not wholly disagree with him theoretically, yet held vague instinctive remnants of the primitive faith of my forefathers; so that I could not help eyeing the corpse with a certain amount of awe and terrible expectation. Besides—I could not extract from my memory that hideous, inhuman shriek we heard on the night we tried our first experiment in the deserted farmhouse at Arkham.

Very little time had elapsed before I saw the attempt was not to be a total failure. A touch of colour came to cheeks hitherto chalk-white, and spread out under the curiously ample stubble of sandy beard. West, who had his hand on the pulse of the left wrist, suddenly nodded significantly; and almost simultaneously a mist appeared on the mirror inclined above the body's mouth. There followed a few spasmodic muscular motions, and then an audible breathing and visible motion of the chest. I looked at the closed eyelids, and thought I detected a quivering. Then the lids opened, showing eyes which were grey, calm, and alive, but still unintelligent and not even curious.

In a moment of fantastic whim I whispered questions to the reddening ears; questions of other worlds of which the memory might still be present. Subsequent terror drove them from my mind, but I think the last one, which I repeated, was: "Where have you been?" I do not yet know whether I was answered or not, for no sound came from the well-shaped mouth; but I do know that at that moment I firmly thought the thin lips moved silently, forming syllables which I would have vocalised as "only now" if that phrase had possessed any sense or relevancy. At that moment, as I say, I was elated with the conviction that the one great goal had been attained; and that for the first time a reanimated corpse had uttered distinct words impelled by actual reason. In the next moment there was no doubt about the triumph; no doubt that the solution had truly accomplished, at least temporarily, its full mission of restoring rational and articulate life to the dead. But in that triumph there came to me the greatest of all horrors—not horror of the thing that spoke, but of the deed that I had witnessed and of the man with whom my professional fortunes were joined.

For that very fresh body, at last writhing into full and terrifying consciousness with eyes dilated at the memory of its last scene on earth, threw out its frantic hands in a life and death struggle with the air; and suddenly collapsing into a second and final dissolution from which there could be no return, screamed out the cry that will ring eternally in my aching brain:

"Help! Keep off, you cursed little tow-head fiend—keep that damned needle away from me!"

V. *The Horror from the Shadows*

Many men have related hideous things, not mentioned in print, which happened on the battlefields of the Great War. Some of these things have made me faint, others have convulsed me with devastating nausea, while still others have made me tremble and look behind me in the dark; yet despite the worst of them I believe I can myself relate the most hideous thing of all—the shocking, the unnatural, the unbelievable horror from the shadows.

In 1915 I was a physician with the rank of First Lieutenant in a Canadian regiment in Flanders, one of many Americans to precede the government itself into the gigantic struggle. I had not entered the army on my own initiative, but rather as a natural result of the enlistment of the man whose indispensable assistant I was—the celebrated Boston surgical specialist, Dr. Herbert West. Dr. West had been avid for a chance to serve as surgeon in a great war, and when the chance had come he carried me with him almost against my will. There were reasons why I would have been glad to let the war separate us; reasons why I found the practice of medicine and the companionship of West more and more irritating; but when he had gone to Ottawa and through a colleague's influence secured a medical commission as Major, I could not resist the imperious persuasion of one determined that I should accompany him in my usual capacity.

When I say that Dr. West was avid to serve in battle, I do not mean to imply that he was either naturally warlike or anxious for the safety of civilisation. Always an ice-cold intellectual machine; slight, blond, blue-eyed, and spectacled; I think he secretly sneered at my occasional martial enthusiasms and censures of supine neutrality. There was, however, something he wanted in embattled Flanders; and in order to secure it he had to assume a military exterior. What he wanted was not a thing which many persons want, but something connected with the peculiar branch of medical science which he had chosen quite clandestinely to follow, and in which he had achieved amazing and occasionally hideous results. It was, in fact, nothing more or less than an abundant supply of freshly killed men in every stage of dismemberment.

Herbert West needed fresh bodies because his life-work was the reanimation of the dead. This work was not known to the fashionable clientele who had so swiftly built up his fame after his arrival in Boston; but was only too well known to me, who had been his closest friend and sole assistant since the old days in Miskatonic University Medical School at Arkham. It was in those college days that he had begun his terrible experiments, first on small animals and then on human bodies shockingly obtained. There was a solution which he injected into the veins of dead things, and if they were fresh enough they responded in strange ways. He had had much trouble in discovering the proper formula, for each type of organism was found to need a stimulus especially adapted to it. Terror stalked him when he reflected on his partial failures; nameless things resulting from imperfect solutions or from bodies insufficiently fresh. A certain number of these failures had remained alive—one was in an asylum while others had vanished—and as he thought of conceivable yet virtually impossible eventualities he often shivered beneath his usual stolidity.

West had soon learned that absolute freshness was the prime requisite for useful specimens, and had accordingly resorted to frightful and unnatural expedients in body-snatching. In college, and during our early practice together in the factory town of Bolton, my attitude toward him had been largely one of fascinated admiration; but as his boldness in methods grew, I began to develop a gnawing fear, I did not like the way he looked at healthy living bodies; and then there came a nightmarish session in the cellar laboratory when I learned that a certain specimen had been a living body when he secured it. That was the first time he had ever been able to revive the quality of rational thought in a corpse, and his success, obtained at such a loathsome cost, had completely hardened him.

Of his methods in the intervening five years I dare not speak. I was held to him by sheer force of fear, and witnessed sights that no human tongue could repeat. Gradually I came to find Herbert West himself more horrible than anything he did—that was when it dawned on me that his once normal scientific zeal for prolonging life had subtly degenerated into a mere morbid and ghoulish curiosity and secret sense of charnel picturesqueness. His interest became a hellish and perverse addiction to the repellently and fiendishly abnormal; he gloated calmly over artificial monstrosities which would make most healthy men drop dead from fright and disgust; he became, behind his pallid intellectuality, a fastidious Baudelaire of physical experiment—a languid Elagabalus of the tombs.

Dangers he met unflinchingly; crimes he committed unmoved. I think the climax came when he had proved his point that rational life can be restored, and had sought new worlds to conquer by experimenting on the reanimation of detached parts of bodies. He had wild and original ideas on the independent vital properties of organic cells and nerve-tissue separated from natural physiological systems; and achieved some hideous preliminary results in the form of never-dying, artificially nourished tissue obtained from the nearly hatched eggs of an indescribable tropical reptile. Two biological points he was exceedingly anxious to settle—first, whether any amount of consciousness and rational action could be possible without the brain, proceeding from the spinal cord and various nerve-centres; and second, whether any kind of ethereal, intangible relation distinct from the material cells may exist to link the surgically separated parts of what has previously been a single living organism. All this research work required a prodigious supply of freshly slaughtered human flesh—and that was why Herbert West had entered the Great War.

The phantasmal, unmentionable thing occurred one midnight late in March, 1915, in a field hospital be-

hind the lines at St. Eloi. I wonder even now if it could
have been other than a daemoniac dream of delirium.
West had a private laboratory in an east room of the
barn-like temporary edifice, assigned him on his plea
that he was devising new and radical methods for the
treatment of hitherto hopeless cases of maiming. There
he worked like a butcher in the midst of his gory
wares—I could never get used to the levity with which
he handled and classified certain things. At times he
actually did perform marvels of surgery for the soldiers; but his chief delights were of a less public and
philanthropic kind, requiring many explanations of
sounds which seemed peculiar even amidst that babel
of the damned. Among these sounds were frequent
revolver-shots—surely not uncommon on a battlefield,
but distinctly uncommon in an hospital. Dr. West's
reanimated specimens were not meant for long existence or a large audience. Besides human tissue, West
employed much of the reptile embryo tissue which he
had cultivated with such singular results. It was better
than human material for maintaining life in organless
fragments, and that was now my friend's chief activity.
In a dark corner of the laboratory, over a queer incu-
bating burner, he kept a large covered vat full of this
reptilian cell-matter; which multiplied and grew puff-
ily and hideously.

On the night of which I speak we had a splendid
new specimen—a man at once physically powerful and
of such high mentality that a sensitive nervous system
was assured. It was rather ironic, for he was the officer
who had helped West to his commission, and who was
now to have been our associate. Moreover, he had in
the past secretly studied the theory of reanimation to
some extent under West. Major Sir Eric Moreland
Clapham-Lee, D.S.O., was the greatest surgeon in our
division, and had been hastily assigned to the St. Eloi
sector when news of the heavy fighting reached head-
quarters. He had come in an aëroplane piloted by the
intrepid Lieut. Ronald Hill, only to be shot down when
directly over his destination. The fall had been spec-
tacular and awful; Hill was unrecognisable afterward,

but the wreck yielded up the great surgeon in a nearly decapitated but otherwise intact condition. West had greedily seized the lifeless thing which had once been his friend and fellow-scholar; and I shuddered when he finished severing the head, placed it in his hellish vat of pulpy reptile-tissue to preserve it for future experiments, and proceeded to treat the decapitated body on the operating table. He injected new blood, joined certain veins, arteries, and nerves at the headless neck, and closed the ghastly aperture with engrafted skin from an unidentified specimen which had borne an officer's uniform. I knew what he wanted—to see if this highly organised body could exhibit, without its head, any of the signs of mental life which had distinguished Sir Eric Moreland Clapham-Lee. Once a student of reanimation, this silent trunk was now gruesomely called upon to exemplify it.

I can still see Herbert West under the sinister electric light as he injected his reanimating solution into the arm of the headless body. The scene I cannot describe—I should faint if I tried it, for there is madness in a room full of classified charnel things, with blood and lesser human debris almost ankle-deep on the slimy floor, and with hideous reptilian abnormalities sprouting, bubbling, and baking over a winking bluish-green spectre of dim flame in a far corner of black shadows.

The specimen, as West repeatedly observed, had a splendid nervous system. Much was expected of it; and as a few twitching motions began to appear, I could see the feverish interest on West's face. He was ready, I think, to see proof of his increasingly strong opinion that consciousness, reason, and personality can exist independently of the brain—that man has no central connective spirit, but is merely a machine of nervous matter, each section more or less complete in itself. In one triumphant demonstration West was about to relegate the mystery of life to the category of myth. The body now twitched more vigorously, and beneath our avid eyes commenced to heave in a frightful way. The arms stirred disquietingly, the legs drew up, and various muscles contracted in a repulsive kind of writhing. Then the headless thing threw out its arms in a gesture which was unmistakably one of desperation—an intelligent desperation apparently sufficient to prove every theory of Herbert West. Certainly, the nerves were recalling the man's last act in life; the struggle to get free of the falling aëroplane.

What followed, I shall never positively know. It may have been wholly an hallucination from the shock caused at that instant by the sudden and complete destruction of the building in a cataclysm of German shell-fire—who can gainsay it, since West and I were the only proved survivors? West liked to think that before his recent disappearance, but there were times when he could not; for it was queer that we both had the same hallucination. The hideous occurrence itself was very simple, notable only for what it implied.

The body on the table had risen with a blind and terrible groping, and we had heard a sound. I should not call that sound a voice, for it was too awful. And yet its timbre was not the most awful thing about it. Neither was its message—it had merely screamed, "Jump, Ronald, for God's sake, jump!" The awful thing was its source.

For it had come from the large covered vat in that ghoulish corner of crawling black shadows.

VI. *The Tomb-Legions*

When Dr. Herbert West disappeared a year ago, the Boston police questioned me closely. They suspected that I was holding something back, and perhaps suspected graver things; but I could not tell them the truth because they would not have believed it. They knew, indeed, that West had been connected with activities beyond the credence of ordinary men; for his hideous experiments in the reanimation of dead bodies had long been too extensive to admit of perfect secrecy; but the final soul-shattering catastrophe held elements of daemoniac phantasy which make even me doubt the reality of what I saw.

I was West's closest friend and only confidential assistant. We had met years before, in medical school, and from the first I had shared his terrible researches. He had slowly tried to perfect a solution which, injected into the veins of the newly deceased, would restore life; a labour demanding an abundance of fresh corpses and therefore involving the most unnatural actions. Still more shocking were the products of some of the experiments—grisly masses of flesh that had been dead, but that West waked to a blind, brainless, nauseous animation. These were the usual results, for in order to reawaken the mind it was necessary to have specimens so absolutely fresh that no decay could possibly affect the delicate brain-cells.

This need for very fresh corpses had been West's moral undoing. They were hard to get, and one awful day he had secured his specimen while it was still alive and vigorous. A struggle, a needle, and a powerful alkaloid had transformed it to a very fresh corpse, and the experiment had succeeded for a brief and memorable moment; but West had emerged with a soul calloused and seared, and a hardened eye which sometimes glanced with a kind of hideous and calculating appraisal at men of especially sensitive brain and especially vigorous physique. Toward the last I became acutely afraid of West, for he began to look at me that way. People did not seem to notice his glances, but they noticed my fear; and after his disappearance used that as a basis for some absurd suspicions.

West, in reality, was more afraid than I; for his abominable pursuits entailed a life of furtiveness and dread of every shadow. Partly it was the police he feared; but sometimes his nervousness was deeper and more nebulous, touching on certain indescribable things into which he had injected a morbid life, and from which he had not seen that life depart. He usually finished his experiments with a revolver, but a few times he had not been quick enough. There was that first specimen on whose rifled grave marks of clawing were later seen. There was also that Arkham professor's body which had done cannibal things before it had been captured and thrust unidentified into a madhouse cell at Sefton, where it beat the walls for sixteen years. Most of the other possibly surviving results were things less easy to speak of—for in later years West's scientific zeal had degenerated to an unhealthy and fantastic mania, and he had spent his chief skill in vitalising not entire human bodies but isolated parts of bodies, or parts joined to organic matter other than human. It had become fiendishly disgusting by the time he disappeared; many of the experiments could not even be hinted at in print. The Great War, through which both of us served as surgeons, had intensified this side of West.

In saying that West's fear of his specimens was nebulous, I have in mind particularly its complex nature. Part of it came merely from knowing of the existence of such nameless monsters, while another part arose from apprehension of the bodily harm they might under certain circumstances do him. Their disappearance added horror to the situation—of them all West knew the whereabouts of only one, the pitiful asylum thing. Then there was a more subtle fear—a very fantastic sensation resulting from a curious experiment in the Canadian army in 1915. West, in the midst of a severe battle, had reanimated Major Sir Eric Moreland Clapham-Lee, D.S.O., a fellow-physician who knew about his experiments and could have duplicated them. The head had been removed, so that the possibilities of quasi-intelligent life in the trunk might be investigated. Just as the building was wiped out by a German shell, there had been a success. The trunk had moved intelligently; and, unbelievable to relate, we were both sickeningly sure that articulate sounds had come from the detached head as it lay in a shadowy corner of the laboratory. The shell had been merciful, in a way—but West could never feel as certain as he wished, that we two were the only survivors. He used to make shuddering conjectures about the possible actions of a headless physician with the power of reanimating the dead.

West's last quarters were in a venerable house of

much elegance, overlooking one of the oldest burying-grounds in Boston. He had chosen the place for purely symbolic and fantastically aesthetic reasons, since most of the interments were of the colonial period and therefore of little use to a scientist seeking very fresh bodies. The laboratory was in a sub-cellar secretly constructed by imported workmen, and contained a huge incinerator for the quiet and complete disposal of such bodies, or fragments and synthetic mockeries of bodies, as might remain from the morbid experiments and unhallowed amusements of the owner. During the excavation of this cellar the workmen had struck some exceedingly ancient masonry; undoubtedly connected with the old burying-ground, yet far too deep to correspond with any known sepulchre therein. After a number of calculations West decided that it represented some secret chamber beneath the tomb of the Averills, where the last interment had been made in 1768. I was with him when he studied the nitrous, dripping walls laid bare by the spades and mattocks of the men, and was prepared for the gruesome thrill which would attend the uncovering of centuried grave-secrets; but for the first time West's new timidity conquered his natural curiosity, and he betrayed his degenerating fibre by ordering the masonry left intact and plastered over. Thus it remained till that final hellish night; part of the walls of the secret laboratory. I speak of West's decadence, but must add that it was a purely mental and intangible thing. Outwardly he was the same to the last—calm, cold, slight, and yellow-haired, with spectacled blue eyes and a general aspect of youth which years and fears seemed never to change. He seemed calm even when he thought of that clawed grave and looked over his shoulder; even when he thought of the carnivorous thing that gnawed and pawed at Sefton bars.

The end of Herbert West began one evening in our joint study when he was dividing his curious glance between the newspaper and me. A strange headline item had struck at him from the crumpled pages, and a nameless titan claw had seemed to reach down through sixteen years. Something fearsome and incredible had happened at Sefton Asylum fifty miles away, stunning the neighbourhood and baffling the police. In the small hours of the morning a body of silent men had entered the grounds and their leader had aroused the attendants. He was a menacing military figure who talked without moving his lips and whose voice seemed almost ventriloquially connected with an immense black case he carried. His expressionless face was handsome to the point of radiant beauty, but had shocked the superintendent when the hall light fell on it—for it was a wax face with eyes of painted glass. Some nameless accident had befallen this man. A larger man guided his steps; a repellent hulk whose bluish face seemed half eaten away by some unknown malady. The speaker had asked for the custody of the cannibal monster committed from Arkham sixteen years before; and upon being refused, gave a signal which precipitated a shocking riot. The fiends had beaten, trampled, and bitten ever attendant who did not flee; killing four and finally succeeding in the liberation of the monster. Those victims who could recall the event without hysteria swore that the creatures had acted less like men than like unthinkable automata guided by the wax-faced leader. By the time help could be summoned, every trace of the men and of their mad charge had vanished.

From the hour of reading this item until midnight, West sat almost paralyzed. At midnight the doorbell rang, startling him fearfully. All the servants were asleep in the attic, so I answered the bell. As I have told the police, there was no wagon in the street; but only a group of strange-looking figures bearing a large square box which they deposited in the hallway after one of them had grunted in a highly unnatural voice, ''Express—prepaid.'' They filed out of the house with a jerky tread, and as I watched them go I had an odd idea that they were turning toward the ancient cemetery on which the back of the house abutted. When I slammed the door after them West came downstairs and looked at the box. It was about two feet square, and bore West's correct name and present address. It also bore the inscription, "From Eric Moreland Clapham-Lee, St. Eloi, Flanders." Six years before, in Flanders, a shelled hospital had fallen upon the headless reanimated trunk of Dr. Clapham-Lee, and upon the detached head which—perhaps—had uttered articulate sounds.

West was not even excited now. His condition was more ghastly. Quickly he said, "It's the finish—but let's incinerate—this." We carried the thing down to the laboratory—listening. I do not remember many particulars—you can imagine my state of mind—but it is a vicious lie to say it was Herbert West's body which I put into the incinerator. We both inserted the whole unopened wooden box, closed the door, and started the electricity. Nor did any sound come from the box, after all.

It was West who first noticed the falling plaster on that part of the wall where the ancient tomb masonry had been covered up. I was going to run, but he stopped me. Then I saw a small black aperture, felt a ghoulish wind of ice, and smelled the charnel bowels of a putrescent earth. There was no sound, but just then the electric lights went out and I saw outlined against some phosphorescence of the nether world a horde of silent toiling things which only insanity—or worse—could create. Their outlines were human, semi-human, fractionally human, and not human at all—the horde was grotesquely heterogeneous. They were removing the stones quietly, one by one, from the centuried wall. And then, as the breach became large enough, they came out into the laboratory in single file; led by a stalking thing with a beautiful head made of wax. A sort of mad-eyed monstrosity behind the leader seized on Herbert West. West did not resist or utter a sound. Then they all sprang at him and tore him to pieces before my eyes, bearing the fragments away into that subterranean vault of fabulous abominations. West's head was carried off by the wax-headed leader, who wore a Canadian officer's uniform. As it disappeared I saw that the blue eyes behind the spectacles were hideously blazing with their first touch of frantic, visible emotion.

Servants found me unconscious in the morning. West was gone. The incinerator contained only unidentifiable ashes. Detectives have questioned me, but what can I say? The Sefton tragedy they will not connect with West; not that, nor the men with the box, whose existence they deny. I told them of the vault, and they pointed to the unbroken plaster wall and laughed. So I told them no more. They imply that I am either a madman or a murderer—probably I am mad. But I might not be mad if those accursed tomb-legions had not been so silent.

THE LITTLE BLACK BAG

by C. M. Kornbluth

Old Dr. Full felt the winter in his bones as he limped down the alley. It was the alley and the back door he had chosen rather than the sidewalk and the front door because of the brown paper bag under his arm. He knew perfectly well that the flat-faced, stringy-haired women of his street and their gap-toothed, sour-smelling husbands did not notice if he brought a bottle of cheap wine to his room. They all but lived on the stuff themselves, varied with whiskey when pay checks were boosted by overtime. But Dr. Full, unlike them, was ashamed. A complicated disaster occurred as he limped down the littered alley. One of the neighborhood dogs—a mean little black one he knew and hated, with its teeth always bared and always snarling with menace—hurled at his legs through a hole in the board fence that lined his path. Dr. Full flinched, then swung his leg in what was to have been a satisfying kick to the animal's gaunt ribs. But the winter in his bones weighed down the leg. His foot failed to clear a half-buried brick, and he sat down abruptly, cursing. When he smelled unbottled wine and realized his brown paper package had slipped from under his arm and smashed, his curses died on his lips. The snarling black dog was circling him at a yard's distance, tensely stalking, but he ignored it in the greater disaster.

With stiff fingers as he sat on the filth of the alley, Dr. Full unfolded the brown paper bag's top, which had been crimped over, grocer-wise. The early autumnal dusk had come; he could not see plainly what was left. He lifted out the jug-handled top of his half gallon, and some fragments, and then the bottom of the bottle. Dr. Full was far too occupied to exult as he noted that there was a good pint left. He had a problem, and emotions could be deferred until the fitting time.

The dog closed in, its snarl rising in pitch. He set down the bottom of the bottle and pelted the dog with the curved triangular glass fragments of its top. One of them connected, and the dog ducked back through the fence, howling. Dr. Full then placed a razor-like edge of the half-gallon bottle's foundation to his lips and drank from it as though it were a giant's cup. Twice he had to put it down to rest his arms, but in one minute he had swallowed the pint of wine.

He thought of rising to his feet and walking through the alley to his room, but a flood of well-being drowned the notion. It was, after all, inexpressibly pleasant to sit there and feel the frost-hardened mud of the alley turn soft, or seem to, and to feel the winter evaporating from his bones under a warmth which spread from his stomach through his limbs.

A three-year-old girl in a cut-down winter coat squeezed through the same hole in the board fence from which the black dog had sprung its ambush. Gravely she toddled up to Dr. Full and inspected him with her dirty forefinger in her mouth. Dr. Full's happiness had been providentially made complete; he had been supplied with an audience.

"Ah, my dear," he said hoarsely. And then: "Preposterous accusation. 'If that's what you call evidence,' I should have told them, 'you better stick to your doctoring.' I should have told them: 'I was here before your County Medical Society. And the License Commissioner never proved a thing on me. So, gennulmen, doesn't it stand to reason? I appeal to you as fellow memmers of a great profession—' "

The little girl, bored, moved away, picking up one of the triangular pieces of glass to play with as she left. Dr. Full forgot her immediately, and continued to himself earnestly: "But so help me, they *couldn't* prove a thing. Hasn't a man got any *rights?*'' He brooded over the question, of whose answer he was so sure, but on which the Committee on Ethics of the County Medical Society had been equally certain. The winter was creeping into his bones again, and he had no money and no more wine.

Dr. Full pretended to himself that there was a bottle of whiskey somewhere in the fearful litter of his room. It was an old and cruel trick he played on himself when he simply had to be galvanized into getting up and going home. He might freeze there in the alley. In his room he would be bitten by bugs and would cough at the moldy reek from his sink, but he would not freeze and be cheated of the hundreds of bottles of wine that he still might drink, the thousands of hours of glowing content he still might feel. He thought about that bottle of whiskey—was it back of a mounded heap of medical journals? No; he had looked there last time. Was it under the sink, shoved well to the rear, behind the rusty drain? The cruel trick began to play itself out again. Yes, he told himself with mounting excitement, yes, it might be! Your memory isn't so good nowadays, he told himself with rueful good fellowship. You know perfectly well you might have bought a bottle of whiskey and shoved it behind the sink drain for a moment just like this.

The amber bottle, the crisp snap of the sealing as he cut it, the pleasurable exertion of starting the screw cap on its threads, and then the refreshing tangs in his throat, the warmth in his stomach, the dark, dull happy oblivion of drunkenness—they became real to him. You *could* have, you know! You *could* have! he told himself. With the blessed conviction growing in his mind—It *could* have happened, you know! It *could* have!—he struggled to his right knee. As he did, he heard a yelp behind him, and curiously craned his neck around while resting. It was the little girl, who had cut her hand quite badly on her toy, the piece of glass. Dr. Full could see the rilling bright blood down her coat, pooling at her feet.

He almost felt inclined to defer the image of the

amber bottle for her, but not seriously. He knew that it was there, shoved well to the rear under the sink, behind the rusty drain where he had hidden it. He would have a drink and then magnanimously return to help the child. Dr. Full got to his other knee and then his feet, and proceeded at a rapid totter down the littered alley toward his room, where he would hunt with calm optimism at first for the bottle that was not there, then with anxiety, and then with frantic violence. He would hurl books and dishes about before he was done looking for the amber bottle of whiskey, and finally would beat his swollen knuckles against the brick wall until old scars on them opened and his thick old blood oozed over his hands. Last of all, he would sit down somewhere on the floor, whimpering, and would plunge into the abyss of purgative nightmare that was his sleep.

After twenty generations of shilly-shallying and "we'll cross that bridge when we come to it," genus homo had bred himself into an impasse. Dogged biometricians had pointed out with irrefutable logic that mental subnormals were outbreeding mental normals and supernormals, and that the process was occurring on an exponential curve. Every fact that could be mustered in the argument proved the biometricians' case, and led inevitably to the conclusion that genus homo was going to wind up in a preposterous jam quite soon. If you think that had any effect on breeding practices, you do not know genus homo.

There was, of course, a sort of masking effect produced by that other exponential function, the accumulation of technological devices. A moron trained to punch an adding machine seems to be a more skillful computer than a medieval mathematician trained to count on his fingers. A moron trained to operate the twenty-first century equivalent of a linotype seems to be a better typographer than a Renaissance printer limited to a few fonts of movable type. This is also true of medical practice.

It was a complicated affair of many factors. The supernormals "improved the product" at greater speed than the subnormals degraded it, but in smaller quantity because elaborate training of their children was practiced on a custom-made basis. The fetish of higher education had some weird avatars by the twentieth generation: "colleges" where not a member of the student body could read words of three syllables; "universities" where such degrees as "Bachelor of Typewriting," "Master of Shorthand" and "Doctor of Philosophy (Card Filing)" were conferred with the traditional pomp. The handful of supernormals used such devices in order that the vast majority might keep some semblance of a social order going.

Some day the supernormals would mercilessly cross the bridge; at the twentieth generation they were standing irresolutely at its approaches wondering what had hit them. And the ghosts of twenty generations of biometricians chuckled malignantly.

It is a certain Doctor of Medicine of this twentieth generation that we are concerned with. His name was Hemingway—John Hemingway, B.Sc., M.D. He was a general practitioner, and did not hold with running to specialists with every trifling ailment. He often said as much, in approximately these words: "Now, uh, what I mean is you got a good old G.P. See what I mean? Well, uh, now a good old G.P. don't claim he knows all about lungs and glands and them things, get me? But you got a G.P., you got, uh, you got a, well, you got a . . . *all-around man!* That's what you got when you got a G.P.—you got a all-around man."

But from this, do not imagine that Dr. Hemingway was a poor doctor. He could remove tonsils or appendixes, assist at practically any confinement and delivery a living, uninjured infant, correctly diagnose hundreds of ailments, and prescribe and administer the correct medication or treatment for each. There was, in fact, only one thing he could not do in the medical line, and that was violate the ancient canons of medical ethics. And Dr. Hemingway knew better than to try.

Dr. Hemingway and a few friends were chatting one evening when the event occurred that precipitates him into our story. He had been through a hard day at the clinic, and he wished his physicist friend Walter Gillis, B.Sc., M.Sc., Ph.D., would shut up so he could tell everybody about it. But Gillis kept rambling on, in his stilted fashion: "You got to hand it to old Mike; he don't have what we call the scientific method, but you got to hand it to him. There this poor little dope is, puttering around with some glassware and I come up and I ask him, kidding of course, 'How's about a time-travel machine, Mike?''

Dr. Gillis was not aware of it, but "Mike" had an I.Q. six times his own, and was—to be blunt—his keeper. "Mike" rode herd on the pseudo-physicists in the pseudo-laboratory, in the guise of a bottle washer. It was a social waste—but as has been mentioned before, the supernormals were still standing at the approaches to a bridge. Their irresolution led to many such preposterous situations. And it happens that "Mike," having grown frantically bored with his task, was malevolent enough to—but let Dr. Gillis tell it:

"So he gives me these here tube numbers and says, 'Series circuit. Now stop bothering me. Build your time machine, sit down at it and turn on the switch. That's all I ask, Dr. Gillis—that's all I ask."

"Say," marveled a brittle and lovely blonde guest, "you remember real good, don't you, doc?" She gave him a melting smile.

"Heck," said Gillis modestly, "I always remember good. It's what you call an inherent facility. And besides I told it quick to my secretary, so she wrote it down. I don't read so good, but I sure remember good, all right. Now, where was I?"

Everybody thought hard, and there were various suggestions:

"Something about bottles, doc?"

"You was starting a fight. You said 'time somebody was traveling.' "

"Yeah—you called somebody a swish. Who did you call a swish?"

"Not swish—*switch.*"

Dr. Gillis's noble brow grooved with thought, and

he declared: "Switch is right. It was about time travel. What we call travel through time. So I took the tube numbers he gave me and I put them into the circuit builder; I set it for 'series' and there it is—my time-traveling machine. It travels things through time real good." He displayed a box.

"What's in the box?" asked the lovely blonde.

Dr. Hemingway told her: "Time travel. It travels things through time."

"Look," said Gillis, the physicist. He took Dr. Hemingway's little black bag and put it on the box. He turned on the switch and the little black bag vanished.

"Say," said Dr. Hemingway, "that was, uh, swell. Now bring it back."

"Huh?"

"Bring back my little black bag."

"Well," said Dr. Gillis, "they don't come back. I tried it backwards and they don't come back. I guess maybe that dummy Mike give me a bum steer."

There was wholesale condemnation of "Mike" but Dr. Hemingway took no part of it. He was nagged by a vague feeling that there was something he would have to do. He reasoned: "I am a doctor, and a doctor has got to have a little black bag. I ain't got a little black bag—so ain't I a doctor no more?" He decided that this was absurd. He *knew* he was a doctor. So it must be the bag's fault for not being there. It was no good, and he would get another one tomorrow from that dummy Al, at the clinic. Al could find things good, but he was a dummy—never liked to talk sociable to you.

So the next day, Dr. Hemingway remembered to get another little black bag from his keeper—another little black bag with which he could perform tonsillectomies, appendectomies, and the most difficult confinements, and with which he could diagnose and cure his kind until the day when the supernormals could bring themselves to cross that bridge. Al was kinda nasty about the missing little black bag, but Dr. Hemingway didn't exactly remember what had happened, so no tracer was sent out, so—

Old Dr. Full awoke from the horrors of the night to the horrors of the day. His gummy eyelashes pulled apart convulsively. He was propped against a corner of his room, and something was making a little drumming noise. He felt very cold and cramped. As his eyes focused on his lower body, he croaked out a laugh. The drumming noise was being made by his left heel, agitated by fine tremors against the bare floor. It was going to be the D.T.'s again, he decided dispassionately. He wiped his mouth with his bloody knuckles, and the fine tremor coarsened; the snare-drum beat became louder and slower. He was getting a break this fine morning, he decided sardonically. You didn't get the horrors until you had been tightened like a violin string, just to the breaking point. He had a reprieve, if a reprieve into his old body with the blazing, endless headache just back of the eyes and the screaming stiffness in the joints were anything to be thankful for.

There was something or other about a kid, he thought vaguely. He was going to doctor some kid. His eyes rested on a little black bag in the center of the room, and he forgot about the kid. "I could have sworn," said Dr. Full, "I hocked that two years ago!" He hitched over and reached the bag, and then realized it was some stranger's kit, arriving here he did not know how. He tentatively touched the lock and it snapped open and lay flat, rows and rows of instruments and medications tucked into loops in its four walls. It seemed vastly larger open than closed. He didn't see how it could possibly fold up into that compact size again, but decided it was some stunt of the instrument makers. Since his time—that made it worth more at the hock shop, he thought with satisfaction.

Just for old times' sake, he let his eyes and fingers rove over the instruments before he snapped the bag shut and headed for Uncle's. More than a few were a little hard to recognize—exactly that is. You could see the things with blades for cutting, the forceps for holding and pulling, the retractors for holding fast, the needles and gut for suturing, the hypos—a fleeting thought crossed his mind that he could peddle the hypos separately to drug addicts.

Let's go, he decided, and tried to fold up the case. It didn't fold until he happened to touch the lock, and then it folded all at once into a little black bag. Sure have forged ahead, he thought, almost able to forget that what he was primarily interested in was its pawn value.

With a definite objective, it was not too hard for him to get to his feet. He decided to go down the front steps, out the front door, and down the sidewalk. But first—

He snapped the bag open again on his kitchen table, and pored through the medication tubes. "Anything to sock the autonomic nervous system good and hard," he mumbled. The tubes were numbered, and there was a plastic card which seemed to list them. The left margin of the card was a run-down of the systems— vascular, muscular, nervous. He followed the last entry across to the right. There were columns for "stimulant," "depressant," and so on. Under "nervous system" and "depressant" he found the number 17, and shakily located the little glass tube which bore it. It was full of pretty blue pills and he took one.

It was like being struck by a thunderbolt.

Dr. Full had so long lacked any sense of well-being except the brief glow of alcohol that he had forgotten its very nature. He was panic-stricken for a long moment at the sensation that spread through him slowly, finally tingling in his fingertips. He straightened up, his pains gone and his leg tremor stilled.

That was great, he thought. He'd be able to *run* to the hock shop, pawn the little black bag, and get some booze. He started down the stairs. Not even the street, bright with mid-morning sun, into which he emerged made him quail. The little black bag in his left hand had a satisfying, authoritative weight. He was walking erect, he noted, and not in the somewhat furtive crouch that had grown on him in recent years. A little self-respect, he told himself, that's what I need. Just because a man's down doesn't mean—

"Docta, please-a come wit'!" somebody yelled at him, tugging his arm. "da litt-la girl, she's-a burn' up!" It was one of the slum's innumerable flat-faced, stringy-haired women, in a slovenly wrapper.

"Ah, I happen to be retired from practice—" he began hoarsely, but she would not be put off.

"In by here, Docta!" she urged, tugging him to a doorway. "You come look-a da litt-la girl. I got two dolla, you come look!" That put a different complexion on the matter. He allowed himself to be towed through the doorway into a mussy, cabbage-smelling flat. He knew the woman now, or rather knew who she must be—a new arrival who had moved in the other night. These people moved at night, in motorcades of battered cars supplied by friends and relations, with furniture lashed to the tops, swearing and drinking until the small hours. It explained why she had stopped him: she did not yet know he was old Dr. Full, a drunken reprobate whom nobody would trust. The little black bag had been his guarantee, outweighing his whiskey face and stained black suit.

He was looking down on a three-year-old girl who had, he rather suspected, just been placed in the mathematical center of a freshly changed double bed. God knew what sour and dirty mattress she usually slept on. He seemed to recognize her as he noted a crusted bandage on her right hand. Two dollars, he thought— An ugly flush had spread up her pipe-stem arm. He poked a finger into the socket of her elbow, and felt little spheres like marbles under the skin and ligaments roll apart. The child began to squall thinly; beside him, the woman gasped and began to weep herself.

"Out," he gestured briskly at her, and she thudded away, still sobbing.

Two dollars, he thought—Give her some mumbo jumbo, take the money and tell her to go to a clinic. Strep, I guess, from that stinking alley. It's a wonder any of them grow up. He put down the little black bag and forgetfully fumbled for his key, then remembered and touched the lock. It flew open, and he selected a bandage shears, with a blunt wafer for the lower jaw. He fitted the lower jaw under the bandage, trying not to hurt the kid by its pressure on the infection, and began to cut. It was amazing how easily and swiftly the shining shears snipped through the crusty rag around the wound. He hardly seemed to be driving the shears with fingers at all. It almost seemed as though the shears were driving his fingers instead as they scissored a clean, light line through the bandage.

Certainly have forged ahead since my time, he thought—sharper than a microtome knife. He replaced the shears in their loop on the extraordinarily big board that the little black bag turned into when it unfolded, and leaned over the wound. He whistled at the ugly gash, and the violent infection which had taken immediate root in the sickly child's thin body. Now what can you do with a thing like that? He pawed over the contents of the little black bag, nervously. If he lanced it and let some of the pus out, the old woman would think he'd done something for her and he'd get the two dollars. But at the clinic they'd want to know who did it and if they got sore enough they might send a cop around. Maybe there was something in the kit—

He ran down the left edge of the card to "lymphatic" and read across to the column under "infection." It didn't sound right at all to him; he checked again, but it still said that. In the square to which the line and column led were the symbols: "IV-g-3cc." He couldn't find any bottles marked with Roman numerals, and then noticed that that was how the hypodermic needles were designated. He lifted number IV from its loop, noting that it was fitted with a needle already and even seemed to be charged. What a way to carry those things around! So—three cc. of whatever was in hypo number IV ought to do something or other about infections settled in the lymphatic system—which, God knows, this one was. What did the lower-case "g" mean, though? He studied the glass hypo and saw letters engraved on what looked like a rotating disk at the top of the barrel. They ran from "a" to "i," and there was an index line engraved on the barrel on the opposite side from the calibrations.

Shrugging, old Dr. Full turned the disk until "g" coincided with the index line, and lifted the hypo to eye level. As he pressed in the plunger he did not see the tiny thread of fluid squirt from the tip of the needle. There was a sort of dark mist for a moment about the tip. A closer inspection showed that the needle was not even pierced at the tip. It had the usual slanting cut across the bias of the shaft, but the cut did not expose an oval hole. Baffled, he tried pressing the plunger again. Again *something* appeared around the tip and vanished. "We'll settle this," said the doctor. He slipped the needle into the skin of his forearm. He thought at first that he had missed—that the point had glided over the top of his skin instead of catching and slipping under it. But he saw a tiny blood-spot and realized that somehow he just hadn't felt the puncture. Whatever was in the barrel, he decided, couldn't do him any harm if it lived up to its billing—and if it could come out through a needle that had no hole. He gave himself three cc. and twitched the needle out. There was the swelling—painless, but otherwise typical.

Dr. Full decided it was his eyes or something, and gave three cc. of "g" from hypodermic IV to the feverish child. There was no interruption to her wailing as the needle went in and the swelling rose. But a long instant later, she gave a final gasp and was silent.

Well, he told himself, cold with horror, you did it that time. You killed her with that stuff.

Then the child sat up and said: "Where's my mommy?"

Incredulously, the doctor seized her arm and palpated the elbow. The gland infection was zero, and the temperature seemed normal. The blood-congested tissues surrounding the wound were subsiding as he watched. The child's pulse was stronger and no faster than a child's should be. In the sudden silence of the room he could hear the little girl's mother sobbing in her kitchen, outside. And he also heard a girl's insinuating voice:

"She gonna be O.K., doc?"

He turned and saw a gaunt-faced, dirty-blonde sloven of perhaps eighteen leaning in the doorway and eying him with amused contempt. She continued: "I heard about you, *Doc-tor* Full. So don't go try and put the bite on the old lady. You couldn't doctor up a sick cat."

"Indeed?" he rumbled. This young person was going to get a lesson she richly deserved. "Perhaps you would care to look at my patient?"

"Where's my mommy?" insisted the little girl, and the blonde's jaw fell. She went to the bed and cautiously asked: "You O.K. now, Teresa? You all fixed up?"

"Where's my mommy?" demanded Teresa. Then, accusingly, she gestured with her wounded hand at the doctor. "You *poke* me!" she complained, and giggled pointlessly.

"Well—" said the blonde girl, "I guess I got to hand it to you, doc. These loud-mouth women around here said you didn't know your . . . I mean, didn't know how to cure people. They said you ain't a real doctor."

"I *have* retired from practice," he said. "But I happened to be taking this case to a colleague as a favor, your good mother noticed me, and—" a deprecating smile. He touched the lock of the case and it folded up into the little black bag again.

"You stole it," the girl said flatly.

He sputtered.

"Nobody'd trust you with a thing like that. It must be worth plenty. You stole that case. I was going to stop you when I come in and saw you working over Teresa, but it looked like you wasn't doing her any harm. But when you give me that line about taking that case to a colleague I know you stole it. You gimme a cut or I go to the cops. A thing like that must be worth twenty-thirty dollars."

The mother came timidly in, her eyes red. But she let out a whoop of joy when she saw the little girl sitting up and babbling to herself, embraced her madly, fell on her knees for a quick prayer, hopped up to kiss the doctor's hand, and then dragged him into the kitchen, all the while rattling in her native language while the blonde girl let her eyes go cold with disgust. Dr. Full allowed himself to be towed into the kitchen, but flatly declined a cup of coffee and a plate of anise cakes and St. John's Bread.

"Try him on some wine, ma," said the girl sardonically.

"Hyass! Hyass!" breathed the woman delightedly. "You like-a wine, docta?" She had a carafe of purplish liquid before him in an instant, and the blonde girl snickered as the doctor's hand twitched out at it. He drew his hand back, while there grew in his head the old image of how it would smell and then taste and then warm his stomach and limbs. He made the kind of calculation at which he was practiced; the delighted woman would not notice as he downed two tumblers, and he could overawe her through two tumblers more with his tale of Teresa's narrow brush with the Destroying Angel, and then—why, then it would not matter. He would be drunk.

But for the first time in years, there was a sort of counter-image: a blend of the rage he felt at the blonde girl to whom he was so transparent, and of pride at the cure he had just effected. Much to his own surprise, he drew back his hand from the carafe and said, luxuriating in the words: "No, thank you. I don't believe I'd care for any so early in the day." He covertly watched the blonde girl's face, and was gratified at her surprise. Then the mother was shyly handing him two bills and saying: "Is no much-a money, docta—but you come again, see Teresa?"

"I shall be glad to follow the case through," he said. "But now excuse me—I really must be running along." He grasped the little black bag firmly and got up; he wanted very much to get away from the wine and the older girl.

"Wait up, doc," said she, "I'm going your way." She followed him out and down the street. He ignored her until he felt her hand on the black bag. Then old Dr. Full stopped and tried to reason with her:

"Look, my dear. Perhaps you're right. I might have stolen it. To be perfectly frank, I don't remember how I got it. But you're young and you can earn your own money—"

"Fifty-fifty," she said, "or I go to the cops. And if I get another word outta you, it's sixty-forty. And you know who gets the short end, don't you, doc?"

Defeated, he marched to the pawnshop, her impudent hand still on the handle with his, and her heels beating out a tattoo against his stately tread.

In the pawnshop, they both got a shock.

"It ain't stendard," said Uncle, unimpressed by the ingenious lock. "I ain't nevva seen one like it. Some cheap Jap stuff, maybe? Try down the street. This I nevva could sell."

Down the street they got an offer of one dollar. The same complaint was made: "I ain't a collecta, mista— I buy stuff that got resale value. Who could I sell this to, a Chinaman who don't know medical instruments? Every one of them looks funny. You sure you didn't make these yourself?" They didn't take the one-dollar offer.

The girl was baffled and angry; the doctor was baffled too, but triumphant. He had two dollars, and the girl had a half-interest in something nobody wanted. But, he suddenly marveled, the thing had been all right to cure the kid, hadn't it?

"Well," he asked her, "do you give up? As you see, the kit is practically valueless."

She was thinking hard. "Don't fly off the handle, doc. I don't get this but something's going on all right . . . would those guys know good stuff if they saw it?"

"They would. They make a living from it. Wherever this kit came from—"

She seized on that, with a devilish faculty she seemed to have of eliciting answers without asking questions. "I thought so. You don't know either, huh?

Well, maybe I can find out for you. C'mon in here. I ain't letting go of that thing. There's money in it—some way, I don't know how, there's money in it." He followed her into a cafeteria and to an almost-empty corner. She was oblivious to stares and snickers from the other customers as she opened the little black bag—it almost covered a cafeteria table—and ferreted through it. She picked out a retractor from a loop, scrutinized it, contemptuously threw it down, picked out a speculum, threw it down, picked out the lower half of an O.B. forceps, turned it over, close to her sharp young eyes—and saw what the doctor's dim old ones could not have seen.

All old Dr. Full knew was that she was peering at the neck of the forceps and then turned white. Very carefully, she placed the half of the forceps back in its loop of cloth and then replaced the retractor and the speculum. "Well?" he asked. "What did you see?"

" 'Made in U.S.A.,' " she quoted hoarsely. " 'Patent Applied for July 2450.' "

He wanted to tell her she must have misread the inscription, that it must be a practical joke, that—

But he knew she had read correctly. Those bandage shears: they *had* driven his fingers, rather than his fingers driving them. The hypo needle that had no hole. The pretty blue pill that had struck him like a thunderbolt.

"You know what I'm going to do?" asked the girl, with sudden animation. "I'm going to go to charm school. You'll like that, won't ya, doc? Because we're sure going to be seeing a lot of each other."

Old Dr. Full didn't answer. His hands had been playing idly with that plastic card from the kit on which had been printed the rows and columns that had guided him twice before. The card had a slight convexity; you could snap the convexity back and forth from one side to the other. He noted, in a daze, that with each snap a different text appeared on the cards. *Snap.* "The knife with the blue dot in the handle is for tumors only. Diagnose tumors with your Instrument Seven, the Swelling Tester. Place the Swelling Tester—"

Snap. "An overdose of the pink pills in Bottle 3 can be fixed with one white pill from Bottle—" *Snap.* "Hold the suture needle by the end without the hole in it. Touch it to one end of the wound you want to close and let go. After it has made the knot, touch it—" *Snap.* "Place the top half of the O.B. Forceps near the opening. Let go. After it has entered and conformed to the shape of—" *Snap.*

The slot man saw "FLANNERY 1—MEDICAL" in the upper left corner of the hunk of copy. He automatically scribbled "trim to .75" on it and skimmed it across the horseshoe-shaped copy desk to Piper, who had been handing Edna Flannery's quack-exposé series. She was a nice youngster, he thought, but like all youngsters she overwrote. Hence, the "trim."

Piper dealt back a city hall story to the slot, pinned down Flannery's feature with one hand and began to tap his pencil across it, one tap to a word, at the same steady beat as a teletype carriage traveling across the roller. He wasn't exactly reading it this first time. He was just looking at the letters and words to find out whether, as letters and words, they conformed to *Herald* style. The steady tap of his pencil ceased at intervals as it drew a black line ending with a stylized letter "d" through the word "breast" and scribbled in "chest" instead, or knocked down the capital "E" in "East" to lower case with a diagonal, or closed up a split word—in whose middle Flannery had bumped the space bar of her typewriter—with two curved lines like parentheses rotated through ninety degrees. The thick black pencil zipped a ring around the "30," which, like all youngsters, she put at the end of her stories. He turned back to the first page for the second reading. This time the pencil drew lines with the stylized "d's" at the end of them through adjectives and whole phrases, printed big "L's" to mark paragraphs, hooked some of Flannery's own paragraphs together with swooping recurved lines.

At the bottom of "FLANNERY ADD 2—MEDICAL" the pencil slowed down and stopped. The slot man, sensitive to the rhythm of his beloved copy desk, looked up almost at once. He saw Piper squinting at the story, at a loss. Without wasting words, the copy reader skimmed it back across the Masonite horseshoe to the chief, caught a police story in return and buckled down, his pencil tapping. The slot man read as far as the fourth add, barked at Howard, on the rim: "Sit in for me," and stumped through the clattering city room toward the alcove where the managing editor presided over his own bedlam.

The copy chief waited his turn while the make-up editor, the pressroom foreman, and the chief photographer had words with the M.E. When his turn came, he dropped Flannery's copy on his desk and said: "She says this one isn't a quack."

The M.E. read:

"FLANNERY 1—MEDICAL, by Edna Flannery, *Herald* Staff Writer.

"The sordid tale of medical quackery which the *Herald* has exposed in this series of articles undergoes a change of pace today which the reporter found a welcome surprise. Her quest for the facts in the case of today's subject started just the same way that her exposure of one dozen shyster M.D.'s and faith-healing phonies did. But she can report for a change that Dr. Bayard Full is, despite unorthodox practices which have drawn the suspicion of the rightly hypersensitive medical associations, a true healer living up to the highest ideals of his profession.

"Dr. Full's name was given to the *Herald's* reporter by the ethical committee of a county medical association, which reported that he had been expelled from the association on July 18, 1941, for allegedly 'milking' several patients suffering from trivial complaints. According to sworn statements in the committee's files, Dr. Full had told them they suffered from cancer, and that he had a treatment which would prolong their lives. After his expulsion from the association, Dr. Full dropped out of their sight—until he opened a midtown 'sanitarium' in a brownstone front which had for years served as a rooming house.

"The *Herald's* reporter went to that sanitarium, on East 89th Street, with the full expectation of having numerous imaginary ailments diagnosed and of being promised a sure cure for a flat sum of money. She expected to find unkempt quarters, dirty instruments, and the mumbo-jumbo paraphernalia of the shyster M.D. which she had seen a dozen times before.

"She was wrong.

"Dr. Full's sanitarium is spotlessly clean, from its tastefully furnished entrance hall to its shining, white treatment rooms. The attractive, blonde receptionist who greeted the reporter was soft-spoken and correct, asking only the reporter's name, address, and the general nature of her complaint. This was given, as usual, as 'nagging backache.' The receptionist asked the *Herald's* reporter to be seated, and a short while later conducted her to a second-floor treatment room and introduced her to Dr. Full.

"Dr. Full's alleged past, as described by the medical society spokesman, is hard to reconcile with his present appearance. He is a clear-eyed, white-haired man in his sixties, to judge by his appearance—a little above middle height and apparently in good physical condition. His voice was firm and friendly, untainted by the ingratiating whine of the shyster M.D. which the reporter has come to know too well.

"The receptionist did not leave the room as he began his examination after a few questions as to the nature and location of the pain. As the reporter lay face down on a treatment table the doctor pressed some instrument to the small of her back. In about one minute he made this astounding statement: 'Young woman, there is no reason for you to have any pain where you say you do. I understand they're saying nowadays that emotional upsets cause pains like that. You'd better go to a psychologist or psychiatrist if the pain keeps up. There is no physical cause for it, so I can do nothing for you.'

"His frankness took the reporter's breath away. Had he guessed she was, so to speak, a spy in his camp? She tried again: 'Well, doctor, perhaps you'd give me a physical checkup, I feel run down all the time, besides the pains. Maybe I need a tonic.' This is never-failing bait to shyster M.D.'s—an invitation for them to find all sorts of mysterious conditions wrong with a patient, each of which 'requires' an expensive treatment. As explained in the first article of this series, of course, the reporter underwent a thorough physical checkup before she embarked on her quack hunt, and was found to be in one hundred percent perfect condition, with the exception of a 'scarred' area at the bottom tip of her left lung resulting from a childhood attack of tuberculosis and a tendency toward 'hyperthyroidism'—overactivity of the thyroid gland which makes it difficult to put on weight and sometimes causes a slight shortness of breath.

"Dr. Full consented to perform the examination, and took a number of shining, spotlessly clean instruments from loops in a large board literally covered with instruments—most of them unfamiliar to the reporter. The instrument with which he approached first was a tube with a curved dial in its surface and two wires that ended on flat disks growing from its ends. He placed one of the disks on the back of the reporter's right hand and the other on the back of her left. 'Reading the meter,' he called out some number which the attentive receptionist took down on a ruled form. The same procedure was repeated several times, thoroughly covering the reporter's anatomy and thoroughly convincing her that the doctor was a complete quack. The reporter had never seen any such diagnostic procedure practiced during the weeks she put in preparing for this series.

"The doctor then took the ruled sheet from the receptionist, conferred with her in low tones, and said: 'You have a slightly overactive thyroid, young woman. And there's something wrong with your left lung—not seriously, but I'd like to take a closer look.'

"He selected an instrument from the board which, the reporter knew, is called a 'speculum'—a scissor-like device which spread apart body openings such as the orifice of the ear, the nostril, and so on, so that a doctor can look in during an examination. The instrument was, however, too large to be an aural or nasal speculum but too small to be anything else. As the *Herald's* reporter was about to ask further questions, the attending receptionist told her: 'It's customary for us to blindfold our patients during lung examinations—do you mind?' The reporter, bewildered, allowed her to tie a spotlessly clean bandage over her eyes, and waited nervously for what would come next.

"She still cannot say exactly what happened while she was blindfolded—but X rays confirm her suspicions. She felt a cold sensation at her ribs on the left side—a cold that seemed to enter inside her body. Then there was a snapping feeling, and the cold sensation was gone. She heard Dr. Full say in a matter-of-fact voice: 'You have an old tubercular scar down there. It isn't doing any particular harm, but an active person like you needs all the oxygen she can get. Lie still and I'll fix it for you.'

"Then there was a repetition of the cold sensation, lasting for a longer time. 'Another batch of alveoli and some more vascular glue,' the *Herald's* reporter heard Dr. Full say, and the receptionist's crisp response to the order. Then the strange sensation departed and the eye bandage was removed. The reporter saw no scar on her ribs, and yet the doctor assured her: 'That did it. We took out the fibrosis—and a good fibrosis it was, too; it walled off the infection so you're still alive to tell the tale. Then we planted a few clumps of alveoli—they're the little gadgets that get the oxygen from the air you breathe into your blood. I won't monkey with your thyroxin supply. You've got used to being the kind of person you are, and if you suddenly found yourself easygoing and all the rest of it, chances are you'd only be upset. About the backache: just check with the county medical society for the name of a good psychologist or psychiatrist. And look out for quacks; the woods are full of them.'

"The doctor's self-assurance took the reporter's breath away. She asked what the charge would be, and was told to pay the receptionist fifty dollars. As usual, the reporter delayed paying until she got a receipt signed by the doctor himself, detailing the services for which it paid. Unlike most, the doctor cheerfully wrote: 'For removal of fibrosis from left lung and restoration of alveoli,' and signed it.

"The reporter's first move when she left the sanitarium was to head for the chest specialist who had examined her in preparation for this series. A comparison of X rays taken on the day of the 'operation' and those taken previously would, the *Herald's* reporter then thought, expose Dr. Full as a prince of shyster M.D.'s and quacks.

"The chest specialist made time on his crowded schedule for the reporter, in whose series he has shown a lively interest from the planning stage on. He laughed uproariously in his staid Park Avenue examining room as she described the weird procedure to which she had been subjected. But he did not laugh when he took a chest X ray of the reporter, developed it, dried it, and compared it with the ones he had taken earlier. The chest specialist took six more X rays that afternoon, but finally admitted that they all told the same story. The *Herald's* reporter has it on his authority that the scar she had eighteen days ago from her tuberculosis is now gone and has been replaced by healthy lung tissue. He declares that this is a happening unparalleled in medical history. He does not go along with the reporter in her firm conviction that Dr. Full is responsible for the change.

"The *Herald's* reporter, however, sees no two ways about it. She concludes that Dr. Bayard Full—whatever his alleged past may have been—is now an unorthodox but highly successful practitioner of medicine, to whose hands the reporter would trust herself in any emergency.

"Not so is the case of 'Rev.' Annie Dimsworth—a female harpy who, under the guise of 'faith' preys on the ignorant and suffering who come to her sordid 'healing parlor' for help and remain to feed 'Rev.' Annie's bank account, which now totals up to $53,238.64.

Tomorrow's article will show, with photostats of bank statements and sworn testimony that—''

The managing editor turned down 'FLANNERY LAST ADD—MEDICAL'' and tapped his front teeth with a pencil, trying to think straight. He finally told the copy chief: "Kill the story. Run the teaser as a box." He tore off the last paragraph—the "teaser" about "Rev." Annie—and handed it to the desk man, who stumped back to his Masonite horseshoe.

The make-up editor was back, dancing with impatience as he tried to catch the M.E.'s eye. The interphone buzzed with the red light which indicated that the editor and publisher wanted to talk to him. The M.E. thought briefly of a special series on this Dr. Full, decided nobody would believe it and that he probably was a phony anyway. He spiked the story on the "dead" hook and answered his interphone.

Dr. Full had become almost fond of Angie. As his practice had grown to engross the neighborhood illnesses, and then to a corner suite in an uptown taxpayer building, and finally to the sanitarium, she seemed to have grown with it. Oh, he thought, we have our little disputes—

The girl, for instance, was too much interested in money. She had wanted to specialize in cosmetic surgery—removing wrinkles from wealthy old women and whatnot. She didn't realize, at first, that a thing like this was in their trust, that they were the stewards and not the owners of the little black bag and its fabulous contents.

He had tried, ever so cautiously, to analyze them, but without success. All the instruments were slightly radioactive, for instance, but not quite so. They would make a Geiger-Mueller counter indicate, but they would not collapse the leaves of an electroscope. He didn't pretend to be up on the latest developments, but as he understood it, that was just plain *wrong*. Under the highest magnification there were lines on the instruments' superfinished surfaces: incredibly fine lines, engraved in random hatchments which made no particular sense. Their magnetic properties were preposterous. Sometimes the instruments were strongly attracted to magnets, sometimes less so, and sometimes not at all.

Dr. Full had taken X rays in fear and trembling lest he disrupt whatever delicate machinery worked in them. He was *sure* they were not solid, that the handles and perhaps the blades must be mere shells filled with busy little watchworks—but the X rays showed nothing of the sort. Oh, yes—and they were always sterile, and they wouldn't rust. Dust *fell* off them if you shook them: now, that was something he understood. They ionized the dust, or were ionized themselves, or something of the sort. At any rate, he had read of something similar that had to do with phonograph records.

She wouldn't know about that, he proudly thought. She kept the books well enough, and perhaps she gave him a useful prod now and then when he was inclined to settle down. The move from the neighborhood slum to the uptown quarters had been her idea, and so had the sanitarium. Good, good, it enlarged his sphere of usefulness. Let the child have her mink coats and her convertible, as they seemed to be calling roadsters nowadays. He himself was too busy and too old. He had so much to make up for.

Dr. Full thought happily of his Master Plan. She would not like it much, but she would have to see the logic of it. This marvelous thing that had happened to them must be handed on. She was herself no doctor; even though the instruments practically ran themselves, there was more to doctoring than skill. There were the ancient canons of the healing art. And so, having seen the logic of it, Angie would yield; she would assent to his turning over the little black bag to all humanity.

He would probably present it to the College of Surgeons, with as little fuss as possible—well, perhaps a *small* ceremony, and he would like a souvenir of the occasion, a cup or a framed testimonial. It would be a relief to have the thing out of his hands, in a way;

let the giants of the healing art decide who was to have its benefits. No, Angie would understand. She was a goodhearted girl.

It was nice that she had been showing so much interest in the surgical side lately—asking about the instruments, reading the instruction card for hours, even practicing on guinea pigs. If something of his love for humanity had been communicated to her, old Dr. Full sentimentally thought, his life would not have been in vain. Surely she would realize that a greater good would be served by surrendering the instruments to wiser hands than theirs, and by throwing aside the cloak of secrecy necessary to work on their small scale.

Dr. Full was in the treatment room that had been the brownstone's front parlor; through the window he saw Angie's yellow convertible roll to a stop before the stoop. He liked the way she looked as she climbed the stairs; neat, not flashy, he thought. A sensible girl like her, she'd understand. There was somebody with her—a fat woman, puffing up the steps, overdressed and petulant. Now, what could she want?

Angie let herself in and went into the treatment room, followed by the fat woman. "Doctor," said the blonde girl gravely, "may I present Mrs. Coleman?" Charm school had not taught her everything, but Mrs. Coleman, evidently *nouveau riche*, thought the doctor, did not notice the blunder.

"Miss Aquella told me *so* much about you, doctor, and your remarkable system!" she gushed.

Before he could answer, Angie smoothly interposed: "Would you excuse us for just a moment, Mrs. Coleman?"

She took the doctor's arm and led him into the reception hall. "Listen," she said swiftly, "I know this goes against your grain, but I couldn't pass it up. I met this old thing in the exercise class at Elizabeth Barton's. Nobody else'll talk to her there. She's a widow. I guess her husband was a black marketeer or something, and she has a pile of dough. I gave her a line about how you had a system of massaging wrinkles out. My idea is, you blindfold her, cut her neck open with the Cutaneous Series knife, shoot some Firmol into the muscles, spoon out some of that blubber with an Adipose Series curette and spray it all with Skintite. When you take the blindfold off she's got rid of a wrinkle and doesn't know what happened. She'll pay five hundred dollars. Now, don't say 'no,' doc. Just this once, let's do it my way, can't you? I've been working on this deal all along too, haven't I?''

"Oh," said the doctor, "very well." He was going to have to tell her about the Master Plan before long anyway. He would let her have it her way this time.

Back in the treatment room, Mrs. Coleman had been thinking things over. She told the doctor sternly as he entered: "Of course, your system is permanent, isn't it?''

"It is, madam," he said shortly. "Would you please lie down there? Miss Aquella, get a sterile three-inch bandage for Mrs. Coleman's eyes." He turned his back on the fat woman to avoid conversation, and pretended to be adjusting the lights. Angie blindfolded the woman, and the doctor selected the instruments he would need. He handed the blonde girl a pair of retractors, and told her: "Just slip the corners of the blades in as I cut—" She gave him an alarmed look, and gestured at the reclining woman. He lowered his voice: "Very well. Slip in the corners and rock them along the incision. I'll tell you when to pull them out."

Dr. Full held the Cutaneous Series knife to his eyes as he adjusted the little slide for the three centimeters depth. He sighed a little as he recalled that its last use had been in the extirpation of an "inoperable" tumor of the throat.

"Very well," he said, bending over the woman. He tried a tentative pass through her tissues. The blade dipped in and flowed through them, like a finger through quicksilver, with no wound left in the wake. Only the retractors could hold the edges of the incision apart.

Mrs. Coleman stirred and jabbed: "Doctor, that felt

so peculiar! Are you sure you're rubbing the right way?''

"Quite sure, madam," said the doctor wearily. "Would you please try not to talk during the massage?''

He nodded at Angie, who stood ready with the retractors. The blade sank in to its three centimeters, miraculously cutting only the dead horny tissues of the epidermis and the live tissue of the dermis, pushing aside mysteriously all major and minor blood vessels and muscular tissue, declining to affect any system or organ except the one it was—tuned to, could you say? The doctor didn't know the answer, but he felt tired and bitter at this prostitution. Angie slipped in the retractor blades and rocked them as he withdrew the knife, then pulled to separate the lips of the incision. It bloodlessly exposed an unhealthy string of muscle, sagging in a dead-looking loop from blue-gray ligaments. The doctor took a hypo. Number IX, pre-set to "g," and raised it to his eye level. The mist came and went; there probably was no possibility of an embolus with one of these gadgets, but why take chances? He shot one cc.of "g"—identified as "Firmol" by the card—into the muscle. He and Angie watched as it tightened up against the pharynx.

He took the Adipose Series curette, a small one, and spooned out yellowish tissue, dropping it into the incinerator box, and then nodded to Angie. She eased out the retractors and the gaping incision slipped together into unbroken skin, sagging now. The doctor had the atomizer—dialed to "Skintite"—ready. He sprayed, and the skin shrank up into the new firm throat line.

As he replaced the instruments, Angie removed Mrs. Coleman's bandage and gaily announced: "We're finished! And there's a mirror in the reception hall—"

Mrs. Coleman didn't need to be invited twice. With incredulous fingers she felt her chin, and then dashed for the hall. The doctor grimaced as he heard her yelp of delight, and Angie turned to him with a tight smile.

"I'll get the money and get her out," she said. "You won't have to be bothered with her any more."

He was grateful for that much.

She followed Mrs. Coleman into the reception hall, and the doctor dreamed over the case of instruments. A ceremony, certainly—he was *entitled* to one. Not everybody, he thought, would turn such a sure source of money over to the good of humanity. But you reached an age when money mattered less, and when you thought of these things you had done that *might* be opened to misunderstanding if, just if, there chanced to be any of that, well, that judgment business. The doctor wasn't a religious man, but you certainly found yourself thinking hard about some things when your time drew near—

Angie was back, with a bit of paper in her hands. "Five hundred dollars," she said matter-of-factly. "And you realize, don't you, that we could go over her an inch at a time—at five hundred dollars an inch?"

"I've been meaning to talk to you about that," he said.

There was bright fear in her eyes, he thought—but why?

"Angie, you've been a good girl and an understanding girl, but we can't keep this up forever, you know."

"Let's talk about it some other time," she said flatly. "I'm tired now."

"No—I really feel we've gone far enough on our own. The instruments—"

"Don't say it, doc!" she hissed. "Don't say it, or you'll be sorry!" In her face there was a look that reminded her of the hollow-eyed, gaunt-faced, dirty-blonde creature she had been. From under the charm-school finish there burned the guttersnipe whose infancy had been spent on a sour and filthy mattress, whose childhood had been play in the littered alley, and whose adolescence had been the sweatshops and the aimless gatherings at night under the glaring street lamps.

He shook his head to dispel the puzzling notion. "It's this way," he patiently began. "I told you about the family that invented the O.B. forceps and kept them a secret for so many generations, how they could have given them to the world but didn't?''

''They knew what they were doing,'' said the guttersnipe flatly.

''Well, that's neither here nor there,'' said the doctor, irritated. ''My mind is made up about it. I'm going to turn the instruments over to the College of Surgeons. We have enough money to be comfortable. You can even have the house. I've been thinking of going to a warmer climate, myself.'' He felt peeved with her for making the unpleasant scene. He was unprepared for what happened next.

Angie snatched the little black bag and dashed for the door, with panic in her eyes. He scrambled after her, catching her arm, twisting it in a sudden rage. She clawed at his face with her free hand, babbling curses. Somehow, somebody's finger touched the little black bag, and it opened grotesquely into the enormous board, covered with shining instruments, large and small. Half a dozen of them joggled loose and fell to the floor.

''*Now* see what you've done!'' roared the doctor, unreasonably. Her hand was still viselike on the handle, but she was standing still, trembling with choked-up rage. The doctor bent stiffly to pick up the fallen instruments. Unreasonable girl! he thought bitterly. Making a scene—

Pain drove in between his shoulderblades and he fell face down. The light ebbed. ''Unreasonable girl!'' he tried to croak. And then: ''They'll know I tried, anyway—''

Angie looked down on his prone body, with the handle of the Number Six Cautery Series knife protruding from it. ''—will cut through all tissues. Use for amputations before you spread on the ReGro. Extreme caution should be used in the vicinity of vital organs and major blood vessels or nerve trunks—''

''I didn't mean to do that,'' said Angie, dully, cold with horror. Now the detective would come, the implacable detective who would reconstruct the crime from the dust in the room. She would run and turn and twist, but the detective would find her out and she would be tried in a courtroom before a judge and jury; the lawyer would make speeches, but the jury would convict her anyway, and the headlines would scream: "BLONDE-KILLER GUILTY!" and she'd maybe get the chair, walking down a plain corridor where a beam of sunlight struck through the dusty air, with an iron door at the end of it. Her mink, her convertible, her dresses, the handsome man she was going to meet and marry—

The mist of cinematic clichés cleared, and she knew what she would do next. Quite steadily, she picked the incinerator box from its loop in the board—a metal cube with a different-textured spot on one side. "—to dispose of fibroses or other unwanted matter, simply touch the disk—" You dropped something in and touched the disk. There was a sort of soundless whistle, very powerful and unpleasant if you were too close, and a sort of lightless flash. When you opened the box again, the contents were gone. Angie took another of the Cautery Series knives and went grimly to work. Good thing there wasn't any blood to speak of— She finished the awful task in three hours.

She slept heavily that night, totally exhausted by the wringing emotional demands of the slaying and the subsequent horror. But in the morning, it was as though the doctor had never been there. She ate breakfast, dressed with unusual care—and then undid the unusual care. Nothing out of the ordinary, she told herself. Don't do one thing different from the way you would have done it before. After a day or two, you can phone the cops. Say he walked out spoiling for a drunk, and you're worried. But don't rush it, baby— *don't rush it.*

Mrs. Coleman was due at 10:00 a.m. Angie had counted on being able to talk the doctor into at least one more five-hundred-dollar session. She'd have to do it herself now—but she'd have to start sooner or later.

The woman arrived early. Angie explained smoothly: "The doctor asked me to take care of the massage today. Now that he has the tissue-firming process beginning, it only requires somebody trained in his methods—'' As she spoke, her eyes swiveled to the instrument case—open! She cursed herself for the single flaw as the woman followed her gaze and recoiled.

"What are those things!" she demanded. "Are you going to cut me with them? I *thought* there was something fishy—''

"Please, Mrs. Coleman," said Angie, "please, *dear* Mrs. Coleman—you don't understand about the . . . the massage instruments!"

"Massage instruments, my foot!" squabbled the woman shrilly. "That doctor *operated* on me. Why, he might have killed me!"

Angie wordlessly took one of the smaller Cutaneous Series knives and passed it through her forearm. The blade flowed like a finger through quicksilver, leaving no wound in its wake. *That* should convince the old cow!

It didn't convince her, but it did startle her. "What did you do with it? The blade folds up into the handle—that's it!"

"Now look closely, Mrs. Coleman," said Angie, thinking desperately of the five hundred dollars. "Look very closely and you'll see that the, uh, the sub-skin massager simply slips beneath the tissues without doing any harm, tightening and firming the muscles themselves instead of having to work through layers of skin and adipose tissue. It's the secret of the doctor's method. Now, how can outside massage have the effect that we got last night?"

Mrs. Coleman was beginning to calm down. "It *did* work, all right," she admitted, stroking the new line of her neck. "But your arm's one thing and my neck's another! Let me see you do that with your neck!"

Angie smiled—

Al returned to the clinic after an excellent lunch that had almost reconciled him to three more months he would have to spend on duty. And then, he thought,

302 *C. M. Kornbluth*

and then a blessed year at the blessedly super-normal South Pole working on his specialty—which happened to be telekinesis exercises for ages three to six. Meanwhile, of course, the world had to go on and of course he had to shoulder his share in the running of it.

Before settling down to desk work he gave a routine glance at the bag board. What he saw made him stiffen with shocked surprise. A red light was on next to one of the numbers—the first since he couldn't think when. He read off the number and murmured "O.K., 674,101. That fixes *you.*" He put the number on a card sorter and in a moment the record was in his hand. Oh, yes—Hemingway's bag. The big dummy didn't remember how or where he had lost it; none of them ever did. There were hundreds of them floating around.

Al's policy in such cases was to leave the bag turned on. The things practically ran themselves, it was practically impossible to do harm with them, so whoever found a lost one might as well be allowed to use it. You turn it off, you have a social loss—you leave it on, it may do some good. As he understood it, and not very well at that, the stuff wasn't "used up." A temporalist had tried to explain it to him with little success that the prototypes in the transmitter *had been trans-ducted* through a series of point-events of transfinite cardinality. Al had innocently asked whether that meant prototypes had been stretched, so to speak, through all time, and the temporalist had thought he was joking and left in a huff.

"Like to see him do this," thought Al darkly, as he telekinized himself to the combox, after a cautious look to see that there were no medics around. To the box he said: "Police chief," and then to the police chief: "There's been a homicide committed with Medical Instrument Kit 674,101. It was lost some months ago by one of my people, Dr. John Hemingway. He didn't have a clear account of the circumstances."

The police chief groaned and said: "I'll call him in and question him." He was to be astonished by the answers, and was to learn that the homicide was well out of his jurisdiction.

Al stood for a moment at the bag board by the glowing red light that had been sparked into life by a departing vital force giving, as its last act, the warning that Kit 674,101 was in homicidal hands. With a sigh, Al pulled the plug and the light went out.

"Yah," jeered the woman. "You'd fool around with my neck, but you wouldn't risk your own with that thing!"

Angie smiled with serene confidence a smile that was to shock hardened morgue attendants. She set the Cutaneous Series knife to three centimeters before drawing it across her neck. Smiling, knowing the blade would cut only the dead horny tissue of the epidermis and the live tissue of the dermis, mysteriously push aside all major and minor blood vessels and muscular tissue—

Smiling, the knife plunging in and its microtome-sharp metal shearing through major and minor blood vessels and muscular tissue and pharynx, Angie cut her throat.

In the few minutes it took the police, summoned by the shrieking Mrs. Coleman, to arrive, the instruments had become crusted with rust, and the flasks which had held vascular glue and clumps of pink, rubbery alveoli and spare gray cells and coils of receptor nerves held only black slime, and from them when opened gushed the foul gases of decomposition.